ALSO BY THOMAS WILLIAM SIMPSON

This Way Madness Lies
The Gypsy Storyteller
Full Moon Over America

the
fingerprints
of
armless
mike

the fingerprints of armless mike

thomas william simpson

WARNER BOOKS

A Time Warner Company

Warner Books, Inc., 1271 Avenue of the Americas, New York, NY 10020

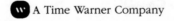 A Time Warner Company

Printed in the United States of America
First Printing: April 1996
10 9 8 7 6 5 4 3 2 1

Library of Congress Cataloging-in-Publication Data
Simpson, Thomas William
    The fingerprints of armless Mike / Thomas William Simpson.
        p.   cm.
    ISBN 0-446-51809-3
    1. Married people—New Jersey—Fiction.   2. Americans—Travel—
Bahamas—Fiction.   3. Criminals—New Jersey—Fiction.   I. Title.
PS3569.I5176F56   1996
813'.54—dc20   95-31880
                                                            CIP

Book design by H. Roberts

To Dr. James C. Hanrahan
aka
"The Hammer"
aka
"The Little Irishman"

Thanks for the title, Doc.

the
fingerprints
of
armless
mike

how sweet the sound that saved a wretch like me

FROM "Amazing Grace" BY THE REVEREND JOHN NEWTON

This one has to do with Money. Cold hard cash. Bread. Bucks. Bank notes. Legal tender. The dark green stuff. Oil of the palm. Fat Jack. You know what I'm talking about. Take Sex out of the cup and the Almighty Dollar quickly rises to the top and turns to cream.

Sex and Money. Money and Sex.

Together they drive men's souls.

What do men think about all day? They think about Sex and Money. And how to get more of both. Come on, don't deny it. You know it's true. Never enough of either one. Always someone out there with more than you. More Sex. More Money.

The more provocative question is: what'll you do to get more? More Money, I mean. Could be more Sex, but right now we're talking Money, coins of liberation. What would you do? How far would you go? Would you lie? Cheat? Beg? Borrow? Steal?

No? Never hid an ace up your sleeve in a penny ante poker game? Never as a kid dipped into Mom's purse or

Dad's billfold? Never worked for an hourly wage and maybe tacked a couple hours onto the OT sheet come the end of the week? Never even thought about pilfering a fiver from the collection plate as that silver tray swept past where you sat solemnly in your pew?

Still no? Well, by God, I must be in the presence of a saint. A first cousin of Gabriel. You never in your whole life did a single solitary thing where the final tally sheet didn't miraculously come out in your favor?

Ah, that's better. So believe it when you hear: if you can take a dime, brother, you can take a dollar.

And now that we're on level ground, let's cut the prattle and drop in on the scene of the crime. That's what we have here, after all, a tale of love, lust, greed, and grand larceny.

There's our perpetrator: Michael Josep Standowski, aka Mike Standish, aka me. That's right: yours truly. Driving an empty U-Haul truck up the long and winding drive to his mother-in-law's Tudor mansion on the hill. Mother-in-law? Never thought I'd have one of those. But what the hell? I'll try anything once.

Oh, so easy to sound glib. Like I'm not in a jam. Like I haven't screwed up Big Time this time. Like I don't have the Law and Iron Kate hot on my trail. No, not me, not Mike Standish. I've got it together. All systems go. At least I'll pull out all the stops to make you think so. Tall and Smooth. Not a crack in sight. A perfect wise-guy grin etched across my Irish Catholic Polack face. Although ask me and I'll tell you my father's English, my mother's Scottish, and Presbyterianism has coursed through our blood since the Reformation.

What's the truth? Where's the old fox hiding?

Behind the wheel of that U-Haul leased under an assumed name, that's where. And believe me, up to no good. No good at all. Pillaging and plundering on my mind. I remember well. Sweat poured off my brow. And not because of the heat. No, mid-March. Cold and gray. A blustery wind.

I had the air conditioner on anyway. Full blast. Windows wide open. All the way down. And still the sweat. Soaking through my tee shirt. Seeping into my cotton flannel (an expensive Ralph Lauren). Running off my forehead. Down my cheeks. I could even feel it behind my knees, between my toes. Nerves all a-jitter. Quivering like hummingbird wings. I dabbed at it with my fine black leather Coach gloves. Driving gloves like the ones I used when I got behind the wheel of Sarah's Bimmer. Gloves that would keep my fingerprints off the booty. The gloves made no difference. A hard rain's a-gonna fall.

I had to drop Brother U-Haul into low to make the grade on that long, steep, winding drive. Up and up, through the woods, brown and bare from the long, dead winter. Finally into a clearing. Dirt, dust, and gravel turned to smooth macadam. My mother-in-law, Katherine Crawford Browne, aka Iron Kate, kept it that way on purpose: dirt and gravel down by the road and for the first hundred yards. Claimed a seedy-looking entryway kept out the creeps and the crooks.

It didn't keep me out.

Sixth-tenths of a mile long that drive. Where I grew up, in Poughkeepsie, New York, we didn't even have a driveway. Parked the car out on the street. When we had a car. Sixth-tenths of a mile, climbing all the time. Right up to Heaven. Rock Candy Mountain. Shangri-la. San Simeon.

TREETOPS the Brownes called their posh estate. Located in north-central New Jersey of all places. Town called Pottersville. Not much of a town: post office, general store, fire house, church (Protestant, of course), a bank. They didn't really need a bank. Greenbacks grew on the trees in that town. I'm not kidding. The maples, oaks, and sycamores didn't have leaves. They had tens and twenties and hundred dollar bills stuck to the ends of their branches. Up at my mother-in-law's spread (one hundred and forty-four acres of lush rolling pasture and hardwood timber), they had trees that sprouted T-bills. So many they used to pick 'em, put in their salads. Colin Crawford (Sarah's uncle, Iron Kate's brother, and my former employer) used to say a rich man should eat something green every day. Then he'd stuff a crisp new ten spot in his mouth and chew it while a sheen of satisfaction spread across his face. Oh how that man loved the color green. They all loved the color green. The whole family. They wore green clothes. Painted their walls green. Frolicked in the green of their gardens. Drove green cars.

In the detached five-car garage at the top of the drive: a 1932 Rolls-Royce Phantom and a 1961 Mercedes-Benz 190 roadster. Both in mint green. Both in mint condition. Both members of the family since they'd been driven out of their glass showrooms decades ago by parents and grandparents. I drove those beauties a time or two myself. Drove the Rolls to the Essex Hunt Club Ball. A pink carnation in the lapel of my tux. Drove the Benz in the antique car show during intermission of the annual charity polo match. Had the top down, Sarah at my side, waving to the masses. Wore an ascot, a top hat. Kept calling everyone old sport.

I guess I'll never get to drive those motor vehicles again. Rags to riches and now back to rags. Easy come, Standowski, easy go.

A Rolls, a Benz, and that day in March, three empty bays. Those bays had to stand empty. No way I would've been anywhere near TREETOPS if those bays had been full. Not driving an empty U-Haul truck. Not with my fingers all sticky. But I knew Iron Kate's forest green Range Rover (fifty grand), Sarah's isle green pearl BMW 325is convertible (forty-two grand), and Lucy's paradise green VW cabriolet (twenty grand) would be off on other adventures. Iron Kate had gone down to Virginia to hunt foxes on horseback. Sarah was off doing her gig with the Literacy Volunteers of

America. And Lucy (the nanny) was taking courses over at the local community college. Barring any unforeseen visitors, I had TREETOPS all to myself.

Backed my U-Haul right up to the front door. Reached to turn off the key, shut down the engine. Another bead of sweat rolled off my chin onto my hand. That hand shook as if I'd been sucking down cups of espresso and not sleeping for the past week or two.

"Easy does it, Mike," I told myself. "You can still back out. All you have to do is put this truck in gear and roll on back down the hill." But I didn't roll on back down the hill. No, I threw open the door and hopped out. Hopped around on the macadam. Fifteen, maybe twenty seconds. Seemed like an hour. The sky, already a dull gray, closed up and turned black. Not cold enough to snow but it sure felt like rain.

The criminal mind? I wondered. What would it do? How would it proceed under the circumstances? Was I a criminal? Am I a criminal? A felon on the run? Where am I anyway? Should I say, or should I keep my whereabouts a secret?

The Bahamas: a lazy, watery land of eternal June. Conjures up visions of passion and romance, of heat and humidity and Gulf Steam breezes, of a mystical, sun-drenched island life. That's where I am. In the Bahamas. That's where I've been driven. Mad. Out on one of the far-flung islands. The Family Islands they call them. At least the Bahamas Tourist Board does. Has a nice homey rhythm to it. But I'm not here with my family. No way. I blew that. Blew it sky high.

I've only really loved three women in my life: my mother, my sister, and Sarah Louise. My mother's dead, my sister's married to Mr. Wonderful, and Sarah has probably written me off as another bad emotional investment. I'll probably never see her again. Unless they drag me back in irons to face my accusers.

Oh yeah, I blew my chance for love and happiness to smithereens the second I quit my procrastinating and stepped up to the front door. I took a deep breath and peered through the glass. I spotted it immediately: the bright red light blinking on the control panel beside the hall closet. Red meant the TREETOPS burglar alarm had been activated. For several days I'd been worried about that light. Sure, I knew how to disarm the beast, the proper sequence of numbers to punch. After all, this was my home too. Where I lived and loved and slept and ate my meals. But some common crook off the street, he wouldn't know how to turn the alarm off. He'd get inside, the alarm would blast, the cops would come a-calling.

Fortunately, I had an ace up my sleeve. See, I knew Sarah had been the last one to leave the house that morning. Sarah trusted people and disliked the alarm, the way she had to arm it, then scoot out of the house at lightning speed. So quite often she conveniently forgot to turn it on. A misdemeanor that inevitably brought upon her the wrath of Iron Kate.

So make no mistake: I knew full well the mother would blame the daughter, but I nevertheless went ahead with the job. I unlocked the door with my key and waltzed into the house. I crossed to the alarm panel. Punched in the right numbers. The red light turned to green. Ah yes: a sharp, vivid green.

The house was safe. The house was mine.

I checked the time on the two-hundred-year-old grandfather clock standing guard beside the front door: 8:42. Not something I had in mind, that clock. Too big. Too bulky. Too fragile. And not all that high on the cost sheet. Only worth six or eight grand. I had my list. Had been working on it for weeks. Knew exactly what I wanted and where it lived. I stretched my fingers into those lightweight leather gloves and went to work.

The physical labor of it all calmed me down. Sure, the sweat continued to flow, but it came now from my exertions. I got the heavy stuff out first, no easy chore running solo. But with the dolly and the hand truck I'd rented back at the U-Haul place, I managed.

I threw the contents (board games, old curtains, tablecloths, photo albums) of the massive cherry chest-on-chest directly onto the living room floor. After all, this had to look like a straight burglary. I carried the drawers two at a time out to the U-Haul. Then the piece itself. First the top, then the bottom. Secured it to the hand truck. Wheeled it outside. Padded it with blankets. Treated that piece of furniture like it was made of solid gold. Damn near was. Iron Kate's insurance policy estimated its value at almost one hundred and twenty thousand dollars. Handmade. Very rare. Over two hundred and fifty years old.

Then upstairs, into Iron Kate's spacious bedroom. Emptied the drawers (bras, panties, slips, cashmere sweaters, jodhpurs) of her walnut highboy onto the thick wool carpet. Carried the drawers down to the U-Haul. Then the piece. Down the wide front stairs on the hand truck, one step at a time. Slow going. Didn't want to lose it, bust it up. Worth too much green. Dark green. Thick piles of green. Close to a hundred thousand dollars. On the open market.

It took time, a lot more time than I'd anticipated. Almost twenty minutes. But finally, after an enormous physical struggle, I got that highboy safely strapped into the U-Haul.

Burglary, I realized, was strenuous work. Physically and emotionally. The sweat kept flowing, both from the toil of my efforts and from the sheer exhilaration of the crime. Every single nerve ending in my body twitched and throbbed with the possibility that at any moment Iron Kate could walk through the front door and demand in her cool, condescending tone, "Exactly what do you think you are doing, Mr. Standowski?"

My mother-in-law loved to let me know she knew my real name. An Anglophile and a closet racist, Iron Kate hated Jews, blacks, Hispanics. Polacks. Had my name really been Standish, maybe a descendant of Myles, had I come from Money, gone to the right schools, behaved like a snob, jumped my Dutch warmblood gracefully over split-rail fences, she no doubt would have embraced me as one of her own.

I checked the clock: 9:24. I had hoped to finish and be back on the road by 9:30, 9:45 at the latest. Decided to hang around until ten. I rode that adrenaline high to my advantage. Moving like a machine, I pilfered only the best stuff, the highest quality merchandise: a cherry drop-leaf table circa 1750. A tiger maple plantation desk circa 1800. A walnut tavern table where Patrick Henry once rested his schooner of ale at the Raleigh Tavern in Williamsburg, Virginia. A set of four Shaker chairs circa 1730. A mahogany writing desk built in Boston in the late 1600s. One of a kind. A simple thing. Not much to it. A flat top, a single drawer, four straight legs. But still worth in excess of fifteen grand. I wrapped it gently and loaded it into the truck.

I took the silver, but not much else in the way of small goods. Too much trouble. Too time-consuming. And besides, I didn't want anyone studying the crime scene and deciding it must've been an inside job.

10:03. Time to move. I decided to make one last trip through the house. Maybe two. By this time I felt quite calm, almost serene. Practically floated through the rooms, noting with a critical eye the messes I'd left behind. I wondered who would find them first: Sarah? Lucy? Timothy? Dorothy?

And then, just as I eased through the front door with a very rare Hitchcock rocking bench, the phone rang. Stopped me dead in my tracks. Five rings before the answering machine took the call. Iron Kate's stern and humorless voice delivered the message. "You've reached the Brownes' residence. No one is available to come to the phone just now. Please leave a brief message with your name, telephone number, and the time you called."

And then a long beep before I heard her voice again, live this time: "It's just me calling to say hello. Hello Sarah. Hello Timothy. Hello Lucy." Pause. "Hello Michael." You could hear the distaste she had for the name. My name.

It took all my powers of self-denial not to pick up the phone and have a nice chat with dear Kate. I could have asked her which pieces might bring the most money with the local dealers. We could have discussed the rising popularity of tiger maple and the sudden decline of pine primitives. But no, I held my ground. Waited for the line to go dead. Then I carried that bench out to the U-Haul, padded it up, and secured it in place.

Time to roll. I could feel the impending threat of peril closing in on me. The rest of the stuff would have to stay. No problem. No need to get greedy. Someday, I figured, it'll all be mine anyway. Mine and Sarah's. I just needed a little something to tide us over, to get us out from under Iron Kate's iron heel. That's how I justified the job. Kept telling myself I was simply stealing from the mother and giving to the daughter—kind of a Robin Hood thing. I wasn't a crook, merely an equalizer.

I decided to make one last trip through the house. Just in case I might've left something interesting.

The mess I'd made looked authentic: a hasty burglar at work. Stuff strewn everywhere: clothes, bedding, important-looking papers. And then I heard it: a car door slam!

I raced from window to window. Peered through the glass. My eyes roaming up and down the drive. Didn't see a thing. Not a car. Not a human. Nothing but my imagination. Damn thing can be such a nuisance.

A long sigh of relief, then straight for the exit. Closed and locked the door. Went out into the yard. Picked up a large rock. Used the rock to smash the window next to the door. The broken glass shattered the silence, destroyed my slippery calm. The time had definitely come to make my escape. But first I reached in through the broken window, unlocked the door, and pushed it wide open.

A job well done.

I closed up the back of the U-Haul. Tried to think what else I needed to do. My brain spit only blanks. Climbed in behind the wheel. Started the engine. Pushed in the clutch. Shoved the transmission into first. Started down that long, winding drive. Oh, yeah, my booty safe and secure, I made my getaway.

So who am I? Where did I come from? How did I wind up living in that big Tudor mansion on the hill? And why am I down here in the islands now, on the run, hiding out, living under an alias? Those and these questions: When is Sarah going to solve the clues I left behind? When is she going to find me? Rescue me? Assure me all is forgiven?

I guess that's my tale, the tale I have to tell. One man's journey through the American landscape. A landscape littered with hills and valleys, Sex and seductions, love and lust, Money and no Money.

Money brought me to America. Money and Fear. Well, maybe not me. But my family. My grandparents. The Standowskis. I could just as easily be living in Poland, slowly starving to death in the aftermath of those stupid, corrupt commies. But no, I was born and raised in the Land of Liberty, a place where a man, any man, can rise up out of nothing and make something of himself: a butcher, a baker, a candlestick maker. A doctor, a dentist, a lawyer. A crook, a con man, a thief.

1939: the year the Nazis rumbled into Poland. The year Adolf sent his young Aryans scurrying across the Oder River and over the Polish plains. The year the Krauts turned Warsaw into rubble in their efforts to eradicate the Jews. We weren't Jews. Just some lowly Catholics. Oppressed by the blessed in Rome for the past thousand years or so. My grandparents lived in Warsaw. In a giant brick colossus. Fifty rooms. Fancy furnishings and fireplaces everywhere. A lavish lifestyle. Just one step below royalty.

My grandmother worked as an upstairs chambermaid. She had to wear a bell around her neck so she couldn't sneak up on the Lord of the Manor when he brought the local maidens over for a frolic. My grandfather worked as a chauffeur. He drove the Lord of the Manor, Mr. Henyk ReLec, around in a Daimler-Benz limousine. Mr. ReLec was a Czech national and a Polish media kingpin. He owned a whole slew of newspapers and radio stations. For a year or more his editorial slant had included aggressive criticism of the Third Reich. Especially its CEO. He had gone so far as to call Adolf an offspring of Attila. So when the Führer's boys rolled into town, the ReLecs had to make a mad dash.

It all happened pretty fast. No time to do anything but pack the gold and go. Undoubtedly my grandparents would have been left behind, save for the fact that the ReLecs needed someone to carry their bags, serve them tea. Even so, old man ReLec refused to allow his servants to bring along their four-year-old son. "Leave the little bastard," is the famous family quote offered by Henyk as the small band prepared for their midnight escape. "He'll slow us down."

"The little bastard" turned out to be my padre, Stanislaw Standowski.

As you can imagine, my grandmother cried and begged and pleaded. The Polish media kingpin slapped her across the face, ordered her to shut up. At that point the pale and lovely Mrs. ReLec intervened, saved the day, paved the way for yours truly to eventually spring forth in the New World. She said the youngster could come, as long as he promised not to make a peep. My grandfather, a practical fellow, had the perfect solution: he secured a length of masking tape over his lad's lips.

The refugees made their way to America, God's Country. They reached New York just in time for Thanksgiving. Too bad there was no turkey waiting for the Josep Standowskis. Within just a few days of reaching the Blessed Land, Henyk ReLec told my grandparents to get lost. No way did he want a couple of ignorant Polacks tending his fancy brownstone on the Upper East Side of Manhattan.

ReLec, benevolent benefactor, handed my grandfather ten dollars (a fiver and five ones) and a soiled scrap of paper. Then he put Josep and his small family out on the street. A cold, windy street swept by a driving rain. Welcome to the Promised Land.

The scrap of paper contained the name and address of a man in Poughkeepsie, New York, who ran a ball bearing factory. My grandfather didn't know it, but war fever had broken out across America, causing the factory to greatly increase the size of its operation. Hundreds of new workers were being hired to man the line, to produce the ball bearings needed to make Jeeps, tanks, trucks, airplanes, and other war toys.

Josep Standowski bundled up his wife and son and headed north. Having just ten dollars to their name, they had no choice but to walk the nearly one hundred miles from Manhattan to Poughkeepsie. Their journey took almost three weeks. They slept in barns. Did odd chores for a few morsels of food. On Christmas Eve, 1939, they reached Poughkeepsie. Spent the night and all of Christmas Day huddled beneath a loading platform at the railroad yard along the Hudson River. And on the morning of December 26, Josep Standowski walked through the front gates of the ball bearing factory. In less than an hour he hit the assembly line, one more cog in the massive military wheel just beginning to rumble through the heartland of America.

Another lofty tale from the Annals of Immigration.

My old man grew up a tough kid in a tough part of town. Poughkeepsie, like a hundred other small Northeastern cities, had a diverse ethnic population. Wops, Micks, Bohunks, Squareheads, Polacks, and blacks lived within swinging distance of one another. Except for the blacks, most had come to America hoping to better their lot. Most had come of their own free will, toting along dreams of liberty, freedom, and economic prosperity. They tried not to think too much about the fact that they lived more or less as indentured servants, laboring six days a week, twelve or fourteen hours a day, for the wealthy factory owner who lived in the fancy mansion overlooking the river. They were in America, and in America a man had the manifest right to dream.

Stanislaw never gave a damn for dreams. When he did dream he dreamed in Polish. He tried to dream in English, but at home his parents always spoke Polish, so that was the last language he heard before bed.

In June of 1953 he graduated from high school. No honors or distinctions. He joined the army to fight Koreans, but the war ended before he could get there; spent most of his hitch inventorying unused war matériel at bases in Georgia, Nevada, and Oklahoma. After two years he came home and went to work in the ball bearing factory. Worked right alongside his pappy.

Stanlislaw lived at home with his parents, but only rarely did he spend time there. He'd stop to shower and change his clothes, maybe eat a meal. Little else. If not at the ball bearing factory, he could usually be found in one of Poughkeepsie's many pubs. At night he slept in a wide variety of beds with a wide variety of women. Stanley had a way with the ladies. In the company of men he presented a hard, gruff, don't-mess-with-me demeanor. But the ladies brought out his gentler, more sensitive side. He knew how to charm them. And once he drew them close, his rugged good looks and muscular physique would lead them beyond temptation.

Then, one beautiful spring afternoon, after almost six years on the line, six years of drinking and carousing, Stanislaw spotted something that just about took his gin-soaked breath away. A Sunday in late May. Warm with the smell of blooming flowers in the air. Stanley had a headache and a hangover. Nothing unusual there. He just couldn't decide if he wanted to go to the bar and drink or lie down somewhere in the grass and pass out.

His eyes wandered. He saw her sitting on the front porch of a house on Innis Avenue. She looked like something from heaven in her white church dress. Long, silky brown hair that fell across her right shoulder and over her breast. The bluest eyes and the loveliest lips Stanley had ever seen.

He stopped, took a step in her direction, conjured up his gentler, more sensitive side. "You're an awful pretty sight. Mind if I ask your name?"

"Jessie," she said and smiled. "Jessie Buell."

"Pleased to met you Jessie Buell," said my old man. "My name's—" And right there Stanley stopped. He didn't want to tell her his name. Wanted a different name, an Irish name, not a stupid Polack name.

"I know who you are," said Jessie.

"You do?"

Jessie giggled, nodded.

They started dating on the sly.

"I'm going over to Eileen's," Jessie would tell her mother. But she wouldn't go to Eileen's. No, she'd go down the street and around the block for a secret rendezvous with Stanley Standowski. All through that spring and summer, they met practically every evening. They'd sit in a quiet corner of the park necking, making plans.

Stanley was twenty-seven. Jessie almost twenty. Stanley had bedded a couple dozen women. Jessie was a virgin. Stanley wanted Sex. Jessie wanted Love.

Jessie's parents would've killed her had they known about her clandestine meetings with this Standowski character. Not only was he a dirty Polack, but he had a terrible reputation. Nevertheless, Jessie told lie after lie after lie in order to feel his strong arms around her tiny waist. And every night, after crawling into bed, that good Catholic girl would pray to God for forgiveness, even though she knew she'd be out there again the following evening, lying and living in sin.

Jessie worked downtown as a secretary in a small insurance office. One day my old man, his heart shoved up into his throat for perhaps the one and only time in his entire life, grew so bold he marched straight into that office bearing a dozen red roses. In front of everyone, insurance agents and prospective buyers alike, he handed those roses to Jessie and professed his deepest, undying love.

My old man didn't love my mother. Not that day. Not any day. He didn't love anybody. He was nothing but a horny bastard willing to do or say anything to get into a girl's pants.

But my mother, she didn't know about men like Stanley. She clutched those roses to her breast and swooned.

Well, Jessie's parents heard about this intrusion even before she arrived home from work. They ranted and raved. Wouldn't let her out of the house. Took her to see the priest who lectured her on chastity, Catholicism, mortal sin, and God's desire to see Irish blood kept pure.

A week passed. A month. Two months. Jessie and Stanley tried to meet, but Jessie might as well have been an inmate at the state pen down in Ossining. Couldn't go down to the corner store without an escort. Security was tight. Irish patrols on every street corner. Like she had some sexual assassin hot on her trail.

Fate, of course, intervened. The parents, the priests, and the concerned Irish community all slipped up at the same time, on the same night: Lent, the beginning of the season of Christ. The whole family prepared for church. The entire neighborhood prepared for church. Everyone but Jessie. She didn't feel well. Earlier in the day she'd thrown up. Twice. Her stomach felt weak. Her head hurt. Or so she said.

"Maybe you should stay home," suggested her mother. "I'll stay with you."

"No, Mama," said Jessie. "You go ahead. I'll be fine."

And so the family went. But they hadn't gone around the block before out of those late winter shadows a figure appeared wearing dark clothing and a leather hat pulled down over his forehead. Slipped into the Buells' small backyard and up the wooden steps to the back door. Knocked softly and entered. They met halfway across the kitchen. Their embrace did not last long for they feared someone might glance in the window and see them locked together. So they beat a hasty retreat to a more secure part of the tiny house. Up the stairs and down the hallway to Jessie's bedroom no bigger than a closet. The room of a cloistered nun. A rosary slipped onto the floor as they tumbled onto her hard narrow bed. Passion unleashed. Kissed, hugged, and scratched while bit by bit their clothes came tumbling off. Their breathing grew fast and deep, especially as more and more of their flesh made contact. She screamed and silently recited her Hail Marys while he pushed against her. Stanley took a little extra time. Not a lot, but at least a little. He knew what to do, practiced in the art as he was. But what he didn't know, what he couldn't know, and nor could she, was that her body was in a state of acceptance, ready and willing to accept Stanley's secretions in a special way. They made love three times in little more than an hour. The exact same number of times the priest passed the collection plate. And now who knows for sure which time conceived the little laddie they would name Michael Josep? But for sure one of those times, since they would not meet again in sexual union until their wedding night four and a half months later.

A shotgun wedding without the shotgun, the marital union of Jessie Buell and Stanislaw Standowski. The Irish gunpowder roared when news of Jessie's condition raced through the streets of Poughkeepsie.

"Did you hear about young Miss Buell?"

"I did, aye, knocked up she is."

"And by a Polack no less."

"Poor girl will be paying for her sins from now till Doomsday."

"And her foal, probably have horns and a tail."

Not so you'd notice.

The wedding went down during my fifth month of gestation. Mama bulged a bit in her white wedding gown. The guests could not take their eyes off her belly. But still, the bride beamed and the groom glowed. Stanley kissed Jessie so hard after the vows that the priest, an Irishman and a racist, actually kicked him in the shin.

God made him do it.

The newlyweds moved into Stanley's bedroom at 26 Kelsey Road. But not for long. With his mama in the next room, Stanley could not perform. So a few months before I made my appearance, they moved into a brand-new garden apartment on Lawrence Lane not far from King Street Park. Not much Money but a whole lot of Sex. They made love at least twice a day right up until the obstetrician told Jessie she should stop until after the birth of her baby. Secretly,

Jessie rejoiced. Stanley had an unrelenting desire to use his member like a jackhammer.

On the day of my grand entry, my old man, Stanley Standowski, was nowhere in sight. Not in the delivery room or anywhere on the grounds of Vassar Brothers Hospital. He was in the last hours of his final shift at the ball bearing factory down near the railroad yard along the banks of the Hudson.

"Can I take the rest of the afternoon off?" he'd asked his foreman during lunch break. "My wife's having our first baby today."

The foreman, a hard-drinking Mick with a nasty disposition, had no use at all for Polacks. Especially Polacks who knocked up Irish girls. "Tell your lass to hold off till tonight, boy. You ain't leavin' the line for nuthin' but death, and maybe, if I'm feelin' religious, the comin' of the Pope."

This did not make Stanley happy. After lunch he went back out on the line, but immediately he began to simmer. Soon he began to boil. Witnesses claim they saw blood vessels bursting in his forehead, smoke curling out of his ears and mouth. He marched up to the foreman and demanded the rest of the afternoon off.

"Not a chance, boy," shouted the Mick. "Now get your lousy Polack ass back out on the line before I dock you a week's pay!"

"Screw you!"

"What did you say, boy?"

They had to scream over the whine of the ball bearing machines.

"I said, screw you, you stinking Irish scumbag!"

The foreman took the first swing. Stanley ducked, set, drove his right fist into the Irishman's gut. A pretty good brawl ensued. Most of the assembly line workers left their posts to watch the action. A good ten minutes passed before security arrived and pulled Stanley off his boss. They threw him out the back door, told him if he showed his face around there again they'd have him arrested. Stanley had a cracked lip and a bloody nose, but he didn't care. Flashed security the Polish victory sign, then turned on his heel and sallied away. He felt great, on top of the world. He stopped to have a drink. Or two. Or three. Bought a round for the bar. Blew his whole wad. Absolutely piss-eyed by the time he laid eyes on his little baby boy.

They christened me Michael Josep Standowski in a blatant attempt to appease my grandfathers. And right away, before ever uttering a word, I began to close the rift between the Standowskis and the Buells, between the Polacks and the Micks.

One look at his grandson and Michael Buell offered his unemployed son-in-law a job in the Poughkeepsie post office. A Polack in the Poughkeepsie post office in the early 1960s may not have been as stunning as a Catholic in the White House or a black on the Supreme Court, but it was nevertheless a small victory for ethnic harmony.

Before long my old man had his own route, the toughest route in the city, the downtown route. Tough because of all the heavy packages the store owners sent and received. But Stanley loved that route. Gave him something to prove. Strong as an ox, he could carry a hundred pounds on each shoulder. And he loved being outdoors, toting those huge blue bags up and down Main Street.

"It's like being Santa Claus," he told Jessie, who had recently become pregnant with their second child. My little sister. Sweet Maggie Jane.

Santa Claus. Right. The Stanley-as-Santa routine did not last long. About six months into Jessie's pregnancy trouble rumbled through the Standowski household. I must've been about two, two and a half. Just a tot. But already I could hear my old man coming. Could tell the good days from the bad.

By that time Jessie had gained close to thirty pounds. She kind of waddled with my little sister rolling around inside of her. She didn't feel very attractive. Her man nevertheless wanted his daily bread. He became moody and sometimes insulting when he didn't get it.

Jessie did her best but without much enthusiasm. Finally she had to tell him a little white lie. "The doctor says we should stop until after the baby's born."

"What?" Stanley demanded. "Why? We didn't stop last time until a couple weeks before you went to the hospital."

Jessie shrugged. "All I know is what the doctor told me."

Very close to Christmas. Stanley had probably hauled a ton of packages up and down Main Street that day. He was tired. Irritable. Totally pissed off. Felt more like Scrooge than Santa. "So what?" he growled. "You're as big as a goddamn house, woman. It would be like trying to fuck a freight train."

Oh yeah, I remember those cruel words spewing out of his mouth. Ugly, vicious words that hung there in the air, destroying forever any fantasies we might've had about domestic bliss.

And before his words had evaporated, Stanley rolled out of the apartment. He headed straight for the local saloon. Promptly got plastered on vodka and beer chasers. The next night more of the same. And the night after that as well. On the fourth night he picked up some bar bimbo. Took her to a cheap hotel down by the bus depot. Humped her, felt guilty, bloodied her nose, threw her out of the room by the scruff of her neck.

Not a good move, Pop. She was injured and insulted. She stopped by and had a chat with the police. The cops came to see Stanley. He got loud and belligerent. They handcuffed him, tossed him in the tank for the holidays.

Merry Christmas! Happy New Year!

After the baby came, Margaret Jane (Maggie) Standowski, Stanley brought himself back until control. With financial help from his father and his father-in-law, he even bought a small house over on Ellsworth Lane at the northeast corner of King Street Park. This simple, two-story, three-bedroom clapboard with the wide front porch and the narrow backyard was where I would pass my youth.

My old man still lives in that house. Alone. All alone.

Let me tell you: my old man was a drunk and a womanizer, and no matter how hard he tried to maintain a sane and sensible family life, he kept reverting to his old selfish, self-destructive ways. Throughout my childhood, Stanley crawled on and off the wagon with a debilitating regularity. While on the wagon, he proved an adequate father. He taught me how to kick a soccer ball. Coached my soccer teams. Took an interest in most of my athletic endeavors: baseball, basketball, track. But Stanley was an extremely moody and unpredictable Polack, prone to fits of anger, sullenness, depression. And when he drank, watch out! The man could grow cold and violent in an instant. He frequently used his fists or the back of his hand. Against me. Against my mother. Even against my little sister.

He beat the tar out of me several times. Probably it was just the booze swinging and flailing. The booze and a general repugnance for his own lousy life. He took his frustrations out on me. Out on us. Maybe I should have been more Christian about it, more forgiving, but as I grew older I came to hate my old man.

I remember one night I snapped. Must be close to twenty years ago, but still as fresh as any memory I own. I was thirteen, maybe fourteen years old. Old enough to defend my turf. Old enough to defend my mother and my sister.

The old man arrived home late from the post office. That inevitably meant trouble. He had the smell of the Idle Hour Tavern wafting off his postman's blues: a dank and sour smell of cigarette smoke, whiskey, and beer. The smell filled our little house, drifted up the narrow stairs and under the door of my bedroom. Smashed into my olfactory nerve and sent a shudder of fear spiraling down my spine.

I stayed up there, pretended to study. Even had a book open. A math book. But I never studied much. Didn't know how. Couldn't care less. I more or less greased my way through school. Good grades and first-class colleges were not high priorities in my neighborhood.

Anyway, that night I considered slipping out my window and down the trellis where Jessie grew roses, but before I could make my move I heard the old man's heavy step upon the stairs. Right outside my door he stopped. "Chow in five minutes," he growled. "Don't make me tell you again." Then he moved along the narrow hall and into the bathroom. I sat there in my room, like some prisoner in his cell, terrified, listening to my old man relieve himself.

Oh yeah, nights like that I kept my eyes and ears wide open. Had to maintain a constant vigil. Stanley could blow at any second.

At dinner he sulked, scowled. His face just inches above his plate. The booze had lost its edge. We all knew it. Could read it in his eyes. No one said much. No one said a word. Except Maggie Jane. Maggie loved to talk, loved to tell us every single thing that had happened to her from the moment her eyes opened in the morning. I wanted her to be quiet, pipe down, get the meal over with so we could escape before Mount Stanley erupted. But not that night. That night my little sister had to tell us all about this experiment they'd done at school. Something about optical illusions. But during the telling, in her excitement, she knocked over her glass of milk. The white stuff turned into a river, washed across the table between the peas and the potatoes, and waterfalled off the edge onto the lap of Stan the Man.

You might've thought the guy'd been electrocuted. He exploded out of his chair like he'd been hit in the groin with a cattle prod. Jessie and I froze in our seats. Didn't move a muscle. But Maggie, she laughed. Hell, it was funny. But you didn't laugh. Not at Stanley. Laughing at Stanley was tantamount to putting a bullet through the head of the President. He went berserk. He roared as he grabbed the table. Hoisted his end right off the floor. The meat, the peas, the potatoes, all of the dishes and silverware, the glasses and the two brass candlesticks—it all went sliding down and off the far side, right onto the lap of my poor, long-suffering mama.

Stanley roared again. The King of his crappy little Jungle. The Maniac of Ellsworth Lane.

My mother tried not to cry. She tried to stay calm as all those dishes and glasses crashed to the floor and shattered around her. She sat there covered with meat and milk and potatoes.

And when I looked I saw tears seeping out of her eyes, running down her cheeks. One wet splotch dribbled off her chin, landed on her hand.

More than I could stand. More than I would bear.

You see, I loved my mother. Worshipped her. She had protected me. Nurtured me. Spoiled me rotten. Time now for me to give a little back. All this flashed through my brain as I sat there staring at the mess and at those tears streaming down her pretty face. My turn to flip out. I was my pappy's boy after all. Part of the same gene pool. Plus I'd recently become a man. Thought so anyway. My hormones raged. Had enough testosterone flowing through my body to fire me to the moon. I fired at my father instead. Leapt out of my chair and went straight for his jugular. Caught him by surprise. Drove the bastard back against the wall. Knocked the air clean out of his lungs. Nothing left for him to breathe. Down he went. Slid along the wall and dropped to the floor.

What did I do next? I just stood there shaking, vibrating. Blood rushing through my veins and arteries. Unable to move. Barely able to breathe. My mother touched me on the shoulder. I must've jumped six feet in the air. When I came back to earth she hugged me to her breast, then told me to go over to my friend Joey's house across the park. She told me to stay inside. To wait for her to call.

I spent two days holed up at Joey's. When I finally went home the old man had pretty much calmed down. He still gave me a beating, but nothing like the one I would have endured had I waited around for him to pick himself up off the floor.

How much of the father rubbed off on the son? Tough to say. I am not a violent or an abusive person. I did not inherit his foul temperament or his disgust for the world. But the rest of it? I don't know. We're all genetic mutants, products of both our parents.

Physically, I am built like my father, rock solid, but I look more like my mother, more Irish than Polish: blue eyes, light brown almost sandy hair. Psychologically, I am a mess. A mix of good and bad, light and dark. Possessed by my old man's selfish, and probably self-destructive, inclinations. But likewise blessed with my mother's eternal optimism and cheerful disposition.

Jessie was a devoted and loving mother. She gave my sister and me unlimited care and affection. Told us every single day how much she loved us. Believed mightily in praise. The drawings I brought home from school were the greatest drawings ever made. I was the best player on the team. The best singer in the choir. Oh yeah, my mom never held back the love she had for us. It was omnipotent. Unconditional.

She taught us that kindness was the only road to happiness. And when I did even some small thing for her, like rub her head when she had a headache or bring her home a wild-flower I'd found growing in a crack in the sidewalk, she'd act as though I'd just handed her the keys to the Taj Mahal.

Jessie did her best under tough conditions. I tell you, I look back on it now, and I cannot believe the stuff she had to put up with. She made the mistake of smiling at Stanley Standowski that one Sunday afternoon, and for the rest of her life she had to pay the piper. Nowadays they'd label my mother a battered wife, both physically and emotion-ally. Nowadays they'd throw Stanley in jail for the stuff he did to her.

An abusive dad and a loving mom. Sets up all kinds of interesting scenarios for those who would dare to delve into my psyche. I have no idea what a normal childhood might be, but I think in the end, after casting stones and laying blame, I had a pretty normal one: public school, Tuesday af-ternoon catechism, Mass with Mom and Maggie on Sunday morning. I messed around with my friends, played sports, caused some trouble. Nothing much out of the ordinary. I might've been a little overzealous with some of my antics, but boys will be boys. Started a fire or two, one at an aban-doned warehouse down along the Hudson. It fanned out of control. Demanded the attention of several local fire depart-ments. But in the end, not much harm done. The absentee owner even made a bundle off the insurance.

For a few years in our early teens we became preoccu-pied with vandalism. No idea why. If the shrinks got hold of me they'd insist it was some kind of anti-authority thing. Probably against my old man. I don't know. Maybe so. We definitely got off on destroying property. Didn't matter whose. Anyone's would do. One night a bunch of us, in possession of a BB gun and a .22, roamed Poughkeepsie blasting out traffic signals and streetlights. Turned the town black. Just before dawn, the entire Poughkeepsie police department descended upon us. We scattered like ants. Ran for our lives. The cops tracked most of us down. But not me. I got away. Got off scot-free.

I've always had a knack for sliding through the cracks. Not a good knack. Just a knack.

And then there was the stealing. Started with a candy bar. A Butterfinger, I think. Mom used to haul Maggie and me along to the grocery. One day I snatched a Butterfinger off the shelf while she chatted up the butcher. Maggie told me not to do it, but I did it anyway. I slipped into the next aisle. Tore off the wrapper. Stuffed the candy into my mouth. Stuffed the wrapper behind some cereal boxes. The thrill of the crime far exceeded the oral satisfaction of the confection.

It went on from there. If I needed something I took it. Not very often. Never very much. A sleeping bag once from a downtown sporting goods store in advance of a weekend camping trip to Bear Mountain. That was a three-man job. Two of my cohorts distracted the guy at the cash register by knocking over a case of hunting knives while I, sleeping bag in hand, slipped out the door.

Still, all told, I wouldn't call myself a juvenile delinquent. Just a rambunctious kid out to have a good time. I grew out of it. Most of it anyway. Look, I came from a blue-collar family. So did the kids I hung around with. Nobody had any money, no extra money anyway. Holidays meant a long weekend over in the Catskills or up in the Adirondacks. One time we spent a whole week on Cape Cod. Now that was a very big deal. Back at school in the fall, I was the envy of my classmates with that Cape Cod sojourn under my belt.

And I'll tell you something else: just about every kid I knew had been knocked around by his old man a time or two. A black eye administered by one's father was a badge of honor; it meant you had gone over the line, bucked authority. And plenty of my friends had fathers who drank. Drank like fish. And plenty of those fathers ran around with women other than their wives. So my old man drank and screwed around and beat me up once in a while. So what? Big deal?

Who am I kidding? I know it was a big deal. I know I've been scrambling all my adult life at least in part because of the abuse my old man inflicted upon me.

But Stanley's part of the deal, part of the package. Take him out of the picture and you can forget college. My grades never would've gotten me in. I hated school, sat in the classroom like a caged leopard. All day long for twelve years I sat at those little desks with my legs shaking and my eyes wandering. I couldn't handle sitting still. Still can't. Prefer being loose, on the run, out in the open, free as a bird.

That's probably why I loved soccer. I could run up and down that field all day long. From end to end, side to side. Stanley had been a soccer player. Played in local leagues well into his fifties. But more than a player, Stan was a student of the game: tactics, strategies, conditioning. Had me kicking a ball before I could walk. Had me on a peewee team before I ever started school. Every night after work, long as he wasn't drunk, he'd be out there in the backyard knocking the ball around with me. Listen, without soccer, I probably *would've* wound up a juvenile delinquent.

My junior year of high school the colleges started coming around to watch me play. The better ones lost interest after one look at my academic record. But plenty of others stopped to talk. They wanted a center forward with speed, agility, and the dexterity to score goals with both the right foot and the left foot. Stanley had taught me well how to dribble and shoot with both feet.

I wound up at Ithaca College, Ithaca, New York. They had very competitive Division II soccer. And pretty easy academically. Right up my alley. They paid my way. Every nickel. No way I could've afforded college without a scholarship. And all I had to do was run up and down the field and stick the ball in the net. Bring some glory to old I.C.

When I got to Ithaca I decided to change my name. I was sick of being a Polack. Hell, I was half Irish. And one hundred percent American. And being eighteen I had the legal right to call myself whatever I wanted. I talked it over with Jessie. She liked the idea. We both knew a Polish name like Standowski could be a hindrance as my future unfolded. But what to do about Stanley? We knew he'd freak out. And, of course, he did. Slapped me across the face when I told him my new name: Mike Standish. Slapped me, then told me I was a traitor and no longer his son. In four years he never once came to watch me play intercollegiate soccer. Not once. Not even the time we played Vassar less than three miles from our front door.

So, do I regret registering for classes at Ithaca College as Michael Joseph Standish? No way. Not for one second.

I walked right into my room and introduced myself to my new roommate. "How you doing? The name's Standish. Mike Standish. Nice to meet you."

My new roomie climbed off his bed, shook my hand. "Cramer," he announced, his voice low and husky. "Graham Cramer."

Right away I could see he was a preppie: the khaki pants, the Izod shirt, the fluffy haircut, the too-firm handshake, the cut of his jaw. Had a stereo on his dresser worth more than my old man's car.

"Graham Cramer, huh?" I stared my new roomie down. Wasn't about to give him an inch. "Kind of like graham cracker?"

"Very funny," he said, then back to his bed, back to his book, some fat English novel written a million years ago.

"What're you reading, Cracker? Any good?"

He ignored me.

I just laughed, set about the business of unpacking my gear. Didn't take me long. Didn't have much: a couple plastic bags filled with clothes, a pillow, a blanket, a clock radio, a cheap lamp for my desk. I pulled a couple wrinkled shirts out of one of the plastic bags. Opened the closet on my side of the room. "Say, Cracker, got any extra hangers?"

He continued to ignore me. So I asked him again.

Without looking away from his book, he said, "Don't call me Cracker."

But hell, I called him Cracker anyway. That day and every day.

Mr. Graham "Cracker" Cramer of Pottersville, New Jersey. Also a soccer player. Although not on scholarship. Cracker didn't need a scholarship. He came from the same town as my sweet Sarah. The town where Money grows on trees.

It would be tough for me to exaggerate Cracker's influence on my life. And I don't just mean because he introduced me to Sarah. Cracker introduced me to Money, real Money, something I might've missed entirely had I hung around Poughkeepsie boozing and carousing, inevitably going to work for the fricking post office. Yup, Cracker and I became best buddies. Eventually. After I came clean.

So where am I? Devil's Cay. Southeastern edge of the Bahamian swirl. Arrived this morning on the weekly mailboat from Eleuthera. The M/V *Seahauler,* an ancient wooden tub, made the passage in less than a day. Seemed like months to me. I might as well have been sailing from the Old World to the New with Columbus and the boys, so lonely and far-flung did I feel aboard that bucket. Farther and farther from home, from Sarah, from all that Sex and Love and Money.

Nothing hour after hour but flat blue-green seas, clear August skies. Heat and humidity. A cancer-causing sun. No land. Anywhere. Until this speck appeared on the horizon: Devil's Cay.

An hour later we chugged into the harbor, a crescent-shaped pond protecting the island's one and only outpost. The engines reversed. The M/V *Seahauler* settled against the rubber-wrapped fender pilings. The deckhand secured her heavy hemp lines to the steel cleats bolted to the crumbling concrete wharf. The old diesel engine coughed and sputtered, then grew silent.

Out of the steer house stormed the captain: an aging brooder with a sun- and alcohol-ravaged face whose best friend lives inside a bottle of dark island rum. An angry cuss, he looked ready to tear the guts out of any man who crossed his path.

"Say, Captain," I asked, nice as can be, "know a nice hotel?"

He growled. Showed off his few remaining teeth: crusty, yellow incisors. "On this godforsaken spit a land?"

I nodded.

Cappy slipped his pint of rum from his pocket, unscrewed the top, took a long swallow. "You got two choices, landlubber."

Landlubber because I threw up on the deck of his stinking diesel tub. Twice: once on the trip from Nassau to Eleuthera, once on the pull from Eleuthera to Devil's Cay. Both times, to display his disgust, cappy spit a wet, syrupy gob of tobacco juice in my direction.

"Two choices, huh?"

"That's right. And ain't neither one the goddamn Waldorf-Astoria."

"I'm not looking for the Waldorf," I told him. "Just some place to close the door and lay my head. You like one any better than the other?"

Too much rum had rotted cappy's teeth, turned his eyes into flaming red fireballs. "I say they both suck a whore's tit. But if yer fool enough to ask my opinion, I say stay aboard the *Seahauler,* make fer Nassau. Gamble, drink, get laid. Life's only pleasures. Cockle yer brains out with some chocolate bimbo, then go back from whence you've come. Forget this Devil's Cay. Damn place is cursed."

"Cursed? How do you mean?"

Cappy took another pull on his pint, wiped the spilled excess off his chin. "Get off my boat now, lubber. I ain't some tight-ass tour guide."

Off the boat. Fine with me. I didn't need trouble. Have enough trouble: love lost and law enforcement hot on my trail. Slung my leather rucksacks over my shoulder, picked up my nylon duffel, stepped onto the wharf.

"Boat leaves soon as we get off-loaded," cappy grumbled. "An hour or less. If you ain't aboard when we draw anchor, there won't be no way off this rock for a solid week. More if I decide to go off on a toot." Then he spit in my direction and turned to his deckhand. "Let's get this load off the deck. We got us a long haul back."

Along the wharf stood most of Devil's Cay's one hundred or so residents. The island has no airstrip, so the mailboat brings not only the mail but most other commodities as well: food, booze, condoms—the whole tangle of human material desire. The islanders meet the boat to get their goods. But they'd come anyway. Need to see who's aboard. Besides the occasional hurricane, visitors give Devil's Cay its sole source of unpredictability. At any time the mailboat can deliver upon the island adventurers, dreamers, outlaws—an endless array of human curiosities. Today the mailboat brought me. I was the object of their boredom, their beady red eyes. Slowly they made way as I mixed among them.

Then one of them stepped in front of me. "Be needing a room tonight, mon?"

I stood face-to-face with a tall, thin black man; maybe the blackest man I've ever seen. Pure black. Pitch black. Absolutely invisible on a moonless night. And with these bright, shiny white teeth hiding behind a set of enormous lips.

"Could be."

"My name's Ferguson. Lewis Ferguson. I operate Lewey's Hotel. It's clean and quiet, mon, and the bed I'll offer you's practically new, not a lump in her."

"How much?"

We bickered for a while. Finally made a deal. Included a free draft of rum at sunset.

I handed him my duffel. Followed him up the street, beneath the shade of the tall banyan trees. Part of the crowd closed in around us. They followed us all the way to the hotel: up the slight rise, along the brick path, passed the hibiscus and the flowing patterns of bougainvillea. Followed us straight through the open archway into the faded pink and lavender lobby of Lewey's Hotel.

They even peered over my shoulder as I signed the leather-bound register with an old-fashioned fountain pen: Mr. Edward Weston, Point Lobos, California.

Oh yeah, Uncle Eddie. Easily the greatest black and white photographer of all time. In my opinion. Definitely my photographic mentor. And a name I've been using as an alias ever since fleeing TREETOPS, let me see, how long's it been? five and a half days. Seems more like five and a half months. Five and a half years. Where, by God, is Sarah? Why hasn't she found me yet?

So now I'm up in my room at Lewey's. Up on the second floor. I try to lock the door but can't. No bolt. No hook. No nothing. Just white walls and pictures of the blue-green sea. A window overlooking the harbor. I sit in a white wicker chair in front of the window. Watch as bags of flour and boxes of cereal and cases of condensed milk are off-loaded from the mailboat. Sweat covers my face. Must be a hundred degrees in here. Ceiling fan won't move. Not an inch. I work the pull string in vain. Think about telling Lewis, complaining, but instead cross to the bed, sit, rub my eyes, feel sorry for myself.

Been doing a hell of a lot of that lately.

My head aches, stomach still feels queasy from the crossing.

I rest a few minutes. Open one of my leather rucksacks. In a padded envelope, under the new Nikon F4S and the wide-angle lens (gifts from Sarah), I find the 8 x 10 color photograph: a portrait I made of her just a few weeks ago, just before the cops started coming around demanding fingerprints from everybody in the house.

God, I love that photograph. Best portrait of her I ever made. Easily. Very tough to take Sarah's picture. A nervous wreck the second anyone points a lens in her direction. Almost impossible to get her to smile. Always the same serious expression on her face. Even in her kiddie pictures. And this from a not very serious girl. Fairly lighthearted, in fact. But I caught her by surprise this time. Down by the stable. Just after a ride. Leaning against the split-rail fence. I snuck up behind her. Softly called her name. Tripped the shutter the moment she turned around. Ah, that face, that angelic face: the auburn hair cut short like a boy's, the high cheekbones, huge brown eyes, perfect lips. Enough to make a man's heart jump right out of his chest. My heart anyway.

But staring at her photograph—that's just too damn depressing. I mean, if she doesn't find me, track me down, I might never see her again. Might never get to hold her in my arms again.

I slip the photo back into the rucksack. Rummage deeper until I find the soft suede pouch. Take out the pouch, draw open the zipper. Count the Money. First the hundreds: twenty grand. Then the fifties: ten grand. The tens and twenties: another six grand. I open my billfold: another two grand. A grand total of about thirty-eight thousand dollars. Thirty-eight thousand dollars: nothing, a mere pittance. For less than forty grand I threw everything away, flushed it all right down the hole.

Forty grand!

And all of it in cash. All of it I have to carry everywhere I go: on cars and planes and boats. Through crowds and customs and stinking crime-infested streets. No bank accounts. No credit cards. Nothing but cash. And new names. False identities.

Thirty-eight grand won't last forever, won't last any time at all as long as I'm on the move, on the run. More Money at home, back in the States, tucked away in banks, but I can't get at it, can't go back and risk getting caught.

I put the cash back in the pouch, back in the rucksack. Two, three, sometimes four times a day I repeat this ritual, this Counting of the Money. Sick, I know.

I settle back on the bed. The springs squeak. I put my hands behind my head, fix my eyes on the ceiling. Plaster cracked and splintered.

After a while I get sick and tired of staring at the ceiling, so I close my eyes and pretend to sleep.

The private, and now, again, the public persona.

Mike, alias Eddie, enters the bar at the back of Lewey's Hotel carrying his two leather rucksacks. Tries to look cool and calm with those bags hanging over either shoulder. But I think the sweat on my upper lip and the way my eyes keep darting around the room pretty much destroy my efforts. I look the way I feel: nervous, jittery, uptight. Still, I have on my brand-new powder blue sports shirt and my spiffy island khakis. Part of the wardrobe I purchased a couple days ago at a fashionable boutique on Duval Street in Old Key West. Was in kind of a hurry, you see, the day I fled TREETOPS manor. Didn't dare walk out of that house toting an arsenal of heavy baggage. Had told the family, as far as I can remember, that I was just going down to the post office to mail a letter.

I glance around the bar. Expect a crowd but see only a single couple sitting by the window. A white couple. The only other whites on Devil's Cay.

And beyond the window night, but enough light illuminates the harbor that I can see the deserted dock. Cappy has taken his mailboat back to Eleuthera. Left me behind.

"Newlyweds."

"Huh?"

"Newlyweds," repeats Lewis. "They're staying on their sailboat moored out in the harbor, but they come into town for supper and to enjoy the sunset."

I nod, take another look at the couple. They sit close, practically right on each other's laps. I, of course, imagine myself sitting there with Sarah on my lap, her arms around my neck, her sweet breath against my cheek. But the imagination this time offers only pain, so I blink Sarah away and walk down to the far end of the bar.

"You miss the sunset, Mr. Weston. Fall asleep?"

I set the rucksacks on the floor, climb onto a bar stool. Situate myself so I can watch the door. "Yeah," I answer, "I fell asleep."

"That's what I told them."

I shoot Lewis a glance. "That's what you told *who*?"

"The locals who come around for sunset, mon, and to have a look at you."

"To have a look at *me*?"

"That's a major pastime here on Devil's Cay. Scope out who the mailboat bring. Hear any news they have to tell."

I think about it. "I didn't bring any news."

Lewis, disappointed, shrugs. "Maybe you remember something later."

"I doubt it." I peer out the picture window overlooking the harbor. See nothing.

"You want that rum I promised you, Mr. Weston?"

Distracted. Then, "Rum? Sure. That'd be good. Rum and Coke. With ice."

"Sorry, mon, no ice."

"Why not?"

"No power. Night before last we had us a fine blow just before sunset. Thunder and lightning as far as you could see. Clear across to Bimini I'd say. The generating station took a hit."

I glance at the ceiling. The fans hang idle. A few bulbs burn dimly.

"A small generator out back," explains Lewis. "Enough to power some lights, but nowhere near the juice to run the refrigerators and the freezers."

"Maybe I ought to renegotiate how much I'm paying for my room."

Lewis shows his white teeth. "You can try, mon."

"Hell, there aren't even any locks on the doors."

"No locks at all on Devil's Cay, Mr. Weston."

"Then how do I keep my stuff from getting ripped off?"

"Is that why you bring your bags to the bar? Afraid of thieves?"

"Damn right."

"Valuable things in those bags, hey mon?"

Nervous sweat runs down my spine. I suppress an urge to make a mad dash for the door. "Valuable enough, yeah."

"Maybe you running from something, mon?"

I glance at Lewis, then at the newlyweds. They haven't heard a word. No one's heard a word. The whole damn thing is so stupid: The U-Haul Caper. The Fence. The Fingerprints. The Running. The Lying. The Money. The Sex. Utterly senseless. Still, my eyes scan the darkness beyond the window. Then the empty space beyond the doorway. Nothing. No one.

"Hell," I say, finally, "we're all running from something."

Okay, so did I tell my new roommate, Mr. Graham "Cracker" Cramer, that I was Michael Josep Standowski, son of Stanislaw Standowski, drunken letter carrier from the wrong side of Poughkeepsie, New York? Not a chance. I wanted a whole new identity to go along with my new name. So I told him a pack of lies. So many lies I had a difficult time keeping them straight. They started flowing out of my mouth on that very first day. And they just kept flowing for most of the next two and a half years, really right up until that night Maggie Jane called crying and said Jessie might not make it till morning.

In a nutshell: Call me Mike. Mike Standish, Malibu, California. Told Cracker and my other Ithaca College classmates Malibu for the simple reason that it rolled off the tongue quite nicely with Mike. Mike Malibu. Malibu Mike. Never underestimate the power of alliteration. So I'd never been to Malibu, never set foot in the Golden State. So what? Suddenly, just like that, just because I said so, I was from there. Born and raised. A California coastal kid. Sand between my toes. Salt between my eyelashes. Surfed before I walked. Learned to play soccer on the beach. All that extra work made my legs like bands of steel. Gave me speed and agility. At least that much I could prove out on the playing field.

But the rest of it: just a story. Spewing from my imagination. And always evolving. An organic mess.

Let's see: Dad was a big-shot Hollywood TV producer. *Mod Squad. Gilligan's Island. Truth or Consequences.* I liked that last one. A nice touch.

Mom was an actress. Very hot in her time. Legs that could kill. Preferred low-budget artsy films. Didn't go for the glitz. But definitely a flaky broad. Drove my old man crazy with her addiction to prescription drugs and her daily visits to the head doctor. Then, when I was like nine, Mom ran off with her shrink. Just went to his office one morning and never came back. We heard they took off for the South Seas, maybe Tahiti, but that could've just been a rumor.

Might as well leave 'em hanging.

On and on I verbally marched, conjuring up a childhood that included dates with Jody F., drinks with Meryl S., joint rolling lessons from Bobby D., front-row seats at the Forum next to Jackie N. Whatever it took. Sure, I wanted to impress, but more than that I enjoyed the re-creation of my Poughkeepsie past.

And my stoic roommate, Graham "Cracker" Cramer— the strong, brooding, silent type—he bought every word I uttered. Lock, stock, and barrel. At least I thought so at the time.

The toughest part of my act concerned my abject poverty. How to explain it? How to make it part of my story? Why I never had a nickel? These questions, for a time, caused me no small amount of consternation. Here I was, son of the inventor of Gilligan and Ginger and Thurston Howell III, and not a single greenback to be found anywhere on my person. A tough sell, but I managed.

"Yeah," I told Cracker, "the old man basically disowned me when I decided to come east to college. He wanted me to go to UCLA, study filmmaking. But I told him no way.

Told him I had to get away from L.A. for a few years. That pissed him off. But I didn't care. I had a scholarship."

Cracker just listened, nodded. Made a few mental notes.

"So the SOB doesn't send me any money. Big deal? I'll get by. I'm not about to beg. And no way am I going back."

Cracker had money. Plenty of green. And more arriving from Mom back in Pottersville, New Jersey, all the time. Every week. Never failed. Came in a CARE package with the homemade brownies, the tollhouse cookies, and the five-pound bags of pistachios.

After a while Cracker just threw the package on my bed. I needed it more than he did. He didn't eat much of that stuff anyway. Stayed clear of salt, sugar, fat. Even as a kid Cracker was into deprivation. Guilt has always been one of his primary motivators. A Calvinist sin to ever have too good a time.

It didn't bother me. I ate those cookies and nuts with all the culinary respect they deserved.

Cracker and I slept in the same room, shared the same head, ate the same bad meals at the same table, listened to the same music, washed our clothes in the same load, sucked the same air into our lungs. We also went to the same parties, hung out with the same people. But Cracker was never much of a partyer. He might nurse a beer along, maybe take a hit or two off a bone if one passed his way. But mostly he stood around at parties looking alternately bored and irritated, waiting to go back to our room where he could read his ancient novels and listen to his vast collection of rock and roll records.

And the coeds, let us not forget the coeds. Cracker and I also gawked at the same lovely young Ithaca College coeds. But whereas I had already been introduced to the joys of female companionship, Cracker still had not. And so, while we both gawked and dreamed, I took the next logical step: pursuit. I pursued night and day. I had no fear of failure. Maggie and I had spent our youth teaching each other what males wanted from females and vice versa. We were practiced in the art. I just tried to get the girls to relax, to giggle, to give me a nice, wet French kiss. Like Stanley, I soon discovered I had excellent powers of persuasion.

Cracker, on the other hand, proved himself to be an uptight white guy without the slightest idea how to make the moves on a member of the opposite sex. Totally inept. You could see the fear in his eyes. Don't ask me why. He stood six feet tall. A lean, hard body from a childhood filled with athletics: soccer, swimming, tennis, horseback riding. Pretty good-looking, even handsome, if you ask me. Simple, straightforward features. Very English. Anglo-Saxon to the core. Blue eyes. An aquiline nose. Perfect teeth. A fortune in orthodontics. Too bad the guy didn't smile much. So damn cerebral. So much stuff on his mind all the time. Always peering out at the world, observing its inhabitants with a wary eye. The pursuit of women did not come naturally. And when finally he did engage one, watch out, he fell wildly in love after the first kiss.

"You're helpless, Cracker," I used to tell him after we had turned off the lights at night. "Altogether useless when it comes to women. One of them's eventually going to wrap her legs around your waist and that'll be the ball game. You'll be stuck with that one forever, sentenced to a lifetime of browbeating and unhappiness."

The future foretold.

I did my best to get Cracker dates. Must've set him up a dozen times. And with some pretty nice girls too. But he always messed it up. Always so somber. Always wanting to talk the serious talk: literature, politics, world events. Very vital topics, I'm sure, but the girls just didn't care. They wanted a few laughs, a spin or two around the dance floor.

I gave Cracker the same advice the rum-sucking skipper of the *Seahauler* gave me just this morning. "Gamble, drink, have a good time. Go after as many of these Ithaca College coeds as you can. There won't be another opportunity like this your entire life."

I think Cracker wanted to take my advice; he has always longed for even a moment of utterly frivolous behavior, but some profound psychological brick wall always stood in his path. Held him back. Every step of the way.

Of course, I didn't know much about his brick wall in those days. I didn't know much about my own brick wall either. Still don't. As far as I knew then, Cracker was just my roomie, a good guy to pal around with in the socially stymied atmosphere of a small liberal arts college.

In our early days, before we figured out we actually cared about one another, maybe even loved each other like brothers, what Cracker and I shared, what brought us together, was our love of soccer. We loved that game. We loved to compete and win.

By the middle of our second season, our sophomore year, we had pretty much taken over the team. With the season on the skids, Coach made a decision to go with the young guys, build for the future. I took over the center forward spot and Cracker moved to left wing. Being a natural southpaw he had a wicked left foot; once saw him splinter a goal post from twenty yards out.

Along with a couple other sophomores and a goaltender from East Germany with reflexes like a cat, we started to win. Won by running, by sprinting relentlessly up and down that field. Ran like young men possessed from the opening gun until the final second ticked off the clock. We ran our opponents into the ground, ran until they collapsed on the turf. Many of our games we won in the last minutes simply because we refused to stop running. Soccer is a game of skill and precision, but also a game that demands enormous amounts of spirit. Long after you are exhausted, long after your brain has started begging you to stop and rest, you must keep running, harder and faster, running until you break the spirit of your opposition. And then you slide the ball into your center forward and watch as he fakes right, dribbles left, and blasts a shot by the goalie's outstretched hands for the winning score.

But then, in the middle of our junior year, nine wins and only a single defeat, a mid-season stat sheet of fourteen goals and eight assists for yours truly, that phone call came from Maggie Jane.

Cracker and I lived in a house down on East State Street with a couple of our teammates. A big old three-story Victorian. Must've been almost midnight when the telephone rang. No big deal. The phone rang at that hour all the time.

I was up in my room. Studying. Trying anyway. I heard Cracker call my name from downstairs. "Standish, phone!"

I picked up the receiver in the upstairs hallway. "Hello?"

"Michael?"

"Maggie?" I could tell right away she'd been crying.

"You better come home, Michael. I think she's giving up. The priest arrived a few minutes ago."

Okay, I knew it was coming. I'd been expecting the call for weeks. Ever since I'd come back to school. Jessie had been sick for almost a year. She had already lived longer than the doctors had said she would. She'd been through the radiation. And the chemo. And more radiation. I'd watched her hair fall out, her body grow thin, her face turn hollow and pale. All summer long, as she grew weaker and weaker, I'd sat with her up in her room, telling her stories, trying to make her laugh, doing my best to act like nothing was wrong.

"Go back to school, Michael," she told me at the end of August. "Neither one of us needs you hanging around here watching me die."

So I went. But I called practically every night. Especially on game nights. I always gave her an in-depth account of our soccer games. She heard about every play, every shot on goal, every score, every victory.

And then, at the end of October, Maggie called. Told me to come home. I went downstairs. Found my buddy Cracker on the couch reading *Madame Bovary*. Not because he had to. Because he wanted to. In preparation for his vocation as Important Late Twentieth Century American Novelist. Cracker had years before set out to read all the important works of fiction ever written. Had started with Homer and was working his way forward.

"I need to borrow your car."

"What?"

Cracker did not often let people borrow his car, a BMW 2002 given to him by his parents as a graduation present from high school. I got a handshake and a check for fifty bucks.

"My mother's dying. I need to borrow your car."

He didn't even look up from Flaubert's opus. "You're full of it. You just want the car so you can go cruising with some babe."

"My mother's dying, Cracker. Now gimme the damn keys."

That got his attention. "What are you going to do? Drive to Tahiti?"

"What?"

"Didn't you tell me your mother ran off to the South Seas with her shrink?"

"She lives in Poughkeepsie. Now gimme the keys."

Cracker never gave me the keys. He drove me to Poughkeepsie himself.

I don't recall exactly when Cracker started to believe my mother was dying in Poughkeepsie, New York, but once he started to believe he stopped asking questions, making sarcastic remarks. Partly, I suppose, he simply wanted to observe, wait, and see what strange scenarios might unfold in the hours and days ahead. But more than any material he might gather for one of his future novels, Cracker grasped my plight and my pain and immediately reached out a helping hand.

Ithaca to Poughkeepsie. In the middle of the night. A long, tough drive along a bunch of winding back roads. Cracker grew sleepy. I took the wheel. Across the Hudson just before dawn. Straight into downtown Poughkeepsie. The city of my youth looked bleak and barren, an old industrial urban hole that had long ago seen its best and brightest days. Thank God I'd escaped. I didn't want to be there. I was scared, and already feeling incredibly alone. After this, I said out aloud, I'm never coming back.

My declaration brought Cracker wide awake. Asked me what I'd said. I told him nothing. Then a few more turns before we entered a residential neighborhood of small houses set close together just a few feet back from the road. My neighborhood. Where I grew up. Tight and Cramped. I downshifted the 2002, slowed, finally stopped. Right in front of a simple wooden house painted white with blue shutters. STANDOWSKI, it said on the mailbox. Cracker glanced at me. I think I might've nodded. We both knew I was home. No need for questions or comments.

We parked on the street. Lots of other cars. Bumper to bumper. Up the porch stairs. Through the front door. The smell of impending death. I wanted to run, run for my life. But the Irish Catholics descended on me before I could make a move. Mama's people. Friends and family. Eyes downcast. Already deep in mourning. Not a Polack in sight. I went quickly up the stairs. Left Cracker to his own diversions. Found out later he got cornered in the kitchen by one of Mama's younger sisters who rambled on and on about what a beautiful and lively girl Jessie had been back in the old days. Back before Stanislaw dragged her through the mud of a rotten marriage. "It was that terrible man," she told

Cracker, "who gave my sister this killer cancer. Twenty years of strain. Twenty years of stress. Enough to make any woman sick to the soul. May he burn in hell."

Cracker, polite white Protestant boy who had certainly never been to an old-fashioned Catholic death vigil before, stood perfectly still and nodded when he deemed it appropriate.

Up in the master bedroom, a ten-by-twelve cell of gloom and disappointment, I knelt beside my mama's bed. She smiled at me as best she could. I took her hand in mine. Limp at the wrist. Bony. Weightless. She looked far worse than she had at the end of the summer. Thinner. More frail. Skin like tissue paper. Eyes buried in the back of her skull. A boy should not have to see his mother like that. No. Makes him crazy. Sad. Angry. Jessie told me she loved me. Assured me she would be watching over me from heaven. She coughed a lot, trembled from the pain.

For chrissakes! What did she do to suffer such an agonizing and humiliating death? Was it her sin of fornicating with that worthless Polack Stanislaw before the proper wedding vows had been exchanged?

I kissed her, held her, told her I loved her too. Thanked her for bringing me into the world. Reminded her of the time she and Maggie Jane and I had floated down the Hudson on inner tubes. And the time she taught me how to dance the cha-cha out in the backyard under the moonlight just an hour before the start of the eighth-grade dance. I would've remembered more but I could see she was exhausted. So I told her I wanted her to meet my friend, my best friend. Probably she didn't want to, so many people in her face already, so much confusion, but loving and considerate to the end, she nodded her consent.

I went downstairs. Found Cracker. He followed me through the house, up the creaky steps, down the hall. I pushed open the door. We went into the room. I could hear

Cracker's heart pounding, could see his hands all clammy, his eyes glazed and dizzy. The room small and crowded: two priests, Mama's mother, my sister, our father. Stanley, huddled back in a corner, scowling, unable to fathom his role in this tragedy. And, of course, Mama, the main attraction, flat out on the bed, tiny and fading beneath a damp white sheet. Cracker looked freaked, like he had lost both the ability and the desire to draw breath.

He followed me over to the bed. I held Mama's fingers, brittle sticks covered with some pale, papery skin. "This is Graham, Mama. I've told you all about him."

Cracker bent down and took her hand. And then, right there, leaning over the deathbed, Cracker started to cry, not buckets like a baby, but still a steady stream rolling down his cheeks.

And my mother, she reached up, looked into Graham's eyes, and whispered, "I'd enjoy a smile much more, son." And then she gently wiped away his tears with the back of her hand.

Cracker needed a moment to get hold of himself. But he managed to give her what she wanted.

"That's much better," she told him. Then, "Now promise me. Promise me you'll watch out for my boy."

Cracker did not hesitate. Not for a second. He nodded vigorously. "I promise, Mrs. Standowski. Absolutely."

I looked at him. I couldn't believe he'd gotten the name right.

"He's a good boy," my mother assured him. "He just doesn't know it yet."

Cracker and I spent six days in Poughkeepsie. On the second day Jessie slipped into a coma. On the third day she mercifully passed away.

And then for three days we waited while the Irish Catholics went through their death ritual. I didn't think they'd ever leave the poor woman alone. Send her on her way. Cover her with earth.

I stayed close to Maggie Jane. I held her when she cried. Together we dealt with the tidal waves of emotion rolling over us. And we dealt with Stanley. As best we could. He paced from room to room looking like some depraved maniac. He was usually drunk by noon. Brow furrowed, he refused to look anyone in the eye.

I asked Maggie if she wanted to come and live with me in Ithaca. She thanked me but said no. She said she had promised Jessie she would stay home and take care of our father.

I thought she was crazy, but I kept it to myself.

To get out of the house, away from all the grief, away from all the aunts and uncles, Cracker and I went over to the park. We kicked the soccer ball around. We missed two games that week. Two defeats. Somehow that made us feel a little better, reaffirmed our importance to the team. We also went for several long walks through Poughkeepsie. I told him my story, my real story, buried forever my TV producer dad and my flaky actress mom. I came clean about my Malibu connection.

"You know, Standish," was about all Cracker said, "I never believed all of it, but I believed a lot of it. You're a hell of a storyteller. Far more creative than me."

And the next day, after I'd finished my confession, he said, "I hate to tell you this, what with your mom passing away and all. But even if from the very beginning I'd known you were nothing but a stinking Irish Catholic Polack from the wrong side of Poughkeepsie, I still would have liked you."

We were getting ready to go bury my mother. Put her in the ground. Forever. I felt pretty bad, pretty gloomy. Sad and confused and abandoned. But Cracker's comment made me smile. "Yeah?"

"Yeah," he told me. "Because you're a funny guy, Mike. And because you're a whole bunch of things I'm not."

He didn't explain what he meant, and I didn't ask.

We walked across the campus of Vassar College. Late fall. A few leaves left on the trees. Most of them brown and blowing around on the ground. We kicked them into the air.

"I applied here," said Cracker.

"To Vassar?"

He nodded.

"So what happened?"

"I didn't get in. Lousy grades. Like you, Standish, I was a crummy student with a bad attitude."

"That old authority thing."

"I guess."

We walked past Rockefeller Hall. Ivy-covered fieldstone walls. The leaves deep red, glistening in the shimmer of the setting sun.

"So what did you want to go to Vassar for?" I asked him. "Don't tell me it was the girls?"

He thought about it, then gave me his answer. "One girl in particular."

"Really? What girl?"

"Just a girl."

"What kind of answer is that? You never mentioned a girl."

"Maybe I didn't want to."

"Don't hand me that. Who is she?"

It took him a while to get his mouth open. Such a reserved WASP. "Sarah," he finally said. "Sarah Browne. Sarah Louise Browne. She grew up near me. Taught me how to ride a horse, how to hit a volley, do a back flip." Cracker was on a roll. This was more than I had ever heard him say at one clip.

I loved it. Listening to him open up. "Yeah? So?"

"So she got married a couple months ago."

"Married?"

"Yeah. To this asshole. Ricky Carlson. A real scumbag."

He looked mad. Maybe hurt. Disappointed. I wasn't sure what to say. I didn't know what my buddy wanted to hear. So for once in my life, I said nothing. I just looked at him, nodded, let him see I was listening, let him know I cared.

Sarah. Sarah Louise Browne. Sarah Browne Carlson. Sarah Browne Cramer. Sarah Browne Standish. Pretty soon probably just Sarah Browne again. She'll unload my appendage like unwanted ballast. Iron Kate will make sure of that. Take an axe to it, chop the bloody limb off. Toss it onto the manure pile along with my fingers and my arms.

Of course, I can easily imagine another scenario. One wherein Sarah frantically tries to find me, track me down, bring me home. I feel certain she'll decipher my clues and appear here on Devil's Cay before too many more days slip by.

There: standing in front of that translucent glass door. Staring at the bold black letters: GLENN SHELDON, PRIVATE INVESTIGATOR. Trying to decide if she should knock on the door or run for her life.

For four or five days now, ever since I disappeared, Sarah has been studying the Yellow Pages. Shocked my wife was to find so many detective agencies; more than twenty in Morris County alone. Who, she wondered, without irony, had so much need for private investigation?

Most of the ads struck her as too impersonal: toll-free 800 numbers, no street address, only regions where they performed their clandestine operations. Others seemed more corporate, interested only in big-money crimes like insurance scams and malpractice suits. She found herself going back again and again to the small listing that said: GLENN SHELDON.

And beneath his name, a list of his services:

DISCREET INVESTIGATIONS

MATRIMONIAL & PREMARITAL

CHILD CUSTODY

MISSING PERSONS

I can see Sarah reading those last two words over and over: MISSING PERSONS, MISSING PERSONS, MISSING PERSONS. And finally, when it became clear that I would not be coming back to give myself up, she decided to stop by and pay Mr. Sheldon a visit at his office on South Street in Morristown.

She takes a deep breath, knocks on the door. No answer. Thinks again about just slipping away. But no, she knocks again. Louder this time. Still no answer. She turns the knob. Pushes the door open. "Hello?" she practically whispers. "Is anyone here?"

My wife, you understand, does not find herself in strange and uncomfortable situations very often. She has grown into adulthood cradled by the protective bosom of her family and its considerable resources. If not for the two divorces, and now this rubbish with me, she would probably still possess her childhood innocence.

"Come in," says a male voice. "Thought I heard someone." And now we meet Glenn Sheldon, Private Investigator, a caricature of the species, a man who has watched *The Maltese Falcon* fifty times, *Chinatown* maybe a hundred times. Thinks often about changing his name to Jake Gittes. Or maybe go all the way and just call himself Spade, Sam Spade. Oh yeah, a scruffy and cynical gumshoe.

He stands in the inner doorway, a cordless phone tucked under his chin. "Be right with you. My secretary's off. Having another baby. Her third, and more, she tells me, on the way. The nineties, I swear to God, a repeat of the fifties."

My wife, look at her, brought up in all the right ways; she smiles politely at this intrusion of words. But inside she's already labeling him a pig: sexist and brutish.

Sheldon smiles back, then retreats into his office. Sarah slips into a leather armchair, the leather old and brittle. She hears him on the telephone, something about surveillance at the mark's apartment, photos "that'll nail his ass to the courtroom door." Sarah tries not to listen, was raised by Iron Kate never to eavesdrop. Still, she can't help but experience a twinge of arousal. Exciting, unfamiliar stuff. Very personal. She looks around the outer office: a desk with a PC and an appointment book, a desk chair that swivels, a fake Persian carpet, some random prints of famous paintings hanging on the walls in cheap frames, most of them slightly askew.

Sarah knows about those paintings, the artists who painted them. Minored in art history at Vassar College. While Cracker pined away for her over at Ithaca. But she doesn't think about those paintings. Not now. She thinks only about escaping before Mr. Sheldon comes back and starts making inquiries about why she's come and how he might help.

Too late.

"Sorry about the delay," says Sheldon, slipping back into the room. "Some rather unsavory business."

Right. He probably didn't even have anyone on the line. Just faking it.

Tall and gaunt, in his early forties, Sheldon could easily pass for an older man. Butts, booze, bad women, and far too much fat in his diet have taken their toll. He introduces himself. "Sheldon, Glenn Sheldon."

Sarah stands, takes his outstretched hand. Smooth and cool, even though the office feels warm and clammy during these hot, dog days of August. "Yes," she says, "how do you do?"

Sheldon likes the sound of that. Gives his young female prospect the once-over, very subtle, knows right away she comes from Money. Can tell not only from those fine, white, chiseled features and the simple but elegant cut of her short auburn hair and the expensive silk dress, but also the question. "How do you do?" The ones with Money, with the proper breeding, they ask, Sheldon has learned over the years, "how do you do?" The rest of them, the trash, the wannabes, they ask, "how ah ya?" never, "how do you do?" But Money, he knows, can be good and bad. Usually good. But not always. More demanding, more arrogant. Still, a young female with dough. Tough to go wrong there. Probably domestic trouble. An unfaithful husband. What else is new? Aren't they all? Yup, she wears a wedding band. Solid gold. And that rock on her engagement ring—could pay the rent for a year with that thing.

"I'm pretty well," he answers. "And you?"

"Oh," says Sarah, all knotted up, a lifetime of repressed feelings, "just fine."

Sheldon sees he will have to hold her hand, at least until he can get her mouth moving. And what a pretty mouth it is. Lips thin but quite succulent. Jesus, this SOB is going to make the moves on my wife.

They head for his office. He gestures for her to go first. The inner office looks a lot like the outer office. More of those famous masterpieces in the cheap frames: Van Gogh's *Sunflowers,* Monet's *Water Lilies,* a portrait by Renoir.

"Have a seat," says Glenn Sheldon, P.I., "and, when you're ready, you can tell me how I might be of service today."

Sarah sits, sighs. She's in it now, no way out. A month ago, even a week ago, she never would've imagined herself in such a predicament.

Sheldon slips around the desk, sits in his metal armchair. Squeaks and moans as it accepts his weight. "I'm glad you dropped by to see me this morning, Miss—"

"Sarah."

"Yes. Sarah. Thanks for coming. May I ask how you learned of my services? A reference perhaps? Or maybe—"

"The Yellow Pages," says Sarah quickly.

Rockets' red glare in Sheldon's brain. The Yellow Pages! That can mean only one thing: desperation. His eyes give away nothing. "It's good to know," he says, calmly, "that I'm getting a return on my investment."

Sarah wants to run, hide, disappear.

"I mean it," says Sheldon. "Those ads aren't cheap."

"Yes, well—"

"Two hundred a month so people can let their fingers do the walking. And with the big boys dominating the action with their full-page color ads, not many walk my way."

Sarah's lips part. "I'm here because, well, because . . ."

Sheldon steps in with the line that always saves the moment. Works every time. Learned it reading Raymond Chandler and Dash Hammett, watching all those Philip Marlowe flicks. "Sarah, let me assure you, what we say here this morning will never leave this office. Glenn Sheldon is well known in this business not only for his superior detective skills, but for his ability to keep his trap shut."

Not so. Glenn Sheldon is actually quite well known in the business for sitting around Lefty's Tavern over on Speedwell Avenue, powering down a few Scotch and sodas, and blabbing the more sordid details of his most tantalizing cases.

"I'm here," she says, finally, "because, well, because I'm looking for someone."

"A missing person?"

The words, muttered with such nonchalance, cause the air to catch in her lungs. "Yes," she whispers, "a missing person."

"And you would like me to help you find this person?"

"I would. Yes."

Sheldon takes a few notes. "The name of the person you wish to locate?"

It takes her a moment. "Standish. Michael Standish."

Sheldon writes down the name. My name. My fake name. My I'm-not-a-Polack name. "And your relationship to Mr. Standish?"

"He's . . . he's . . . he's . . . my husband."

Sheldon does not miss a beat. "I see. And how long has he been missing?"

"Almost a week now . . . Well, five days."

"And do you have reason to believe something has happened to your husband, something beyond his control?"

"I'm not sure I know what you mean."

"Do you think, Mrs. Standish, he's been kidnapped, abducted, taken against his will?"

"Oh, no, absolutely not. Nothing like that."

"So we can conclude that his disappearance is . . . of his own choosing?"

Sarah drops her eyes. "Yes."

"Your husband has run off?"

Hey, Glenn, let's show a little finesse here. A little tact. The woman's hurting.

"No . . . but . . . yes . . . but . . ." Sarah wants in the worst way to try to explain.

"With another woman?"

Sarah suddenly laughs. Not a real laugh, just something to keep herself from crying. "Oh no, I'm quite sure he hasn't done that."

But experience has taught Sheldon another woman is always involved. But he decides to keep his experience to himself. At least for the time being. Later, if he turns out to be right, this sweet young thing might need a shoulder to cry on. Worm. "All right then, tell me, why do you think your husband has disappeared?"

"I know exactly why."

"You do? Would you care to share that information with me?"

For the first time since she arrived at Sheldon's office, Sarah feels bold, even assertive. "No," she answers, "I wouldn't."

Sheldon balks. He hadn't expected defiance.

"I just want you to find him," says Sarah. "None of the rest of it matters."

Sheldon nods. He knows how to coddle a client. "Of course, I understand."

A tear very nearly slips from Sarah's right eye. She moves to wipe it away. "I just want to find him. That's all. And soon. Before too much time passes."

Sheldon allows a moment or two to pass. Then, "I think I should warn you; it can be very difficult and time-consuming, as well as expensive, to locate someone who has disappeared. Especially someone who does not wish to be found. It's a big world out there."

Sarah's eyes narrow. She does not care for Sheldon's condescending tone. "I know that, Mr. Sheldon. But I think my husband wants to be found."

Oh yeah, found and forgiven.

"On some level, some subconscious level, he wants me to find him."

Christ, thinks Sheldon, just what I need, another distraught woman in touch with the mystics. But what the hell? It pays the bills. Beats sitting around nights watching the tube. "And why do you think that?"

"Because he loves me."

Glenn Sheldon suppresses a sigh. He can barely disguise his disgust for the word. Another moment passes. "I see."

"He does."

"I'm sure."

Time hangs there in the moist heat of the office, then slips out the open window. Sheldon clears his throat. "All right, do you have any idea where your husband might've gone, where we might begin to look?"

Sarah nods. "I do, yes." She reaches into her handbag. "I found something."

"A clue?"

"Yes, a clue."

Sheldon leans forward, extends his chest out over his desk.

Sarah draws a small notepad from her handbag. "This might help make the world a slightly smaller place."

Yes indeed. Shouldn't be long now before the cavalry comes riding my way.

We buried my mother. Six feet under. Standing there next to her grave, with the priest pontificating in Latin, I felt a twinge of joy. Yes, joy. Very soon I imagined Mama's spirit rising, up and out of that damp hole, soaring heavenly. Once and for all out from under the sadistic heels of the Pope and her sweet loving Stan.

Jessie used to daydream about venturing out in the world, exploring, seeing new places, meeting new people. This, finally, was her chance.

I hung around after the funeral long enough to squeeze my little sister, tell her I loved her, tell her once again that she could always come to Ithaca if things got rough at home. I didn't even bother to say goodbye to Stanley. Feared if I did that during the farewell I might accidentally drive my kneecap into his groin, my thumb into his eye socket.

Then the drive back to Ithaca. Very quiet in the Bimmer. Only a few words passed between us. Not even the radio on. But just before we reached the house on State Street, Cracker asked me if I wanted to spend Thanksgiving with him and his family.

I jumped at the chance. New places. New people.

My first visit to the Cramer Compound in Pottersville, New Jersey: it changed my life. At least pulled it in another direction. Twenty years old that fall, but I had no idea people lived like that. Not really. A million miles from our row house in Poughkeepsie. Affluence personified. The Money may have fallen off the trees by that time of year, but someone had obviously raked it up, stuffed it into the walls. The beds. The sofas. The cars. The Cuisinart food processors. The green stuff showed its face everywhere I turned.

We drove down the long straight macadam drive lined on both sides with tall red maples. Beyond the maples, fenced pasture. Horses to the right. Cattle to the left. Black Angus, Cracker told me. Excellent steak makers. Lean and tender.

We parked the Bimmer behind a couple of Mercedes-Benzes: a bright red SL coupe and an enormous sedan that looked big enough to live in. I also spotted a 'Vette, a pickup truck, and another 2002 similar to Cracker's.

The Cramers called their dwelling a farmhouse. Right. A sprawling two-story affair with half a dozen bedrooms, almost as many bathrooms, and a kitchen as big as the entire downstairs of our Poughkeepsie digs. It had once, decades ago, been a small wooden farmhouse. Served the dairy farm that surrounded it. But that was back before the Cramers moved in and started expanding.

There was a modest two-story farmhouse on the other side of the one-hundred-and-twenty-acre spread. Occupied then by the estate manager, the guy who took care of the horses, the cattle, the hay fields. Occupied now by Graham and his wife, Alison, and their two kids, Molly and Tracy.

Another dwelling on the compound as well. A cottage. Just a tiny one-bedroom affair out back under the white pines. I lived there once myself for a few months a few years back, before I married into the Browne family and moved across the valley to TREETOPS. But all of that is story still to come.

Thanksgiving around the Cramer table. All the trimmings. All we lacked was a few Indians. I guess they figured they had me.

At either end of the big table: Mary and Walter Cramer. Mom and Dad. Mary came from Money. Inheritrix of a sizeable trust fund. Very sizeable. Plenty left over for Cracker and his two siblings: younger sister Karen and older brother Ron. Rotten Ron. The dough came down from a couple generations back. Heavy industry of one kind or another. Nothing particularly exciting. Maybe ball bearings. Not that it really matters. What matters is the way it pulled in the green. Piles and piles of green.

Yup, the Cramer clan was flush, no doubt about that, no need to worry about putting chow on the table: a twenty-pound turkey that day, plus ten pounds of bloody roast beef, stuffing, and gravy, two kinds of potatoes, baked beans, green beans, waxed beans, squash, carrots, pumpkin pie, cherry pie, apple pie, ice cream, cake, coffee, and just about any alcoholic beverage that exists here on God's intoxicated earth: bourbon, Scotch, beer, wine, sherry, port, cognac. Oh yeah, the Cramers liked to imbibe. They needed to imbibe. About the only way they could get through the meal without scratching each other's eyes out. Wealth, in the Cramer case, did not equal happiness. This was not a close-knit clan.

All that food, enough to feed the Family Standowski for a week, went mostly to waste. I, of course, ate my weight. And Walt, he could put it away. A human garbage disposal. But the rest of them, they just picked. And complained.

About the food. The weather. The politicians. The illegal immigrants. The poor.

Sister Karen was on this anti-meat-eating kick. Spent a half hour describing in deliberate detail the brutal conditions under which cattle and poultry live their measly lives so we can consume their dead flesh. Rotten Ron, one of sweet Sarah's future hubbies, kept calling her a radical and telling her to shut up. Cracker sat there with his eyes down, pushing the food around on his plate with his fork and looking both agitated and embarrassed. Mary kept smiling at me, passing me more meat, more potatoes, more beans. And Walt, à la Stan the Man, he pretty much kept his mug buried in his food. Had something akin to a scowl on his face when he glanced up in search of more vittles. And when he finished he pushed back his chair, stood, and left the dining room without a word. Straight to the TV and a three-hour teleconference with the National Football League.

"Jesus," I said to Cracker later that afternoon, "your family's more screwed up than mine."

Cracker sighed, shook his head. "Tell me about it."

Walter Cramer shouldered most of the blame. A very uptight fellow. No sense of humor. Seemed to have very little use for human beings. Preferred his calculator, slide rules, and protractors. Walt was an inventor, one of those guys with a huge IQ and a big brain but zero social skills. He possessed a dozen or more patents. Mostly on techno stuff dealing with transistors, computers, remote control devices.

Walt had one of those life-altering experiences while still a teenager. It may go a long way in explaining why he was so fouled up emotionally. Why he never held his kids. Why he never gave them affection. Why Cracker's relationship with his old man might've been more psychologically damaging than the one I had with mine.

Walt had a nickname: Big Walt. Big Walt stood six feet four and weighed in at a solid two hundred and thirty pounds. But long ago Walt had learned to control his massive size, to make himself appear physically small and harmless. He did this because in grammar school he tackled his best friend during a backyard football game. Just a simple, straightforward tackle. Had done it a thousand times. But this tackle left his best friend with a broken neck and a wheelchair for life. Big Walt blamed himself, saddled his ego with prodigious amounts of guilt. Since then he has pretty much suppressed his enormous physical attributes. Suppressed them because he feared them. Feared the harm they could inflict. All this suppression, however, came with a price. Big Walt, his huge body swollen with nervous energy, had to find other ways to vent his angers and frustrations. And since he couldn't do it physically, he wound up doing it mentally, emotionally. Just ask his wife and kids. I watched them, all through that Thanksgiving weekend. They feared the big bruiser. Went out of their way to give him space. Keep him calm. Make him comfy.

Cracker and I, over the years, have spent countless hours discussing our loving papas. It has strengthened the bond between us. Made us allies forever. But whereas Graham later took on the burden of trying to befriend his father, seek out some common ground upon which they both could tread, I never did. To this day I've kept my distance from Stanislaw Standowski. It has probably been a mistake. But then, I've made my share of those.

By the end of that Thanksgiving weekend I had worked my way into Mary Cramer's heart. Probably she just felt sorry for me, but by Sunday afternoon, just before Cracker and I headed back to Ithaca, Mary ordered me to call her Mom. This after she had me tell her all about Jessie, as many details as I could recall, even the details surrounding her death. When I was through, all choked up, tears running down my face, Mary Cramer held me against her breast and whispered in my ear, "From now on, Michael, you call me Mom. Everyone needs someone to call Mom, and I want to be that someone for you."

And so I did. And so I have for all the years since. Called her Mom. So similar emotionally to my own mother. Give Jessie a trust fund and a red Mercedes coupe and she and Mary could easily have been sisters.

Why, I wonder, do good, kind, decent women marry such shitty men? Is it a weakness? A tragic flaw in their characters? Or do they feel sorry for us? Want to reform us? Bring us into the fold?

Back at school the CARE packages started coming in pairs. One for Cracker, one for me. Always a short note enclosed as well. A brief reminder to study hard and keep a positive outlook even during difficult times.

I wrote back to Mom Cramer at least once a week. To thank her and bring her up to speed on all our latest college antics. I would tell her in great detail about the wild affairs her son was having with Ithaca's most beautiful coeds.

A port in a storm, Mom Cramer, a port in a storm. But I needed something a little closer to home, someone a little closer to my own age.

And quite by chance I met Alison Witte. She filled the bill. To a tee. A music major at I.C., Alison played a wide variety of instruments. Mostly things with strings: violin, cello, harp, classical guitar. She had grown up in northern Vermont, cold country. Her parents were a couple of ex-hippie types. Artists. Ran a small business out of their basement: hand-painted tee shirts, sweatshirts, baseball caps. One hundred percent preshrunk cotton. Nonpolluting dyes. All natural. SAVE THE EARTH. LOVE THY NEIGHBOR. PEACE NOT WAR.

Alison was an all-natural girl. One hundred percent. As down-to-earth as they come. No makeup. Not even mascara. She had never shaved the hair under her arms or on her legs. Soft and blond. You could barely see it. Smooth as silk.

Alison and I fell pretty hard for one another. One of those times when two needy people meet, kiss, and latch on for dear life. I doubt we had been together a week before we had Sex. But I did not really want to have Sex with Alison. I just wanted to curl up at her side and lay my head against her breast. This is not to say I did not enjoy making love to Alison. I did. Thoroughly. I loved being inside of her. It made me feel warm and safe and secure. But I never felt much passion. My erection felt more like an umbilical cord than an organ of sexual stimulation.

When I spoke to Maggie Jane about this, she told me, "Jessie only died a few months ago, Michael. You're looking for an emotional connection to take her place. Be careful you don't hurt this girl."

Alison and I spent enormous amounts of time together. Day and night. Cracker used to say we might as well get joined at the hip like a pair of Siamese twins. He was just jealous. In June he went home for the summer.

Alison moved into the house on State Street. Right into my bedroom. I went to summer school so I could graduate on time. Alison played the fiddle three nights a week at a Cornell coffeehouse. We swam naked in the deep pools at Taughannock Falls. We went sailing on Cayuga. Hiking out at Tremen State Park. We had a good time together.

Too bad the fighting started a week or so before summer ended. I wanted to stay with my soccer mates at the house on State Street. Alison wanted us to get a place of our own. I won out, but Alison turned into a totally different person right before my eyes. Her true self came pouring forth. A spoiled brat used to getting her own way. Tough and uncompromising beneath that mild exterior. No siblings. Doting parents who thought their love child would save the world.

Oh, right, and I was Prince Charming. Nothing wrong with Mike Standish. Sane and stable. Psychologically sound.

I hadn't been using Alison to fill a void, plug a wound. No way. Not me.

The good times were over. But relationships, once there's been Sex, never die a peaceful death. First Allie and I had to hassle each other for a few months. Ten months, if anyone's counting. Right up until that day I disappeared into Edinburgh's famous fog.

Oh yeah, I have a history of disappearing when the going gets rough.

During spring break of our senior year, Cracker asked me if I wanted to go to Florida. Alison wanted me to go to Vermont, meet her parents. I chose the Sunshine State.

We drove down in the 2002. Drugs and alcohol all the way. How we survived I have no idea. Somebody watching over us I guess. God. Maybe Jessie. The entire two weeks remains in my memory as nothing but a blur. Up all night, sleeping on the beach during the day. Daytona. Fort Lauderdale. The Keys. Cracker had credit cards and plenty of cash. And a brand-new camera. I'll never forget that camera. That camera gave me a vocation, an artistic inspiration. It set in motion my ambition beyond kicking a soccer ball through a net.

I remember it like it happened yesterday. Marathon Key. On our way to Key West. Gonna get drunk with Hemingway's ghost at Captain Tony's Saloon. But first we needed a swim. Sombrero Beach. I fished through the trunk of the Bimmer looking for a towel. Instead I found a large plastic shopping bag. I opened it up. And inside, a veritable gold mine of camera equipment. A brand new Nikon F3 with three lenses: a 28mm, a 105mm, a 200mm. Plus a gear bag and a wide assortment of gadgets: filters, film, a shutter release, a book on how to take beautiful color pictures. All of it still in the boxes.

I'd never taken a photograph in my life. But the stuff beckoned, whispered that I should come closer.

"Hey, Cracker, where did you get all this stuff?"

He slouched in the driver's seat, sunburned, bleary-eyed. "All what stuff?"

"All this camera stuff?"

"Oh that. I told Mom I wanted a camera to take some pictures in Florida."

"So she bought you this? Jesus. There's enough gear in here to go on location for *National Geographic*."

"Whatever's in the bag."

"You mean you haven't even looked at it?"

"Been meaning to. Just haven't been sober long enough to get the bag open."

I got the bag open. The boxes open. Ran my hands over the cool black steel of that Nikon F3. Few things had ever felt so right. So perfect.

I spent the rest of the afternoon reading the manual, learning about lenses, shutter speeds, aperture openings. Loaded in a roll of Kodak color. Set the ASA. Advanced the film. Popped off my first shot: Cracker lying in the sand, sound asleep, his mouth hanging open. When we got home I had it blown up, framed, hung it in the front hall of our house on State Street.

For the rest of the trip you couldn't get that camera out of my hands. I had the viewfinder smashed up against my eye night and day. It brought my surroundings suddenly and clearly into focus. For the first time in my life I started to see the World. I mean really see it. Grasp it. Colors. Shapes. Sizes. Patterns. Everything looked so amazing: the sea, the sky, the birds flying overhead, the swirl of the surf lapping onto the sand, people jogging, swimming, shelling, soaking up the sun. It all looked like the Perfect Picture. So I kept tripping the shutter. As fast as I could advance the film. Boom! Boom! Boom! Couldn't shoot fast enough. In five days I shot ten rolls, two hundred and forty negatives. All the film Mom Cramer had provided for her boy's Florida flight of fancy.

I got hooked. And I stayed hooked. Still hooked to this day. Photography has provided me with a clear path through the chaos.

Devil's Cay: out on the Atlantic rim of the Bahamas, north of San Salvador, east of Cat Island. But that doesn't tell you much. You'll need a damn good map if you want to find me. Want to track me down. Even on the most detailed maps of the Bahamas, Devil's Cay shows up as nothing more than a cartographer's unmarked blot of ink.

One small town. Doesn't even seem to have a name. You're just in town or out of town. Not much out of town. Sand and coral, a few scrubby pines. A ramshackle shack or two. Not much in town either. A cobblestone street with more than a few missing cobblestones. A row of one- and two-story buildings. Most made of cinder block and stucco, the rest of clapboard and cedar shingle. They give off an air of casual neglect. Once-bright pastel colors have faded and peeled in the steady waft of salt air and humid, subtropical heat. Home sweet temporary home.

So what do I do? I sit around the bar drinking, waiting, worrying, jawboning with my host. "Say Lewis, ever been to the States?"

Lewis stands behind the bar lining up his bottles of booze, glass soldiers in his alcohol army. "Just once, Mr. Weston. A long time ago. My daddy took me."

"Where did you go?"

"Idaho."

"Idaho! How come Idaho?"

"You know the writer, Hemingway?"

"Ernest Hemingway? Yeah, sure."

"My daddy knew Hemingway. He used to drink at my daddy's hotel on Bimini."

"That's something. But what's it got to do with Idaho?"

"When I was a boy, this Hemingway, he stuck a gun, a shotgun, in his mouth and blew his brains out. Up in Idaho. My daddy took me up there because he wanted to see where this great man would do such a cowardly thing."

"Cowardly, huh?" Then, "So did you get to see?"

Lewis shakes his head. "No, mon. We flew on all these airplanes. Finally got to Idaho. A big place, high mountains, some with snow on top even in summer. We looked around awhile, but then my daddy got mad because everywhere we went people kept calling us niggers, saying, 'What do you want here, nigger?' and 'We don't allow no niggers in here, nigger.' So we gave up, come back to the islands."

I think about it. "That's some story, Lewis. Is it true?"

Lewis smiles. "What do you think, mon?"

"Me? I don't know. The truth is a slippery business."

Lewis smiles again with those big white teeth.

"I know a little something about prejudice, Lewis."

"That so, Mr. Weston?"

"Oh yeah. You see, I'm a Polack. Calling a guy a Polack is like calling a guy a nigger."

"An ugly thing, mon."

"Where I grew up lots of people didn't like Polacks. Maybe they liked us more than they liked niggers, but not much more. A Polack has to put up with a lot of Polack jokes. Tell me, Lewis, you know the only thing dumber than a Polack?"

Lewis shrugs. "No, mon. What?"

"Two Polacks."

Lewis laughs. "I hear the same joke about niggers."

I sigh, look out the window, don't have a clue what to do all day. Hot here on Devil's Cay. A hot breeze slipping through the windows. I slept in this morning, owing mostly to the fact that I didn't sleep much last night. Used to sleep like a baby. But since becoming a felon last March, I've turned into a borderline insomniac. Suffer from the most wretched nightmares. The one where I don't have any arms, just a couple of stumps hanging off my shoulders, constitutes the worst of the lot, the one that brings on the heavy sweats, the brain-jarring anxiety.

Turn back to Lewis. "The mail boat captain said something to me yesterday about Devil's Cay being cursed. What do you think about that, Lewis?"

"You believe in the devil, Mr. Weston?"

"Never used to. Lately I'm not so sure."

"Folks here, they believe in the devil. On Devil's Cay the devil be alive and well."

"So you think the island's cursed?"

"I don't know, mon. What do you think?"

"I think when I was in the Bahamas on my honeymoon a couple years ago, I read that Devil's Cay was one of the last places in the islands where they still practice Obeah."

Lewis finally wipes that smile off his face. Replaces it with a frown. "And what do you know about Obeah, mon?"

"Not much," I tell him. "Just that it's sort of like voodoo."

"Sort of like voodoo, huh?" He gives me a long look. "Is that why you come to Devil's Cay, Mr. Weston? To check out this Obeah?"

"Maybe, I don't know." I reach down, pick up one of my leather rucksacks. "I mostly came to take photographs."

"Photographs?"

I pull out my old Nikon F3. Yup, the same one I found in the trunk of Cracker's Bimmer all those years ago on Marathon Key. He told me I could use it as long as I took care of it. I'm still using it. "I plan to take some pictures, Lewis."

"Of the island?"

"Right. Think anyone'll mind if I start poking around with my camera?"

"I don't know, mon. Folks on Devil's Cay pretty private."

"Is that right?"

"Oftentimes."

"That's not what I wanted to hear, Lewis. I came to Devil's Cay to shoot some photographs. Less than a hundred Bahamians live on this island. I want to shoot every single one of you, make a kind of photographic chronicle of island life, capture the essence of this one small, out-of-the-way corner of the planet."

"You talking ambitious, mon. I thought you just come to Devil's Cay because you running from something."

"Running? Hell no, Lewis, not me. I'm a professional photographer. Freelance mostly, but right now I'm on assignment for *Life* magazine."

"*Life* magazine, hey? I don't know, Mr. Weston, that sound like some slippery business."

I give Lewis a smile for that one while I clean the filter on the end of the camera lens. Then I set the camera on the bar, glance out the window again, see sea and sky, figure it must be almost noon. Close enough. "Maybe I'll have a little pinch of rum, Lewis. Just a couple fingers to take the edge off the morning."

Lewis does his duty. Tosses a cardboard coaster onto the bar, sets the glass of rum carefully on top of the coaster. Right in front of me.

"Thanks, Lewis." I lift the glass, tip it against my lips, allow a small amount of the smooth amber liquid to slide down my throat. "Tell me something, Lewis."

"What that be, Mr. Weston?"

"How would I drink this if I didn't have any arms?"

"Say again, mon?"

"If I didn't have any arms, how would I lift this glass to my mouth?"

"You talking crazy, mon. You got two perfectly good arms."

"But let's just say I didn't. No arms at all. How would I do it? How would I eat? Drink? Take pictures?"

"You been smoking the ganja, mon? Sound like you been smoking the ganja."

"No, I'm just asking you a simple question. How would I drink this rum, how would I bring it to my lips, if I didn't have any arms?"

Lewis takes another long stare at me. Looks kind of concerned. Wonders, I'm sure, if I might be a little off my rocker. "You couldn't, mon. Without arms you couldn't drink that drink."

"Exactly, Lewis. Right on the money. I couldn't do it. Not without help. No man's an island, Lewis."

Content with my profundity, I raise the rum to my lips, take another sip. How long can I go on like this?

Lewis turns his back on me. Goes about his duties: rubs clean the beer mugs and wine glasses, places them in the overhead rack.

I turn around. Take another look out the picture window. A boat enters the harbor, an old twin-engine trawler. In large letters across the hull it says: B.C.E.C.

"Who's this rolling into town, Lewis? That a local boat?"

Lewis takes a look. "No, mon, that be B.C.E.C. Bahamas Cooperative Electric. Those boys gonna restore power, make it so you can have ice cubes in your rum and Coke."

I stare for a while longer at the boat, hoping, I guess, that Sarah might be on board. Not a chance. I unleash a mighty sigh. "That's good, Lewis. That's just fine."

Cracker and Alison and I, along with the rest of our Ithaca College classmates, graduated in early June. Maggie Jane came. She sat in the front row. Cheered and whistled with her fingers between her teeth when I walked up to the podium to receive my sheepskin. Never felt so proud in all my life. Even though Stanley didn't make the trip. Couldn't be bothered. Too much on his plate. Mail to deliver. TV dinners to stick in the oven. No-name vodka to pour down his miserable gullet.

Alison's parents came. Don and Madeleine Witte. Down from their communal outpost in northern Vermont. Arrived, believe it or not, in a brand-new Caddy Coupe de Ville. Fashionably dressed in contemporary safari wear. Seems the tee shirt biz had turned big time after L.L. Bean had picked up their line. They wore their newfound Money well. Gave me hugs and kisses, real touchie-feelie types, told me how happy they were to finally meet me. And I them. Or so I said.

The Cramers came. A sizeable contingent. Mary, of course. But no sign of Big Walt. Down in D.C. plugging his latest invention to the patent office. Replaced by a couple grandparents. Aunts and uncles. The siblings: Karen and Ron. Rotten Ron, I think you'll like this one, had a young lady with him. His sweetheart. Introduced to me, even though I don't really remember, as his fiancée. A pretty girl. Tall and thin and poised with striking auburn hair.

"Michael," Mom Cramer said, "this is Sarah Browne. Ron's fiancée. Sarah, this is Michael Standish. A friend of Graham's. A member of the family."

I honestly don't recall. Nothing but a vague recollection of that lovely chestnut mane. I wanted to touch it. Reach out and run it through my fingers. Feel it against my cheek. Almost did. Almost took a handful. But held back. Lucky for me. Ron, a borderline sociopath, probably would've clocked me. Under the influence, I was, of two tabs of Electric Sunshine. Peaking as the graduation ceremony grew near. I had on dark glasses to hide my huge black pupils. Many of my classmates did as well. Early that morning some generous chap had started dispensing free LSD in celebration of our successful efforts to gain college diplomas.

That night a bunch of us had dinner together. Some smoky steakhouse up in Collegetown. A whole room to ourselves. Must've been thirty of us. Mary Cramer picked up the tab. A couple grand I feel sure. Peanuts. Mere peanuts. Walking Around Money.

I didn't eat a thing. Food looks absolutely disgusting while riding on the wings of lysergic acid. But I drank my share. Probably did a couple bottles of red and a bottle of white all by myself. Everyone loaded and having a good time. Talk turned to what we might do with the rest of our lives now that we had taken this giant step. Alison wanted to play Carnegie Hall. Cracker to pursue his literary demons. And me, I just wanted to point my Nikon at the world and say, "Smile!"

Mom Cramer had a few ideas. At least in the short term. During the tail end of our many-course meal, she made an announcement. Cracker and I sat on either side of her. She stood up, tapped her spoon on her glass of port. Her guests grew quiet. "Young people," she said, "need to travel. Visit foreign ports. See how the other half lives. This way they can overcome prejudice, provincial pettiness." Then she handed first Cracker and then me a soft leather pouch. "Go," she said, a tad tipsy. "Go forth and discover who you are."

In the soft leather pouch: tickets and vouchers. Plane tickets, train tickets, boat tickets. Vouchers for hotels, car rentals, restaurants. A European odyssey, our graduation gift. For a brief instant my brain told me to refuse this present, to say thanks but no thanks. A very brief instant. I gave

Mom Cramer a big wet kiss on the cheek. A warm embrace. Thanked her profusely.

God, how lucky had I been to get Graham Cramer as a roommate? Pretty damn lucky. A shot in the dark. Could easily have been assigned to another room, another floor, another dorm. Amazing how fragile are the wheels of fate. No Cracker, no Sarah. No Sarah, no U-Haul. No U-Haul, no trip down to Devil's Cay.

Three cheers for Graham and Mike. Then more drinks for everyone. Noisy discussions about where we'd go, what we'd see: the Tower of London, the Eiffel Tower, the Leaning Tower of Pisa. Towers and mountains and museums.

Down at the far end of the table I saw Cracker in deep conversation with the Wittes. Don and Madeleine. On and on they chatted. More than once that ex-hipster-turned-nouveau-riche tee-shirt-maker slapped my good buddy on the back. I wondered what was going on. Finally ventured down there to find out. Didn't take long. They let me in on it right away. This European thing sure sounded like great good fun. Mom and Pop Witte wanted their little girl to get in on the action. Hell no, was my first thought, no way. But they had the bucks now to send her, a Coupe de Ville stuffed with green. And weren't we all such great good friends, the Three Musketeers and all that scat.

Cracker, don't ask me why, thought it sounded like a grand idea. Maybe the guy already had his eye on her, I don't know. Maybe it was just the booze and the acid and the atmosphere making him so agreeable. Whatever. I don't know. All I know is that before Mom Cramer paid the tab it had been decided: we would make our European sojourn together, as a trio, a graduating triumvirate.

We flew to London in early July. Had tickets the next day for the All England Tennis Championships. Wimbledon. Quarterfinals. Sat in Center Court cheering while a couple of white guys even younger than us wearing white shirts, white shorts, white socks, and white sneakers ran around on the burned-out grass flailing at that little white ball.

I quickly grew bored. My head on a string as my eyes followed the ball back and forth, back and forth. Cracker loved it. Couldn't get enough. Soaked up all that Anglo-Saxon atmosphere like a sponge. Of course, he played the game. Had been playing all his life. Played at Ithaca. Third singles. He sat there in Center Court until long after the matches had finished for the day. Sat there until some English usher came over and told him to get the hell out. Nicely.

We did London. All the important sites. Can't remember them now but I feel confident we saw them: Westminster Abbey. St. Paul's Cathedral. Buckingham Palace. The War Room. Saw them all. Together. Mike: the photographer. Alison: the musician. Graham: the writer.

Too bad I didn't feel like being with either one of them. They were both so, I don't know, needy. They had to know every second exactly what we would be doing, exactly where we would be going. No way did one of us do something without the other two. All together or not at all. Cracker didn't sleep in the same bed with us, thank God, but he often slept in the same room. Not that it mattered. Alison and I didn't have Sex anymore. The act for us had worn itself out. After a long day of sightseeing we preferred to just turn out the light, roll over, get some z's.

By the time we'd motored through Oxford, Stratford-upon-Avon, and the English countryside, I longed to get away from my fellow travelers. If only, I kept thinking, they were the Couple and I was the Odd Man Out. Then I could just quietly slip away, slide into oblivion. But it was not that easy. Not with these two. I needed a plan. A clever plot.

We headed north for Scotland. I kept saying I wanted to do this and that. Go here and there. Kept waiting for them to disagree, to put up a fight. But like a pair of sheep, they kept going along with my suggestions, fearing, I suppose, that terrible things would happen if our triad became divided.

Still, I left them alone more and more. In the walled city of York I took off in the rain for an entire afternoon. Lost, I became, on those narrow winding streets. Lost and lustful of every solitary step. And when finally I found them, in a bakery sharing a raspberry tart, they looked content, deep in conversation. Lovers. Barely more than a nod when I made my presence known.

Edinburgh: Cool. Damp. Drizzly. Depressing. Fog as thick as roofing tar. Up at the ancient Castle high above town, fog so thick you couldn't even see the Scottish tour guide as he lambasted his Limey cousins to the south. Maybe not the violence of Northern Ireland, but plenty of antagonism and resentment there in Scotland.

After three days in the drizzle and fog the troops grew restless. They'd seen enough of the United Kingdom. Ready to invade the continent. Across the North Sea to the Netherlands, to Amsterdam.

The night before departure I made my move. Came back to the room after a visit to the local pub. Told my mates I'd just met a man who said we simply had to visit the Highlands before we left Scotland. Had to see them. Experience them. No way around it. Cracker and Alison looked dubious. They did not want to change the plan, hated changing the plan. I gave them a few seconds to think it over. Then I gave them a nudge, "If you guys would rather skip the Highlands, fly to Amsterdam, I could understand that."

They seemed relieved. Each gave a little nod.

I pounced. "If that's what you'd rather do, I could cruise up to the Highlands for a few days by myself. Up and back. Quick as a cat. Then rendezvous with you over in Amsterdam. No big deal. That way we'd all be happy. I'd really like to get some pictures of that country."

Groans and moans. Panic on their faces. We discussed my plan deep into the night. Both Cracker and Allie had long lists of reservations. They thought we should stick together. Go forward as a unit. I did my damnedest to reassure them. Give them strength. Quite bizarre as another foggy dawn approached. Finally they relented. A detailed itinerary was drawn up before any of us dared go to bed. Where we would be and exactly when we would be there was committed to paper. Our own private Magna Carta. I could hardly believe these two. So damn dependent.

Relief finally came when I boarded the Highland Express late that afternoon at the Edinburgh train station. Cracker and Alison stood on the platform just outside my window. In the fog they looked pale and pitiful. Gave me a forlorn wave. I pretended not to know them.

Alone at last. In Europa. On someone else's tab. Mikey's Big Adventure. I roamed like a lion who'd been held captive in a cage. Roamed and hunted. Hunted with my viewfinder. Hunted for women. For life. Sucked the life out of every scene I stumbled upon. Slept little. Ate less. Absorbed the endless streams of stimulation.

A few days in the Highlands. Lush. Wild. Desolate. Then on to Amsterdam. The Whores, my God, with their curly blond locks. Up and down the Dam. A man could drive himself to an early death. In and out all day and all night long. I gave them Money. They gave me Sex. Sex and Money. Oh, the Sex they gave me. Anything I wanted. Things I hadn't even dreamed of at my innocent age.

Then, sexually satiated, south to Brussels. The hash. You should have seen the hash. Gigantic chucks of Lebanese blond. The size of softballs. I gave the man some Money. He gave me some hash. Break a piece off. Stuff it in a pipe. And off to Never-Never Land.

Paris. Geneva. Zurich. Always at least one step behind my mates. If their detailed itinerary gave a Thursday departure, I made sure to arrive no earlier than Friday or Saturday. Always a note at the front desk from Cracker. Telling me they were moving on, sticking to the plan, having a good time, missing me lots. Usually a money order for me as well. Enough to keep me going. Whores and hash and healthy amounts of fermented grape and malted barley. And, of course, film. I had to keep buying film. Had to keep shooting my life. Roll after roll after roll.

Almost stumbled upon them in Lucerne. Just outside our hotel overlooking the Vierwaldstätter See. Me going in. Them coming out. Damn near bumped right into Cracker. But he had his attention diverted. By my darling Alison. She had my buddy laughing, cackling up a storm, something to do, I gathered, with the concierge, his pompous manner. Alison doing an impression of him: the voice, the walk, the tilt of the head, the whole bit. I stepped quickly out of the way, behind a marble pillar, and watched. Had never seen her do anything like that before. Anything so . . . so loose . . . so frivolous . . . so funny. A twinge of jealousy. Almost called out to them. Almost. Not quite. Knew if I made my presence known I would never get away again.

I spent the next several weeks on my own. Italy. Spain. Portugal. All those different people. Different languages. Different cultures. Different food. I hate to admit this, but I grew weary. Lonely. Anxious.

Then Cracker quit leaving notes. Not a word. Just the money orders. Bless his WASPy heart.

So somewhere between Rome and Madrid the tide turned. I grew tired of going solo. I got tired of wondering if Cracker was making love to my girlfriend. The time had come to rendezvous, to re-form our triumvirate.

Too late, Mikey Boy, too late.

Cracker and Allie now danced one step ahead of me. At hotels in Madrid, Seville, Lisbon, Pamplona I missed them by inches. Didn't catch up with them until the end of August. Back in London. At Heathrow. Just before the flight home. I spotted them across the terminal. Arm-in-arm, snug as a couple of bugs in a rug.

I was pissed. Jealous. Hurt. As though I had done nothing to bring about this union. Oh yeah, a union had been forged between them during the six weeks they had traveled without me through the Old World.

On the plane, while Alison slept, Cracker said, "I don't know, Mike. Hard to explain. We just hit it off."

"You mean you humped her."

He didn't look at me. Couldn't. "No, I mean, well—"

"You humped her, Cracker. Just admit it."

"We were just going along, seeing stuff, waiting for you, and—"

"And one night you both got looped on wine and started screwing like a couple of wildcats."

I wanted to bloody Cracker's lip. But at the same time I wanted to give him a great big hug and a kiss. I hated the SOB and loved him at the same time. All in one's perspective.

"I'm sorry, Michael," said Alison just before we landed at Kennedy. "But I think you made it pretty clear that you were no longer interested."

Right. I guess I did.

The next thing I knew they announced their engagement. Followed very soon thereafter by a wedding date: October 15.

"What the hell is the big hurry?" I asked Cracker.

He shrugged. He didn't really have an answer. Mumbled something about no reason to wait.

So they did it. At a small Unitarian Church up in Vermont. Already winter up there. A dusting of snow the night before the exchange of vows. The leaves long gone from the trees. M. Standish: best man. Pretty good-looking guy wearing a black tux with a red vest and a red rose in his lapel. I stood beside my good buddy and said not a word while I watched him throw his bachelorhood away on a bitch.

Or was I just jealous? Envious? Fretful I'd let something fine slip through my fingers?

All kinds of weird and wild dynamics at work in that tiny wooden church: Alison marrying Graham to get back at me, to kick me in the private parts for being such a louse. Graham marrying Alison because just a few weeks earlier his brother had married Sarah, the true love of his young life. Alison marrying Graham for the Money, his lovely little Trust Fund. Graham marrying Alison to prove that their six-week European Sex fling had not been a fluke, a simple matter of Sex for its own sake. The two of them marrying out of fear: fear of loneliness, fear of the unknown, fear of the outside world.

The preacher called for the ring. I had it tucked away in my vest. Solid gold. Twenty-four-carat. Worth at least a grand. More than I had to my name. Thought about just leaving the thing in my pocket. Acting like I'd lost it. Hawking it for cash in a day or two. Of course, I didn't do it. No, I pulled it out, handed it over.

Graham slipped it onto Alison's finger. Man and Wife.

Graham and Alison: still married after all these years. Hard to believe.

I wonder if Graham's heard about my hasty flight from TREETOPS? Surely the rumors have started to circulate.

There he is: walking the edge of the alfalfa field with his older daughter, Molly, age eight. Another hot, steamy August morning. The hay's been cut, drying now in windrows. Cracker stops, bends, picks up a blade of alfalfa. He examines it, rubs it between his fingers, chews an end.

"How is it, Daddy?"

Graham Cramer: quiet, dependable, in harmony with the earth, at odds with some of the humans who inhabit it. Especially his pappy and his spouse. But not his daughters. He loves his daughters. Apples of his eye. "I think we'll make some bales today, kid. Just as soon as that sun climbs a little higher."

Graham Cramer: manager of the Cramer Compound. He runs the whole show now: Crops. Cattle. Gardens. Lawn care. Building maintenance. Of course, Big Walt's still the boss. When Big Walt says jump, Cracker . . . well, he at least takes a little hop. He's held that post, for . . . God, it must be close to four years now. Four years this fall. Unbelievable. Time sashays on.

Daddy and daughter reach the end of the hay field. Cut through a wind break of white pines into their own backyard: freshly mowed grass, a big sugar maple with a rope swing hanging from one of the lower branches, a couple of kid's bikes, a vegetable garden with tomatoes, peppers, melons ripening on the vine. Beyond the garden the two-story clapboard farmhouse: small, simple, functional. Like the marriage between Cracker and Ms. Witte-Cramer. Maybe not so simple.

Up the porch stairs, through the back door, into the kitchen. I can see it all as clear as day. There's Alison, the uptight farm manager's wife, sitting at the kitchen table with their younger daughter, Tracy, age five. Maybe six by now. A pile of asters and zinnias rests on the table between them. Alison, still looking fine, just a few crow's-feet around the eyes from too much frowning, too many attitudes copped on a world beyond her grasp. Trims the stems with a pruning shears while Tracy carefully places the flowers in a glass vase.

Cracker heads straight for the sink, grabs a glass out of the drainer, fills it with water. Good, clean, clear well water.

Molly crosses to the table, immediately starts to help with the flowers, a good kid. "Daddy says we're going to make bales today."

Tracy jumps out of her chair, races across the room to her father, a skinny-as-a-rail lightning rod of fledgling energy. "Can I ride in the hay wagon, Daddy? Can I? Can I? You said last time maybe this time I could."

Cracker drinks his glass of water using one hand, picks up his daughter with the other. "I never thought it would be this time so fast."

"What does that mean?"

"It means you can ride in the hay wagon as long as either your mother or I is back there with you."

Tracy, already privy to the benefits of being agreeable, kisses her father on the face, says, "Okay," and squirms out of his arms. Heads back to the table.

But not before Alison stands, shoos the two urchins toward the back door. "Go swing on the swing," she tells them. "Ride your bikes. I have to talk to your father."

"About what?" Molly, the Inquisitive One, wants to know.

About me.

"Stuff," answers Alison. "Important adult stuff. Now go."

The kids head for the door. Dawdle for a minute or two on the back porch, then wander into the yard where they find the cat prowling through the grass like some lion on the hunt in deepest, wildest Africa.

Cracker refills his glass. "So what's the deal you had to get rid of the kids?"

"I had a phone call a little while ago."

"A phone call? From who?"

"Never mind from who. It's what they said that matters."

The Pottersville Grapevine: alive and well, spreading the word.

"Yeah, so what did they say?"

"When was the last time you saw Mike?"

Here we go.

"Mike? I don't know. A few days ago. Last weekend. When we took the kids up to the trout farm. Why?"

"Because he's gone."

"What do you mean, he's gone?"

"I mean he's gone. Vanished. Without a trace."

"What are you talking about? Says who?"

Alison does not hear his questions. No, she has her own agenda. She has been working on her own agenda ever since I vanished into Edinburgh's thick gray fog. "I told Sarah not to trust him. Two years ago I told her. I told her not to get involved with him. Warned her he was selfish and undependable, that all he knew how to do was play games."

Games. Right. You win a few. You lose a few.

"Wait a second," says Cracker, my good buddy, coming instinctively to my defense. "There must be some explanation, some reason—"

"I knew it was just a matter of time before the pig left the trough."

"But wait, I—"

"No one's heard from him for a week. He just disappeared without a word to anyone, not even Sarah."

Cracker takes a few seconds to think it over. "God, I can't believe this."

"You better believe it."

My old college roomie can't do anything but shake his head.

"You should call Sarah," his wife tells him.

"Me? Why me?"

"Because he's your friend. And she's your sister-in-law."

Cracker lets loose a long and mighty sigh. He takes some more time to think it over. Finally decides he kind of likes the idea of calling Sarah. If what his wife says is true, maybe, just maybe, Sarah might need a shoulder to cry on.

Still carrying a torch after all these many years.

"But what'll I tell her? What'll I say?"

Alison doesn't care what he says. She just wants the inside scoop, all the gory details. Picks up the roving phone, thrusts the receiver into her hubby's hand.

Yup, I'm hearty grist for the local gossip mill now.

After their lavish Caribbean honeymoon, Barbados of all places, nothing but poor blackies kowtowing to rich whiteys, Cracker and Alison headed west. Go west, young lovers. Colorado. Boulder. The thing to do in those days for young, disgruntled Easterners. Cracker to write the Great American Novel. Alison to fix his breakfast and fiddle in a classical quartet. Mozart and Johannes Brahms. A splendid, creative life. Filled with love and fresh mountain air. And no need at all to worry about the color green. The green arrived promptly every fortnight, hand-delivered by a breathless and grungy Pony Express rider from Morgan Guaranty Trust back in the Big Apple. The green would follow Cracker to the ends of the earth. And so too my sweet.

But what about me? What was I supposed to do with the rest of my life? What did I do after returning my tux to Dante's Rent-A-Tux in Burlington, Vermont? Where did I go?

God, it's tiring to remember, to dredge up the memories. Enough to make me want to go upstairs, lie down on my bed here at Lewey's Hotel, fall fast asleep for a few days. Sleep until Sarah arrives.

Okay. I went out to the airport, cashed in the ticket Mom Cramer had bought to fly me home. Home? Wherever that was. Poughkeepsie? Not a chance. I hadn't seen Stan the Man in a year or more. Maggie Jane lived outside of Boston. She was a junior at Boston College, worked as a researcher in a hotshot law office. She'd made the Great Escape, survived the Standowski Reign of Terror.

I took the two hundred bucks for the plane ticket and started south using my thumb as a transportation device. Hitchhiked back to Ithaca. Only took me a couple days. Three at the most. I wasn't in any hurry. I had my camera, a few rolls of film, a change of clothes. Decided right then and there, right out along Highway 9 just south of Fort Ticonderoga, to chronicle my Life in Pictures. In full-color photographs. A Day in the Life of Mike included self-portraits morning, noon, and night; shots of virtually every man, woman, and child I shared a word with; images of food I ate, beer I drank, ground upon which I walked.

So began my Life on the Road. A restless, wandering life.

I moved back into the house on State Street. I still had most of my few meager possessions there: some clothes, a few books, sports gear. I slept on the sofa. The bedrooms inhabited now by a fresh stream of Ithaca College soccer fiends. They liked having Standish in the house. A living legend. I.C.'s goal-scoring king. Plus my bawdy tales, my caustic wit, my one-handed, two-fingered joint-rolling skills.

Coach gave me a job. Working with the team. Went right through the season, then into the gym for winter workouts. It didn't pay much. Five hundred a month. Still an excess of green for a poor boy like me. A hundred for rent. Four hundred for film, food, booze. What more could a twenty-two-year-old guy want?

I discovered the Ithaca College library, a place I had rarely visited during my undergraduate days. I read every single book the library had on photography. And after I exhausted the I.C. collection, I ventured over to Cornell to peruse the Big Red machine. Gave myself an education on the history of picture taking. Learned the who, what, and when. I studied the famous images, the people who made them: Stieglitz, Steichen, Strand, Evans, Adams, Margaret Bourke-White, Edward Weston. Edward Weston! The man's photographs made my eyes pop right out of my skull. His stark, striking portraits. They reached right down and grabbed his subject's soul. And his nudes. Penetrating beyond the superficiality of surface. That's what I wanted to do: explore, examine, expose the human body.

Bonnie. Poor Bonnie. I didn't mean her any harm. She was such a pretty Irish lass. A frosty day in May when she ran into the likes of me. She worked at the Cornell library, a graduate student in medieval studies. We met because I looked lost. I had no right being in that library, wandering among those sacred Ivy League stacks. My trespassing must've showed on my face for suddenly this young lady requested a look at my student ID. I tried to distract her with a smile and a joke, the one about the lion who ate the lovely librarian. But she didn't see the humor so I scrounged up my old I.C. ID.

"This won't do," she said, her voice terse, her backbone ramrod straight. Just a tiny thing with short brown hair, big brown eyes. Looked about fourteen. Trying real hard to look and sound like an adult. I wanted to give her a squeeze. So on the way to the exit I tried another smile, asked a few questions. She liked that. Told me she was writing her master's thesis on the perception of reality in the legend of King Arthur's court. Whoa! I worked to recall the old tale. I told her I loved those guys: Arthur, Merlin, Sir Lancelot.

"Basically a bunch of sexist pigs," she replied.

That's when I laughed, called her Guinevere. I caught her eyes in mine, asked her if she might like to have a beer and some conversation sometime.

Bonnie liked wine. Not beer. And she loved to talk. I didn't mind listening. We just went right ahead and fell for each other. Nothing to it.

Bonnie had a small third-floor apartment at the end of Stewart Avenue. Very small. Starving-college-student digs. Barely enough room for us to get our clothes off at the same time. But we managed. A serious girl Bonnie. An even more serious lover. Battle of the Sexes stuff. She had to ride on top. I figured she must've been suffocated by some huge linebacker early in her sexual development.

Still, I enjoyed that girl. The way she could chatter. Make love to her, give her a glass of red, and watch the verbal river flow. Bonnie had all kinds of thoughts and theories swirling around in her brain. Stuff about why men needed to control and dominate women. And why women let them. I didn't know. I just listened.

Bonnie finagled me a card so I could check books out of the Cornell library. She could see I was a serious artist. Closing me off from the materials I needed to pursue my art would've been sacrilegious. "Artists," she told me, "are our true creators."

That sounded good to me.

I took lots of photographs of Bonnie. Black and white. Some color. Mostly head shots. Usually while she sipped a glass of vino and dredged up the details on the more important female deities. Several of those shots quite complimentary. I gave them to her as gifts. She found them very flattering. Did not even notice, even with all of her feminist defenses on red alert, that I had an angle. Of course I had an angle. I wanted to shoot Bonnie in the buff. Never for a second did I stop telling her what a great body she had. This was only a little white lie. Bonnie had an okay body. Kind of scrawny and boyish. Still, I found her beautiful. Sexy. Erotic.

"If you take pictures of me naked," she asked, finally warming to the idea after several months of subtle arm twisting, "who will see them?"

"You and I will see them."

"Who else?"

I kissed her neck. "If you want, Guinevere, the whole world will see them."

She closed her eyes, fantasized about the world running its eyes over her naked body. Then she snapped back to reality. "I get the negatives," she announced. "The second you get the film developed, I get the negatives."

Absolutely. No problem.

She agreed to two rolls: one color, one black and white. We did the shoot right there in her tiny apartment. Mostly on the bed. A few on the floor.

Jesus, what a disaster!

I wonder if Weston started out like that.

First problem: Bonnie posed like a mannequin. Only stiffer. Not a supple line or muscle in her body. Tension pouring out of every visible orifice. Every smile faked, forced. Incredibly self-conscious with her tiny breasts and tuft of light brown pubic hair exposed to the camera's unfeeling eye.

I didn't know how to make her relax. Didn't have a clue. Point and shoot. You mean there's more to it than that? Hey, look at me, I'm a photographer, an artist. A couple times, if memory serves, I think I actually said, "Smile! Say cheese."

Good God.

But it gets worse. I didn't know the first thing about lighting. Just turned on all the lamps, attached my flash, and went to work. Everything looked okay through the viewfinder: soft and smooth. But when the prints came back from the lab: shadows from hell! Cruel and harsh.

In the black and white shots Bonnie looked like a corpse. I mean she looked dead. And like she'd been dead for quite a while. A week or more. Rigor mortis. Half expected to see flies and maggots crawling around on her as I stood in a corner of the photo lab rifling through the prints.

And the color shots: not much better. The artificial room light combined with the bright light cascading off the flash did some weird stuff. Made Bonnie look all washed out. Like a ghost. And in every shot: red eye. Big-time red eye. Big bright red dots where her eyes should've been.

My intentions had been perfectly sincere. Both loving and professional. But here were a sick bunch of photos. God, I didn't want her to see them. No way. I had every intention of burning them at the first possible opportunity. But she was waiting for me right outside the lab, poised to take possession the second I stepped through the door. I looked for a back way out. Nothing. Not even a window. Finally went out through the front. Tried immediately to explain. The words came pouring forth. But in this case the pictures told the story. The whole story. Worth a million words.

Bonnie snatched them from my hand. "I'll take those."

I should've grabbed them back, headed for the hills. I never should've let that poor girl see those naked images. Never.

One look and her eyes exploded. Tripled in size. One after another she scanned those photos, those nudie pix. Must've been about halfway through the stack when she finally flipped out. Who could blame her? This was disgusting stuff. Bottom of the pornography barrel. She could've decided the whole thing was funny, checked it off as another of life's strange experiences. But Bonnie was a serious girl. An intellectual. A feminist.

God, I should be thankful she didn't have me killed.

Her face turned bright red. I thought she was angry. But then I saw the tears streaming out of her eyes and down her cheeks. I touched her shoulder, tried to calm her down. Smooth things over. That's when the anger rose up and showed its ugly head. Bonnie knocked my hand away. Slapped me across the face. Turned. Took off. I pursued. I tried to explain, apologize. A waste of time. Energy. Bonnie kneed me in the testicles. Hard. I doubled over.

Then, right out there on the sidewalk, for all of Ithaca to hear, she told me never ever ever was I to come around and see her again. "If you do," she shouted, "I'll hire someone to torture you! To pluck your eyes out!" Then she kicked me again and fled, photos and negatives safely in hand.

I gave her a couple days to simmer down. I knew I'd screwed up. But I had not done so on purpose. Or had I? Had I subconsciously sabotaged those photos? And by so doing struck our relationship a fatal blow? I don't know. I don't think so. I wanted those pictures to be beautiful. I wanted them to represent the sensuous feelings I had for Bonnie. But maybe not. Maybe I somehow knew, or at least hoped, that she would find them insulting and drive me from her life. So damn difficult to know for sure, to fully understand our motives and desires.

I went to see her. That much I know for certain. Tail between my legs. A soft knock upon her door. She wouldn't let me in. Wouldn't even talk to me. She told me to get lost. Forever. Threatened to call the cops.

That's when my brain flashed on the image of my old man slapping around that bar bimbo at the sleazy hotel next to the Poughkeepsie bus depot. Right after that is when I decided to leave Bonnie alone. Let her go in peace.

Next came Carla. Rough and tumble Carla. A female bodybuilder. I met her when she came to Ithaca for a competition. At the State Theatre. The whole soccer team went. Drunk. To gawk and whistle at the muscular babes in their gold chains and string bikinis. What a display.

After the show I went backstage. Nikon around my neck. Big talk spewing out of my mouth. Something about being a photojournalist for *Sports Illustrated*. Most of those glistening girls flexed their biceps for me, tossed off their best smiles. Just in case. Not Carla. Carla got right in my face. Glued her green eyes to mine. "*Sports Illustrated!* Right. And I'm Ms. Universe." Then, twinkle in her eye, towel in her hand, she started to rub the sweat and oil from her thick, fibrous thigh.

I stood there, staring, practically drooling. Finally managed to ask, "Want some help with that?"

Carla laughed. She had a big, booming laugh. Then she twisted that wet towel tight, told me to turn around, and snapped off a couple good ones right on my left cheek. Later, back at her motel room, she soothed my battered buttocks with some cool aloe cream.

I followed her home. All the way to Connecticut. Thought I might stay for the weekend. Wound up staying more than a year.

Washington Depot, Connecticut. A small town in the western part of the state. Litchfield County. Close to the New York border. Probably only fifty miles as the crow flies from Poughkeepsie. I never made the trip though. Might as well have been clear across the country. On the other side of the globe.

Carla lived above an art gallery. Basically one big room. Physical fitness gear everywhere: dumbbells, rowing machine, stationary bike, chin-up bar, chest pull, sweat suits, weight-lifting magazines. Carla spent every waking moment developing one muscle or another. Often in the midst of lovemaking I would catch her doing deep knee bends, upper thigh squats, push-ups, chest presses, abdominal rolls.

She worked as a carpenter. Did trim work. Hung doors and moldings. Kitchen cabinets. She had her own crew. All female. Three of them. Drove around in an old Dodge panel truck. Ladders on the roof. Tools in the back. Jazz on the radio. The whole thing blew me away. Another stop on the road to enlightenment.

Carla never asked me how long I planned to stay. She just gave me the bottom drawer of her dresser and asked me to respect her space. She wasn't really around much. Up and out of the house by seven. Worked till dark. Then straight to the gym in New Milford for some work on her quads, pecs, biceps. Then dinner out. Usually at this health food restaurant where they served tofu, squid, seaweed, stuff like that. Sometimes she'd eat Italian. Once in a while Chinese. Then home for some telephone work. Had to get the next day's business settled. She used to squeeze a pillow between her legs while she yakked on the phone. Might as well build up those adductors as long as we have some time to kill.

And what about me? What did I do in Washington Depot, Connecticut, besides stare in stunned silence at Ms. Carla? I peered at her through my viewfinder quite often. Every chance she gave me. Popped off numerous shots of her posing and flexing in her tight little spandex outfits. Never in the buff. She told me flat out it would never happen. And it never did.

It must've been late summer when I landed in Washington Depot. I spent my days wandering around, taking photos, communing with nature. Autumn hit quickly, the foliage exploding with color. That, I suppose, would be my Leaf Period. I must've taken three hundred pictures of leaves: leaves on trees, leaves in piles on the ground, leaves floating through the air, red leaves, yellow leaves, brown leaves. I wrote Cracker a long letter. I was always writing him long letters. I should probably write him one now. I told him all about my leaf photos. Then I asked him in a postscript if he could lend me a few bucks so I could get the film developed. He sent me two hundred and fifty dollars, plus a note saying all was well, Allie was pregnant.

I shook my head at that news, then made haste down to the custom color lab in New Milford. All those photos, and believe it or not, a few good ones. I had a dozen of them blown up. 8 x 10. I sent copies of the best ones out to Cracker. He was my best buddy and my patron, after all. Vincent had Theo. I had Cracker.

I showed the rest of the prints to the woman downstairs who owned the art gallery. "Very nice," she said. "Would you like to hang them?"

That simple question justified my existence, gave my life meaning. It was true after all: I was an artist.

But the designation did not carry much weight with Carla. "We're all artists," she informed me. "You have to be an artist to get out of bed in the morning and look at yourself in the mirror." Then, a pair of twenty-pound dumbbells balanced over her head, "What about the artist paying his share of the rent and utilities? It's been a couple months."

I tried to act indignant, the artist as a creature beyond such mundane cash considerations. But, of course, Carla had a point: I had been freeloading. So I dug out my cash sock shoved into the back of my bottom drawer. I loathed bank accounts. Too confining. I gave her half the rent for the following month. That left me busted, less than fifty bucks to my name.

Carla helped me out. She introduced me to Doris. Doris was a mason. She needed a helper. I rode to work in the back of the panel truck. With the buzz saws, nail guns, and air compressors. Like going off to do battle. Wore jeans, boots, flannel shirt, a brand-new down vest for armor. Had splotches of mortar all over the vest by the end of the first day. I also had arms that felt like dead tree limbs. Must've mixed a couple tons of sand, cement, and water. With Doris constantly barking at me in the background. "Too dry! Too wet! Too stiff! What the hell's the matter with you, Standish? This mud's like soup! I can't put up stone with soup!"

Mud: that's what we called it. Mud. Never mortar. Always mud. I was the main mud maker for Mudd Masonry. The only mud maker. All day long. From sunup till sundown. I mixed the mud. Doris put up the stone. Doris Mudd. A big girl. Strong as an ox. Arms of steel. Had kind of a sweet face. Freckles on her nose and cheeks. She hated those freckles though. Hated men as well. At least pretended like she did. But oh how she loved to work with mud and stone. Good at it too. An artist if you ask me. She made stone walls of exquisite beauty. Her talents were in heavy demand. You might wait a year or more to get Doris to build you a stone wall.

Still, I did not enjoy my work. Day after day, every day but Sunday, it left me filthy dirty and sled dog tired. So tired I often could not execute my sexual duties with Ms. Carla. My insufficient output did not sit well with her. She basically viewed me as another piece of exercise equipment, a living sexual device, a human dildo. The fact that I spoke, soiled the bathroom, and drank the last of the orange juice only made matters worse. She would've preferred someone that folded up and tucked away in the corner, someone she could drag out when the craving for sexual stimulation moistened her loins.

In the spring Maggie Jane came for a visit. After three days she took me aside and said, "Michael, you're coming back to Boston with me. Find a way to tell Carla, and let's get out of here."

Maggie never liked my girlfriends. No, I shouldn't say that. That's not true. She liked some of them fine. But she never found one just right for her big brother. Until she met Sarah. She felt the chemistry between Sarah and me the very first time she saw the two of us together.

But now look at us: separated by time and distance and half the Atlantic Ocean. Me down here on Devil's Cay and Sarah still sitting in that private eye's office up in Morristown, New Jersey. What was his name? The name I gave him? Sheldon?

Right. Glenn Sheldon.

She's up there showing him the clue she found, the clue I left behind. Quite a simple clue. One I felt certain Sarah would find lickety-split. In the trash can of the guest room across the hall from our bedroom at TREETOPS. I sometimes used that bedroom as an office, as a place to escape from the Family Browne. The room had a telephone, an easy chair, a good reading lamp. I called Continental Airlines from that chair. Asked about flights south to Florida, specifically to Fort Myers. I wrote the information down on a scrap of paper. Made a reservation on Flight 1182. To add a little intrigue I gave the woman on the phone a false name, a name I knew Sarah would easily spot. Then I tossed the scrap of paper with all the vital info into the trash basket.

All this happened last week. Just a few short days ago. Just as the law and Iron Kate started to close in on me. Oh yeah, I could feel their mandibles around my neck and ankles. My fingerprints were everywhere, all over everything.

"I found this in the trash," Sarah explains to Glenn Sheldon, P.I. She hands him the scrap of paper, half a Post-it note.

Sheldon, his hands twitching away after five cups of Colombian Supreme, takes the scrap of paper, studies it, runs his eyes over it:

CONT. AIR.
FM—7:40, 11:45, <u>6:50</u>

"So," he says, finally, "this FM business. What do you think it means?"

"I know what it means," Sarah tells him. "It means Fort Myers. That's a city on the west coast of Florida."

Sheldon can't stand her knowing, him not knowing. Does some more twitching, shoulders and neck. "Yeah, I know. South of Tampa. So what do you think? That he flew to Florida? On the flight he's got underlined?"

Good work, Sherlock.

"Yes," says Sarah, princess of patience, "I think there's a good chance that's exactly what he did."

Sheldon nods, thinks it over. Takes a long look at my luscious wife. Wonders what kind of moron would run out on this lovely piece of tail. But Glenn Sheldon, P.I., does not dwell on this issue for long. Been around long enough to know a pretty face and a slim waist can hide one whining, nagging, demanding broad. "Okay," he asks, "so when do you think he took this flight?"

"On the fourteenth."

"Of this month?"

"Yes."

"You're sure?"

"That's the day he disappeared."

Sheldon writes it down. "It's a place to start. I'll go out to Newark Airport, see a friend of mine who works for Continental. We'll find out if your husband was on that six-fifty flight to Fort Myers. Of course, it might not be easy. He might've used an alias to book his reservation. It's easy enough to do on a domestic run."

Atta boy, Glenn. You're on the ball now. One step closer to Devil's Cay.

"But I should warn you," he adds, "this kind of operation takes time. And it can get expensive." Sheldon can smell the green lurking in my wife's purse. It makes his nasal hair tingle.

"I don't want you to waste my money, Mr. Sheldon," Sarah tells him. "But as long as you think we can find him, I want you to keep looking."

Sheldon figures the time has come to drop the cash bomb. "It'll cost you three hundred a day, plus expenses."

Sarah doesn't even blink. Why should she? This is why the rich have Money. To get themselves out of jams. She opens her purse, pulls out a checkbook. "All right, Mr. Sheldon, I'll pay you one week in advance. What else will you need?"

"Some pictures of your husband. Preferably something recent."

Sarah, always prepared, pulls a manila envelope out of her pocketbook. "I took this picture of Michael just last month."

Sheldon opens the envelope, finds a stack of photographs, a dozen copies of the same print, a portrait of me sitting out by Iron Kate's swimming pool, tennis racket in hand.

M. Standish: man of leisure.

Sheldon studies the photo. I can tell by his expression that he expected this guy Standish to look older. Older than his honey of a wife for sure. Middle-age crisis kind of thing. Overweight. Probably balding. But the guy in the picture looks like a kid, barely out of his twenties.

"These will do just fine," says Sheldon. He pushes the photographs back into the envelope.

"I can get more copies if you need them."

"We're okay for now."

Sarah sighs, hands him the check, stands.

Sheldon quickly stands also. He grasps the check between his thumb and index finger. It has a real nice feel.

Sarah prepares to go. "If you find out my husband did in fact fly to Fort Myers, how soon before we can fly down there?"

"*We,* ma'am?"

"Yes, Mr. Sheldon, *we*. I expect to be involved."

"That's not normally how I work."

"Well, maybe this time you can make an exception."

My bride's intonation does not leave much room for Sheldon to argue. She's a tough woman my wife. You'd be surprised. Soft and subdued. A voice that rarely rises above a whisper. But as tough in her own right as Iron Kate. And with an uncanny ability to get her own way. She wanted me, after all. And all the opposition in the world couldn't block her path.

I lived with Maggie off and on for the next few years, all through her days at Harvard Law School. That's right, Harvard Law. My little sister had studied hard and made good. She even had some high-powered law firm paying her tuition and part of her living expenses in exchange for future services.

We lived in Cambridge, in half of an old house a couple blocks from the Charles River. I did the food shopping, not quite my share of the cleaning, and virtually all of the cooking. Maggie used to tell me I'd make some woman a fine wife. Except for this bad habit I had of packing my bags and taking off at a moment's notice.

I worked for an architectural photographer in Brookline. His name was Al Lane and he had a contract with the state of Massachusetts to photograph old buildings slated for historical preservation. It wasn't the most exciting work in the world, but we traveled all over the state, worked outside in good weather, and best of all: Al didn't much care when I disappeared for a few months.

Which I did on a regular basis. Call it wanderlust.

The second I had a few extra bucks in my pocket, I would hit the road. It didn't matter where I went. I was not really into destinations. They always seemed like a contrivance. I kept my personal possessions to a minimum. Rarely owned more than I could carry. Photography equipment mostly. A couple extra lenses for my Nikon F3 (one of them borrowed but never returned, the other one swiped from a camera store in Raleigh, North Carolina). Let's see, what else? A sturdy tripod, some waterproof cases. Darkroom equipment by and by. That's about it. Never had more than a couple changes of clothes. Traveled light, and when I moved on, I gladly left all excess behind.

Cracker called me Stray Wolf. I would drop by and see him several times a year. Always out of the blue. He preferred it that way. I never stayed long. Just a few days, maybe a week. That was about as long as Alison could handle me.

We also spoke regularly on the telephone. We'd talk for an hour or more. He always wanted to know where Stray Wolf was, who Stray Wolf was with, what Stray Wolf was doing, if Stray Wolf had learned any new sexual positions. My old buddy got a vicarious pleasure hearing about my musings and meanderings. But the truth is: I needed Cracker more than he needed me. He, along with Maggie Jane, provided me with a kind of emotional cushion, a soft place to land whenever I started to run low on guts or love or Money.

Cracker and Alison did not last long in Boulder. Allie got nervous as the birth of their firstborn approached. Flew east to her mommy's side a month or so before Molly arrived. Flew east and never flew back. Cracker soon followed. They bought a little farm. Twenty acres. Just down the gravel road from the tee shirt tycoons. I visited them often. An emotional oasis. A small stone farmhouse. Very cozy. Fireplaces in every room. Cracker didn't do much farming. Too damn cold. Only warm enough to grow anything from the Fourth of July until maybe, if you're lucky,

Labor Day. Two months of warmth and ten months of freeze your ass off.

They had a couple cows, sheep, chickens. Cats and dogs. A vegetable garden out back. A few fruit trees. But Cracker was really just a gentleman farmer. And the only farmer in all of New England driving ten thousand dollars' worth of computer equipment. Kept it up in the spare bedroom on the second floor. All the latest techno stuff (modems, faxes, CD roms, spell checkers) for his bookwriting endeavors. Only thing lacking: books. Cracker could never quite get himself motivated to write those novels he had always wanted to write. Plenty of talk. Copious amounts of notes. But very little prose.

During one late summer visit I broke into his hard drive. Wanted to see exactly what my old buddy had been up to creatively over the years. Middle of the night. All others in that stone house fast asleep. It took some time but I finally punched the right keys, pushed the right buttons, found my way in. Nothing but a Thief, a Peeping Tom. Peeping Mike. Found a story, a pretty long story, more than fifty pages, called "Overland." All about this guy who roams the country taking photos, romancing women, doing whatever the hell he pleases. A guy called Stray Wolf.

Poor Cracker. Proves himself a rather pitiful SOB from time to time.

Don't we all.

Not long after she graduated from Harvard Law, Maggie Jane told me she was getting married. I was not surprised. I had seen it coming for a year or more. Still, I voiced my displeasure. At least in jest.

"You can't get married, Maggie," I told her. "You're supposed to marry me."

"We'd have weird children," she replied. "And besides, you're too wild for me, Michael. I need someone quiet and stable."

She needed Tom Anderson. Tom was a lawyer too. From a prominent Boston family of lawyers. Tom was quiet and stable. Tom was polite and kind and very well bred. And he didn't drink a drop. Tom came from well-educated English Protestants, as far removed from Stanislaw Standowski as any man could be.

I gave Maggie Jane away. A charming custom. Stanley had told her he would do it, had promised her he would attend the wedding, but the bastard never bothered to show. Yet another reason why I hate that stinking Polack.

Tom and Maggie got hitched out on Cape Cod. Orleans. Where Tom, fine WASPy boy from an affluent family, had spent all of his twenty-six summers. A little white Methodist church by the sea. Warm. Sunny. The smell of salt air wafting through the open doors. I led my little sister down the aisle. God, she looked beautiful. A taller, happier version of Jessie Buell. I found myself beaming. Proud big brother. Even shed a few tears as they exchanged vows. Maggie looked filled with joy. Overflowing with glad tidings. She'd done a couple years of therapy by that time. Working out stuff to do with Stan and Jessie. Childhood stuff. Encouraged me to do the same. But I was too stubborn, probably too scared. So I'm doing my therapy now. Cold turkey. Down here on Devil's Cay. At the bar of Lewey's Hotel.

I met Robin at the reception. Tom's sister's friend. Tiny, pretty, feisty. Stole my heart away in an instant. "Want to marry me?" I asked.

"Do you have money?" came the reply.

"Not a nickel," I answered.

"Then," she said, a hint of a Southern accent in her vivacious voice, "marriage is out. But everything else is in."

My sentiments exactly.

"Norfolk, Virginia," she cooed when I asked where she'd grown up. "My daddy's a Navy man."

"An excellent branch of the service," I think I told her. And then out came my Nikon. Snapped a few pictures of her. All smiles and straight white teeth as I tripped the shutter. My loins pushed against the tight woolen weave of my tuxedo trousers. I felt a powerful desire to put my arms around Robin's narrow waist, draw her lips flush with mine. Asked her if she wanted to dance. She said absolutely. I ran my fingers up and down her spine as we spun around the dance floor. Had ourselves a delicious kiss or two. Of course, we'd been imbibing. Glass after glass of champagne. I pressed my maleness against her hips.

Robin hit me with a reprimand. "Naughty boy, Mr. Standish. What would your sister say?"

Robin proved a flirt, but no easy mark. Made me chase her around the Cape for two or three months. Broke, as usual, I needed to find work. Hired on with Captain Claw. Helped him drag his lobster traps up off the bottom of Cape Cod Bay. Poor guy had lost his left hand. Just above the wrist. Not in a lobstering accident either, as you might expect, but while ripping plywood out in his garage with a table saw. Slipped on a puddle of oil left by his old pickup, stumbled against the saw, and, in a flash, zip, adios left hand. That saw blade cut it off clean.

Captain Claw (real name Jimmy Teems) took it in stride. A stolid Yankee with a very dry sense of humor. Enjoyed drinking beer with his steel claw. Told me he even occasionally used it to masturbate. His wife taught grade school over in Barnstable. So Jimmy didn't have to rely on the crustaceans to earn a living. We checked the traps once, sometimes twice a day. Hung around the fishing piers shooting the breeze, sipping the suds. I always had my Nikon at the ready. Took many a photo of the sea and those crusty New England salts who sucked a living out of her.

In my spare time I pursued Robin. She enjoyed the chase and had become quite good at it. Knew all the moves. Could manipulate a man as well as any woman I've ever known. Okay by me. I certainly was not above occasionally calling on my skills as a strategist. Finally caught up with her one night after the summer people had gone home to their real lives. Out on Nauset Beach. Perfect late summer evening: a gentle breeze off the Atlantic, nice and warm, no moon, heaven full of stars. I brought a blanket, a bottle of wine, a joint as fat around as a cigar. We smoked the whole bone, giggled from the first toke to the last. Made love wrapped up in that blanket, the sand giving way beneath us as we pushed and rolled our way around the beach.

We moved in together a few weeks later. The middle of October. A small two-bedroom bungalow right on Wellfleet Harbor. I could walk down to the Captain's boat from there in less than five minutes. Robin had herself a spiffy little red Mazda Miata sports coupe (a gift from her Navy dad) to haul her over to Orleans where she worked in a big girls' boutique that sold overpriced clothes to rich fat women.

One could easily say that Robin and I had a two-pronged relationship: Sex and recreational drug use. We copulated (frequently), smoked grass, and drank beer over at the Wellfleet Pub. Within walking distance of our bungalow so we never had to drink and drive. A good thing too. Wellfleet had a constable whose greatest joy came from issuing DUIs. He literally glowed as he penned the summons from the driver's seat of his aging patrol car.

Sex, Booze, Drugs. Beyond that, after our first few months as a Couple, we had little to do with one another. Nothing else in common. The problem, of course, with so many relationships founded on the old in and out. We went our separate ways. Robin had her friends. I had mine. I never really knew what Robin did all the time. I know she liked to go to the movies. Something I loathed. Two hours of tedium. Fictional people's lives inflicted upon me on the big screen. She loved shopping. Something else I tried not to do more than once a year. And the cups of spiked cappuccino at the bistros up in Provincetown. I know she enjoyed that. And maybe she fooled around. I don't know. I don't think so. I think that came later.

As for me, well, I did what I always do when I settle in a new place: I sought out the sports junkies, the athletes. I played hoops at the local high school in the winter, soccer in the Cape League spring and summer. I did some fishing. Surf fishing. Spear fishing. Deep-sea fishing. I rowed several days a week in Captain Claw's old wooden dory. It had been his father's. And his grandfather's before that. Of no use to the Captain. Tough to row a boat with a claw. Beautiful piece of work too. Long, graceful lines. Once I got my arms and shoulders in rowing shape, I could make that craft cut through the water at a splendid clip. I liked to take it out early in the morning, the fog still draped over the harbor, no one around but the gulls and the pipers. Gave me time to think. To contemplate what I wanted to be when I grew up.

I did some traveling as well. With a guy named Harry. A photographer. The real McCoy. Had sold his stuff to *National Geo, Smithsonian, National Wildlife, The Outdoorsman*. Sixty, maybe sixty-five. Retired. Enjoyed wandering around, popping off a few shots. Used to invite me to tag along. Mostly as his lackey, but hell, I had plenty of opportunities to trip the shutter of my aging F3. We ventured all over the Cape, out to the islands (Nantucket and Martha's Vineyard), up to the Adirondacks, up and down the coast of Maine. Had ourselves a hell of a good time. Old Harry knew how to have a good time. He'd been everywhere, seen everything. Would stop and talk to anyone. Had some oft-repeated advice, however, that grew a little thin, "Stay away from women, son. All they do is slow you down, little by little eat you up. Remember, God gave us whores for a reason."

So much stimuli in life. So many people coming at me from so many different directions, different angles, different attitudes. Enough to drive a poor boy crazy.

I must've been on the Cape, copulating with Robin, hauling traps for Captain Claw, shooting photographs with old Harry, for a year and a half or more when I ran into Wesley Mack at the Wellfleet Pub. Late May. Middle of the afternoon. I had a bunch of my photos spread out on the bar. Had my buddies (barkeep, cook, one of the waiters) gathered around for a look. Some new stuff I'd taken up in Maine. During a swing with Harry. The wild, rocky coast. Storm clouds and lathery surf.

We noticed when he came in. Tough not to notice. He sat down at the end of the bar. Big as a house. Ordered a beer and a burger. "Rare." Had a deep, raspy voice. A pair of shoulders like a prizefighter. Neck like a pro football player. Wore a black leather jacket, black leather pants, black boots. A black motorcycle helmet first under his arm, then under his seat. And oh yeah, a face as black as the ace of spades, a rare and unusual sight in the overwhelmingly white enclave of Wellfleet. And he also had this scar, this prominent purple scar running from his right earlobe across his cheek to the corner of his mouth. Sucker stood out for all the world to see.

"Bullshit," he said after he ordered his meal, after he drained a couple drafts, literally sucked the beer out of the mug, after he took some time to study my prints.

My buddies had pretty much drifted back to work.

"Excuse me?" I asked.

"Pretty good technique," said my latest critic. "Adequate composition. But the images: bullshit. The ocean. The sky.

The fucking surf. Gimme a break. You could train a chimp to shoot that shit."

I stood there, stunned, not real certain what to say. Finally decided I better introduce myself.

He shook my hand. Had himself a huge paw. Like a bear's. Nearly crushed my wet rag. "Mack," he roared, "Wesley Mack."

Wesley Mack and I spent the rest of that day and most of that night cozied up to the bar of the Wellfleet Pub. Drank ourselves several gallons of beer. More than a few shots of tequila. Talked about taking pictures. Debated for hours whether or not photography was a bona fide art form. I gave it a yea. Wesley a nay. Said a camera in the hands of all but a few was an instrument of visual destruction. But later, after our blood alcohol levels had soared off the charts, I argued nay while Wesley pushed for yea. Around and around we went. Going nowhere. Solving the problems of the Art World. The Whole World.

Finally, I had to ask. Couldn't keep it in any longer. Had to know. Couldn't take my eyes off it. "Tell me something, Wes," my words slurring and sloshing all over the bar, "how did you get that scar?"

He stroked it with his thumb. "What? This?"

I nodded.

"Got this little beauty mark in a knife fight."

"No shit?"

"That's right," he told me. "In Newark, New Jersey. When I was sixteen years old. Sweet, ain't it?"

I just whistled softly. Gave him a nod.

That's when Wesley pointed at my prints. Stabbed his index finger down onto the pile. "Why don't you throw this cutesy-ass crap away, Standish. Go down to Newark. Take some photographs with grit. Get your damn camera bloody. Find out what's really going on in America."

My eyes and thoughts swam through the alcohol haze.
"Newark?"

Wesley nodded. "Goddamn right."

"Don't think I've ever been to Newark." Thought about
it. "Except maybe to the airport."

"Time you went, boy. Way past time you went."

We talked it over. At great length. Wesley got me all
revved up. Told me I could go "way beyond the stilted Puritan bullshit of Weston and Adams. Those two honkies shot
nothing but waves and tits and trees. Where's the drama in
any of that?"

I had no idea. I had lost all sense of reason.

"You have to hit the streets, Standish. The drama's on
the streets. The mean urban streets."

"You think so?"

"I know so."

I had more than enough booze bubbling through my
system to believe him. It gave me strength, courage. Balls as
big as balloons. Ego all swollen up, raring to go, ready for a
fight. "Yeah," I said, "yeah, yeah, yeah. Let's do it. Let's go
for it."

Wesley slapped me on the back, headed for the pay
phone. Had the whole deal sewn up before I slipped in and
out of the men's room. Called his brother Ernie down in
Newark. Got me a job and a room.

I found myself rolling on a southbound train before I'd
even recovered from the hangover. My Wellfleet Period had
abruptly come to a close.

Newark, New Jersey. Jesus! What was God thinking
about when he put together this little corner of his earthly
paradise? What was I thinking about when I agreed to pass
some time there?

Ernie's Bar & Grill. Small neon sign in the dusty window said so. At the corner of Broad and Broome. Helen

Keller could have sensed Trouble in the air in that neighborhood. Trouble oozed out of the cracks in the sidewalks, wafted from the cracked and grimy windows up and down the street. Don't ask me for explanations. I ain't no sociologist. Slavery. Poverty. Raging unemployment. Alcohol and substance abuse. Broken families. Of course, these last two excuses permeate every American neighborhood. Even the rich ones. But most neighborhoods don't look like this. Hell on earth. Junk all over the place. Broken bottles. Piles of garbage. Homeless vagrants picking through the fetid refuse. Men, grown men, hanging around on stoops in the middle of the workday, sucking on bottles of cheap wine, cussing and screaming at each other, buying and selling bags of dope. Grass. Crack. Speed. Heroin. Anything you want. Always in minuscule quantities because no one has more than a few welfare shekels in their pocket.

When you're white, brother, you watch your back. Every second. Thank God I had Ernie as my protector. He picked me up at Penn Station. Walked around the 'hood with me. Told the brothers I was a distant cousin from down on the plantation and they damn well better leave me alone.

I had a room behind the bar. Triple lock on the door. A safe little cave tucked away in the alley next to the dumpsters and Ernie's old T-Bird up on blocks.

For seven long weeks I lived and worked at Ernie's. Six nights a week I stood behind his bar pouring shots and beers, changing the channel on the overhead TV, doing my best to stay out of Trouble. Always Trouble brewing at Ernie's. Every single second. The air stank of spilled beer, stale cigarettes, violence, and vomit. The wild-eyed black dudes and the few crazy Portuguese who hung around Ernie's gave me a hard time. Rode me without mercy. Made a hobby of it.

"What the fuck you doin' in this shithole, white boy?"

"You gonna get messed up you don't watch your skinny white ass."

"You bein' here in Nigger Land mean only one of two things: either you a cop or you plain dumb stupid."

"Stupid," I assured them. "A total moron." All the time smiling while doling out the freebies. "On the house," quickly became my favorite expression. Watching my back, spinning in circles. The crackheads loved to sneak up behind you, clock you over the head with a brick or a bottle, steal the coins and the crumpled-up dollar bills from your pocket.

During the day I roamed the streets of Newark. Usually with Aaron, Ernie's twenty-two-year-old son. Aaron did his best to keep Trouble at bay while I tried to capture that urban hellhole on film. Did the best I could, but man, you just don't know until you've seen it with your own eyes. I swear to God, the teeming masses out in suburbia would be horrified. Danger and decay everywhere. Tough to imagine anyone in Beirut or Mogadishu living in any worse conditions. The filth. The fear. The freaking degradation of human life. I did my best to tell the story with pictures. But I couldn't do it, couldn't come close. Not with the hopelessness and the urgency that the story demanded, deserved. So what did I do? I started digging deeper, taking more chances. I started taking pictures right inside Ernie's Bar & Grill. Portraits of the patrons. A dicey business. Very high-strung subjects. Could turn on you in an instant.

Then I got really crazy. Decided I had to shoot at night. Out on the streets. No way around it. The only way to fully capture the Drama. The Tragedy.

Sometime around one o'clock in the morning. Middle of June. Warm, muggy, overcast. Most sane, law-abiding citizens (especially ones as white as me) would not have stood on the corner of Broad and Broome in broad daylight, much less in the dark hours before dawn. They would have feared for their middle-class lives in that urban militarized zone. But me, I liked the location. And since I worked till midnight, I didn't have much choice about the time. Not if I wanted to shoot the night owls.

Besides, the lighting was perfect. The harsh glare cast by the overhead street lamps provided excellent contrast for my black and white images. The artificial light gave the pictures a sharp, violent punch. You could look at those prints and smell the Trouble. Wesley Mack, I realized, had been right. My Cape Cod stuff was crap. A couple hundred prints of the sea in various phases of quiescence and rage. Had even sold a few of those prints at a local gallery in Truro. Not any of the black and white stuff. Nothing but the full-blown color shots of waves crashing onto the beach with maybe a seagull in the foreground to appease the buying public.

But now, in the middle of Newark, in the middle of the night, the sound of sirens wailing in the distance, I stood right smack in the middle of the action. Watched through the viewfinder of my F3 as the regulars over at Ernie's Bar & Grill pushed through the door, stumbled along that cracked and dangerous sidewalk. I knew many of those drunks by name, all of them by reputation.

The Big Trouble started when the sound of those police sirens suddenly grew louder. Then closer. That's when I heard the first shot. I couldn't tell at first from where. The brick buildings caused the shot to echo. Could've come from over at Ernie's. Tough to tell.

I looked away from the viewfinder to see what I could find. Nothing. Just the sirens, slicing through the warm, humid night, growing closer and closer. Then the door over at Ernie's burst wide open. Half a dozen drunken brothers poured out onto the sidewalk. Running, shouting. "The fucker has a gun! The fucker has a gun!" Then another shot. Definitely from inside the bar. More of Ernie's boys raced through the door. Out into the street. For a second or two I froze. Couldn't decide if I should look with my eyes or my viewfinder. Finally, thank God, decided on the viewfinder. I knew most of the great action images captured on film had happened in a single blurry instant. No time to focus or think.

I had the camera mounted on my sturdy aluminum tripod. I swung the camera, fiddled with the focus, started shooting. As fast as I could trip the shutter. Then a third shot. And a fourth. Two cop cars, their lights flashing, their sirens wailing, raced around the corner and came to an abrupt halt right in the middle of Broad Street, directly between Ernie's and where I stood.

I kept tripping the shutter, knowing I wouldn't find out what I had until the film could be developed. That's when I spotted Ernie. He came slowly through the door, followed by a man with a gun. A .38 Magnum. Held that weapon tight against Ernie's head. Ernie was a big dude, even bigger and broader than brother Wesley. But the other dude had the piece.

I recognized him. They called him Slammer. The guy in the neighborhood who almost reached the NBA. Six feet five, quick as a cat. Played college ball for St. John's. Got involved with crack his senior year. Hadn't been right since. Bad temper, legendary mood swings. Everyone knew he carried a piece. Ernie had more than once refused to give Slammer drinks, and for reasons no one knew, Slammer had it in his head that Ernie was tooling his Puerto Rican girlfriend.

Now Slammer had gone over the edge. Two people already lay on the floor of the bar bleeding, bullet holes in critical areas. One of them looked like he probably wouldn't make it. The cops out of their patrol cars demanding Slammer drop his weapon, release his hostage. But Slammer couldn't hear a word. The crack had turned his brain to mush.

By this time I stood there vibrating from the adrenaline rush. But I kept shooting, happy I'd stuck in that fresh roll of T-Max 3200 before hitting the streets. This was definitely the action I'd been waiting for, that I'd come all the way from Cape Cod to capture. Zoomed in on Ernie and Slammer. Popped off a shot or two. Then I swung the rotating mount on the tripod, popped off a couple shots of the police sergeant issuing orders through a megaphone that Slammer couldn't hear. Then back to Ernie and Slammer just as Ernie, fed up with that cold steel stuck against his head, elbowed Slammer in the ribs and made a run for it. He didn't trust those cops or anyone else to save his hide.

Slammer raised his pistol, fired as fast as he could pull the trigger. The first shot hit Ernie in the back. Knocked him down. The second shot slammed into the side of one of the cop cars. The third shot whistled past the cop car and smashed into my right shoulder. More or less shattered my clavicle. And the fourth shot: it went straight up into the air as Slammer flew back against the door of the bar after those Newark police officers emptied their weapons into the assailant's vital organs.

Oh yeah, quite a night. Quite a scene.

Cracker sat in the kitchen of his safe, quiet, peaceful farmhouse on the Cramer Compound, forking leftovers (black bean and cilantro salad) into his mouth, when the phone rang.

Finally, to stop the ringing, he picked it up. "Hello?"

"Cracker?"

"Mike?"

"Your old buddy."

"Where are you?"

"I'm in Newark."

"Newark, New Jersey?"

"Right."

"Where? At the airport? You want me to pick you up?"

"Listen, Graham, I'm in a jam. I was wondering—"

"Look out, here we go again. How much this time?"

"Maybe," I told him, "you better bring your checkbook."

That same night Cracker and I sat in his kitchen drinking beers. Ice-cold ones. I had my right arm in a sling, my right shoulder hidden beneath several yards of white cotton gauze.

Cracker kept his eyes on me. "You ready to tell me yet?"

"Soon as Alison gets here. No use going through this twice."

Cracker sighed, took a hit off his Coors.

A couple minutes later Alison came into the kitchen. Almost had a smile in her eyes. Probably thinking about her two beautiful little daughters she'd just put down for the night. But one look at me and wham! she ripped that hint of a smile off her face. "Okay," she demanded, "what happened to you this time?"

Ah, the sweet joys and satisfactions of an old lover.

I spent the next hour or so telling them all about the Mack Brothers, about my adventures in Newark.

Cracker stopped me from time to time to demand more detail, but the question I remember best came from my old college sweetheart. "Are you telling us that just because some stranger said your photographs were lousy you packed your bags, threw away the life you'd been leading, and moved to an entirely black neighborhood in Newark, New Jersey?"

I shrugged, very cool, cracked another can of Coors. My right shoulder reacted with a shot of pain. A pretty fair wince raced across my face.

"Sounds to me," said Cracker, "exactly like something Standish would do."

Alison looked disgusted. I could see our past in her eyes. "So basically," she announced, not a question, "you just got up and walked out on Robin."

"There were," I assured her, "extenuating circumstances."

"Oh right," said Alison, sarcasm foaming out of her mouth. "No doubt."

"Come on, Standish," said Cracker, "get on with the story."

The story. Right. My story. Maybe first I should say something about those extenuating circumstances. Something I never bothered telling Cracker or Alison or anyone else.

I may have told the Cramers that I simply packed up, moved out of Wellfleet, and headed south for Newark, but that statement, like many of my statements over the years, was not entirely true. Not fully grounded in reality. I suppose most lies are unfathomable, and so too was this one. Maybe I told it to maintain my reputation as a ladykiller, a reputation I always enjoyed flaunting around Alison. But something else might've been working as well. A man, after all, has many reasons why he lies: ego, insecurity, testosterone. And often he doesn't even know why; lies just spill from his mouth as naturally as the air he expels from his lungs.

The truth in this particular case is worth dispensing. A week or two prior to my long discussion with Wesley Mack concerning the quality of my photography, I'd returned to Wellfleet after a month-long shoot with Old Harry up along the coast of Maine. I had originally told Robin I'd be gone four or five days. The days quickly turned into weeks. The day we finally got back to town, I stopped at the pub for a beer. Tony, the barkeep, told me I ought to head for home.

"That scumbag Bonner's old VW van," he said, "has been parked outside your house for close to a week."

I nodded, gave that bit of news some thought. Drank three quick beers and a shot of Old Grand-Dad. Paid my tab, left the pub, more or less marched down Main Street to our bungalow along the harbor. And sure enough, parked there in the gravel drive: Bonner's rusty piece-of-crap VW van. Right behind Robin's spiffy red Mazda Miata. Bonner was a shit. Everyone knew Bonner was a shit, a real lowlife sleazeball who would probably steal from his own mother. But then, lots of people around town had said the same thing about Robin. And probably about me too. So who knows from nothing?

Just after dusk. A light mist filled the air. Fog rolled in off the bay. A light snapped on in the bedroom of the bungalow. I kind of half walked, half stumbled up to the front stoop. Carefully turned the knob, pushed open the door. Right away I heard Robin giggling in the bedroom. Had heard that giggle a million times. Oh yeah, I knew how to make her giggle. Had always had the power to make the girls giggle. I slipped through the living room, crept down the narrow hallway. The bedroom door hung wide open. I stepped right into the room. My room. Where I rested my head at night. Robin and Bonner were all finished up for the evening, just hanging around naked in the sack now licking a bottle of Smirnoff's fresh from the deep freeze.

And that, as they say, was that. Except for these two addendums: The first took place right there in the bedroom. I crossed to the bed, pulled down my Levi's, and relieved my aching beer-swollen bladder all over the sheets and blankets. My audience could only gape in wonder. Then, a minute or so later, back outside, hammer in hand, I methodically shattered the windshields in both Bonner's van and Robin's spiffy little sports coupe.

For these misdemeanors, our local constable charged me with absolutely nada. Not only did the man dislike Bonner intensely, but he, along with virtually everyone else in town, agreed the two lovebirds deserved new glass.

So Robin screwed me over. Nooky on the side. These things happen. Always have. Always will. But before we purge yours truly of any and all responsibility, let us consider his track record during the year and a half he and Robin cohabited. He spent almost half that time out of town, wandering hither and thither, snapping photos, surely at least peeking at good-looking women. And being a rather virile young fellow, one might assume he occasionally did more than just peek. And, of course, let us not forget the night he got looped on tequila sunrises and tried to seduce Robin's younger sister Peggy up visiting from Norfolk, VA. Had his hands inside Peggy's blouse when big sis slipped into the room.

All in all, not a pretty picture. Maggie Jane warned me from the very beginning that Robin was not the right girl for me. She insisted we would only cause one another emotional distress.

So you see, by the time Wesley Mack rolled into town on his black Harley, I was sleeping on a buddy's sofa, hungry and restless, looking for inspiration, searching for a way out of town.

But all this is a sideshow. A sideshow that went unannounced that evening at the home of Graham and Alison Cramer. I told them instead about getting shot.

"That bullet threw me backwards, knocked me cold. I woke up in the hospital and found the doctor removing the slug, patching me up. He put my collarbone back together, wrapped it so tight I couldn't move it, then sent me to recovery to deal with the pain. But no matter how much painkiller they gave me, that sucker throbbed and pounded for a week."

"They had you in the hospital for a whole week?"

"Ten days altogether."

Cracker, impressed, whistled softly. "So how did you wind up in jail?"

Oh yeah, that facet of the story.

"On my ninth day at Newark General they found out my health insurance was bogus. I'd falsified my admissions forms. But since I'd been shot on the street, the city of Newark was taking care of most of my medical bill. An excellent public relations move. Still, a week in the hospital is an expensive holiday in modern America. When the smoke cleared I had a personal tab of almost fifty-five hundred bucks."

"So you slipped out of the hospital without paying?"

"Hey, what else could I do? Pawn my photography equipment to pay my bill because some wacko freaked out, almost blew my arm off?"

"Okay, so you slipped out of the hospital. How did you get caught?"

"That's the stupid part. I had to get my stuff, my camera gear. I had to go to the police station, sign a bunch of papers—"

Alison, feigning disinterest in the whole affair, suddenly perked up. "You walked right into the police station after sneaking out of the hospital!"

"They'd taken my Nikon after I got shot. I wanted it back. They didn't know I'd left the hospital without paying. I just signed some release papers and they gave me my stuff. Then I walked over to my room behind Ernie's Bar and Grill to collect my clothes. By the time I had everything together my shoulder was hurting pretty bad. I decided to lie down for a few minutes before getting the hell out of Newark. I must've fallen asleep because all of a sudden I opened my eyes and found these two giant cops hovering over my bed. They read me Miranda, hauled me downtown."

"Where you called me?"

"Actually, Cracker, I called my old man first."

"Your old man! You're kidding me?"

"Nope, I called Stanley. Just to see what he'd say. See how he'd react."

"And?"

"And, well, I hadn't talked to the SOB in a long time. Years. He listened to my tale of woe, then told me maybe jail would be good for me. Calm me down. Make a man out of me. Just the place to learn a few life lessons. Then he hung up without even saying goodbye."

"Jesus," said Cracker, "he's a piece of work, your old man. Makes Big Walt look like a prince."

I shrugged.

"So then," asked Cracker, "you called me?"

"That's right, old buddy," I said. "Then I called you. And just like always, you pulled my irons from the fire. I owe you another one."

"You owe him," announced Alison, having heard enough, ready for bed, on her way up the stairs, "fifty-five hundred dollars."

More or less.

And look: there they are again. The Happy Couple. Still in the kitchen. In the present. Cracker and Allie. Discussing the miserable no-good rat Standowski. The one who disappeared, who ran off without a word. Cracker with telephone in hand. His lovely bride browbeating him into submission. "Call again. Just call again." Cracker, the human doormat, actually does what he's told. He calls again, lets the phone over at TREETOPS ring and ring until the answering machine picks up. But he has no desire to leave a message. So he hangs up. Turns to his wife. Shrugs.

Alison spews fire. Pissed and impatient. She wants the story on Mikey Boy's disappearance. The whole story. "Maybe you should just drive over there."

"But no one's home. Sarah's not there."

"Maybe she's out by the pool. Or down at the barn."

Cracker sighs. For over an hour, ever since Alison told him about my latest maneuver, he's had to listen to his wife vilify and belittle his best buddy. Not that Mike doesn't deserve it, if what she says proves true. Just drive over there, he thinks to himself. Yeah, I'll just drive over there. Get away from this— He blocks the canine nickname he has recently, and silently, given his wife. "Okay," he says. "I'll go over and see if I can find her."

Once safely away in the family's Grand Wagoneer, Cracker relaxes. Sometimes Alison puts him right out on the edge of anxiety. Sometimes he can't wait to get away from her. She's become, over the years, especially since the move from Vermont down to Jersey, so demanding, so petty . . . so unhappy. Hey, I tried to warn him. Years ago I tried to tell him. Tried to tell him some bitch would sink her claws into him and never let go. Of course, he didn't listen. Not to me. Poor Cracker. A man who just wants to slide along, inhale and exhale, come in contact with the earth, dig in the dirt. But all too often he feels surrounded by personalities who need power and control. He loves Alison, at least he thinks he does, but sometimes he feels like backhanding her across the cheek or stuffing a dish towel in her mouth. He never would, never could, but he still thinks about it. And more and more he finds himself drifting, wandering, even hiding, seeking out ever more creative ways to escape her company. If not for Molly and Tracy. No, he doesn't want to think about that. Not now. Slaps himself on the head. For chrissakes, Cramer, think about this thing with Standish. What's that damn Polack gone and done now?

He switches on the radio. Nothing but negative talk from the shock jocks, noisy ads for beer, cars, sugar water. Pops in a CD. U2, *The Joshua Tree*. Cranks the volume. That frantic Irish rhythm section explodes through the speakers. Just a few miles from the Cramer Compound to TREETOPS, but Cracker figures he has time for a tune or two. The first one about a guy who still hasn't found what he's looking for. A lyric that always jars Cracker's brain. He rarely gets to listen to music anymore; the kids with that damn TV set blaring, Alison always talking the day to death. Blah blah blah blah blah. Used to, back in his college days, listen to a couple hours of rock and roll every day. Loved to escape into a wild bass line, some playful lead guitar licks. Oh yeah, here's that Bono lyric about not being able to live with or without her. Makes Cracker crazy, thinking about that stuff.

A turn onto Hollow Brook Road. Dips, bends, forks. He takes the right fork. The road climbs under tall shade trees until Cracker reaches an inconspicuous driveway on the left. The bottom of the drive: packed dirt and gravel, no wider than a car. No mailbox, no house number, no indication whatsoever that the Brownes might live up that rutted track. But on the side of the drive, among the wild rhododendrons, a small metal sign, decorated with painted yellow daisies: TREETOPS.

Cracker turns in, starts climbing. He clears the potholed mess after a couple hundred yards. Hits the smooth macadam. Slows for a look at the hay fields, the horse pastures. Split-rail fence crisscrossing a green late summer landscape. Cracker crests the hill. Dead ahead he sees the massive Tudor perched atop the high point on the ridge. Built by Thomas Browne, Sarah's daddy, in the early 1960s, the house occupies nearly six thousand square feet. Deep green English ivy covers the entire front facade. Dark red chimneys flare into the sky.

Cracker parks the Wagoneer next to the detached five-car garage. Look: the '32 Rolls and the '61 Benz. Still shiny and green. Looking like a million bucks. Cracker crosses the parking area, cuts through a break in the row of cedar trees enclosing the backyard. Once through the trees, he enters onto a vast sweep of manicured lawn broken only by a gazebo, a swimming pool, and a Har-Tru tennis court outfitted with lights for night play. He looks around but doesn't see a soul.

He takes a moment to enjoy the view before knocking on the back door. To the northeast, across the valley, he can see part of his father's land, land he hopes one day will be his own. At least sometimes that's what he hopes. Other times he wants nothing to do with that land, with the expense, the responsibility, the memories of Old Walt ranting and raving. Sometimes he just wants to climb into his Wagoneer and drive. And keep driving. Drive until he's someplace where he's never been, where no one knows him. Somewhere where he can hole up, write that damn novel he's been wanting to write for God knows how many years.

Cracker takes a deep breath, knocks softly on the back door. Half hopes no one is home. What'll he say? "Hello Sarah, Mrs. Browne. How are you? I hear Mike's run off." He sighs, figures Iron Kate will hold him at least partly responsible for this mess. After all, he's the one who introduced that stinking Polack into the family.

No one answers his knock. Relieved, he turns away. Decides to take a ride over to the stable. Back down the drive. Halfway down, another road, a gravel road, forks to the west. Bisects more fields, more pastures, runs through a thick wood. Then a clearing with several outbuildings: sheds, hay barns, a caretaker's cottage, an indoor riding ring, a magnificent horse stable. Beyond the stable: a large outdoor ring with lights and a wide assortment of professional jumps. Cracker sees the ring is empty, no one in sight. Still, he takes the time to check inside.

The stable has stalls for sixteen horses. Used to all be occupied. But Katherine no longer gives lessons or takes boarders. Now only the family horses remain: three geldings, two mares, Timothy's feisty gray pony. All well-trained foxhunters. But today the stalls stand empty. Today the horses have been turned out to enjoy the sun, the fresh summer grass. The family may be in crisis, but their valuable beasts still need attention.

Cracker wanders through the stable. No hurry now. Nowhere to go. Nothing to do. For a few minutes anyway. He soaks up the silence, the smell of hay and well-oiled leather. He learned to tack, groom, and ride a horse here. Learned from his instructor, Miss Sarah Browne, an accomplished equestrienne by age twelve. She gave him a riding lesson every Monday afternoon after school for almost three years. He hated riding, loved his teacher. The only reason he kept coming. All that time he had a boyhood crush on her. And years later, when she began to date his older brother, he found those boyhood yearnings continued to linger. And linger still. Oh yeah, Cracker's a guy who never moves very far beyond his past.

Now, standing here in the cool quiet of this empty stable, memories exploding off the wooden walls, Cracker thinks about desire, about longing, about responsibility, about freedom. But as quickly as the thoughts come, he drives them away, shakes them loose. This, he tells himself, is no time to be questioning the validity of his dry, dusty existence. Although, if he's honest about it, there has never been a good time for such deliberations. Closed up, young Graham "Cracker" Cramer; choked off from his own emotions since adolescence.

He hurries out into the bright sunshine, climbs into his Grand Wagoneer, takes the dirt trail back up to the main house. Primarily used as a bridle path, the trail runs behind the stable, up along the ridge. Steep and rocky. Cracker slips into four-wheel drive. When he reaches the crest he stops to take a look at the beauty, to feel the serenity. Cannot believe his old buddy Mike has messed up his hold on this incredible piece of real estate. Worth a few million. But then, he thinks, maybe all this land, all this affluence, is its own form of bondage. Maybe Money isn't the only prize. For just a moment he thinks maybe I did the right thing, made the right choice.

He feels the heat of the sun on the side of his face. A line of sweat runs down his cheek. He wonders what he should do next. No way does he feel like going home, dealing with Alison. Questions and accusations.

"Goddammit, you stupid son of a bitch!" Cracker shouts loud enough for me to hear. But I have no idea if he's talking to me or talking to himself.

Probably talking to both of us.

Much to Alison's profound displeasure, I did my shoulder injury R&R up in the spare bedroom of her precious little farmhouse on the western fringes of the Cramer Compound. Many more than one conversation between the blissfully wedded pair went something like this:

"Come on, Allie. Where's the guy supposed to go?"

"I don't know, Graham. But is he supposed to stay here for the rest of his life?"

"I wouldn't call a couple months the rest of his life."

"A couple months!"

Cracker shrugged. "The doctor told him today if he wants to regain full use of that shoulder he has to stick to a rigorous program of physical therapy for the next six to eight weeks."

"Six to eight weeks! He never even clears his plate off the table."

"That's because the girls jump up and clear it for him."

"They're like his little slaves."

"Look, if you want him to help out, just ask him."

Alison stuck her head behind her gardening magazine. Pretended to read. But she had to ask, had to know. "So who paid for the doctor?"

Cracker took a few seconds to answer. "I did."

"You did?"

"I did, yeah."

"So we have to give him room and board *and* pay his medical expenses?"

"I don't know, Allie. I'm just trying to help the guy out."

They lay in bed, side by side, but separated, physically and emotionally. Their reading lamps cast shadows on the wallpapered walls.

Down at the end of the hall, the subject of their conversation had himself fully entrenched in the guest room. Surrounded by virtually all of his worldly possessions. Clothes and photography equipment mostly. Plus a couple of leather rucksacks and a nylon duffel (the very same bags, by the way, I have with me here at Lewey's swanky Devil's Cay hotel). Also a few books, some personal belongings, not many of these: wallet, penknife, nail clipper. Mike Standish: material minimalist.

And that night I had a girl in my room, two girls actually, although one of them kept running down to the basement to see if Oodles the half-Siamese, half-Persian cat was ready to give birth to her first litter of kittens.

"You're wasting your time, Tracy," Molly kept telling her little sister, "she won't be ready for at least another day or two. The vet said."

"I just want to see if she's okay," said Tracy. She raced into the hallway, then stopped. "No more reading till I get back."

"Not a word," I assured her. Then, "Grab another handful of cookies on your way up!" I earmarked the page in *The Phantom Tollbooth,* placed the book on the nightstand. I lay on the bed, stripped to the waist on the early summer evening some two years and two months ago. Just two years and two months. Nothing but a spit back into the wind.

Molly rubbed my scalp, my good shoulder. My injured shoulder was still bandaged, but earlier that day the doctor had told me to quit using the sling, start getting the whole arm back in shape.

"Work my neck a little, kid. The muscles are stiffer than steel."

Molly rubbed her tiny hands over my neck, exactly the way I'd taught her.

The younger one, Tracy, reappeared in the doorway, hands filled with freshly baked chocolate chip cookies. She handed two to me, one to her sister.

"Everything okay with Oodles, kid?"

Tracy nodded, plopped down on the edge of the bed. "She's asleep."

"That's good," I told her. "You guys should probably go to sleep too."

"No," they protested. "One more chapter."

"Okay, one more chapter. But you have to rub my feet while I'm reading."

"Your feet!" Molly held her nose. "Your feet smell."

"No way. Nothing about Mike Standish smells."

Tracy already had her hands wrapped around my heel. Molly, reluctantly, took up the other foot. The slight hint of a breeze blew through the open window.

I picked up *The Phantom Tollbooth,* began to read. While down the hall the mother listened over her magazine to the voices of her children. "They're still up."

"He's reading to them," said their father.

"They should be in bed. It's after ten."

"So they'll sleep later in the morning."

Alison didn't buy it. She pulled back the satin sheet and put her feet firmly on the floor. Wearing nothing but a long tee shirt over her thin, thirty-year-old frame, she marched out of the bedroom, down that creaky wooden hall.

I could hear her coming. Hell, I could feel her coming. Probably I should've shooed her kiddies away. At least had them sitting on the floor at the moment their mommy arrived in my private chamber. But no, the devil made me leave well enough alone. Those two innocent little girls were energetically pulling and rubbing my toes when Alison, having worked herself into quite a tizzy, stormed through the door. The moment she spotted their hands upon my flesh, she freaked.

"What is this!" Ordinarily a passive person, especially physically, Alison that night actually crossed the cluttered room, grabbed her daughters by the arms, and pulled them forcefully away from the bed. "Molly! Tracy! Go to your rooms! Now!"

Young Molly, used to more predictable behavior from her mother, pulled away, demanded to know, "Why?"

"Because I said so."

"But why? We were just—"

"Be quiet! I don't want you rubbing his feet!"

Upon hearing this, I let loose with a laugh. Couldn't help myself. My cackle echoed through the room.

"Why can't we rub his feet?" Molly sounded both curious and defiant.

"Because I said so."

"But, Mom, that's so stupid. Mike reads to us and we rub his feet. Dad would call that a square deal. And you're always telling us: to get you have to give."

Back down the hallway, good old Dad, my best buddy, all ears, smiled. I could see that smile shining right around the corners.

"I don't care what I'm always telling you!" Alison turned, steered her girls for the door. "Now I'm telling you to go to bed!"

Molly, miffed, pushed her little nose into the air, turned on her heel, headed down the hallway. "Good night, Mike," they both called. "See you in the morning."

"Right," I shouted. "Sleep tight. Don't let the bedbugs bite."

Alison spun around, glared at me. Didn't faze me in the least. She'd been glaring at me for years. "You're so damn smug."

"Gimme a break, Allie. You're just mad because your kids are showing some attention to someone other than you. You never could stand competition."

"You're ridiculous."

"I'm ridiculous? What about you? Charging in here, making a scene. I thought you had more self-control."

"I don't think it's appropriate for them to be in here rubbing your half-naked body."

"I'm not a child molester, sweetie pie."

"It wouldn't shock me if you were."

I showed her my pearly whites. "Maybe you're just jealous. Maybe you wish *you* were in here rubbing my half-naked body."

That's when Alison gave me the stare of a cold-blooded killer, a stare that more or less said, "Watch your step, bub, or I'll blow a hole in the other shoulder." Then she turned, marched out of the guest room. Slammed the door as she went.

Too bad the latch was broken, causing the door to swing wildly on its creaky old hinges.

Molly and Tracy were not the only Cramers I read aloud to that summer. As the warm days rolled along, I also read to Mom Cramer. Out by the swimming pool in the shade of the tall magnolia tree. Cooler under there sipping our iced tea flavored with fresh mint from Mom's herb garden. She was horrified when she learned that I'd been shot. Spoiled me rotten that summer not only with fresh iced tea but with filet mignons charred to perfection on the barbecue. Recently she'd undergone eye surgery for a cataract. She could see okay but had difficulty focusing up close for any length of time. So I read to her. Almost every afternoon. Usually from the *New York Times* or the latest edition of *The New Yorker*. She especially enjoyed the book reviews and the latest political snippets. Would just lie back on her chaise lounge, eyes closed, smile on her face, listening to the melodious tones of my voice. Often she would just nod off, have herself a little nap, wake up happy to find me still sitting there at her side.

Once her vision stabilized, I showed her some of my photographs from various stages of my picture-taking career. Like my own dear mother, God rest her soul, surely would have done, Mom Cramer marveled at my creations. Told me repeatedly I was definitely a genius. Oh yeah, very easy for me to love that woman.

One day after I'd been hanging around the Cramer Compound for a month or so, lounging and healing and reading to Mom, Cracker told me he wanted to show me something.

"What?"

"Just come with me."

I climbed into the rusty old pickup truck used to haul hay and debris around the estate. We drove out past the farmhouse along the dirt fire road. Cut through one of the alfalfa fields, then into a forest of white pines. At the edge of the pines stood a small wooden cottage. Kind of creepy-looking. Like something from the Brothers Grimm.

Cracker pulled up outside. Stepped out of the pickup. "Home sweet home."

"What? You're exiling me to this dump?"

"It was Mom's idea. Come on, let's have a look."

"Mom's idea! I thought she liked me."

"She does. She loves you." He headed for the door.

I followed. I had to climb across the seat, exit through the driver's door. The passenger side door had long ago been crushed, rendered useless by some accident no one could recall. I walked across a mossy lawn littered with pine needles. Took a closer look at the cottage. Buried in deep shade from all those white pines. A thick green film of mildew covering the red cedar shakes. Cracker kept calling it the cottage but to me it looked more like a shack, though it did have a gabled roof and a screened-in porch off to one side.

"Place looks pretty funky to me."

Cracker looked hurt. "It's nice inside. Even has a fire-place."

"For what? Those quiet romantic evenings?"

"You never know."

No, you never do.

Cracker led the way up the stoop to the door. The wooden step broke when he put his weight on it. I laughed as he caught himself on the rusty wrought iron railing.

"That's nothing," he said over his shoulder. "We can fix that."

"Right," I said. "You can fix that."

Cracker opened the door, stepped inside. Me right behind. We stood in the middle of what passed for the living room, a small rectangular space maybe twelve by ten with a seven-foot ceiling. The air smelled close, damp, musty.

"Jesus," I wanted to know, "somebody die in here?"

"Just have to get the windows open. Air the place out." Cracker moved quickly through the space, threw open every window he could find. Not too many. Maybe half a dozen in the whole place. Small. Grimy.

I looked around. Didn't take long. Not more than ten or twelve paces from one end to the other. Off the living room, a bedroom, a closet-like cubicle that might, with a little engineering prowess, handle a queen-size bed. No closet. I pushed open the room's one small window.

A narrow hallway ran off the other side of the living room. It led to the dining room–kitchen area. A pleasant enough space with the screened-in porch off the end and a small fireplace tucked into the corner. Kitchenette looked like it had recently been remodeled: new fridge and stove, a sparkling clean stainless steel sink.

"Fireplace work?"

"Far as I know. The flue might need cleaning."

I felt like a prospective buyer, Cracker my uptight, praying-for-a-sale real estate hawker. I pushed through the door to the porch. Most of the screens torn, full of holes. Bird greetings decorating the floor. "So tell me, Cracker, when's the last time humans inhabited this shack?"

Realtor Cramer looked hurt again. "Not that long. The guy just moved out a couple months ago. He lived here for two years. I think he made paintings, but I never saw any. Hell of a stone wall builder though. You can see his handiwork lining both sides of the main drive."

I stood there, thought about what life would be like in that shack. Then asked, "So what's the deal? What have you and Mom cooked up?"

"We want you to stay. For as long as you want."

"As long as it's out here in the shack?"

"We'll rent it to you."

"Rent it to me!"

"Right."

"For how much?"

"Don't worry about it. Not much."

"What does that mean?"

"It means we usually don't charge rent."

"No? Then what do you charge?"

"You just give us a certain number of hours every month."

"Oh, I get it. I'm like your indentured servant. How many hours?"

"Just relax, Mike. Take another look. If you're interested, we'll talk."

"I just like to know what I'm getting into."

"You're not getting into anything."

Okay. So I took another trip through the shack. Paused awhile in the tiny bedroom. Started to see the possibilities. "I could set up a darkroom in here. Sleep out in the living room."

"Whatever you want."

"I want to get to work on those rolls I shot in Newark."

"Perfect place to do it."

Back to the living room. "Looks like a hell of a lot of trouble though. I don't have a lick of furniture." I'd abandoned the little I had accumulated up in Wellfleet to Robin and her beau Bonner.

"So what do you need? A bed? A table? A couple chairs?"

I headed for the great outdoors, pulling away, putting some distance between myself and any commitments, any responsibilities.

Cracker followed close behind. Right on my heels. "Alison and I have some stuff in storage. We might not have a bed, but I'm sure we have everything else you'd need to get started."

Did he just want me out of the farmhouse? Away from the wife and kids? Or was he really looking for me to stick around? Be his sidekick at the Compound?

I kept moving. Reached the back of the pickup. Messed with the rusty tailgate latch till it popped open. Dropped the tailgate, took a load off. My shoulder felt pretty good. All the bandages had been removed. I didn't have much strength in my right arm, very little range of motion in the shoulder socket, but each day Slammer's bullet became more a source of storytelling and less a source of pain.

I pulled a joint from my shirt pocket. Struck a match and lit up. The sweet, pungent smell of marijuana filled the air, overpowering the fresh scent of evergreen. I inhaled, held the smoke in my lungs, exhaled.

Cracker stood beside me. "The old herb. I don't see it around much anymore."

I smiled, handed the joint to my old buddy.

Cracker chose not to take it. "I don't know, Mike. Hell of a lot to do today. If I smoke that I'll be worthless."

I shrugged, took another hit. All I had on my plate was a one o'clock rendezvous with Mom out by the pool. Gonna work on the *Times* editorial page.

Cracker watched me inhale, then exhale, then the smoke curling up into the lower branches of those white pines. "So where did you get that stuff? I wouldn't even know where to buy it anymore."

"I just bought this yesterday."

"Yesterday? Where? From who?"

"Some guy I met down at the Oldwick General Store."

"You're kidding me?"

I shook my head. "Guy named Harris. Billy Harris. Said he knew you."

"Billy Harris had reefer for sale?"

"He had several measured bags in the trunk of his Saab. Selling the stuff right out in the parking lot as though they were vacuum cleaner bags."

Cracker looked alarmed. "I've known Billy for twenty years. Never even knew he smoked grass, much less peddled the stuff."

I took another hit. "You're an innocent, Cracker. Always have been. All that green is a great source of insulation."

That's when he took the reefer from me. Took a few short tokes, then a long, deep one. We smoked that joint right down to the nub. Sat on the tailgate for a while then, not talking, listening to the breeze work its way through the pines, watching the shadows creep across the mossy ground as the late morning sun reached higher into the pale blue summer sky.

"So what do you think?" he asked. "Want to give the place a try?"

"I'm thinking on it," I told him. "But I don't know. This place has hassle written all over it."

"What hassle? I don't see any hassle."

"There: up on the roof. Written in fat blood red letters."

"Gimme a break, Standish. We spend a few days fixing the place up, throw in some furniture, and presto, you have a great place to live."

I thought about it. "Listen, Cracker, I appreciate your position. I know Alison wants me out of the house. But you don't have to set me up with my own digs. My shoulder's feeling pretty good. You can just tell me to shove off."

"So you don't want to do it?"

I thought about it some more. Although really, because the narcotic in the marijuana had my synapses all riled up, I spent more time thinking about the tiny red ants crawling around on the pine needles beside my sneaker. "Okay, tell me this: how many hours a week do I have to labor for the privilege of living in this broken-down shack?"

"Twenty."

"Twenty! What's my hourly wage? A buck an hour?"

"I'll pay you fifteen bucks an hour. And you know as well as me, Standish, you ain't worth half that."

I nodded, knew he was right. Still, I did some quick calculations. "Twenty hours a week times fifteen bucks an hour equals three hundred bucks. Multiply that times four weeks in a month, and christ, Cracker, you're charging me twelve hundred bucks a month for this dump."

"No, I'm not. I'm charging you six hundred bucks a month for this dump. And for that six hundred bucks I'll also give you use of the pickup."

"What a prince. And what about the other six hundred? How does that figure into the equation?"

"We'll apply that six hundred to the money you owe me for paying your hospital tab and springing you from jail."

"Jesus, Cracker! Is that your wife's voice coming out of your mouth?"

I bought the package. After thinking it over, I decided it sounded like a pretty good deal. Not only was I sure Cracker would back off on the twenty hours a week, but I needed a place to lay low, regenerate, work on my prints. And with Mom's home cooking just an alfalfa field away, well . . .

I immediately went to work. I removed the mildew with bleach, then gave the cottage a fresh coat of red paint. I repaired the steps on the front stoop and replaced the screens on the porch. Inside I scrubbed and repainted the walls. I fixed the doorjambs, replaced any missing trim around the windows and floorboards. I repointed the stonework in the fireplace, then had a man out to clean the flue. Once finished, I brought the Family Cracker out to have a look.

"The place looks great," my good buddy told me. "It hasn't looked this good in years." Then to his lovely bride, "Didn't I tell you he was a handy guy?"

Alison shrugged. "A regular Mr. Fix-it."

I laughed. "Thanks Allie. I've always counted on your support."

"So when are you moving in?"

"You mean, when am I moving out?"

"Whatever."

"Soon," I assured her. "Very soon."

She looked delighted.

Molly came out of the bedroom. "Why are all the walls and windows in there painted black?"

"Because that's my darkroom, kid."

"What's a dark room?"

"A darkroom's where Uncle Mikey develops his photographs."

Alison rolled her eyes. She hated my guts. At least she thought she did.

I didn't waste any time clearing out of her farmhouse. Early the next morning I coaxed that old pickup north to Wellfleet where I had my darkroom equipment stored in Captain Claw's garage. I stayed a few days to catch up with my old pals. Several times I told my tale of booze, cops, and guns in Newark, New Jersey. Each time the action grew bolder, more violent, my own role more heroic. More than once I even pulled off my shirt, put my bullet hole on display.

The night before my return to Jersey, I ran into Robin at the Wellfleet Pub. My old flame sat at the bar nestled up tight against her latest love merchant: the dashing and delightful Bonner. I could smell her sexuality, almost taste it on my tongue.

She didn't seem at all surprised to see me. "Hey Mike."

"Hey Robin."

"Someone said you were in town."

"Yeah."

Bonner turned, gave me a look. Fixed his arm around his woman. Stinking slimeball. "You ain't gonna piss on me tonight, are you, dude?"

I gave the pig a little smile. "Maybe. Gimme time."

"We heard you got shot."

"Yeah," said Robin, all Sex and Concern, "we heard you got shot."

"I did." And I pointed. "Right there. In the shoulder."

Bonner didn't want to make too big a deal about it, not in front of his woman. "That's rough."

"I guess."

Bonner turned away then. Needed to have a word with the bartender.

Robin gave me a long, I've-been-worried-about-you stare. We had been lovers, after all. Pretty good tumblers. It might've been my imagination, but I had the feeling she would've enjoyed watching Bonner disappear, watching me slip right back into her life. Humans are such morally corrupt creatures.

"So," she asked, "are you okay?" Her voice sounded soft, sensuous, intimate.

I saw and heard. I had eyes and ears. I'd been around. I knew how fouled up the game could get. How screwed up human beings were about their emotional and sexual relationships. Still, I gave her a smile. Didn't cost me a dime. Besides, we'd had some good times together, both in and out of bed.

"Yeah, sure," I told her. "I'm fine. Couldn't be better. What about you?"

Robin, small, blond, and oh so tough, a military brat, glanced over her shoulder at Bonner. Busy as a bee ordering his next bourbon and beer chaser. "Oh, I'm peachy, Mike," she said, her smile wry, maybe a little weary. "Just peachy."

And so it goes, the broken hearts and twisted minds of boys and girls who dare to get involved.

*　　*　　*

I left the Cape early the next morning. By noon I'd reached my new digs on the Cramer Compound. Found Cracker waiting for me, his Grand Wagoneer overloaded with furniture. Plus every last lick of gear I'd left behind in the spare bedroom.

"Alison," said Cracker, looking a tad sheepish, "sent your stuff over."

That was worth a laugh. "And she's now fumigating the room."

We hefted and hauled, a prelude to my antics to TREE-TOPS not all that many months later. Although that day Cracker and I carried in, whereas I spent my solo career as a mover carrying out. I wonder what Cracker would've said had I asked him to help me pull the job?

He would've said, "Don't even think about it, Standish," and then, of course, I never would've done it, never would've rented that U-Haul, never would've left my fingerprints all over that solid cherry chest-on-chest.

As we carried in my borrowed dining room table, I said, "I've been meaning to ask you about my benefits."

"Benefits! What benefits?"

"Hell, Cracker, a working man has to have benefits. What if I get sick? It's expensive getting sick in this country."

"So don't get sick."

"Plus I have this lower back thing that could use attention."

"Find some woman to rub it."

Oh, if only he'd foreseen the woman I'd find; he gladly would have added my name to the Cramer health plan.

"And what about dental?" I asked after we'd set the table in place. "I've got this screaming molar on the lower left. Had it for months. Probably a root canal and a crown to fix it up. That's a quick eight or nine hundred bucks."

Cracker headed for the door. "If you get hurt while you're working, we'll take care of you. Otherwise you're on your own."

"All you rich slobs are the same," I told him. "No idea how a simple decayed tooth can lead a poor man to wrack and ruin."

"You're tearing my heart out."

"I mean it. You have no conception of reality. You people have insurance policies for everything. Hell, you probably have insurance policies protecting your insurance policies."

"Damn right we do. Now pick up the end of that sofa."

We hauled in a sofa, a set of chairs, a bureau, a bookcase, a few lamps, a wide assortment of boxes containing books, pictures, doodads, and enough kitchen junk to at least make the room usable.

Next we unloaded the pickup, the stuff I'd hauled down from the Cape. The heavy item was my old warhorse of a print enlarger; my most prized possession: a Beseler 23C with a motorized chassis on a solid steel adjustable table. I'll probably never see that beast again. Down in my custom-made darkroom in the basement of TREETOPS. Waiting for me. Wondering if I'll ever return. It doesn't look good.

I also had a fireproof filing cabinet where I kept my negatives, and a small fireproof safe where I kept my prints. Half a dozen cardboard boxes contained lenses, trays, lamps, filters, chemicals, and several different types of photographic paper.

After we had everything inside, Cracker said, "I never realized how much stuff you need to make photographs."

"A hell of a lot of stuff," I told him. "And plenty of cash. It ain't cheap making good prints. Wanna be my sugar daddy?"

"Bugger off."

We stood in the living room. I took a look around. "Guess the only other thing I need's a bed."

So that night, after dinner, we drove up to a discount bedding store in Chester. Just before we walked through the door, I said to Cracker, "Let's make the salesman think we're gay. A couple of gay guys out buying a new bed."

But Cracker didn't bite. "What? No way."

Fine. I'd let him play the reluctant one. Still hiding in the closet.

I tried every mattress in the store two or three times. I bounced on the edge, sprawled across the middle, squirmed from side to side. Hey, I rarely buy anything, so when I do buy something I like to enjoy the experience. Make the most of it. That's why I kept urging Cracker to lie down beside me.

But Cracker, tense and scowling, stayed on his feet, stayed clear over on the other side of the store, arms folded, trying to look manly. I kept patting the edge of the mattress, asking him to *please* come over and try the *firmness*. His eyes just glared at me. Poor Cracker. Another missed opportunity. Been playing the same controlled middle-class WASPy role his entire life. Never varies. A thirty-year run.

I finally made my decision. Then I got to haggle over price. Another of life's small pleasures. It took time. The salesman worked on commission. Obviously didn't like homosexuals. Probably had never even known one. Definitely didn't like thinking about Cracker and me soiling his nest of Beautyrests. But I kept working on him. A solid half an hour. It eventually paid off: a Simmons queen size for a song. Delivery in a few days. I handed over the cash, inspected the receipt. Then I turned to Cracker, who had ventured a little too close. I squeezed his wrist, cooed in his ear, "Okay, hon, time to go home and feed the tiger."

Cracker was not amused. The second we got outside he slapped me a good one across the back of the head. "I live around here you stupid son of a bitch."

I laughed at him. "That's not it. You're just afraid of your latent potential. One or two hormones away from giving up your bride for some stud."

"What are you babbling about now?"

I climbed into the Wagoneer. "Come on, all this buying has made me thirsty. I need a cold one."

"I have a six-pack in the fridge."

"No way. I'm sick of Alison counting how many beers I drink. Let's go cozy up to a bar. Some place with a little action."

Cracker nodded, but without much enthusiasm. We wound up in Oldwick at the Tewksbury Inn. Not much action, especially in the middle of the week, but at nice bar with high wooden stools and plenty of cold beer both in bottles and on tap. Cracker suggested mugs of Watney's on draft.

"So this is the local hangout, huh?"

Cracker nodded to two men about our age sitting down at the end of the bar. "I guess, yeah. But I'll tell you, with a couple young kids you don't get out much."

We drank our beers, ordered another round. Cracker started to relax. Waved to a couple sitting at a table over by the front window, then nodded to an older man who came in and sat at the bar. Small-town life.

"Looks like you know a few folks around here."

"I ought to. I've lived in this township my whole life."

We sipped our beers. I glanced around the bar. Whiskey bottles and old wooden beams. A Yankee game on the tube. I felt comfortable, at ease. Like I'd been there before. Like this was a place I could spend some time.

Then I saw something that changed my life, sent me swirling into yet another of my frequent emotional whirlwinds. A woman this time. It usually is a woman. A young woman. Not too young. Right around my age. A real looker. Standing in the doorway. Just suddenly appeared there as if by magic. I fixed my eyes on her. She brushed a handful of hair out of her eyes, squinted into the semidarkness. Her hair short and wavy, the color of strong tea. I kept staring at her.

"Hey Cracker?"

"Yeah."

"Take a look at this."

Cracker turned. Saw immediately what I wanted him to see. Tall and thin in her tight tan riding britches, high black riding boots, a dark green canvas shirt.

"Pretty sweet, huh?"

"Yeah," said Cracker, very quietly. "Pretty sweet."

"Think she'd marry me?"

"A poor slob like you?" His voice sounded a bit more venomous than necessary.

"Yeah, a poor slob like me."

"Not a chance."

Still, I could dream. "My oh my," I said, "a long and lanky equestrienne."

The young woman's eyes adjusted to the dim light. She looked directly at us, at me. Smiled, gave a little wave.

"You see that?" I asked Cracker. "She wants me."

"I think she's just being friendly."

Another woman appeared in the doorway, an older woman, but also tall and thin. Attractive. Also dressed in britches and riding boots. The younger woman looked at the older woman, said something, then pointed over at us.

The older woman appeared to frown, but only for a moment. She recovered, gave a little smile, waved. The younger woman started toward us. The older woman followed, a definite reluctance in her step.

"You can have the old dame," I told Cracker. "I'll take the young one."

"Whatever turns you on, Standish."

Cracker stepped off his bar stool as the women approached. The guy has always had impeccable manners.

Smooth and chiseled faces on these women. Handsome and refined. Definitely, I realized, a mother-and-daughter team. They walked, almost glided, with dignity and confidence. They had Money written all over them.

I held the younger one in a lustful gaze when all of a sudden I heard Cracker say, "Hello, Sarah. Hello, Mrs. Browne."

My eyes flicked over at my old buddy.

"Hello, Graham," they both said.

My eyes darted all over the place. Up and down. Side to side. I tried to take the whole scene in at once. I saw the younger one, Sarah, smile. At Cracker. The older one, the mother, trying hard not to frown.

Then Cracker kissed them both on the cheek. Just like that. Simple as can be. Gave their shoulders a squeeze.

They returned the kiss. Quick pecks.

I found my mouth hanging wide open. A gaping hole.

Cracker did his thing. Made the introductions. "This is an old college friend of mine, Mike Standish. Mike, this is Sarah Browne and her mother, Katherine."

The ladies shook my hand, very polite, told me how nice it was to meet me. I returned the pleasantry, but then, still off balance, I grew mute. A rare occurrence.

I heard Cracker ask, "You've been out riding?"

"Yes," answered Sarah Browne, her voice soft and perfectly measured. "It was a beautiful evening. Not so humid as it's been."

"Timothy didn't make the trip?"

"Not tonight," she answered. "He's off with one of his friends."

Mine eyes, eyes that had just glimpsed glory, narrowed. Who, I wondered, was this Timothy character? I figured it must be a husband. I was immediately irked.

"How are your mother and father?" I heard Mrs. Browne ask Cracker. "I haven't seen them for ages."

I checked Sarah's hand, slim and lovely, for a wedding band. Didn't spot one.

"They're fine," I heard Cracker answer. "Staying busy."

But this one can't be unattached, I thought. No way. Not a chance.

"I'm sure we'll see them at the annual charity barbecue?"

Impossible.

"I heard them talking about it just the other day."

Has to be a man in her life.

"And you and Alison will be there? With the kids?"

Probably some stinking millionaire.

"Absolutely."

Katherine Browne suddenly turned on me, having surely read my wicked thoughts regarding her luscious daughter. Ready to bite my head off, tell me to mind my own business. But no, nothing so dramatic. She just wanted to invite me to a party. An invitation she would no doubt later regret.

"Mr. Standish, as a friend of Graham's, let me invite you to our barbecue as well. Will you be in the area a week from Saturday?"

I needed a second or two to get my mouth open. "A week from Saturday? . . . Oh yeah, sure . . . I think so . . . I know so . . . Actually, I've just moved to town. I'm sure I'll, you know . . . be here."

These were polite, well-bred people. They ignored my bumbling. "That's fine then," said Mrs. Browne. "We would love to have you join us."

"Right. Thanks," I managed to say. "That would be great."

"Come, Sarah," commanded the mother. "Let's eat. I'm famished."

Sarah offered first Cracker, then me, another smile. A pleasant, friendly smile. She turned then and followed her mother across the bar to the dining room.

I watched her until she disappeared. "Lord have mercy on me, Cracker. Where have you been hiding that one?"

Cracker shrugged. "Who? You mean my sister-in-law?"

"Sister-in-law!"

"Well, ex-sister-in-law."

"That's the one Ron ran out on?"

"I wouldn't exactly say he ran out on her, Standish. I'm afraid it's a little more complicated than that."

Oh yeah, always is. "Whatever. You know what I mean."

"I know you sounded like an idiot just now, practically drooled on yourself while you stared at her."

"Hey, every once in a while a beautiful woman does that to me."

I tried to get another glimpse of Sarah, but she was long gone. I blew the air out of my lungs. "God, that was something!" I looked for her again. "Is she available?" I drank off the rest of my beer. "I didn't see a ring on her finger. Maybe she takes it off when she rides." And then I kept right on going. "So who's Timothy? Don't tell me it's a new husband." I didn't wait for an answer. Just kept on babbling. "Your brother must be a damn idiot letting that one slip away. Even I wouldn't be dumb enough to let that happen."

No, I'll just mosey on out the door myself.

Cracker didn't say a word. Just sat back and listened to my motor runneth over. That, he was no doubt thinking, is one female Standowski will never get his lecherous little Polack hands on. Not a chance.

☙

Devil's Cay. Another day on the horizon. After another long and labored night of tossing, turning, more armless nightmares. Cracker assured me that evening at the Tewksbury Inn that Sarah and I had met before. But I didn't think so, couldn't recall, couldn't imagine forgetting such a lovely face as that. Still, he was right: I had met her before. At our graduation. But we've been through all that. Let's face it: the memory is at best a fickle and flawed instrument.

Now Lewis has me up and at 'em before dawn. Did I really agree to this? I suppose I did. Last night after half a dozen margaritas. Down the stairs, out through the front door. Lewis leading the way. Me right behind. Still dark outside as we start down the cobblestone street. I yawn, try to shake myself awake. Adjust the cameras slung over my shoulders: my F3 with a 28mm wide-angle lens, and my spiffy new, top-of-the-line F4S, a birthday gift last year from my sweet Sarah. This morning, just before leaving my room, I attached the 80–200mm autofocus zoom to the F4, another gift given by my love. The camera and the lens: just a couple of the many pieces of photography equipment Sarah bought for me. She wanted me to have the best gear possible so I could pursue my art without limitations.

And don't for one second think I don't dwell on this as I make my way along the rough cobblestone street. Sarah, and the things she gave me materially, physically, emotionally, occupy my thoughts virtually every second of every day. I can't pass an instant without something reminding me of her smell, her warmth, her eyes, her generosity. No matter how hard I try, no matter how many Bahama Mamas I consume, she's right there with me. Last night, I have to tell you, I nearly broke down and called her. Once, from the small office behind the front desk, I even tried, made the attempt. I had the receiver in hand. But long-distance service from Devil's Cay is at best a hit-and-miss operation. Sometimes it takes an hour or more to get a call through to the States. No luck last night. And thank God. I mean, what would I have said? How would I have explained? It would've been the booze talking. The booze and the guilt and the self-pity. No, I won't call again. Can't call again. Not now, maybe not ever.

All around me I see shapes moving through the darkness. Slowly, cautiously. I hear doors open and close. The sound of children giggling. Feet shuffling along the cobblestone street.

Lewis grabs my arm. I shudder. "Easy, Mr. Weston. It just me, mon."

We cross the street, go down a narrow alley between two old dilapidated brick warehouses. Lewis leads. I follow. Not my normal shtick. Lewis carries my tripod, one of my leather rucksacks filled with accessories: lenses, filters, film. Don't worry: I've got my greenbacks in constant contact with my flesh. Ain't a soul on Devil's Cay, I feel sure, who wouldn't kill for my wad.

"Still awful dark out here," I tell Lewis. "We could have slept another hour or two." A twinge of paranoia rumbles through me. Wonder if this might be a setup. If all of a sudden a couple goons will explode out of the darkness, rob me blind, leave me in a ditch. It's the Money. The Goddamn Money. Nothing but Trouble since the day I got it. Stole it.

"Be light soon enough, Mr. Weston," Lewis assures me. "Just enough time to set up your camera before that ball creeps out of the sea."

The alley ends. We walk beneath a canopy of casuarina trees. The feathery branches with their long flowing needles brush against my face. Like spiderwebs. I frantically brush them away.

"Easy does it, mon," says Lewis. "The beach just ahead."

But first we have to cross some outcroppings of coral. Crunchy underfoot. All around me now I can hear the crunching. I still can't see the black faces through the darkness as we ascend a series of low dunes made from coral and sand. More than once I slip but stay on my feet. "When the hell are we getting there, Lewis?"

Again Lewis laughs. So do several other invisible voices. "Sorry, mon," Lewis says, "I forget, you never make this trip before. I made it so many times I could do it in my sleep. Oftentimes I think I do."

Heading down to the sea for sunrise. A daily and almost religious experience for the residents of Devil's Cay.

Finally we reach the last rise before the Atlantic. And sure enough, the first faint traces of dawn show on the horizon. I follow Lewis down to the beach. We kick off our shoes. The fine, soft sand feels cool on our feet. I remove my shirt, spread it on the sand, carefully set the cameras on top of it. Take the tripod from Lewis.

Lewis looks pleased to lose the load. "Feeling like a pack mule, mon."

I extend the legs on the tripod, set it firmly in the sand. Feels good to have some work to do. I attach the F4, then pause for a look around. Up and down the beach the residents of Devil's Cay spread themselves out in a long, thin line. Most stand, a few sit. Some talk in quiet voices. All eyes face the sea.

I remove the lens cap from the F4. Switch on the camera, put my right eye to the viewfinder. Not much light. But maybe enough for the effect I want: specters at sunrise. Open the aperture as wide as it'll go, then set the shutter speed for two full seconds. Using a cable release, I pop off a couple shots of the islanders waiting for the sun to show. As the light slowly but inevitably brightens, I quicken the shutter speed, stop down the aperture. Take a dozen frames.

Hope one might capture the religious eeriness of this morning ritual.

An orange glow shimmers over the surface of the sea. I swing the tripod, make a few adjustments. The very top of the sun peeks over the horizon. For just a moment it seems to slow, to hesitate, to wonder if retreat might be possible. I don't think so. The relentless cycle of night and day, as these islanders well know, offers only a single, inexorable option. Same as my flight from TREETOPS. Only one way out.

I study the sunrise through the viewfinder. In no time at all the sun, huge and orange, rises out of the Atlantic, reaches into the sky. As it pulls away from the earth, it yellows and grows smaller. I capture the illusion on film.

Finally, when the roll runs out, I disconnect my eye from the viewfinder. Scan the beach, now bathed in bright morning sunlight. Already many of the islanders have started to retreat. I watch them disappear back over the dunes.

"Where are they going?"

Lewis laughs. "Where do you think, mon? They going home. Back to bed."

Back at the hotel I fall asleep on the sofa in the lobby. Since arriving on Devil's Cay I haven't been getting enough sleep. And when I do sleep I immediately slip into one of my limbless nightmares: no arms, no legs, sometimes no head. Last night I had one starring Cracker and Alison and Sarah. They were using my head as a soccer ball, kicking it back and forth across the Brownes' lush green lawn. My mouth kept screaming, but the more I screamed the harder they kicked. Finally Sarah took a shot on goal, but the goalie, in the guise of young Tim, blocked my head away with his fingertips. My head rolled across the grass into the swimming pool and sank.

I woke up from that one in a cold sweat.

And now a breakfast of orange juice, toast, fresh conch fritters. The conch feels rubbery and still alive in my mouth, but I eat it anyway, every last bite. I need to keep up my strength. Can't afford to run out of fuel.

After breakfast I hit the streets. Almost two days, forty-eight hours, on Devil's Cay, and still I haven't toured the town. Other than my morning trip out to East Beach, I've been holed up at the hotel, staring out the windows, missing my woman, worrying about my troubles.

I have my F3 loaded with T-MAX 100, my F4 loaded with Kodachrome 25. Already decided to shoot the islanders in black and white, but the sky, the sea, the faded pastels deserve low-speed, fine-grain color transparencies.

Across from the hotel, on a slight rise overlooking the harbor, stands St. Andrew's Parish, a small white stucco church with baby blue shutters. 1803 states the wooden sign over the door. I try to find a shot, but the sun hangs too high, too bright. The image would look like a sterile post-card: VISIT THE BAHAMAS! I hate that stuff, nothing but photo-graphic prostitution.

Next a row of stucco and brick buildings, one and two stories high, right smack on the street, directly across from the harbor. Looks like the government must be a formidable employer on the island. A shingle advertising one ministry or another hangs outside practically every doorway: Ministry of Tourism, Ministry of Finance, Ministry of Education, Ministry of Youth, Sports, and Community Affairs, Ministry of Agriculture and Fisheries. Who, I wonder, needs all these ministries on this lazy little island? I step back, find an angle, pop off a couple shots. A scene flashes through my brain: Sarah and I sitting on our bed back at TREETOPS, snuggling, looking at pictures of my trip to the Bahamas when sud-denly we come across one of the ministries. We have a good, long laugh over the absurdity of swollen bureaucracies. But the scene dissolves the second I realize I'll never share these photographs, or our bed, with Sarah again.

Unless I go back. Turn myself in. Give myself up. Make a full confession. All the felonious details.

I sigh. Loudly. For several minutes I wander through town in a stupor. Dogs, cats, chickens, goats wander up and down the street. But it dawns on me: I haven't seen any humans, not a soul since leaving Lewey's. I head back to Ministry Row. Try a few doors. All locked. Eddie's Edgewater Eating Club: also locked. So is Lyle's Tailor Shop. Gelin's Dress Shop. Nigel's Ice Cream Parlor. And Devil's Cay Supply, where, according to the faded plywood sign, they sell appliances, housewares, lumber, all things electrical. But the door: locked tight. When I peer through the window, I don't see any bodies, just deserted aisles and mostly empty shelves.

I turn away. Become aware of the sun. It hangs directly overhead, cruel and oppressive, nothing like that benign orange ball I photographed at dawn. It beats down on me, frying my pale white skin. White men don't belong down here in the tropics. We belong in the northern climes, huddled in our houses with our pale white women and our accounting ledgers. It must be a hundred degrees out here. Not a wisp of wind. Not even a ripple on the surface of the aqua green sea. Across the harbor I spot the Devil's Cay Inn, a two-story stucco house painted turquoise with white trim and shutters. I make a beeline for the wide front porch hoping to find shade, maybe something cool to drink.

The front door stands wide open. I go inside: a large sitting room with a three-stool bar at the rear. An enormous black woman naps in a wooden rocker beside the bar. I can't take my eyes off her. She must weigh three hundred pounds. Yet her face, light brown, smooth as silk, is practically thin. Light passes through a nearby window, illuminating her face. I take a step or two closer, quietly bring my F3 into the firing position. But just as I'm about to trip the shutter, her huge eyes open wide.

She snarls at me. "You do dat, mon, and I be forced to fix you." Her voice sounds like it comes up out of a steel kettle drum.

I pull the camera away from my face. "Fix me?"

She slowly nods her huge head up and down. The fat jiggles on her neck. "You steal my soul with dat ding. For dat I be forced to put my mouf on you."

"I just wanted to take your picture."

"Nuthin' come free, mon."

Ah, so that's it. Money. Same as everywhere else. They want Money if I'm to take their picture. "How much?"

The fat woman shrugs. "I let you know."

"When?" I see now that the woman not only has a thin face but pretty eyes as well. They sparkle, vast and black.

"Later. Right now time to sleep."

"I think the whole island's asleep."

She shrugs again.

"Can I get a beer?"

"Not now, mon. Bar closed. Come back later I give you a beer. I also give you a room cheaper than you got at Lewey's."

So, I have some power being the only visitor on the island. The honeymooners on their sailboat sailed away yesterday. "How much cheaper?"

"Ten dollars a night cheaper."

"Maybe I'm only paying that much a night at Lewey's."

"I know how much you pay."

"I'll bet you do."

I give her a smile, tell her I'll see her later, turn to go. But suddenly, out of the blue, just for the hell of it, just because I can't resist temptation, never could, a friend of the devil and all that jazz, I bring the F3 into the firing position.

In a flash, I focus and shoot. Pop! Pop! Pop! Three shots of the fat lady in six seconds.

Her face goes from surprise to shock to anger. Her big black eyes narrow and frown. "Dat very dangerous, mon. You get fixed for dat. No choice now. For dat you pay a price."

I just smile, nod. Assure her I'll send a print. 8 x 10. Then back out into the heat through the open door. Like stepping into a furnace. How long will I be able to cope with this hellish climate? I feel weak, sapped, like maybe I have a fever.

Now back at Lewey's, at the bar, sipping an ice-cold Kalik. "I tell you, Lewis, I think you and I are the only two people awake on this entire island."

"Might be," says Lewis from behind the bar.

"I took a turn around town, didn't see a soul."

"Maybe they hiding from you, mon."

"You think so?"

"No, Mr. Weston," says Lewis. "I just messing with you."

I nod. Sip. Think a few things over. "I stopped by the Devil's Cay Inn."

"Oh yeah, mon. You meet Mama Rolle?"

"I think I did."

Lewis shows his teeth. "Good size woman with a deep voice?"

"That's the one."

"How she making out today?"

"She offered me a room at a lower rate."

Lewis shrugs. "Mama Rolle always pulling stunts like that."

"I told her I'd think about it."

"You do that, mon. But remember, Lewey's sits on higher ground. My rooms got better views of the sea."

"I'll keep it in mind," I tell Lewis. Then, "I took her photograph."

"You pay her for that?"

"Nope."

"Oh Jesus. I bet she didn't like that none."

"Not a bit," I tell him. "She snarled at me. Told me she was going to fix me."

"You shouldn't take that picture, Mr. Weston."

"So what does she mean, she's going to fix me?"

"Mama Rolle be an Obeah woman, mon. She does white magic. Has the power to cast spells and such."

"So you're telling me this fat broad with the baby face has put some kind of curse on me?"

"Sound that way, mon. She say she going to put her mouth on you?"

I nod. "She did, yeah. That's exactly what she said."

Lewis shakes his head. He looks mighty concerned. "Mama be over there right now concocting some herbal mess, reciting certain Psalms from the holy book. One aught nine and one ten be my guess. That's the way she does it."

"Does what?"

"Fixes you."

"Jesus," I say. "Just what I need on top of everything else. Some fat mama casting spells on me." I chug down the rest of my beer. "Better let me have another one of those, Lewis."

"No problem, mon. We make you cool today. Make you forget your troubles."

Right. That's why Stanley used to drink. To forget his stinking troubles. Maybe I'll start introducing myself around town as Stanley. "Hi. How you doing? The name's Standowski. Stanley Standowski. Friends call me Stan. Stan the Man."

Maybe I should give Stanley a call. Ask him if he'd like to join me down here in exile, on my own private St. Helena.

Party Time up at TREETOPS. A happier, gentler time for the widow Browne. A time before her daughter took up with an unemployed Polack of dubious character. A time when the future still looked bright. A time when all those fancy antiques still stood upon sacred ground. A time when the Cramers' Grand Wagoneer still held its showroom luster, was two years and thirty thousand miles newer . . .

Alison behind the wheel as we wound up the Brownes' driveway. Cracker beside her. Me in the back sitting between my two babes: Molly and Tracy. We'd all dressed casually for this summer outing.

Parking attendants swarmed as Alison pulled the Wagoneer up to the front door of the grand Tudor. The Cramers and their friend, Mr. Michael Standish, stepped out. And there, on the wide front portico, stood Katherine and Sarah Browne, smiling, waving, welcoming their guests to the Brownes' fifteenth annual charity barbecue to benefit the Matheny School for handicapped children.

We had to wait in line for several minutes to greet our hosts. Half a dozen other guests had arrived before us, including an ex-governor of the Garden State. Close to two hundred guests would be in attendance by the middle of the afternoon, many of them from some of New Jersey's most prominent and affluent families.

Don't think I wasn't impressed. Until I got downwind from them.

I had all my attention focused on Ms. Sarah Browne as we stood on the slate walk leading to the portico. I watched as she greeted her guests. She looked even better than I remembered. I had been thinking about her almost constantly since we'd met at the Tewksbury Inn just over a week earlier. I wanted in the worst way to ask her out, win her over. What fool wouldn't? The only question left was how to make my move. Just that morning, while working in my darkroom, I had decided to use my camera as a connecting tool, as a kind of Cupid's arrow.

Some men use their wealth to break the ice with women they desire. Others use power. Or fast cars. Some even use dogs. Cats. Stuffed animals. I didn't have any of these goods at my disposal. But I had the sensual allure of my camera lens. I would use it to draw Sarah close.

We reached the front of the line. The Cramers and Brownes exchanged hugs and kisses. The kids, I noticed, called Katherine and Sarah, "Auntie Kate" and "Auntie Sarah."

I stood off to the side, absorbing the scene, my Nikon at the ready. I thought about popping off a shot or two, capturing this moment on Kodak Gold, but decided it might be too much of an intrusion. Normally that wouldn't stop me, but I didn't want Ms. Browne labeling me rude before we'd even said hello.

Besides, Katherine (her nickname had not yet taken root), a model of propriety and good manners, was not about to let her guest languish for long. "Mr. Standish," she said, remembering my name while taking my hand, "thank you for coming."

Now I may be speculating here, but Katherine, besides finding her guest young and attractive, also believed that with a surname like Standish, he undoubtedly came from a fine and upstanding White Anglo-Saxon Protestant family. He was, after all, a friend of the Cramers, blue-blooded WASPs to the core. And she surely assumed he had Money, either inherited or earned. Few people could afford to live in that neck of the woods without generous amounts of green. Probably thought I fed on Wall Street, or maybe Madison Avenue.

Poor Kate, in for such a shock. "I see you brought your camera."

"Yes."

"Well," said Katherine, "take lots of pictures. But only of people smiling. And please, none of me."

Oh, right, I knew this game. Played it very well. "Mrs. Browne," I said, "forgive me, but any photographer worth his shutter speed would be a fool to ignore such a beautiful subject. It would be like visiting Yosemite and ignoring El Capitan."

Katherine grabbed my arm, squeezed. She was a good-looking woman. Hell of a fine-looking woman. Listen, you can't let my general distaste for my mother-in-law cloud your opinion. Katherine Browne has many fine qualities. Not least of which is the fact that she recently turned fifty-nine, but with that thin frame and fine English skin, she could easily pass for a woman in her late forties. And contrary to popular opinion, she occasionally remembers how to have a good time. She may not ever let her hair down entirely, but give her two or three glasses of sherry and the right company, you might just hear a frivolous laugh fall from her mouth. The woman loves children, her own, of course, but also those less-fortunate kiddies who need a helping hand. She gives generously of her time and money to various local charities. She also cares for her horses, her dogs, any stray animals that might cross her path. All in all, not a complete Bitch. And quite smitten with yours truly that sunny afternoon on her front porch. "Now, Mr. Standish," she said, beaming, her hand still squeezing my arm, "flattery will most definitely get you everywhere."

"Merely the truth, ma'am."

Another squeeze before she released her grip. "Go," she commanded. "Swim. Eat. Play tennis. Enjoy yourself." She smiled at me, then turned her attention to Mr. Kenyon, a former Cabinet Secretary in a recent Republican administration.

I found Alison and Sarah eyeing me closely. Sarah had kind of a wry smile on her face; Alison more of a sneer.

"What did you say to my mother, Mr. Standish? I haven't seen her face light up like that in years."

"Oh, nothing. I just paid her a small compliment."

"And what small compliment would that be?"

"I couldn't possibly let that cat out of the bag, Ms. Browne."

Sarah shook her head, didn't lose that smile. "I think, Mr. Standish, we'll have to keep our eye on you."

Fine with me.

It would've been nice to stand there and make Sarah smile some more, all day long, but the former Cabinet Secretary from the Grand Old Party (no Dems allowed up at TREETOPS), one of those windbags who use power to seduce women, had come to this picnic to drool over young Ms. Browne. The pol practically pushed me out of the way to reach his destination. "Sarah, my dear, you look ravishing."

Sarah glanced at Alison, rolled her eyes.

I caught this reaction, realized immediately that false flattery might win a point or two with the old girl, but with this young thoroughbred it would not win many favors. She had no doubt heard every line in the book. Every variation of every line in the book. I'd have to tread lightly, be very nimble on my feet.

The former Cabinet Secretary grabbed her hands. "Yes, good enough to eat."

Sarah gave Alison another look, then whispered, "Talk to you guys later. Duty calls."

Duty. Right. After hanging around the Brownes' backyard charity barbecue for a couple hours with the other guests, I had the distinct impression the whole bunch of them had shown up to do their Duty. Like this picnic was some kind of penance for God knows what sins: Greed? Avarice? Adultery? That lush sweep of lawn felt like a white-collar prison yard. Never in my life had I seen so many white people with access to so much free food and free booze having such a bad time. They stood around in small clusters practicing the art of polite and utterly inane conversation.

Hot topic number one: the heat.

"Hasn't it been dreadfully hot?"

"Ghastly."

Hot topic number two: the humidity.

"Isn't this humidity stifling?"

"I feel like I'm swimming."

And hot topic number three: sagging real estate prices.

"I don't think we will ever see a boom like that again."

"Absolutely not. The eighties were an anomaly."

"An aberration."

I tried to go with the flow, stick to the party line. I was, after all, just a guest. A friend of a friend. Only recently invited. But my God, the day would die a painful death without a real smile having been cracked. And so I took on the role of Jester, made an effort to infuse the conversations with a touch of humor, a dash of social satire. Such as when I suggested that perhaps the severity of the heat and humidity was a result of humans fouling the environment with too many chemicals and pollutants. You know, funny and poignant at the same time. Well forget it. Those rich white folks did not wish to discuss such matters. The subject made them very uncomfortable. They no doubt owned large amounts of stock in all the big petrochemical companies. They smiled nervously at my digs, then quickly slipped away.

Oh yeah, I caught on real fast: nothing controversial. To utter even a single innocuous political statement, other than to belittle those who rode donkeys, was a no-no. Could cause feathers to ruffle. Blood pressure to rise. Frivolous conversation to turn suddenly meaningful.

Things did grow a tad more interesting when I stumbled upon hot topic numero cuatro: other people's business. Now this was good stuff. Excellent fodder. High drama. Usually unfolded as a private moment between two women standing off in a corner, their mouths whispering furiously.

Yes, the rumor mill was alive and well at the Brownes' barbecue. And those in charge of the mill had no shortage of grist. They may not have had me yet, but they had plenty of others to feed through the wheel.

To gain access to the mill, I had no choice but to eavesdrop.

"I hear she's been sleeping with the gardener."

"No?"

"Yes."

"That quiet young Italian boy they hired last fall?"

"The very same. I understand he's quite a handful in the sack."

Controlled laughter.

"After eleven years with that husband, she could stand a little excitement."

"He's such a bore."

"A bore, yes dear, but rich. Filthy rich."

They acknowledged this profundity with curt nods. I waited for more, but the two bitches turned their attention back to the weather, to the grass turning brown without proper irrigation. I moved on, in search of more fertile ground. And not long after, while standing on the back patio discussing the humidity with a couple of dour-looking gents, I fell privy to this exchange between a couple of aging biddies.

"I hear they're fucking like foxes."

"I hear it too. It's so disgusting."

Oh yeah, nothing quite so stimulating as hearing a gray-haired dame utter the word fucking. Makes the hair stand up on the back of my neck.

"Betty heard them doing it in the ladies' room at the hunt club last week before they went out cubbing."

"Before!"

"Yes, before."

"It must have been five o'clock in the morning."

"Or earlier."

"I'll bet they're upstairs in one of the bedrooms at this very moment humping their brains out."

I peered over my shoulder at the two gossips: stern, cold mugs. Both looked like they could use a good roll between the sheets. Then I glanced up at the house, hoping for a glimpse of the couple under discussion. I searched the windows until the thought occurred to me that the female in this tryst might be Sarah. My eyes combed the patio. The backyard. She was nowhere in sight. Wait. There. Standing over by the tennis court. Performing her role as the gracious hostess. Still surrounded by guests and admirers. I'd been unable to get anywhere near her all afternoon.

When the eavesdropping routine grew boring, I retreated to the creative pleasures of my Nikon. If the rich and mighty wanted to talk about the weather, then sneak off to whisper about who was diddling who, so what? I'd use my camera to stir things up, invade a little privacy, maybe rip off a few masks by tripping my shutter, capturing this bunch of pompous white phonies on film.

"I'm the official court photographer," I told the small groups of picnickers as I waded in among them while they daintily ate their grilled beef tenderloins and three-bean salads. "Smile."

I focused and shot with lightning speed. I've never been shy about sticking my camera in someone's face. Sure, it was obnoxious, but that didn't bother me. A good photo mattered a hell of a lot more than good manners. Besides, the good manners lurking in the Brownes' backyard were dreadfully superficial, false fronts disguising all kinds of risqué behaviors, racist attitudes, and an almost manic need to know who was screwing who and who possessed the most Money.

It wasn't me. I wasn't screwing anyone and I had like five or six bucks wadded up in my pocket.

I did my best to shoot Sarah. But she proved elusive. Each time I found her in the viewfinder, she slipped away. At first I dismissed it as simply bad luck. But then I caught her watching me, following me with one eye as she performed her duties with the other. This excited me, both as a photographer and as a sexual predator, until I realized she was not so interested in me, as in avoiding my lens. Every time my index finger hovered over the shutter release, she turned her head or danced away.

Was she playing a game? Playing hard to get? Messing with my head? Or was the whole thing just my imagination?

I tried to get close enough to pose these questions, or to at least sift for a few answers, but it proved impossible. A constant flow of humanity, mostly horny-looking young bucks wearing Brooks Brothers seersucker shorts and Ralph Lauren Polo shirts, demanded her attention.

And then I ran out of film. So I put away the Nikon, went looking for Cracker. I found him standing by the swimming pool, sipping a Beck's.

"What's up?"

"Not much," he told me. "Just playing lifeguard."

Tracy, Molly, and several other kids frolicked in the pool playing water tag.

"Which one belongs to Sarah?"

Cracker pointed "That little guy there."

"So that's Timothy, huh? How old is he?"

"Must be seven by now. Maybe eight."

I checked out the kid, a skinny bundle of nervous energy. Then, "I could use a beer. Want one?"

Cracker checked the level in his bottle. "Sure."

I returned with a couple of cold ones. "So tell me, Cracker, what's up with this crowd?"

"What do you mean?"

"What do I mean! Hell, did somebody die? Is this a wake and nobody told me?"

"It's just a picnic, Mike."

"I thought people were supposed to have fun at a picnic. The kids are the only ones having any fun."

"It's just a picnic to raise money for a good cause."

"Oh," I said, stretching out the vowel, "right. A good cause. That explains it."

Cracker glanced around, took note of the sedate mood, the general lack of good cheer. "They do look a little solemn, don't they?"

"Solemn? I hate to tell you this, old buddy, they look dead. So do you. This place is turning you into a corpse. Might be time to make a run for it."

An offhand remark. Tossed off, as usual, with nary a thought. But Cracker got all wound up. Wanted to discuss it. At great length. Wanted to know if I really thought he should move away, seek new pastures. But I didn't feel like talking about it. I'd had enough talking for one day. I prefer action. So I sucked down my beer, pulled off my shirt, kicked off my sneakers, and dove into the pool. When I came up for air, I splashed as much water on Cracker as I could before my old college roomie moved back out of range.

A few of the guests around the pool actually smiled at my rowdy display, but most showed their disapproval by frowning, shaking their heads. I ignored the whole lot. I joined the kids in a round of water tag, then taught them to play the game in a whole new way: with their eyes closed.

*   *   *

Late in the afternoon, after many of the guests had made their getaways, I took another walk around the grounds hoping to find Sarah. Instead I found a couple of older guys sitting in the gazebo out beyond the swimming pool, yukking it up, working on a bottle of Chivas.

"Finally, someone who's actually having a good time."

They stopped laughing. Stared at me. Stared as only Rich White Males from Old Families can stare. Like there ain't a damn thing in the world that can hurt them, make them feel inadequate. A good thirty seconds passed. I wasn't sure if I should make a joke or a quick retreat.

"We're not having a good time, you dumb son of a bitch," one of the gentlemen announced. "We're getting drunk."

"Cowed."

"Slammed."

"Pickled."

"Pissed."

"Pig-eyed."

"Yeah," I said, "I can see that. What's the occasion?"

One gentleman slapped the other gentleman on the back. "Yeah, Colin, what's the occasion?" He pretty well slurred his words.

Colin thought about it. "Screw you, Bill Winslow! Whoever said we needed an occasion to get drunk?"

Bill Winslow pointed at me. "He did."

"Who the hell's he?"

"Hell if I know. Never laid eyes on him before."

"Probably one of those young capitalist pinkos trying to decide if he should vote his fricking conscience or his fricking wallet."

They waited for me to say something. I'd recovered by this time, just stood there grinning at them, didn't say a word.

"Arrogant son of a bitch, ain't he?"

"I think we better give him a drink."

"He doesn't have a glass."

"He has a bottle."

"Of that piss-ass German swill."

"Let him pour some in the bottle."

Colin handed me the bottle of Chivas. I tried to take it. He only let go after a brief tussle.

I poured out the beer, poured in the Scotch. "Thanks." Raised the bottle, made a toast, "To the dullest damn picnic I've ever been to."

Glasses chinked. We all had a snootful.

Colin licked his lips, looked me dead in the eye. "So, you think we're a dull lot, hey kid?"

"I didn't say that. Never said *you* were dull. Don't know you. Just said this picnic was dull."

"You're right," said Colin, "we are dull. Dull as dishwater. Dull as old paint. Dull as reel fishing." He took another sip of Chivas. "Dull, kid, but rich. Layers and layers of green." Then another sip. "Never underestimate the power of money, kid. It goes a long way in dealing with dull."

"So who were those two old-timers?"

"Bill Winslow and Colin Crawford."

"Man were they stewed."

"You look pretty well fried yourself, pal."

I couldn't deny it.

I followed Cracker through the row of cedars, out into the parking area. Only a few cars remained. The charity barbecue had all but faded into that great forgettable party past.

"So what's the deal anyway?" I wanted to know. "I finally find a few laughs and you pull me away."

"The deal is, Alison wants to go home."

"So let her go. We'll stay here, tip a few with the old boys."

"Maybe next time."

"Pussy-whipped faggot."

Cracker didn't like that. Not one bit. Too close to home. Threw his arm around my neck, tried to wrestle me to the asphalt. I beat back his attack, worked my way to the edge of the grass. Collapsed under Cracker's weight. He put me in a half nelson, pressed my back and shoulders into the turf. But I knew the way out. Years and years of wrestling, playing grab-ass. I used my free arm to leverage my body off the ground. Kicked my leg up, wrapped it around Cracker's neck. A quick snap at the knee and down went Cracker. Face plant. A mouthful of dirt. But he recovered quickly, before I could pin him. We wrestled and rolled across the lush green lawn.

Over the years we've had our share of entanglements, one or two fired by real anger or resentment, but most of them, like this one, nothing but boys being boys.

The bout finally ended when Cracker sent me sprawling into a thorny tangle of pyracantha. The bush drove its fiery thorns into my arms and legs. I swore the devil's anthem. Struggled to my feet, dusted myself off. "Next time, my ass," I told him. "The only next time is this time."

Cracker laughed, gave me a shove. "Michael J. Standowski: Photographer. Philosopher. Fuck-up."

"Don't call me Standowski," I said, only half kidding. "I'll rip your eyes out."

"I'm shivering in my boots."

We went around the side of the house then, arm-in-arm. Found Alison and the kids saying so long to Sarah. I had to concentrate to walk a straight line.

Alison spotted her husband. "So," she asked, "where did you find him?"

"In the gazebo. Having a word with Colin and Bill Winslow."

Alison took a closer look. She spotted the sweat on our brows, the grass stains on our clothes, the tiny clots of blood on my arm where the pyracantha had snagged me good. "Have you two infants been fighting again?"

Cracker, the chump, actually dropped his eyes. "He started it."

I showed my teeth. "And proud of it."

"A couple of vile creatures," mumbled the wife.

"What's the matter, Allie?" I asked. "Don't like the idea of your hubby wrestling with another man?"

She spewed smoke and fire into my eyes. "It's time," she announced, "to go."

"What's the hurry?" I wanted to know. "We just got here."

And then I launched myself in Sarah's direction. "All day long I've been trying to have a word with our pretty hostess." I had this enormous grin on my face, due in large part to the amount of beer and Scotch I had flowing through my bloodstream. I promptly reached the bottom step of the front porch and stumbled.

Sarah, the vague hint of a smile on her face, caught me before I made contact with the hard gray slate. "Careful, Mr. Standish, you'll fall." She tried to let go, but I stumbled again. She caught me again. "I think you did that one on purpose."

"Absolutely not," I assured her. "I'm weak from the vicious beating inflicted upon me by Mr. Graham Cramer. You'll have to look after me."

A slightly wider smile this time, and then, "I don't think so." But she continued to accept my weight.

"Ms. Browne, if you let go of me I'll crumble to the ground like the scarecrow in *The Wizard of Oz*." Hey, it just popped into my head, out of my mouth.

"The Wizard of Oz!" shouted Tracy as the yellow brick road flashed through her little brain. "Mommy, can we

watch *The Wizard of Oz* when we get home? Can we, please, can we?"

Alison, the bad witch, glared at me but snapped at her daughter. "No."

And Sarah, her eyes still smiling, "I doubt you'll crumble to the ground, Mr. Standish. Somehow you don't strike me as the crumbling sort." But she endured my weight nevertheless.

"Oh, but I am. I fall apart almost every day, then have to find some way to put myself back together."

Sarah gave me a curious look. Was this, I'm sure she wondered, a spontaneous confession or just a quick con job?

Alison, of course, did not have to wonder. Not for a second. "Oh please," she sneered. "Let's go before I throw up."

The kids snickered. Cracker looked downright uncomfortable.

But Mike and Sarah: we missed Alison's slur entirely. Her words passed right through our bodies. Nothing but sound waves.

I looked into Sarah's eyes. She looked into my eyes. Something on this great green planet shifted. Only a moment or two slipped by, but a moment or two that I think sealed our fates.

Arm-in-arm for the rest of the evening we might've lingered had not Cracker moved forward, relieved Sarah of her burden. "Let's go, pal." He only made his move after Alison gave him the evil eye.

We struggled, Sarah and I, back to reality.

Am I kidding with all this romantic, smoky-eyed nonsense? Putting you on?

No way. Something happened in that moment. A spark flickered. A connection was made.

Cracker dropped Alison and the kids off at the farmhouse, then drove me out to the cottage. I'd been stretched out in the back of the Wagoneer, sleeping it off, but with the family gone, I climbed into the front seat. "So who's this guy Colin?"

"Colin Crawford?"

"Yeah?"

"He's Sarah's uncle."

"Really! Her uncle? The old girl's brother?"

"Right."

"He can put away the booze. That Winslow guy as well. Another half hour with those two I'd've been crawling around in the bushes on my belly."

Cracker laughed, swung the Wagoneer down the grass and gravel lane. Pulled up behind the rusty pickup. "How's the truck running?"

"It's a piece of junk," I told him. "Why don't you get Big Walt to buy me a new one? Maybe a big Chevy with a V-8 and four-wheel drive."

"Right," said Cracker the Ironist. "I'll call him when I get home. Bet he'll do it too. You've been on the job now almost a week. Probably given us six or eight hours of your precious time."

I smiled, shrugged. "Hey, you never know unless you ask."

Cracker put the Wagoneer in park. "About tomorrow," he said. "We have some clearing to do out behind the old hay barn. I'd like to get an early start. Before it gets too hot. I thought by six or six-fifteen we could—"

"Hang on a second there, pal. I have something to tell you."

"What?"

"I got a job offer."

"A job offer? From who?"

"From Uncle Colin."

"What? You're full of it."

"Not this time. That's why I wondered who he was."

"Colin Crawford made you a job offer?"

"That's right," I told him. "Colin said, and I quote, 'Kid, I don't know who you are, but you got balls. Young men today don't have balls. Life's too damn easy. When I was a young man you had to have moxie. Me, I like a man with moxie. I need a man with moxie in my business. A salesman. A salesman with balls.' Then he slapped me on the back, poured some whiskey in my beer bottle, and offered me a position."

"He was drunk," insisted Cracker. "Just letting his lips flap. Tomorrow he won't even remember he met you."

"I'll remind him."

"He'll tell you to piss off."

"No he won't. What does he do anyway?"

"Colin Crawford? He's into all kinds of things. Stocks and bonds. Real estate. Commercial development. He was in business with Sarah's father. Crawford and Browne Investments, Incorporated. It's still Crawford and Browne, but now it's just Crawford running the show."

"What happened to Browne?"

"He died in a boating accident. God, it must be ten or twelve years ago."

"So the old girl's a widow?"

Cracker answered with a nod.

"And now her brother runs the whole show. And you say it's a pretty big show?"

"A goddamn big show."

"How big?"

"Jesus, I don't know. Millions in assets. So what's the deal? You really going to pursue this job offer thing?"

"I wasn't planning on it. But now I'm not so sure."

"Yeah? Why not? Why the change of attitude?"

"Because now you tell me the guy is Sarah's uncle."

"So he's Sarah uncle? So what?"

It took my old buddy a minute or so to catch on. The light of another summer day slipped away. It grew dark inside the Wagoneer. Cracker reached up, turned on the light, gave me a pretty good snarl. "Jesus Christ, don't tell me you're interested in Sarah. For God's sake, Standish, give the poor girl a break. Leave her be. She's had enough stinking, selfish men in her life. Including my brother. She doesn't need another one. She definitely doesn't need you."

From where I sit now, it sure looks like my old college roomie was right.

The next morning my name slipped into the conversation around the Brownes' breakfast table. My ears began to flap and hum the second their mouths mentioned my name. But the real reason I know they were talking about me is because Sarah told me so herself. Told me this and plenty more as our intimacy deepened.

The Brownes' breakfast table: a two-hundred-year-old drop-leaf solid cherry gem serving the family since back before the War of 1812. Worth in excess of ten grand, it would later become part and parcel of my booty. But that August morning it still sat in a small, cozy nook on the southeast side of the sprawling kitchen. Early morning sunlight poured through the floor-to-ceiling windows. Very early morning sunlight. Katherine Browne liked to get up with the sun. Usually got the rest of the crew up as well. She couldn't stand to see people sleeping too far beyond the dawn. It irked her no end. Probably some old Puritan thing.

6:38 A.M.: "So, Timothy, did you have a good time at the barbecue yesterday?"

"Yes, ma'am. I spent almost the whole day in the pool."

Half glasses on a string around her neck, a smile for her grandson. "I know you did. This morning I feared you might come downstairs with gills."

"Not all fish have gills, Gram."

"No?"

Young Tim shook his head. "And fish don't have nerves. So when you catch a fish on a hook, the fish doesn't even feel it. Insects don't have nerves either. You can pull the legs right off a daddy longlegs and he won't feel a thing. It's still not a very nice thing to do, so don't worry, I never would. I don't like to hurt things. In fact, I've been thinking about maybe wearing a little white mask over my mouth like those people in China or India or someplace so I won't suck any flies or gnats or mosquitoes down my throat by accident."

Timothy finished his soliloquy, then he turned his attention to his bowl of whole grain cereal. The women in the kitchen made eye contact. Their heads shook. They had come to expect these performances. Never did he cease to amaze them with his wide and indiscriminate circle of knowledge.

Timothy had four women who doted over him. His mother, of course. And his grandmother. And twenty-year-old Lucy, his nanny, who had joined the family a year or so ago from her home in northern England. She had wanted for years to live with a family of Yanks. Lucy was quiet, dependable, totally devoted to the boy. And let us not forget Dorothy. Dorothy kept the household on an even keel. She cooked, cleaned, shopped, made sure everyone made it on time to wherever they had to go. She'd been with the family for over thirty years. Long enough to remember Sarah in diapers. A baby-sitter back in those days. Later a housekeeper. Had her own family then. Lived down in the village. But by and by her kids grew up, moved away. Then her husband, after forty-one years inhaling Lucky Strikes, curled up and died after a long illness, so Katherine asked the widow if she wanted to come live with the family.

These four women made Timothy's life heaven on earth. They spoiled the kid rotten. Didn't really mean to, just couldn't help themselves. Occasionally they'd hold powwows in his absence wherein they would reprimand one another for being too lax with discipline, too free with compliments and confections, too eager with hugs and kisses, too generous with their time and energy. They instinctively knew this avalanche of attention would, in the long run, damage the young whippersnapper, cause him to develop an exaggerated sense of his own importance. Nevertheless, the avalanche continued to rumble.

What Tim needed was a papa. Rotten Ron, his biological father, had flown the coop. A rooster on the wing. Tim needed a guy around the house, a man to teach him about guy stuff: farting and belching and scratching, throwing and catching and hitting. All the women in the world can carry an eight-year-old boy only so far.

Tim worked on a few spoonfuls of cereal, then muttered, "I learned a new game yesterday."

"Don't speak with your mouth full, Timothy." His granny.

"You did? What game was that?" His nanny.

"A swimming pool game." Here's where I pop up. "Water tag with your eyes closed. Mike taught us."

Sarah, never a morning person despite her mother's best efforts over three full decades, perked up at the sound of the name. (Hey, she told me this herself.) "Mike? Mike who?"

"I don't know," said Tim. "He just told us to call him Mike."

Sarah closed the Miller's equestrian catalogue she'd been leafing through. Decided that new saddle could wait. Looked across the table at her son. "Child or adult?"

"Well, he acted like a kid, but he was a grown-up."

"Kind of tall? Light brown hair? Blue eyes?"

Katherine gave her daughter a set of curious eyes. Dorothy did the same.

Timothy scrunched up his face. "I don't know, Mom. I don't notice stupid stuff like that."

But Sarah had noticed. She wouldn't have admitted it that morning, but she'd drifted off to sleep the night before with my weight still resting in her arms.

"Mike Standish," announced Katherine. The Iron One kept a steady gaze on her daughter's reaction. "He spent quite a lot of time in the pool with the children. I understand he found the adult company rather tedious."

Sarah did her best to show nothing. "Oh, Graham's friend?"

"I should think so," said Katherine. "I found him very charming. An excellent quality . . ." She paused here to gather her audience. ". . . except in someone upon whom you need to depend." Another pause, then, "I also understand he did a bit of imbibing with my brother and that Bill Winslow. You think he could have made it through one picnic without stumbling upon those two."

Often when Katherine spoke she did not necessarily desire a response. Only wide-open ears from her subjects. A royal decree kind of thing.

The others went back to their cereal or their toast or their coffee. A minute or two slowly ground by. Lucy was the first to rise. "I should go down to the stable and get Ruby ready for pony club."

"That's fine, Lucy," said Katherine. "And Timothy, you go with her. You're plenty old enough now to groom and tack that pony."

"Yes, ma'am."

Lucy and Timothy said their goodbyes, then out through the back door. Sarah hesitated a moment, then excused herself, hurried after them. She caught up out near the garage.

Timothy jumped into her arms. "You want to come, Mom?"

Sarah gave her boy a squeeze. "God, you're getting heavy. Like a man. Soon I won't even be able to lift you." She set him down, turned to Lucy. "Lucy, does Alison Cramer usually stay with Molly at pony club? Or does she just drop her off?"

Lucy shrugged. She thought a question was simply a question. Had not learned yet the subtle nuances of the double-entendre. "Sometimes she stays."

"Listen," said Sarah, "why don't we all go down and get Ruby ready. Then we'll hook up the trailer and I'll take Timothy to pony club this morning. I've only been once or twice all summer."

Okay, maybe Sarah had an ulterior motive for taking Timothy to pony club. She admitted as much to me in the days and weeks ahead. But don't for one second get the wrong idea about Ms. Browne. She did not need any special motivation to spend time with her son. She loved that kid more than anyone or anything in the world. But that particular morning what she really wanted to do was have a chat with Alison Cramer: wife of Graham, friend of Mike.

She got her wish.

The two young women leaned against the post and plank fence surrounding the pony club ring at the equestrian center. They watched Timothy and Molly and half a dozen other kids circle the ring on their ponies while the instructor, stern Mrs. Pierson, barked orders. "Sit up straight! Shorten your reins! Heels down! Hands in!"

Sarah had taught Timothy to ride soon after he learned to walk, but pony club sharpened his skills. If he could improve his jumping, Sarah hoped to take him out foxhunting this season. But right now she had a man on her mind. A mystery man. A man who had conspicuously shown some interest in her. But she had to broach the subject cautiously, with a certain decorum. Alison and she were friendly, but not really friends. They had their kids in common.

"Molly's doing well," she said. "It looks like she's starting to get her seat."

Alison watched her older daughter post. "She's more comfortable now."

"And confident," added Sarah. "I can see it in the way she holds her neck."

Alison nodded in agreement, but not because of Molly's neck. She was merely deferring to a higher authority, something she loathed doing. Alison was not a horse person. She had not grown up with horses. Did not really like horses. Rather scared of the beasts actually. When Graham had said he wanted the kids to learn how to ride, she'd resisted. Loss of control and all those emotional knickknacks.

Sarah knew this, sensed it anyway, and so quickly moved the conversation in a different direction. "Did Molly and Tracy have a good time at the picnic yesterday?"

Alison nodded. "They wound up exhausted, as usual. Both of them fell asleep in the car on the way home."

Sarah smiled. Saw her opening. She took a moment to watch Timothy take Ruby over a jump. Slightly off balance, otherwise okay. Sarah is not a manipulative person, certainly she does not think of herself as a manipulative person, but even she has to occasionally slide in through the back door. "Well," she said, "at least you had two strong young men to carry the kids inside."

Alison thought about it, then, "Oh, you mean Mike?"

Sarah continued to watch Timothy. "Yes. Wasn't he riding with you?"

"He was riding with us all right," said Alison. "He's been riding with us for a while now. But don't get me started on Mike."

Sarah felt a rush of blood to her brain. Avoided shifting her eyes. She looked dead ahead at those trotting ponies. "Sorry, I didn't mean to touch a nerve."

Alison shrugged but said nothing.

Sarah, anxious, took a chance. "He seems nice enough."

Alison had just been simmering, waiting to turn up the heat. "Oh, he's plenty nice. A real charmer. Charm the last nickel out of your pocket. Charm you right out of your pants."

Sarah wondered about that. She thought it might possibly be pleasant. It had been so long since she'd been with someone she really desired, someone who made her toes curl. Those few brief moments with his body pressed up against—

"It's just too bad," continued Alison, "he doesn't have any scruples. Not a moral bone in his body. He only cares about one thing: himself. Men are generally a selfish and disgusting species, but this one takes the blue ribbon."

Sarah could feel Alison's anger itching to break loose. She didn't want that anger to explode and fizzle before she could probe for a few answers. "Didn't you and Graham and Mike all go to college together?"

Alison nodded. "Four years at Ithaca. He was just the same then. I went out with him for a while. Quite a while actually. Off and on for a couple years. He charmed the pants off me, I can tell you that. Bastard."

So, thought Sarah, this anger has some scorn behind it. But she didn't have time for all the details, not today. Mrs. Pierson would be wrapping up the lesson. "And now he lives around here?"

"Temporarily, I'm sure. He pops in and out on us. Usually when he wants something from Graham. Like money."

"Money?" The word rattled Ms. Browne. "What does he do for a living?"

"Good question. He doesn't do much of anything. Never has."

"What do you mean?"

"I mean he's a snake oil salesman. A con man. Floats along, living here and there, doing odd jobs. Coming and going as he pleases. Usually I find out he has some woman paying the bills, taking care of reality."

Poor Sarah. She found her mouth hanging open. This was not what she wanted to hear, not about a guy to whom she felt attracted. A bit of mystery, okay, maybe even some intrigue, but financial security and gainful employment needed to fill out the picture. For some uncharted reason, Sarah had concluded that I was an architect working on several new and innovative designs. Between her silk sheets the night before she had concocted this scenario. And had rounded it out with assumptions like Money, Rank, Respectability. All the tangibles.

I had my work cut out for me.

And then good old Allie again. Digging my grave a little deeper. Shoveling in the dirt. "Like a few months ago."

Sarah snapped back to the moment. "A few months ago?"

"He was living with this girl up on Cape Cod. We met her a few times. A real sweetheart." Oh, right. The pick of the litter. "Much better than he deserved. And then one day he just upped and left her. Moved to Newark."

"Newark? Newark, New Jersey?"

Alison nodded. "Yes. You see, Mike fancies himself an artist, a photographer."

This made Sarah feel a little better. She'd studied art at Vassar. She knew artists often had unusual temperaments, odd lifestyles. And the rest of it, well, it could just be Alison's wrath. Maybe Mike had dumped her once and she had never quite gotten over it, never forgiven him. Two sides to every story and all that.

"So what was he doing in Newark?"

"I don't know. He had some kind of epiphany that he needed to go to Newark and take pictures of black men getting drunk and killing each other."

"What?"

Alison was on a roll now. "So what does he do? He winds up getting shot."

"Shot!"

"Yes, shot. By a bullet. Right in the shoulder."

Sarah, I have to tell you, because she told me, found this image of me getting shot incredibly autoerotic. Her sex hormones surged as she imagined a bullet piercing my flesh. She had never known anyone who'd been shot. "How did that happen?"

"God, who knows? He got mixed up in something horrible. Nothing unusual for him." My dear Allie, making me a hero and not even trying. "Then he tried to slip out of the hospital without paying his bill. He's always trying to slip out without paying his bill. But the police caught him. Graham had to go down and bail him out. He's been with us ever since."

In a swirl of confused sexual signals, Sarah managed to ask, "So he's staying with you?"

"He was staying with us. Now he's living out in the old cottage on the Cramer place. Out of sight but not out of mind. The girls go see him all the time. He fascinates them. It makes me sick."

"And what's he doing? Does he plan on staying?" Sarah worked to suppress the panting enthusiasm in her voice. No way did she want Alison to sense her interest in this man.

But Alison didn't sense a thing. Too busy foaming at the mouth. Give her an inch and she'll rake me over the coals all day long. One of her favorite pastimes. "Who knows how long he'll stay? As long as it's in his best interest."

Sarah wasn't sure what to say. She'd heard an earful, far more than she'd anticipated. Out in the ring the kids started to dismount, walk their ponies. Sarah felt relieved that it would soon be time to go home. She felt calmer now. Past that sexual explosion upon hearing I'd been shot. She decided it was better to find out sooner than later that I was essentially a creep and a ne'er-do-well. But still her loins tingled.

Alison had a bit more to say. She continued to smolder and fume, a few flames yet left to spew. "Men are just little boys in big bodies. Dangerous little boys. So full of treachery and deception. That liar doesn't even have the guts to go through life with his real name."

Sarah had started to drift, to think about the things she had to do later in the day. Things to keep busy. "Huh? Who?"

"Mike," said Alison. "His name's not Mike Standish."

Sarah looked confused. "It's not?"

"No. It's Standowski. Michael Josep Standowski. But he couldn't stand being Polish, so what does he do? He sweetens it to the more Anglican Standish. What does that tell us about him?"

Sarah shrugged. She wasn't sure. She didn't have a clue. But as the kids led their ponies out of the ring, she found herself wondering about her own name: Sarah Louise Browne. And the surnames of her two ex-husbands: Cramer and Carlson. Such good clean proper English names. From good clean proper English families. White Anglo-Saxon Protestants to the bone. And both of them cruel, selfish bastards. Ugly, mean, and violent. Standish. Standowski. What, she asked herself almost out loud, does it matter? What's the difference? All she wanted was a man to love her, respect her, treat her kindly and with tenderness. His name? She couldn't care less about his name.

*   *   *

While all this went on, Cracker and I hacked away at the dense undergrowth behind the barn with various tools: sickles, machetes, loppers, pruning saws, gasoline-powered weed whackers. The variety of weapons didn't make the job any easier, only slightly less tedious. I swore frequently at the foliage, my profanity growing ever more coarse and creative as the morning wore on. Sweat poured off my brow under the rising August sun. Cracker barely perspired a drop. He went about his work calmly, methodically. Since moving back to the family compound, the guy had spent hundreds of hours clearing old growth. Part of his penance.

"Easy does it, Mike," he kept telling me. "You're going to kill yourself. Slow and steady's the only way to win this race."

I wiped the sweat off my forehead. Small blotches of blood dotted my arms and neck where the thorny brambles had fought back against my onslaught. I turned and glared at Cracker, narrowed my right eye. "Watch yourself, boss, or when you ain't looking, I'll lop off your stinking head with this machete."

Cracker smiled. "Go ahead, lop it off. I'd be better off without it. But until then, slow down. It's been years since anyone cleared this old pasture. We're not going to clean it up in an hour."

"Why are we cleaning it up anyway?" I wanted to know. "You people already have more lawns and gardens than the White House."

"I want to build a grape arbor back here. The sun and soil are perfect."

"A grape arbor? Shit." I shook my head and went back to hacking the foliage.

Brambles, wild roses, vines, and an assortment of weeds had taken hold of the earth behind the barn. Cracker wanted it back. He'd already reclaimed several acres of the Cramer Compound since returning to his boyhood home.

Where there had been weeds, now there were flower gardens. Where wild roses had once flourished, now a wide variety of hybrid teas and grandifloras bloomed throughout the summer. Where there had been neglect, now signs of care and cultivation. Cracker had been working hard to make the grounds thrive on one hundred percent organic compounds. A slow process after decades of harsh chemicals and synthetic fertilizers, but little by little he intended to win the war.

He took pause from his labor, wiped his face with a bandanna. Looked up to check the position of the sun. Not much past nine, but already plenty hot. "Let's take a break. Get some water."

I lopped through a thick kudzu vine. "You'll get no argument from me, boss."

We'd parked the pickup in the shade on the far side of the hay barn. Took our break sitting on the tailgate. Drinking ice water from a thermos. Shoving down some plums, apricots, bananas.

I figured to get Cracker talking. Maybe keep him going till lunch. "So did you mean what you said last night?"

"Mean what I said about what?" He peeled a banana and ate it.

"About Sarah."

"What about her?"

"I want to ask her out."

"She won't go out with you."

"Why not?"

"You're a bum."

"So what? So are you. You just caught the luck of the draw getting born into a rich family."

Cracker smiled, popped a plum, sucked down the juice and the meat, spit out the pit. "I still don't want you going out with her. Go find some bimbo to play with till you're ready to move on." He glared at me. "Don't mess with my sister-in-law."

"You sound a little possessive there, Cracker. She's the one, isn't she?"

"The one what?"

"The one you told me about when we were in college."

"What are you talking about?"

"It took me a while to remember. To put it all together. But Sarah Browne's the one you were in love with. The one who got away."

"Screw you, Standowski."

"Oh, so it's Standowski again, huh? What's the deal, old buddy? Still have some hidden desires lurking in your pants?"

"Go to hell." Cracker ate another plum. Then he went to work putting an edge back on his sickle.

"What about these ex-husbands of hers?" I asked. "Your brother and this other guy?"

Cracker did his best to ignore me. But the subject was too close to home, buried but not very deep. He kept honing the edge of that sickle as he worked himself into a frenzy. "A couple of sons of bitches. That's all you need to know."

"What was the first one's name?"

"Carlson. Ricky Carlson." Cracker spit the name out of his mouth. "He came from a local family with money. Had a fat job on Wall Street. But he was a sleazeball and a psychopath."

"Psychopath?"

"A goddamn narcissist with a mean streak."

"Care to throw me a few more details?"

"The stories vary. But it's pretty clear he started beating her up emotionally even before the honeymoon. Within a few months he took a few swings at her. Just little stuff at first. Pushed her around, slapped her across the face. Sarah was like twenty-one or -two years old. She didn't know any better. So she kept it to herself, didn't tell anyone, figured it would pass."

"This guy Carlson beat her up?"

Cracker nodded. He still refused to look my way. Eyes riveted on that cold steel blade. "That's right. That's what he did. He beat her up. Then one night the bastard lost control. He hit her with his closed fist. The first shot broke one of her ribs. The second shot cracked her jaw. The third shot blackened one of her eyes."

"Jesus."

"Nice, huh? A real swell fellow."

"I'll say."

"Fortunately, the following morning, Katherine showed up for an unexpected visit. One look at her daughter and, brother, that was the end of that marriage. She had that scumbag thrown in jail for assault. Insisted Sarah press charges. He wound up with fourteen months in Rahway State Prison. A lot less than he deserved. I would've strung him up by his thumbs, cut off his balls, and let him slowly bleed to death. You can't go around beating up your wife."

My old man beat up my mother. I wonder if Ricky Carlson's father beat up his mother? While Ricky watched? One decent thing you can say about me: I've never laid a hand on a woman in anger. Atta boy, Mike. Solid gold.

"So how long were they married?"

Cracker thought about it. "Not long. Not even a year."

"And how long after that did she marry your brother?"

I might as well have punched my old buddy in the face. The memory I'd stirred was obviously not a happy one. Eyes and mouth taut as drum skins, Cracker bore down even harder with that whetstone. "Don't get me started on my brother."

"Hey, I always thought Ron was an okay guy. A little tightly wrapped maybe, but still okay."

Cracker frowned, scowled. "You got it wrong, Mike. Ron's not okay. Not even close. He's a drunk and a lunatic."

"Hell, Cracker, he's your brother."

"I don't give a damn."

"Where is he anyway?"

"Who knows? No one knows. He just disappeared. Dropped off the face of the earth."

"Does he ever see his kid?"

"Timothy? No. He hasn't seen him in two or three years."

I thought about that. And about all the private stuff in people's lives that we never get a handle on, that we never even hear about. Then, "So what did he do to Sarah? He didn't beat her up, did he?"

"Not physically, no."

"Tell me about it."

Cracker sighed, really blew out a lungful. Then he tossed that whetstone into the bed of the pickup. Stood and glared at me. "No, dammit. I don't feel like telling you about it. The whole thing sucks. Besides, it would take too long. Time to go back to work."

"Ease up, Cracker. Those thornbushes aren't going anywhere."

But Mr. Graham Cramer had uttered enough mumbo jumbo for one day. He was all pissed off now. Pissed off at his brother. Pissed off at this guy Carlson. Pissed off at me. I'd ruined his nice mellow day with the weeds out behind the barn.

"Fuck it," he announced. "Just fuck it." He glared at me again. "And you, pal, you keep your stinking Polack hands off Sarah. You got it? Keep them off." Then he marched back to the bramble patch, took up his razor-sharp sickle, and flailed at the undergrowth under that steamy August sun.

*   *   *

I chose not to cooperate with my old buddy's wishes. I did wait, however, until the end of the week to call Sarah. It must've been close to the end of the month as well. Almost September. Almost, I can't believe it, two years ago. Unbelievable. The past two days seem like they've lasted longer than the past two years.

I would've called Sarah sooner, wanted to call sooner, but I had to wait that long to have a phone installed in the cottage. Something to do with my credit rating not being the finest in the land. Of course, I could've used the phone over at Cracker's or out in the barn. I could've gone into town, used a pay phone. But here's the rub: a case of cold feet and raw nerves. A phenomenon I hadn't experienced since grade school.

Also, although not really, I did feel a certain ambivalence in connection with Cracker's request that I leave his old crush alone. Ambivalent but nevertheless attracted. Plus my love of the chase. At that time I had absolutely no idea if I'd be able to successfully corral that thoroughbred. Little did I know that she'd been waiting fretfully, eagerly, for some wild stallion to come charging into her stall, sweep her off her feet. She had been surrounded too long by emotional as well as sexual geldings.

So finally, late Friday afternoon, I picked up the telephone, found a dial tone. A moment of hesitation, then I punched in the seven numbers I'd looked up in my brand-new directory and memorized a few days earlier.

"Hello?"

"Tim? Is that you, Tim?"

"Yes."

"Hi, Tim. How's it going?"

"Okay."

I wondered if I should identify myself. Decided against it. "Is your mom home?"

I heard Tim turn away, shout, "Mom, telephone!"

And then Sarah's voice in the distance, "Who is it?"

"I dunno. Some man."

And a few seconds later, "Hello?"

"Sarah?"

"Yes?"

"It's Mike."

"Yes?"

"Mike Standish. Graham's friend."

What was that? Her pulse quickening? Her breath catching in her lungs?

"Yes. Hello. Hi." Oh yeah, she'd been hoping I'd call. No doubt about it. She had spent, I felt sure, more than a few minutes remembering our brief embrace on the front steps at the tail end of the charity barbecue.

As for me, well, I had the nerves working overtime: trembling hands, sweaty palms, legs a-jitter. "So," I asked, "how's everything going?" Jesus, what was that? A tremor in my voice? I knew then I had the bug with this one.

"Oh," she answered, doing her best to sound ho-hum, probably recalling that conversation with Alison at the pony club meet, "you know, pretty well. Kind of busy with Timothy getting ready for another school year."

"Third grade, right?"

"Yes, right. Third grade." Me knowing that small tidbit seemed to please her, put her at ease. I'd hoped it would. That's why I'd interrogated the kid at poolside during the picnic.

I managed to pull myself together after that. My panic attack passed. Time to move on. Time to try and make her laugh. I finally got her to admit the barbecue had been kind of boring. Made her confession in practically a whisper. Fearing, no doubt, that Mama Kate might be out on patrol, searching for any and all persons spreading dissent.

When the mood felt right, I popped the question. The centuries-old question that has kept many a man distant from the woman of his desires. Fearing rejection, he lets the question go unasked, keeps it buried deep within his heart. Not me. I've always believed in plowing straight ahead.

"So," I ventured, my hands almost steady, my palms practically dry, "what do you think about, you know, maybe going out sometime?"

Silence for a second or two, then she asked, "Like on a date?"

"Right," I said. "Like on a date." Then, so she wouldn't have to think too long or hard about it, "We could go to a movie. Or out to eat." And finally the clincher, "Tim could come along too. He could entertain us."

That pretty well settled that.

"How can I refuse?" came the response. "Timothy would never forgive me."

Nor would I. Although now, of course, guilt and misery cascading off me like water over Niagara, I wonder if I should've followed Cracker's edict: left Ms. Browne well enough alone. It would appear she has a weakness for wicked and pernicious men. And I am just the latest in an advancing line.

Sarah had plans for Saturday night: a date with another man (no big deal, she took the time to tell me, an arrangement that had been made weeks ago).

Nothing I could do about that. So what about Sunday night? Yes, she assured me, Sunday would be fine.

The phone rang late Sunday morning. I figured it would be Cracker. Or maybe Maggie. No one else called me. No one else knew I had a telephone. Only a handful of people even knew I was in New Jersey. But it wasn't Cracker. Nor Maggie Jane. It was Sarah. Plotting, I found out later, her evening escape from TREETOPS. She did not want to tell Mother Kate about her date with the new boy in town.

"I hope," I said, "you're not calling to tell me you fell madly in love last night and so you're canceling our date?"

I got a nice laugh out of her with that one. Then, "I don't fall madly in love," she informed me.

"Never?"

"Never."

"Maybe we'll try and change that."

A short pause to think this over, and then she said, "I was just calling to see if you wanted us to pick you up."

I hesitated. I had hoped to keep my humble digs a secret, at least until I'd had a chance to explain my role on the planet. Whatever role that might be. Financially humble starving artist would undoubtedly be my part in this particular play. No way around it. Sarah obviously had plenty of access to men with Power and Money. But what about men with Passion and Creativity?

"Sure," I said. "Pick me up anytime."

"Great," she replied, her enthusiasm unveiled. "Timothy and I have an errand to run this afternoon. We'll come straight over after that. Around six."

Oh yeah, there was an errand, I found out later, if you want to call dropping her annual donation check to the Vassar Alumni Fund into the mail on a Sunday evening an errand. A check that had been sitting on her bureau for two weeks.

"Do you know where I live?"

This time she hesitated. "Well . . . I think so . . . Yes. Alison told me."

That's when I first learned she'd been talking to Ms. Witte-Cramer. I wondered how that might round out the action. Whether it would be good or bad. Good, I figured, that Sarah had been asking. Bad, however, that nasty Alison had been providing the answers.

*   *   *

We went for pizza at the Wonder Bar in Whitehouse. Young Tim's choice. And just fine with me. Right up my financial alley. A twenty dollar bill would probably bring me change. We ordered a large pie with sausage and green peppers. Tim wanted a Coke. Sarah said no, too much sugar, too much caffeine. An argument ensued. I stayed clear.

Tim finally settled on a glass of cranberry juice. Then he raced off to play with the video machines. "That's why he likes to come here," explained his mother. "They have one where he gets to play a race car driver."

"Formula One Racers," I said. "Pretty good graphics. Excellent crashes."

Sarah gave me a look out of the corner of her eye. She wasn't sure if she should be encouraged by my knowledge of Formula One Racers, or concerned.

The waitress brought us a pitcher of beer. I filled our glasses, raised mine to make a toast. "To us," I said. "May we both find love, and maybe even happiness."

Sarah smiled, but at the same moment I thought I saw a twinge of sadness in her pretty eyes. "You can't have one without the other."

"Sure you can."

"I don't think so."

"They're just words," I said. "Silly notions."

Sarah started to respond but stopped. A curious twinkle in her eye. An odd curl to her lip. And then, "I can see I'll have to stay on my toes. Love, philosophy, and video games all in less than a minute."

I kind of shrugged, smiled. I didn't know, couldn't tell, if she was amused by my offerings, or annoyed. It didn't really seem to matter. We had something far more potent in the works. Something neither of us could deny. Our eyes met. And held. Held fast. For ten seconds. Fifteen seconds. Half a minute. An eternity. Something growing there. Something emotional. Something physical. Taking root.

Somewhere a glass shattered on the floor. We looked away from one another, in the direction of the crash. When we returned we fell back on the few things already familiar: Graham and Alison, last week's barbecue, Vassar College, Poughkeepsie, New York. Safety in these subjects, if only temporarily.

Tim returned to the table. He made some funny faces at me. I made some faces back. Then he told some jokes. "How do you catch a squirrel?"

I knew that one but didn't let on. "I don't know."

"Climb a tree and act like a nut. What do you call a sleeping bull?"

"You got me."

"A bulldozer. What's a volcano?"

"No idea."

"I know," said Sarah. "A mountain with hiccups."

"Mom! Be quiet. I already told you that one."

The kid, I realized, was a vital piece of the puzzle.

While we ate our pizza, I told my shot-in-the-shoulder story, embellished for the local audience, of course. By the end of the story I had transformed into young Tim's hero, a regular superman who had taken a slug and lived to tell about it.

But Sarah, much to my amazement, also looked at me with awestruck eyes. The story had been for the kid, but I had obviously struck a nerve with the mother as well.

After pizza we drove to the ice cream parlor for double-scoop cones. We took our cones outside and sat on the curb to eat them. Tim (he liked that I called him Tim and not Timothy) got all worked up telling me about his pony, Ruby, how Ruby sometimes bucked, but when Tim did a simulated buck his double scoop slipped off its cone and plopped onto the sidewalk.

"Timothy!" His mother scolded. "Look what you've done."

"I didn't mean to."

"You have to be more careful."

"I want another one."

"No."

"Why not? It was an accident."

"I said no."

A standoff settled in for a few seconds. I kept out of this one as well, just watched, took in the dynamics of this mother-son duet.

But I did take some time to wonder what I'd be like as a father. Better, I hoped, than my old man. Of course, the old cliché insists you never know how the suit fits till you try it on. Oh yeah, a big part of my problem, I have recently realized, is a deeply ingrained fear that if I stick around anywhere too long, I will wind up re-creating the horrors of Stan the Man.

We can't have that. No way. So we have to foul things up. Self-destruct. Then hit the road.

A woman walked by with her yellow Lab. The Lab smelled the ice cream, yanked hard on its leash, buried its muzzle in the melting pile of mint chocolate chip. We had a good laugh over that, even Sarah, then I slipped Tim a couple bucks. The kid went inside, bought himself a fresh cone.

"You shouldn't have done that," said Sarah.

"Why not?"

"Because he has to learn."

I gave my rocky road a good lick. "You're not one of those people who's never done anything wrong, are you?"

Sarah narrowed her eyes. A moment passed. A slight smile broke across her pretty face. "Well, maybe one or two things."

"That's a relief," I told her. Then, "Besides, I didn't buy that cone just for him."

"No?"

"No, I also bought it for me."

"For you?"

"Absolutely. So he'll like me. See, I figure if he likes me there's a better chance you'll like me." No use trying to hide the psychology angle from a Vassar girl. They're too smart. Better to put the goods on the table. Let 'em know what you're up to.

Sarah found my eyes, but this time she pulled away before that eternity thing could settle in again. She licked her cone, looked kind of coy, and oh so beautiful. "Very clever."

"I hope so. Because believe me, I want you to like me."

She enjoyed hearing that. Even made her blush.

We headed home in her BMW 325is convertible. The isle green pearl one. A warm night. The roof down. It felt fine inside that German cockpit. Just right.

I thought about asking her if I could take the wheel, but decided it might be premature for such a request. So instead I just sat back and listened to Tim talk a blue streak from the back seat, something about saving the rain forests and the whales and the ozone for future generations. But then, practically in midsentence, he grew silent.

I looked over my shoulder. Found the kid had conked right out.

"Timothy," said his mother, "has only two speeds: on and off."

We passed the next few minutes talking about the boy: height, weight, grade, birthday, favorite things to do, all the vital statistics. Then, as if by magic, we found ourselves in my driveway, parked behind the rusty old pickup, a dim yellow porch light burning beside the door of the cottage. And suddenly we had to talk about something besides the kid.

I found myself slightly off guard. It must've been the close proximity of such a fine and lovely woman. I could smell her perfume. Soft and muted. Like a rose. Oh yeah, I was fully smitten. Out of my mind. I worked hard to pull myself together. "So, did you have a good time?"

"I did, yes."

"A loaded question."

Sarah nodded.

I looked over my shoulder again at the kid. "He's sound asleep. Want to come in for a minute?" A minute. Right. "I have a nice bottle of wine in the fridge."

She considered the temptation. "I probably shouldn't."

"You're right, you probably shouldn't. But do you want to anyway?"

That stopped her. Gave her something to think about. Covered up her thoughts with a confession. "I did have a good time, you know."

"So does that mean you want to come in, but you're not coming in because you want to and that kind of scares you?"

She had to give that verbal circus a chance to settle. "I just think it's late."

I checked the clock on the dash. "Oh my God, look at that. Almost ten minutes after nine."

A nice big smile. Then, "Maybe some other time."

Bingo. A foot in the door. All I really wanted.

I thought about leaning over, kissing her on the mouth. But I don't know, I felt kind of scared. Like what would happen if she rejected me? I'd be devastated.

So instead I asked, "What about tomorrow?"

"Tomorrow?"

"Sure. Tomorrow is some other time. What do you want to do tomorrow?"

We could see each other clearly in the white light cast by a rising moon. Sarah looked mildly confused, but also kind of excited, maybe even exhilarated. Thinking, no doubt, that it would be far simpler to just say thanks but no thanks, back off now, let life go on as before, try again another day, with another date, let some power greater than herself take control. But at the same time she felt this attraction, powerful and physical, shouting at her to take a chance.

"I don't know," came the voice of ambiguity. "Maybe . . ." and she saw my eyes reflected in the moonlight, "maybe you should call me."

Yes, maybe I should. Maybe I will. Tonight. From Lewey's office.

"I'm sorry, Mrs. Standish," says Glenn Sheldon, P.I., "your husband was not on that six-fifty flight from Newark to Fort Myers."

"You're sure?"

"Not if he was traveling under his own name. And he wasn't on any other flight to Fort Myers that day either. In fact, he wasn't on any Continental flight to Florida that day, the day before, or the day after. Not as Michael Standish."

Wanna bet?

It's not quite eight A.M. up in central Jersey. Already Sheldon sips his third mug of joe. A nasty brew. Super-espresso. At least, he tells himself, I'm not smoking those filthy Camels. He leans back in his chair, feet propped up on his cluttered desk. The office empty, he has his client on the speaker phone.

Sarah sits on the edge of her bed. Our bed. Where she sleeps now alone. She holds the phone to her ear. At this hour she would normally be out foxhunting with her mother, maybe Tim. Maybe me. But not today. Not this morning. This morning she made an excuse, told her mother she had other things to do.

"What?" Iron Kate wanted to know.

"Things," said Sarah.

The Iron One stared at her. Frowned. "I don't want you sitting around the house moping. What's done is done."

Ah, so easy for her to say. Less than a week gone and already the old biddy has written me off. Probably feeling ambivalent about the whole mess: upset she lost her precious pieces of old wood, but overjoyed to have that Standowski creature out from under her roof. So tough to know in life exactly what we really want.

"But what," Sarah asks Sheldon, "if he was traveling under another name?"

"Since it was a domestic flight," answers the P.I., "it would be easy enough to do as long as he paid cash for his ticket."

"So what happens now?"

"It took some time and effort," says Sheldon, "but I managed to get passenger lists for all Newark–Fort Myers flights for the day you think your husband headed south. There are six or seven hundred names, but a lot of them we can eliminate right off the bat: women, couples traveling together under the same name—" Sheldon cuts himself short. Wonders if he should ask, then figures, what the hell? "You're absolutely sure your husband would have been traveling alone?"

Sarah cannot believe she has to put up with this invasion of her privacy. All week long she's been trying to decide what terrible sins she must have committed in this or some other life to undergo such emotional trauma from the men she simply tried to love. First Ricky, then Ron.

Now me.

"Do you mean," she wants to know, "is it possible Michael ran off with another woman, and could they be posturing as a married couple?"

Sheldon's glad he has her on the phone because he can't hide the smirk on his weathered face. "The thought crossed my mind."

"Well, it's impossible. I'm sure he's traveling alone."

Sheldon drains his mug. "Then we can eliminate couples traveling together. We can also eliminate reservations booked several weeks in advance. It sounds like your husband made his move in a pretty hasty fashion. Do you have a fax machine?"

"A fax machine? Yes, we do."

"I'll fax over these passenger lists. I've checked off the names you might want to take a closer look at. They're primarily men, traveling solo, who purchased their tickets less than a week before departure. Take your time, and if you find something interesting, call me. I'll be in the office all morning."

Sarah gives Sheldon the fax number. Says goodbye, hangs up. The fax machine sits down in Katherine's study. Sarah heads downstairs through the vast, empty house. No one else is home. Lucy is off with Katherine and Timothy to help with the horses. And Dorothy is down at the church in Pottersville where she helps out at the day-care center three mornings a week.

Oh yeah, I know their schedules. Right down to when they brush their teeth. I studied them for weeks before moving in with my U-Haul.

Sarah hears the whine of the fax machine as she enters the study. It used to be her father's office. Dark cherry paneling covers the walls. A large desk dominates the space. An antique desk, made of burled walnut, built in Philadelphia before the War for Independence. Too much for me to carry or it wouldn't be there at all.

Inside that walnut desk was where I first glimpsed Iron Kate's insurance policy protecting her nest of antique goodies. Right then and there I made myself a copy of that policy. An important moment along my road to damnation.

The fax machine sits on an old table beside the desk. Sarah picks up the sheets of paper. Drops into the leather desk chair. One glance at the long list of names makes her weary. Sighs. Thinks about Katherine and Timothy out with the hounds. Today, this early in the season, they would be roading, not hunting. Sarah has always enjoyed the peace and serenity of roading. Just ambling along on her trim and muscular gelding, Jabberwocky. Walking and trotting. No jumps, no long runs. Just the horses and the hounds. The gentle morning air.

She studies the list. Sees nothing but an endless blur of strange and unfamiliar names. So many people in the world. Too many. Michael, she knows, would've hunted this season. Last year he learned how to ride: to trot and canter. With his strength and athleticism he proved a quick study. Of course I did. No big deal. All you need's the guts to get up there and do it. And in the summer, after a long search, I found my own mount: a big Dutch warmblood with excellent manners and an easy gait. Thunder, I named him. After some story about horses Jessie had read me as a kid.

Sarah sighs. She tells herself, for the millionth time since I disappeared, that this whole rotten mess is her fault. She thinks she should've seen it coming, should've recognized my insecurities, my need to provide.

She rubs her eyes, looks again at the list. Nothing on the first page. Nothing on the second page. What, she wonders, am I looking for? How will I possibly know what name he might have used?

But even before she finishes this thought, the name leaps off the page, smacks her right between the eyes. "My God!"

She picks up the phone, dials Sheldon's number.

"Sheldon here."

"Mr. Sheldon. It's Sarah Standish."

"Problem with the fax?"

"No, I received it."

Sheldon works on his fifth cup of coffee. Look at him. He's actually vibrating right in his chair. "You have something already?"

"I think so. About halfway down page three."

Sheldon picks up his copy of the passenger list. "I got it."

"Where it says first-class passengers?"

"Right."

"Weston. Edward Weston."

"I see it," says Sheldon. "You think that might be your husband?"

"I'm sure of it."

Sheldon checks his notes. "It fits the profile: a one-way first-class ticket that was purchased on the same day as the flight. But why Edward Weston? What's the significance?"

"I'll explain on the way to Fort Myers."

Now it's Sheldon's turn to sigh. "You're sure you don't want me to go down there and see what I can dig up? If I find something I'll call and let you know."

"I told you yesterday, Mr. Sheldon, we're in this together."

Sheldon takes another gulp of coffee. The guy can't stand Florida, especially in the summer. Too damn hot. Too damn humid. "So when do you want to go?"

"Today," says Sarah. "This afternoon. I just need to take care of a few details first. I'll call you later this morning."

The telephone rings before Sarah gets halfway out of the study. She feels sure it will be me. "Hello?"

"Sarah?"

"Yes?"

"It's Graham."

"Hello, Graham." She hides her disappointment. No way does she want him to know what has happened. "How are you?"

Cracker has not been looking forward to this call. Up most of the night thinking about it. About me. He would prefer to have nothing to do with this business. But Alison keeps insisting it's his obligation to find out what happened, what I've done, how he might help. Even now she lurks at his side. Last night she kept bugging him to call, to get the inside dope from his ex-sister-in-law. Cracker refused, said it could wait till morning. And sure enough, soon after sunrise, Alison started following him around the house with the cordless phone.

"I'm pretty well," he tells her. "What about you?"

"Just fine," lies my sweet. "How's Alison? And the kids?"

"Everyone's great." Cracker wishes this whole conversation would go away. He keeps thinking about his brother. And that bastard Carlson. And about Mike. I told him to stay away from her. And his wife, Alison, right in his face, scowling, waving her arms, mouthing some inaudible orders. He wonders how far he would get if he just made a run for it, headed for the hills with the clothes on his back, his pockets stuffed with Money. Not very far. He knows he'd go crazy in a day and a half without Molly and Tracy. Guilt. Fear. Loneliness.

"They're great kids, Graham. You and Alison are very lucky."

My sweet Sarah: always reserved, polite, concerned for others.

Cracker can feel his wife's hot breath on the back of his neck. "Sarah, listen, I . . ." He searches for the right words. "I heard that Mike, well, I heard he—"

"You heard what, Graham?"

Cracker glances at Alison. Her mouth moves a million miles an hour but no words come out. He answers very quickly. "I heard he left town."

Sarah has been anticipating a conversation like this one for almost a week now. "Left town? Who told you that?"

Cracker wonders if the whole business might be a rumor. "Well, I don't know. Alison heard something . . ."

Alison waves him off. No way does the Bitch want her name dragged into this.

"You mean Mike didn't tell you?" asks Sarah.

"Tell me what?"

"He had to go up to Poughkeepsie. His father's sick."

"Really? No, he didn't tell me."

"It was very sudden. They're not sure what it is yet. He's having tests."

So unlike my love to tell a lie. Almost painful to watch.

A great wave of relief washes over Cracker the Gullible. Then he remembers old man Standowski, that rough-and-tumble Polack. "Is he going to be okay? Mike's father, I mean."

"I'm sure he'll be fine. Listen, Graham, I hate to run but Timothy's waiting for me out in the car."

Another little white lie. Two in one day. That might be a record.

"Well," says Cracker, "okay. Maybe have Mike call me when he gets back."

"I will. Definitely. Bye." Sarah hangs up quickly.

The sound echoes in Cracker's ear. He hangs up the receiver, turns quickly on his wife. "We should get our facts straight before we start jumping to conclusions."

"Why?" demands Alison. "What did she say?"

"Mike's up in Poughkeepsie. His father's sick."

Alison takes a second or two to think about it. "That's bullshit."

"What! Why do you say that?"

"Did Mike say anything to you about his father being sick?"

"No. But it sounds like kind of a sudden thing."

"Give me a break. We know all about Stanislaw Standowski. He's never done a lick to help his son. Do you really think Mike would run to his side if he took ill?"

Good point, Allie, my old flame. Excellent point.

"Yeah, I think he would."

"So let's call and find out."

"Call who?"

"Mike's father in Poughkeepsie."

Cracker's heard enough. "Sarah told me Mike was with his father. That's good enough for me. So let's just leave it alone. Put it to rest."

"What's the harm in calling?"

"No, goddammit!" Cracker heads for the back door, exits, slams it closed.

It looks as though I have everybody riled up.

And there's Sarah: plotting and planning before she runs off to Florida in search of her thieving and wayward husband. First she calls her grandmother Rebecca down on Sanibel Island just west of Fort Myers to make sure the old girl would like a visitor.

Rebecca Crawford laughs. "I'm just sitting here waiting for you, dear. Are you bringing those two handsome men along with you?"

Sarah is relieved to learn her mother has not yet told her grandmother about my vanishing act. "Not this time," she says. "I'm on my own."

"Even better," says Rebecca. "We'll drink whiskey and smoke cigarettes and prowl for men. Mostly blue hairs down here, honey, but a few of them can still dance the two-step." This from a woman in her eighties.

Sarah tells her grandmother she should be there sometime this evening.

She hangs up and packs a suitcase while waiting for Katherine and Timothy to return from the hunt. She goes over in her mind what she will tell her mother. Decides to keep it simple, to say as little as possible.

Early afternoon before she finally gets her mother alone. She finds her in the study. Goes in, closes the door. "I need to get away for a few days."

Iron Kate is immediately suspicious. "Away? Where?"

"To Florida. Sanibel."

"With Timothy?"

"No. Just by myself."

Katherine fixes her eyes on her daughter. Long ago she mastered the art of extracting information from reluctant children, even children who have wandered into their thirties.

Sarah avoids her mother's eyes, but soon launches into an explanation. "I'm always standing by the phone . . . Waiting for him to call . . . Wondering where he is . . . I'm going crazy, Mother. I need to get away."

Katherine does not even bother to blink. A woman who can hold her eyes open for hours. A gift from a lifetime of earnestness. Finally she asks, "You're not going looking for him, are you?"

Sarah's eyes drop to the floor. Little white lie numero tres about to be served up on a silver platter. "Of course not. Where would I look?"

Katherine ignores the question. "Because if you are, Sarah Louise, I just want you to know, you're wasting your time. He's not worth it. Trust me, he's not worth the trouble and aggravation."

Thanks, Kate. I knew I could count on you. Hey, I mean it. It's a psychological thing. The more Mama Kate runs me down, the harder her daughter will work to bring me back into the fold. At least this is how I read it.

Sarah sighs. She wants in the worst way to get away from her mother. She knows now that I was right: we never should have agreed to live at TREETOPS. We should have moved out right after the wedding. We should have found our own place, been on our own.

I wonder though: Would it have changed anything? Would it have made any difference? Would our own home, our own house, have made me more secure? Would I have stayed put? Left my mother-in-law's antiques well enough alone?

I don't know. So tough to say.

I know this: I did not bother to call Ms. Browne after our first date. At least not on the telephone. On the morning after our evening of pizza and ice cream, I decided to just show up at her door. In person.

But first I had to see Cracker. I found him weeding the azalea bed out by the swimming pool.

He looked up from his work. "Where you been, Mike? I thought you were supposed to help me today."

"I'm having some trouble with the pickup. Looks like a bad distributor. Do you think I could borrow the Wagoneer for a trip down to the auto parts store?"

Cracker stood up, straightened his back. "You sure that's all it is?"

The pickup ran like a top. I just didn't want to wind up the Brownes' driveway in that rusty old piece of sheet metal. "Pretty sure, yeah."

Cracker, my old buddy, reached into his pocket, dug out the keys, and tossed them to me. "Try to get back before lunch, okay? I need some help taking some dead limbs off that old Norway maple over by the tennis court."

I nodded. "No problem. Just one other stop I need to make. I'll be back in a snap."

Half an hour later, all showered and clean-shaven, I knocked on the Brownes' front door.

Dorothy pulled it open. "Yes?"

I gave her a smile. "Good morning. I'm looking for Sarah."

Dorothy is almost as protective of Sarah as Mother Kate. Had practically been the girl's wet nurse. "You are, are you?"

"Yes, ma'am." I could see I'd have to soften her up.

"Is she expecting you?"

"Absolutely."

"And you are?"

I feigned a disappointed sigh. "Oh, how quickly they forget. I'm Mike Standish, Dorothy. We met at the barbecue."

Dorothy couldn't hide her pleasure upon hearing me remember her name. "Oh yes, I remember now."

"No," I said, and shook my head, "I don't think so. But that's okay, you had a flock of men around you when we met."

Dorothy, not a day under sixty, actually blushed. "I was probably carrying a tray of hors d'oeuvres."

"You know, I think you're right. Some kind of pasta shell stuffed with crab meat. Delicious. A little touch of heaven. I'll bet I had a dozen of them."

Dorothy tried to wipe the smile off her face. No luck. "I can see you're a talker, Mr. Standish."

"Not me, Dorothy. Now what about Sarah?"

"She's down at the stable."

"And where would that be?"

Dorothy told me, adding that I could walk or drive.

I chose to walk. It would give me time to clear my thoughts. I'd been up most of the night, tossing and turning, an emotional whirlwind.

I followed Dorothy's directions: across the lawn, through the woods, down the bridle path. As I neared the end of the path I spotted the stable. And on the near side of the stable I spotted Sarah. Dressed once again in riding britches and high black riding boots. She stood next to a large gray horse, a hose in one hand, a long-handled brush in the other. The animal whinnied, tossed its head from side to side. "Oh Jabber, stay still. Don't make such a fuss."

I slipped into the shade of a nearby oak. I watched as Sarah washed that beast carefully, even lovingly. Washed his back, his neck, his belly, his chest, his legs, his loins, his flowing white mane. And all while she talked to him: told him how wonderful he was, how beautiful, how sweet. I'd never heard anyone talk to an animal that way before. My old man hated animals, same as he hated people. We never had pets. Not even a hamster or a goldfish. I stood there with my mouth open as that pretty girl spoke to her horse with perfect intimacy. And when she finished she threw her arms around the great beast's neck, covered his snout with kisses.

I felt an ambiguous explosion of emotion: attraction and repulsion, clarity and confusion, a pull to move forward and a push to retreat. I wanted that pretty girl down there, that beautiful young woman, to put her arms around my neck. I wanted her to love me the same way she loved that beast.

A man came out of the stable. He was short and slight, walked with a limp. He wore overalls and work boots. One shoulder hung lower than the other. He crossed to Sarah. "Want me to turn out Jabberwocky now, missy?"

Sarah smiled at the crooked little man. "That would be nice, Wiley. Maybe we should put him out in the east pasture where he can find some shade under the apple trees. It looks like another scorcher."

"Absolutely right there, missy. Hot, hot, hot."

Sarah attached a lead rope to the horse's halter, handed the rope to Wiley. The man led the horse away. Sarah watched them go. Her expression almost forlorn. As though she might never see that animal again.

I wanted her to someday look at me that way. Another desire ominously satisfied.

After a few moments she disappeared into the stable.

I slipped out of the shade, hopped over the split-rail fence. Cut across a dusty paddock. Stopped in front of the large open door of the stable. Inside, out of the bright sunshine, only darkness and shadows. I couldn't see a thing. Squinted. Took a step or two forward, passed through the open doorway.

And suddenly, there she stood. We bumped right into each other.

"Mike!"

"Sorry, I didn't mean to scare you."

"I didn't think anyone was here."

"Just you and me."

Sarah avoided my eyes. She stepped outside, into the bright sunlight. Glanced past me, down the gravel drive in a vain search for her four-legged friend.

I turned, took a look as well. "Good-looking animal," I told her. "I saw you giving him a bath as I came down the bridle path."

Sarah smiled. "That's my boy. Jabberwocky."

"Jabberwocky?"

"It's from a poem my father used to read me."

"Sounds like a pretty wild name."

Sarah glanced at me. "So, do you ride?"

"Horses?"

She nodded.

"Not a lick."

"You should learn. It's great fun. And good exercise."

"Always seemed kind of rough on the horse."

"Not at all," said Sarah. "They love it."

My heart, I swear to God, raced at a full gallop. I could feel it pounding against my rib cage. I took a long deliberate look at her. Couldn't help myself. She was lean from head to toe. Not an ounce of fat anywhere on her body.

She held a bridle in her right hand, focused her attention on it. All those straps and buckles.

I kicked at the dirt. Struggled to find the right thing to say.

And finally, after what felt like an hour or more, I said, very softly, practically a whisper, "I've been thinking about you."

She kept her hands and eyes riveted on that tangle of leather and steel. "You have?"

I nodded. And knew I had to go for it. Nothing to lose. "Ever since I stepped out of your car last night."

She glanced up then, took another look for Jabberwocky. Couldn't find her friend anywhere.

"You kept me awake," I told her, "until the wee hours of the morning."

Probably she didn't want to trust that line. But she liked the way it sounded. It earned me a small, brief smile.

That smile gave me confidence. "I couldn't get your beautiful eyes out of my thoughts."

She gave me a look then, her head tipped slightly to the side. Not sure if she should buy this line either.

"All night long," I told her, "I kept thinking I'd made a terrible mistake."

Her eyes narrowed. "Mistake?"

We stood very close. Only a couple feet apart. "Yeah," I told her. "Last night sitting in the car, I had this overwhelming desire to touch your cheek, to kiss you on·the lips. But I chickened out, didn't have the guts to do it. And then you drove away and I spent the next several hours thinking I'd missed my chance."

A moment of silence. It could have gone either way. She could have laughed right in my face. But it didn't happen. Sarah, you see, had been up most of the night as well, having similar thoughts about me. Admitted as much in the not too distant future.

Now, hearing my confession, she allowed herself to relax.

I took a step toward her. Leaned forward. Our faces close. Only a few inches apart. We tipped our heads, licked our lips. Knew exactly what was coming. Our eyes fell closed. Our lips met. Gently. Softly. Oh yeah, nothing on earth quite like a first kiss. Makes the body feel alive. Electric.

In the middle of the kiss I opened my eyes. Found to my surprise Sarah staring straight at me. She liked this all right, liked it just fine.

I slipped my arms around her waist. Drew her close. Pressed her chest against mine. The air ran out of our lungs.

A fortnight came and went. Two weeks. Fourteen days. Fourteen nights. In the long and often tempestuous history of Western civilization, those fourteen days, if memory serves, proved remarkably benign. No wars. No floods. No earthquakes. No important decrees from the White House. Or the State House. No significant increase in the number of homicides. No more acts of domestic violence than usual. No drastic shifts in the earth's rotation or in the Milky Way.

Unless, of course, I missed something. I was, admittedly, preoccupied; no more concerned with political or social events than with the rings circling playfully around planet Saturn.

What's that old cliché? Love makes the world go around. Perhaps it does. That and Sex and Greed and Gravity. And Money most assuredly.

Oh yeah, up in those monied, rolling hills of Pottersville, New Jersey, love was definitely in the air.

Sarah and I had by that time sought out one another's company every day for fourteen days. Sarah told me, in a whisper, that she hadn't seen the same man every day for fourteen days since her marriage to Graham's brother, Ron.

What did we do? I don't know. I can't remember. We kissed and talked and yukked it up. I made Sarah laugh. Laugh and giggle. As simple as that. Girls like boys who make them laugh. At least at first. I made Sarah laugh with my stupid faces, my dirty jokes, my slightly skewed sense of humor.

Mix the laughter with the passionate kisses we placed upon each other's lips, and suddenly you've got romance knocking at the door.

Who knows why these things happen? Chemistry? Opportunity? The luck of the draw?

Sarah told me that my kisses made her weak in the knees. "And not many men," she added, "have been able to do that."

"How many?" I wanted to know.

But she wouldn't say. She kept the magic number to herself.

Oh yeah, we spent time together, lots and lots of time. Much of it down at the stable. Sarah gave me riding lessons on Jabberwocky. But a one-hour lesson seemed to take all afternoon. Even into the evening.

I remember us sitting outside, our backs against the wall of the stable, the sun setting beyond the sycamores, and Sarah saying, "I can't explain why, Michael, but I feel so comfortable with you. It's only been a week but I feel like we're old friends, like I've known you for years."

That night, late, after midnight, all worked up, unable to sleep, I called Maggie Jane.

"I'm in love," I told her.

"What? It's the middle of the night."

"She's beautiful, Maggie. And sweet. And smart. Definitely smarter than me."

"Michael! What are you babbling about?"

"Sarah Louise, Maggie. I want you to come down and meet her."

She told me she would. As soon as she could get away.

At the end of that first fortnight, Sarah and I took a bold and scary step forward.

It happened over at my place. At my palace beneath the pines. The first time she'd actually ventured inside my domain. For two weeks we'd rendezvoused almost exclusively over at the Brownes' stable. We made quite a show with those horseback riding lessons to cover our true intentions. I responded by learning to trot and canter with surprising speed. But on the thirteenth day not much progress was made. On the thirteenth day we didn't even bother to put a saddle on Jabberwocky. We just allowed the mellow-mannered gelding to wander around the ring while we climbed the ladder to the hayloft.

We lay in the hay, kissing and goofing around, when suddenly we heard Wiley call from out in the paddock. "Missy, are you about! Is there something you want done with the Jabber?"

I began to imitate the stable hand's delivery. Sarah began to giggle. I put my hand over her mouth. She put her hand over mine.

Wiley kept calling. We kept giggling. Finally he went away.

That's when we realized we needed a tad more privacy. So I invited Sarah for lunch. And reluctantly, but with enormous anticipation, she accepted.

The next day, the fourteenth day, we sat at the small wooden table out on the screened-in porch sipping lemonade and picking at some chicken salad sandwiches I'd bought that morning. Mostly we stared into each other's eyes. I imagine we both had exactly the same look on our faces that fledgling lovers have been casting for the past millennium.

Anyone familiar with that look, and let's face it, most of us are, could clearly see we had taken the plunge.

Sarah, in time, shook herself loose from our latest trance. Her practical side stepped to the fore. "I really think you should go see him."

This threw me. "Go see who?"

"Uncle Colin."

"Oh, right." I smiled, leaned my elbows on the table. "I told you I would."

"I could call. Let him know you're coming."

A few days earlier I'd made the mistake of mentioning Uncle Colin's job offer to Sarah. Mentioned it not because I intended to pursue it, but because I thought she'd be impressed. But ever since I'd told her, she'd been pushing me to go see him.

"Don't call him," I told her. "I'd rather just pop around and see him."

"But you'll go?"

"Sure. I'll go. As soon as I have time." Sarah, my sweet, didn't know yet that I really don't like being pushed.

"I think you should."

I gave her another smile, then leaned in a little closer. "Of course you think I should. But that's only because you can't believe you're falling for some guy with no job and no money who lives in a shack out in the woods."

"That's not true."

"You mean you're not falling for me?"

Sarah's face gave a little flush. "No," she said. "I mean, yes. I mean, that's not what I mean. I mean, it's a good opportunity. Working for Crawford and Browne. You said he offered."

"He did offer. In a moment of profound drunkenness."

"Well."

I had to laugh. Couldn't help myself. "I feel sure, Ms. Browne, that you would like to spiffy up my past. Dress me in a suit. Make me more respectable. Introduce me around as your special friend, Mr. Michael Standish, young Wall Street tycoon, Madison Avenue exec."

Sarah smiled and frowned at the same time. She would not have admitted this, but my future bride had already become keenly aware of both the social and financial chasms dividing her world from mine.

I pushed aside our chicken salad sandwiches. "And that's okay," I told her. "It's perfectly natural. In fact, I find your desire rather touching. And your solution quite reasonable. But a real job? With Crawford and Browne? That might be more load than this mule can bear. I'm a starving artist. Dedicated to his art. Not much interested in the materialist struggle. There: I've warned you in advance."

Then, before she could respond, I crept up onto the table, put my right hand around the back of her neck, and drew her close. A soft sigh slipped from her mouth. Her eyes fell closed. I kissed her hard on the lips. After half a dozen kisses, I slipped off the table, took her by the hand, and led her into the living room. The brand-new queen size bed loomed there, massive and omnipotent, practically filling the space.

But Sarah, almost as a reflex, steered clear of the mattress and its profound emotional entanglements. "The artist," she said, "promised to show me some of his creations."

Indeed I had. I loosened my grip on her waist. "Follow me."

We stepped gingerly around the bed and into what would normally have been the bedroom. I flipped on the light. The room, even the windows, had been painted jet black. I closed the door, turned off the light. Total darkness consumed us. The middle of the day outside but inside not a single speck of light.

"Pretty neat, huh?"

"Pretty dark."

I flipped on the light. "To make fine prints you need a split second of properly controlled light followed by a pure supply of absolute darkness. Anything less and all you achieve is mediocrity."

Sarah took a long, slow look around the room. She could see everything had its place. A good darkroom demands order, cleanliness, simplicity. There was a dry side and a wet side. The enlarger dominated the dry side. It stood on its own steel frame, massive, and, to my eyes anyway, magnificent. The wet side had a large stainless steel sink and a long Formica counter. I'd recently installed the sink and counter with the help of the Cramers' plumber.

I opened the small fireproof safe sitting on the floor behind the enlarger, pulled out a metal box. "Here's some prints I've been working on."

The box contained the photographs I'd taken in Newark before getting shot in the shoulder. Working night and day, I had made close to fifty prints, a few 5 x 7s, but most of them 8 x 10s. Sarah's eyes locked on to the black and white picture lying on top: two black men standing on a sidewalk at night, the one black man with a gun held firmly against the other black man's head: Slammer and Ernie outside of Ernie's Bar & Grill.

"See that guy with the gun?"

Sarah nodded, her eyes and mouth pretty much wide open.

"That's the guy who blew the hole in my shoulder. It happened just a minute or so after I popped that shot."

It was an impressive photo. Maybe the most powerful photograph I have ever taken. Full of tension and clarity and impending violence. And the print itself: perfect. Clean and sharp and focused. A splendid blend of purpose and contrast.

One by one Sarah went through the prints in the box. An art major at Vassar, she had studied photography. Possessed an intellectual knowledge of the craft. I stood at her side and watched nervously as she looked at the photographs. My photographs. I wanted her to like them, to be impressed. I wanted her to think I had talent.

Most of the photos were of black men drinking booze and smoking cigarettes, talking jive and playing pool, hanging out at Ernie's and on their front stoops. These men had an almost desperate need to look cool and collected, utterly unaffected by the urban decay crushing their lives. But in at least a few of the shots I had managed to dig beneath this veneer. Fear screamed out from many of the photos. You could read and feel the fear sometimes in their eyes, sometimes in their mouths, sometimes in their body language. But it was definitely fear. Raw, unadulterated fear.

Sarah went through the entire box. Slowly and methodically. Without hardly saying a word. This was a world she did not recognize, that she only superficially knew existed.

Finally, she cleared her throat and said, rather softly, "These are incredible, Michael."

I breathed a sigh of relief. I thought they were pretty good myself. But believe me: I'd been working my tail off on those black and white prints into the wee hours of the night in full anticipation of Sarah's visit. They had been meticulously prepared and arranged. I definitely wanted Sarah to think I had a purpose in life.

Sarah had more to say. Much more. She wanted to praise. Sarah, like Jessie, is a praiser. A firm believer in building self-esteem. Undoubtedly another reason why I fell in love with her.

"These are important photographs," she said. "Not only powerful, but relevant from a sociological point of view. They should be on display."

I think I shrugged. Like the black men depicted, very cool. At least on the surface. "I don't know. I'm not really into social causes. Whitey captures Darkie on film during rough moment. I just like a good photograph. One that kicks you in the pants when you look at it with your eyes."

"But, Michael," she protested, "these images transcend photography. Don't you see? An entire culture is under the gun here. This is an amazing portrayal of black urban life."

"Whatever you see is okay with me. I just look through the viewfinder and pop the shot." Again, very cool and detached. Then, to show her I had some history behind me, I threw this into the mix: "I agree with Edward Weston. He said photography is the mirror of a man's mind."

"Edward Weston . . ." Sarah thought about the name. "I remember some of his work from college."

"I have whole books of his stuff," I told her. "But let's not look at them now."

I flipped off the light and led Sarah back into the living room. The bed loomed even larger than before. But this time she made no effort to avoid it. No, this time we sat on the edge of the bed, upon my thin cotton blanket. We shared a kiss. And then another kiss. And another. In no time at all we reached a horizontal state. Our bodies, so tame for the past two weeks, quickly became entangled. We rolled from one side of the bed to the other. Finally, the tempest ebbed. Momentarily. We both needed a few seconds to catch our breath.

Sarah, I could see by the wonder in her eyes, could hardly believe her lack of inhibition. Some deep physical attraction was at work here, one that she had rarely if ever experienced before. She had dated men for months without actually lying down on a bed with them. And then she had often only done so out of a sense of obligation, a woman's role in the relationship. But here, with me, as she admitted later, she both wanted and needed to feel her body close against mine.

We kissed and caressed some more. Slowly this round, as though we possessed all the time in the world. I kissed her neck. She kissed my ears and my eyelids. I felt weak, sapped of strength.

We wrapped our bodies together. Arms and legs.

Don't ask me to explain. I have no idea why two people can so suddenly and unexpectedly connect physically and emotionally.

We lay side by side, our faces just inches apart, our noses almost touching. I smiled. Sarah smiled back. God, she was beautiful. I touched the tip of my nose to her nose.

"Eskimos," she said.

Our hands became more active. We had on shorts and short-sleeve shirts. We ran the tips of our fingers up and down each other's thighs. I put my hand under her shirt, gently touched her stomach, drew circles around her belly-button.

I felt all the air run out of her lungs.

"You know," she whispered, "we can't make love."

I looked at her, for a moment confused. Then, "Sure we can. Of course we can."

"No," she said, "we can't."

"Why not?"

Sarah fixed her pretty eyes on mine. "AIDS," she mumbled.

I felt myself pull away. One desperate little word fell from my mouth. "What?"

"We can't make love," Sarah told me, "until we get tested for AIDS."

I relaxed. Had myself a nice deep breath. "Tested. Right."

"It's the responsible thing to do. I feel pretty strongly about it."

"You're right," I said. "These days you never know."

"I think it's prudent to have a test before getting involved with a new partner."

I wasn't sure how much I wanted to hear about Sarah's other partners. I just wanted to be her lover. The best and most satisfying lover she'd ever had. "Have you been tested before?"

"Yes."

"I haven't."

She smiled, touched my face. "Don't worry, it doesn't hurt."

"So what do I do?"

"You go to the doctor. You can go to my doctor if you don't have one. I'll give you her name and number. She's great."

I felt my skin crawling with all this AIDS talk. The dreaded disease was not my favorite topic of conversation.

I tried to lighten the load. "So let's go down and get tested. We'll be making love by midnight."

Sarah gave me another smile. "It takes a week or more to get the results."

"A week or more! We'll never make it."

"We'll make it."

"Not if we keep climbing into bed like this we won't."

Sarah laughed, kissed me on the mouth, assured me it would be well worth the wait. Then she bounded off the bed. "I have to go," she announced. "Timothy hates when I'm late picking him up at school."

We pulled ourselves together. I walked Sarah out to the car. And who do you think drove up just as we indulged in a passionate goodbye kiss? Why my good buddy and her ex-brother-in-law, of course.

Sarah and I stood at the door of her Bimmer, lips glued together, as the Grand Wagoneer came cruising in beneath the canopy of white pines. We both heard the wheels rolling over the gravel. Sarah tried to pull away, put some distance between us, but I, bad boy that I am, held her close, kissed her again.

Cracker got a good look at us. No doubt it made him angry. He didn't know, couldn't decide, if he wanted to run me down or zoom away without saying a word. But being a polite, well-bred, upper-middle-class white boy, Cracker did neither. He parked the Wagoneer, stepped out, and did his best to engage us in courteous conversation exactly as his mother had taught him.

He nodded, even tried to smile. "Sarah. Mike."

Sarah blushed. "Hello, Graham."

"How you doing, Cracker?"

"Me? I'm doing okay." Another smile. This one slightly twisted. And then his facade cracked. "What about you two? How are you two doing?" Emphasis on the word two.

We could all three hear the bite in Cracker's voice. Couldn't miss it.

"We're doing great, buddy. Just had ourselves some lunch."

"Is that right?"

"Yup. Sorry I didn't invite you. Maybe next time."

"I can't wait."

I laughed. But Sarah blushed. Again. Then she checked her watch. "God, it's almost three. I have to run. Timothy will kill me."

Cracker practically scowled at her. "Alison left more than half an hour ago to pick up Molly." His tone had turned icy, as though this offense at being a few minutes late picking up her son proved beyond a reasonable doubt that her secret tryst with the scoundrel Mike was not only disgusting and amoral, but proved her inadequacy as a parent.

Graham Cramer: closet moralist.

Sarah, however, did not appreciate the insinuation. "Well then," she said, her displeasure only faintly veiled, "I guess Alison is just a superior mother."

Cracker, rebuffed, did not respond.

Sarah opened the door of her BMW. I had my hand on her waist. She knew I wanted a goodbye kiss. She wanted one as well. But not with her ex-brother-in-law standing guard. Glaring at her. Oh, she thought (I could feel her thinking it), to hell with him. To hell with all of them. I have been so good for so long. She turned then and kissed me mightily on the mouth.

Before I could explore for more, she slipped into the coupe and turned the key. That finely tuned German engine fired immediately. She put the transmission into gear, waved goodbye, and drove off.

Ah, the subtle nuances and thoughtful innuendoes of lovers, friends, and foes at work and at play. They make the daily grind so much more entertaining.

We watched the Bimmer disappear in a haze of dust and evergreens. And then Cracker turned on his old pal. All pretense at civility ran away.

"You're fucking her, aren't you?"

"That's none of your damn business."

"You son of a bitch."

"I don't think I deserve that."

"I can't believe you're fucking her already."

"I didn't say I was."

"But you are?"

"Not a chance."

"You're not?"

"We're just friends."

"Bullshit. Are you or aren't you?"

"Let's put it this way, old buddy: if not yet, soon." He deserved it. Still, I ducked, just in case he tried to deck me.

"I thought I told you to keep your grubby little Polack hands off her."

"Ah, so that's the nut. It's an ethnic thing. I'm too dirty to touch the precious white meat."

"No, that's not it at all. I just know what a slimy rotten scumball you are when it comes to women."

I shook my head. "You got it all wrong, pal."

Cracker turned into a mimic. "You got it all wrong, pal."

"What's the matter, Cracker? You jealous?"

"No, I'm not jealous. I just don't want to see her get hurt."

I turned almost serious. "She's a big girl, Graham. Older and wiser than either you or me."

"That's very touching, Standish. Too bad she has no idea yet who she's dealing with."

"And who's she dealing with?"

"A selfish, reckless, irresponsible prick."

"Very nice, old buddy. Although, I think you're getting yourself all worked up over nothing. We've had lunch a few times. What's the big deal?"

He glared at me. Then, finally, "I've known you a long time, Mike."

Whatever that meant.

I figured we'd said enough. Better now to redirect the conversation. "Didn't you want me to help you do something this afternoon?"

"Yeah. That's why I drove over here in the first place. I need some help cutting down some dead limbs."

"Sounds like a very vital project. We better get after it right away. Before the sun goes down on the Cramer way of life."

Cracker ignored my digs. All he wanted was the last word. "Just watch your step. Sarah's like family. She's like a sister to me."

More like a gilded lover, thought I, but I kept the notion to myself.

A few days later I went to see Sarah's doctor over in Far Hills. I would've gone sooner, but feared, I suppose, failing the test. Coming up positive.

I also had to wait a few days because of Cracker. He kept me laboring like a dog. From sunup till sundown. Hauling and shoveling, digging and cutting, planting and pruning. My punishment for kissing Sarah.

Probably it's some kind of third-generation immigrant thing, but I profoundly loathe manual labor. Hate it with a passion. I've done it over the years to put a few pennies in my pocket, but never with any great joy or fervor. My granddaddy, Josep Standowski, broke his back in that filthy ball bearing factory for most of his adult life. Worked himself to a frazzle so some fat cat could live the life of Riley up in the hills above the Hudson. And my old man, even though he probably deserves worse, has spent the better part of his life hauling a sack stuffed with electric bills and L.L. Bean catalogues up and down the streets of Poughkeepsie. A well-trained chimp could have done the same. I decided when still a lad that the time had come for the Standowski clan to take it easy, put their feet up, stop and smell the roses.

Maybe that's one of the reasons why, after my visit to the doc's, I decided to drop by for a visit with Uncle Colin. His office stood practically right next door to the doctor's office. On a quiet side street lined with mature maples and expensive late-model imports.

I say one of the reasons because surely I had other reasons as well. I was sick and tired of manual labor, yes, but I also had a pretty girl on my mind. And I wanted to make that girl happy. So I went to see her uncle.

The offices of Crawford & Browne Investments, Inc. did not look like much. Not from out on the street. Nothing but a big old three-story house: drab, light brown paint on the clapboards, drabber, dark brown paint on the trim and on the shutters, some ratty-looking bushes lining the foundation. It did not impress. I guess I had expected something far grander. It looked like the kind of house where I might rent a room up in the attic for a hundred and fifty a month. No way did it look like a place where people made fat wads of cash. But the small sign hanging on the front porch assured me I'd come to the right place: CRAWFORD & BROWNE INVESTMENTS, INC.

I straightened my collar, gathered my lies, stuffed them into my pockets, and set forth to see if I could talk my way into a cozy corner office.

An older woman occupied the desk just inside the front door. Anne Compton, I found out later, had been with the company for twenty years. Short and plump, but with long, slender fingers that could type a million words a minute, Anne served as secretary, receptionist, bouncer, and confidante. She basically ran the show.

I stepped up to her desk, gave her a smile. "Good morning."

She glanced over her half glasses. "Good morning. May I help you?"

"Yes. Mike Standish to see Mr. Crawford."

"Do you have an appointment?"

Another smile. "No," I said. "No appointment."

She gave me the once-over. "I'm afraid Mr. Crawford is very busy this morning, Mr. Standish. It might be better if you had an appointment. This is a business call, I assume."

"No, not really. Just in town and thought I'd drop by to say hello."

Her steely blue eyes gave me an inquisitive stare. She'd been around awhile, had seen and heard it all. "So this is a social call?"

"Yes, ma'am. A social call."

Now Anne undoubtedly knew Mr. Crawford was up in his office doing importance business, probably practicing his putting or his fly casting. But she also knew he did not like being interrupted. Her job was to run interference, protect her boss from all lawyers, bankers, and solicitors.

I gave her a nudge. "Go ahead, give the old boy a buzz."

Anne, I like to think, could not resist my smile. She pressed the intercom. "Mr. Crawford?"

Colin Crawford's voice came through loud and clear on the speaker. "What is it, Anne?"

"A Mr. Mike Standish here to see you."

"Standish? What's it about?"

"A personal call, sir."

"I don't know any Standish. Ask him what he wants."

I had to think fast. Leaned in close to the desk. "Good morning, Mr. Crawford. It's me, Mike Standish. We met at your sister's barbecue a few weeks ago. Out in the gazebo. You and me and Bill Winslow."

I heard Colin laugh. Oh yeah, he remembered. "Right. You and me and Winslow. Send him up, Anne. Just make sure he doesn't have any whiskey on him."

Colin Crawford's office occupied the entire third floor of that old house. The second floor housed various engineers, architects, brokers, and salesmen, but Colin kept the top floor for his own use. He used to share it with his partner and brother-in-law, Sarah's father, Thomas Browne, but after Thomas died Colin decided to drive the company solo.

A wide spiral stairway led to the third floor. I wound my way up. Colin met me on the landing. He was a tall man, still trim and fit, with a red face and a short crop of sandy hair. Carried one of those long-shafted putters in his left hand, the kind that lets you stand upright. His right hand reached out to me. I shook it. It tried to crush the bones in my palm. I forced myself not to wince.

"Okay," Colin Crawford roared, "sure. I remember you. Come on in. Tell me what I can do for you today."

I followed Colin into his office. A vast wide open space: massive mahogany desk on the far side of the room between a pair of floor-to-ceiling windows. A leather sofa and two leather armchairs in front of the desk. A drafting table against one of the walls. A wooden box filled with rolled blueprints. Some bookcases crammed with books and magazines. And that was about it. A putting green made out of artificial turf filled the middle of the room. Half a dozen golf balls lay scattered across the green.

"You play golf, Standish?"

I hated golf. "Sure, when I can find the time."

"Has to be the most boring game man has ever invented," announced Crawford as he stood over a ball and knocked it squarely into the cup. "A game designed primarily to drive men insane. But an excellent business tool. You invite your prey to your private club, force him out under a hot summer sun, get him snookered with a few chilled martinis, make him think he's the funniest, wittiest son of a bitch in the land, and then, BOOM!, you take the sucker for a ride down Money Lane, stick him for every dollar he's got." Crawford knocked another ball into the cup. "Get the picture, Standish?"

I nodded, then, realizing my mouth hung open, I closed it.

"So what's up, kid? Something on your mind? Or is this strictly social?"

I figured it wouldn't do me much good to beat around the bush. Not with this guy. "I have a job on my mind."

"A job, huh?"

"Yes, I'm getting bored with my present position. That day at your sister's, you mentioned something to me about a sales job." I waited for him to respond, but when he didn't, I quickly added, "A few days ago I was talking with your niece. She thought it would be an excellent idea if I came by to talk to you."

Crawford took a break from his putting. Gave me a glance. "Sarah?"

"Right."

"Now there's one hell of a fine-looking girl," said Colin. "You got designs on that one?"

"Sarah?" I shook my head. "No, we're just friends."

"Don't bullshit me, son. No man's just friends with a woman like that."

"No, really, I—"

"Maybe she's a pain in the ass like her mother," Uncle Colin continued. "I don't know. But I get the feeling she's more like her old man, a little more easygoing. Tom Browne was one easygoing guy. Best friend I ever had. He loved a good time. Now Kate, she's my little sister, but I swear to God, even as a kid, she never knew how to have any fun. As serious as the damn Pope that one." Crawford knocked his next putt past the cup. "Shit! So tell me, Standish, what do you sell?"

"Medical supplies," I answered, without a moment's hesitation. "For J&J."

"So what's the problem?"

"I'm sick of selling surgical gloves and sutures. I'd like to try my hand at selling something a little less depressing. And I'm tired of working for such a big outfit. Too much politics."

Crawford looked me in the eye and nodded. "I know what you mean. We built an office building for J&J about ten, twelve years ago. What a bunch of ass-kissing, pass-the-buck schmucks they were. Not a man among them. No balls at all. So we screwed them good on the cost overruns. Made a killing." He got a big charge out of this. Had himself quite a belly laugh. "I wouldn't want to work for the bastards. A bunch of girls in fancy suits if you ask me."

Crawford didn't wear a suit. Wore khakis, loafers, a blue golf shirt. Handed me the putter. "Go ahead, give it a go."

I did as ordered.

Crawford crossed to that big mahogany desk. Opened a few drawers, searched around inside for a minute or so. Swore a few times. Finally found what he was looking for. Closed the drawers, walked back to the putting green. He held up a brand-new, unused pencil. Just a regular, yellow, number two, lead pencil. "Okay, Standish, here you go."

I took the pencil from him. Waited a second or two for an explanation, then asked, "You want me to fill out an application?"

"Hell no."

"So what do you want me to do with the pencil?"

"I want you to sell it to me."

"Sell it to you?"

"That's right, kid."

"Now?"

"Right now. If you can sell me that pencil, even though I already own it, then I might be able to find you a spot here at Crawford and Browne."

Hotter than dripping candle wax here on Devil's Cay. Too hot to think. Middle of the day. High noon. Nothing to do till dusk but hang around Lewey's bar with a glass of ice water in one hand and a bottle of beer in the other.

Maybe this would be a good time to pause, take a look at Sarah's roots. This whole Crawford & Browne business. Crawford and Browne: blue bloods to the bone. Oh yeah, Sarah's familial story strikes a stark contrast to my own. Go back just a few generations and you'll find my ancestors digging potatoes in the Irish muck, cleaning out other people's crappers in downtown Warsaw.

But my bride's family, now that's a loftier tale. To catch up with them, we need to go back, way back, in fact, to one of the first incursions of Europeans upon these New World shores. Remember the *Mayflower*? Well, one of the passengers was Mr. Peter Browne, twenty-year-old bachelor from Sussex. Not much is known about what Pete did before boarding the *Mayflower* on September 16, 1620, but we know he survived the journey to America and became part of the original settlement headed by Mr. John Alden and Captain Myles Standish (no relation, as I've said before, to yours truly). For a hundred years or more it was believed Peter Browne died in 1633 without leaving a wife or heirs. But in truth he had a son. And that son begat another son who begat another son, right up through the end of the twentieth century, some twelve or fourteen generations of Brownes.

Now all this talk of direct *Mayflower* descendancy may leave you either waxing nostalgic or feeling sick to your stomach depending upon your ancestral point of view, but believe me, it meant a hell of a lot to the Brownes. They've had their noses in the air for three hundred years because their ancestor rode over here on that rickety old sailing ship. The fact that Pete may have been a common crook (à la their latest in-law) or a religious fanatic did nothing to squelch their pride or enthusiasm.

Was I impressed when I learned of their *Mayflower* connection? Yeah, I guess so. Beats being forced out of Warsaw in the middle of the night by the Nazi horde. But once I began to know the family better, I wondered what difference it really made. I mean, what did it prove? Mama Kate, direct *Mayflower* darling, scion of one of our founding families, Daughter of the American Revolution, was still a snob and a bitch and a racist.

But I don't want to get personal here. Just want to keep moving.

We don't want to get bogged down trying to trace a dozen or more generations of Brownes. We'll just go back a generation or two, just far enough so you can see how profoundly different were the lives of Sarah's grandparents compared to mine. Trust me: we won't find any Brownes trudging penniless on foot from Manhattan north to Poughkeepsie in order to spend thirty years toiling in a ball bearing factory. Nope, the WASPs you are about to meet never once trudged or toiled. They had others do the trudging and toiling for them.

All four of Sarah's grandparents were born right here in the good old U.S. of A. They all came from solid English stock with a touch of the old German thrown in to make them tough, stubborn, and uncompromising. All were pure Protestants of the Presbyterian faith who, like most good Presbyterians, attended church services on a semiregular basis regardless of whether they wanted to or not.

Sarah's maternal grandmother, Rebecca Peabody Crawford, residing now on Sanibel Island, Florida, was the only grandparent not born with a sterling silver spoon in her mouth. Her father, Mathias Peabody, was a professor of economics at Sarah Lawrence College. Becky earned a degree in comparative literature from that same school. A rebellious young lady, and, they say, an independent thinker, Becky enjoyed smoking cigarettes and talking deep into the night about the vital new work being done by the expatriate American writers like Gertrude Stein, Sherwood Anderson, and John Dos Passos. Fancied herself a writer, but in truth she was a far better talker.

The man who would marry Becky, Mr. Richard Crawford, found Miss Peabody irresistible. Proposed a week after their first date, a riotous affair culminating at the Cotton Club up in Harlem wherein several blue bloods were arrested and charged with drunkenness and disorderly conduct. Becky laughed right in Richard's face when he asked for her hand.

"You can't be serious," she said. "I have far more interesting and entertaining things to do than become your whore and domestic servant."

After graduating Becky sailed for Paris where she wrote a sexually explicit novel that never found a publisher and entered into a lustful, scandalous affair with a married band-leader of Italian descent. Their romance faded after Becky became pregnant and had an abortion in a hotel room just off the Rue de la Paix.

After the abortion Becky tamed her wild ways. Sailed for America. Married Richard Crawford. Why not? He was persistent, handsome, filthy rich, and yes, okay, a stuffed shirt. But hey, one rarely satisfies all of one's desires. Compromise has its role in life. Besides, Becky felt quite confident his trust fund would make them happy, happy, happy. And she knew they'd have beautiful children. Which they did. Three of them. Two strapping lads, Richard Jr. and Colin, plus a daughter, Katherine, who would, of course, eventually become my mother-in-law. Colin took after his fun-loving mama, Katherine after her rather dour father, and Dick Jr., well, he died while fighting the Koreans along the 38th parallel.

But what about Dick Crawford Sr.? Katie's papa? Where did he get his dough? He inherited it, most of it anyway. His father and grandfather had been in the retail biz, dry goods. But Dick found retail tedious, so he decided to try stocks. Did extremely well. And he was smart enough, or lucky enough, to get out of the market before the bottom fell out in '29. Took his fortune and bought real estate. Lots and lots of real estate. Out there in north-central New Jersey. Mostly dairy farms and second-growth timber in those days. To most folks without foresight, that land seemed too far from New York City to ever be worth more than a song.

Well, here's the very brief tale of how one family grew very rich: In the late 1920s and early 1930s Dick Crawford bought hundred-acre parcels for five thousand dollars or less. Now, half a century later, five-acre parcels of that same land bring in a quarter of a mil. Or more. So you can see how he and his descendants have managed to lead the Good Life.

Dick built his family a mansion up in the Bernardsville Mountains. Retired at the ripe old age of thirty-eight to live the life of a country gentleman. Just sat back and watched his assets soar. An avid tennis player and sailor since his youth, he sought out new athletic endeavors to fill his expanded leisure time. Took up archery, horseback riding. Filled his barn with the finest four-legged beasts. Joined the Essex Fox Hounds. Eventually became one of its Masters. Died, Dick did, at eighty-two, while out hunting up a fox. His gelding stumbled while jumping a brook, sending the old boy flying, head over heels. He landed on his neck and broke it. Everyone on the hunt heard it snap. Died right out there in the woods.

But his widow lives on. Becky hit eighty-five not long ago, but she hasn't slowed down since her days back in gay Paris. The old girl, and this is certainly not meant as an endorsement for the foul practice of smoking preserved tobacco, still puffs away on a pack or more a day. Drinks like a fish too, gin mostly, but an occasional belt of bourbon still passes through her lips. She's a feisty old dame. Plays a hell of a game of tennis. Golf. Even sails her own skiff. Loves to argue. Argued with me for hours the very first night we met. About politics and art and why soccer has never caught on professionally in the United States.

Rebecca really couldn't bring herself to like me. Not after she found out I was a Polack who had changed his name. But she could see Sarah's happiness, so she cut me a break. Never bowed entirely to Iron Kate's assessment that I was "a panderer and an opportunist." She could relate to my situation, probably because she herself had married for the green all those years ago. But Becky, once she'd made her play, forever after remained a loving and devoted mate. No stealing the in-laws' sterling and running off to Paris or some other faraway port.

Important also to remember that Becky's the matriarch of the family now, the oldest surviving voice. She relishes the role. Loves to give advice, pry into everyone else's business. I figure once Sarah arrives on Sanibel, Becky will be telling my bride exactly how to handle her thieving, conniving, wandering husband.

And look: Sarah has already arrived. Has already settled into her room on the second floor of Casa Rosa. An open, airy, and spacious south Florida home. Pink stucco with white storm shutters, surrounded by royal palms, overlooking el Golfo de México in Sanibel's poshest neighborhood.

Yes, my sweet already has her traveling garb off and her swimsuit on. A one-piece. Quite a sight. She goes down the stairs and out the back door where her granny awaits with dueling tumblers of gin and tonic over crushed ice. "A little sustenance, dear," says Grandma Becky, "after your long flight south."

Long flight indeed. What with that obnoxious Glenn Sheldon, P.I., sucking down one Jack Daniel's after another. Must've consumed half a dozen of those little bottles between Newark and Fort Myers. And each one made him slightly bolder, slightly more aggressive. Kept flirting with her, breathing his whiskey breath right in her face, a couple times even laying his big clammy hand on her thigh.

Sarah sighs, takes a swallow of the gin and tonic, allows her grandmother to lead her down the sandy path to the beach. The sun hangs low, preparing for its daily dive into the Gulf.

Becky Crawford has never been big on idle chitchat. Likes to move straight to the meat of the matter. "Your mother called," she says, "while you were en route."

Sarah sighs again. "I assumed she would."

Becky's just a wisp of a woman now. Maybe five feet two, ninety pounds. A strong breeze could blow her into the middle of next week. But still she's a dynamo, a regular powerhouse. I wouldn't want to tangle with her. "Katherine gave me, as you can imagine, quite an earful."

They kick off their shoes, reach the water's edge. The waves lap onto the shore, wash up around their ankles. The water warm, warmer even than the air.

"Mother," says Sarah, "never could mind her own business."

Becky laughs. "Care to tell me your side of the story?"

"What's left to tell? I'm sure Mother gave you all the gruesome details."

"Do you think he did it?"

Sarah stops, glances at her grandmother. "Do I think he did what? Do I think he committed the burglary?"

Becky hesitates, then nods.

Sarah shrugs.

They walk the beach, sip their drinks.

"These damn men," says Becky, finally. "They hold such incredible power over us. All out of proportion to the actual joy we derive from them. If I had it all to do over again, I'd make myself a million and just keep some young stud in a cage for when my sexual desires flared out of control."

Sarah manages a smile. This is why she wanted to visit her grandmother. The old girl saw the world more clearly than anyone else she knew.

"So why," asks Rebecca, "do you think he did it?"

Sarah takes a moment before answering. "I don't know. But somehow I think he did it for me."

"For you?"

"Yes, for me."

"So you think he did it for love? Not for money?"

"I think he did it because he wanted to give me things. Things only money could buy."

The Damn Money. Always rearing its ugly head.

Rebecca decides not to push it, not to point out some of the stark realities of the situation. Like: if he did it for you, sweet granddaughter of mine, why did he suddenly quit the coop? Head for the hills? No, Becky keeps her attitudes to herself, puts her arm around her granddaughter's waist. Gives her a nice squeeze.

They keep walking through the soft sand, through the pools of warm water.

A couple hours later, back at Casa Rosa, the telephone rings. It's Sheldon.

Sarah takes the call in her bedroom. "Yes?"

"I found something."

"Already?"

"Hey," boasts the private eye, "I know how to stay focused. Besides, you pay me to work around the clock."

Sarah tries to forget about his boozy breath and groping hands on the flight south. "So what did you find?"

"The same day your husband arrived in Fort Myers, he rented a car right here at the airport. Using his own name."

Sarah is not surprised. To her it is just more evidence that I want her to find me. "And?"

"Well," Sheldon explains, "you need a major credit card to rent a car. I figure he got to the counter and suddenly realized an alias wouldn't fly. He had to whip out the plastic. Rented a Chevy Corsica from Avis. Charged it on an American Express card also bearing the name of his employer, Crawford and Browne Investments, Inc."

That Sheldon's a sharpie. Can't take that away from him.

Sarah, of course, knows I don't have any credit cards of my own. I tried last year to get one, but ran into a bad credit history. "So do we know where he went in this Chevy Corsica?"

"Yup," answers Sheldon. "We know exactly where he went."

Sarah, my sweet, feels her heart pound a little faster.

"On his contract with Avis it said he was taking the car to Miami, but he never went to Miami. At least he didn't drop the car there. A day and a half later he dropped the car at the airport in Key West."

"Key West!"

"That's right."

"So when do we leave?"

"First thing in the morning," says Sheldon. "I've already rented a car, procured the necessary maps."

"Why don't we leave now?"

"We could, but hell, it's pretty late. Almost nine o'clock already."

"I want to leave now."

"You're the boss."

Sarah insists, hangs up, turns around, finds Becky standing in the doorway.

"Good news?"

"Maybe. I know now that Michael rented a car in Fort Myers and drove it to Key West."

"So your mother was right. You did come down here to look for him."

"Mother's always right."

"Not always."

"I know you probably think it's a dumb idea, but I have to try. I have to—"

Becky puts her bony finger over her granddaughter's lips. "You're right, Sarah Louise, I probably do think it's a dumb idea. But I also know you love this man. Love makes us crazy. Utterly mad. That's why I think you better follow this as far as it goes or you'll never have another moment's peace."

A kiss and a hug and a promise to stay safe, be careful.

Another hour passes. And there's my bride in the passenger seat of a Lincoln Town Car heading south on Interstate 75. Sheldon behind the wheel, half in the bag, working to keep his eyes open, sucking on a cup of super-caffeinated joe.

And look who else is behind the wheel. Of his Grand Wagoneer. Flying north on the New York Thruway. Stereo blasting an old one by The Band. "Chest Fever." Cruise control on eighty mph.

Where the hell's he going? And why's he in such a hurry?

Last night Cracker fought with his wife until almost midnight. Although he and Alison don't actually fight. Mostly Alison lectures him on his deficiencies while he sits there and takes it. Last night began with a verbal castration owing to the fact that the local rumor mill had been hard at work earlier in the evening, spreading the word about my unexplained disappearance. And fresh grapes growing on the vine had talk of Sarah slipping out of town as well. Alison was pissed. Felt out of the loop. Wanted to know what Graham planned to doing about it.

He wanted to say, "Not a damn thing, it's none of my business," but he knew that would only lead to another round of abuse wherein she would call him weak and impotent. So instead he gathered his courage and said, "Alison, I want you to shut up now so I can get some sleep."

This counterattack struck with such surprise, and was so out of character, that Alison, wounded, actually grew mute.

But Cracker didn't sleep. Not for a second. He lay there motionless for several hours, staring at the ceiling, occasionally checking the clock on the nightstand. As the illuminated hands worked through the early morning hours, Cracker worked through his life. The whole mess. Decided he was a miserable and useless loafer, utterly devoid of ambition or purpose. That old wide-awake-at-three-A.M. thing.

Finally, a little after four, Cracker climbed out of bed and went down the hall to look in on his kids. They slept peacefully, smiles on their little faces. He gave them each a kiss, pulled on some clothes, went downstairs, drank a cup of coffee left over from the day before, then went outside. Just to suck some fresh air into his lungs. A damp coolness hung in the air. Another autumn on the way. He decided he wanted to drive. Somewhere. Anywhere. With the radio on. Some good old rock and roll blasting in his ears. Climbed into the Wagoneer. Backed down the driveway. Headlights off till he hit the road. Wound through the hills. Finally reached the highway. Knew exactly where he was going. Damn right he knew. Heading north. For his wife. For Sarah. For his old buddy. For his own peace of mind.

He leaves the Thruway now at exit 18, crosses the Hudson River, and enters the city of Poughkeepsie just after dawn. Goes up this street, down that street. The streets I played on as a kid. Tag. Running bases. Stickball. It takes him a while to remember the way, locate the house. His only visit the time we came to watch Jessie die. But Cracker has an excellent memory. Eventually, with a little patience, he finds it. Spots the worn sign on the mailbox: STANDOWSKI.

He parks along the road out in front of the house. Looks around for my car, my Ford Taurus provided by Crawford & Browne, Inc. Doesn't see it. Wonders if maybe he should wait until it gets a little later before he knocks— But then, his emotions all revved up from no sleep and too much stimuli, he practically jumps out of the Wagoneer, marches up our short front walk. Climbs the wooden stairs. Crosses the porch. Takes a deep breath. Pushes the buzzer. Waits. Nothing. Not a sound from inside. He pushes the buzzer again. For several seconds. Impatient now. Impatient and pissed. At me. At his wife. At his father. At himself. He pulls open the screen door. Peers through the window. His view blocked by an old frayed curtain. Pounds on the loose glass.

Then, suddenly, he hears someone, Mike?, coming down the hall. Messing with the door. Cursing at the lock. Fiddling with the knob. Several seconds pass before the door swings wide open. A man once tall but now bent and twisted stands there. His bloodshot eyes scowl and squint. He looks dirty, disheveled. Like he probably slept in his clothes. A cloud of alcohol hangs over him, the smell oozing from his pores and mouth. And his face: red and swollen, pocked from a lifetime of beer and whiskey.

"What the hell you poundin' about? Whattaya want?"

Cracker stares at the man in the doorway. Swallows hard, can hardly believe his eyes. "Mr. Standowski?"

"Who wants to know?"

Cracker thinks about holding out his hand, but decides against it. Doesn't want to have physical contact with this seedy-looking creature. Seems almost impossible to him that this man could be his best friend's father.

Seems pretty damn unlikely to me too, old buddy. But if I don't watch my step, I could wind up rowing that same leaky boat.

"Graham Cramer," answers Cracker. "I'm a friend of Mike's."

Dear Old Dad's eyes scowl a little deeper at the sound of my name. "Yeah? So? You here to tell me he died or somethin'?"

Nice, Pop. Real classy.

Cracker knows instantly his trip north this morning has been in vain. Probably he knew it all along, but now, the cold truth stares him in the face. No way, he tells himself, did Mike come up here to take care of this stinking old rummy, this sorry son of a bitch who didn't even have the decency to attend his own son's wedding. Alison, thinks Cracker, was right. Sarah told me Mike's father was sick just to throw me off the scent.

Still, he figures he better ask. "Actually, I was wondering if Mike was here."

"Hell no he ain't here."

"Have you seen him recently?"

"Haven't seen the bastard for years. Don't wanna see him."

"Do you know where he is? Any idea where I can find him?"

Stanislaw takes his right index finger and thumps it hard against Cracker's chest. "I don't know where he is. You hear me? Don't give a damn neither. Now get the hell off my porch and leave me alone. I got things to do."

Cracker can't imagine what. But he quickly retreats all the same. Back to his Wagoneer. Back to Jersey. Back to the Compound. Back to his little family. Tells his wife a few lies when he gets there late in the morning. Doesn't want to tell her the truth. Can't bear the thought of listening to her lecture and gloat. But he wonders now all the time why I left. Where I went. When I'm coming back. See, he doesn't know about Vince. Or the U-Haul. Or my fingerprints all over that chest-on-chest.

*　　*　　*

I'm down here, Cracker. On Devil's Cay. Sucking on a cold one. Waiting for you to come down and pull me out of the fire. Again.

I've been daydreaming a lot lately. Mostly about Sarah. About the first time we made love. Oh yeah, I remember well. It happened just hours after we got the results of our AIDS tests. Negative all the way. Plenty of reason to celebrate. So we did. In the cottage. On my brand-new queen size bed.

Late summer. Still pretty warm. Sarah didn't have much on. I pulled it off as slowly as I could. White tennis sneakers and socks. I kissed her ankles and behind her knees. I pulled her red tee shirt up over her head. She let it fall off her shoulders onto the floor. I kissed her breasts and licked her—

"Hey, Mr. Weston, what you grinning about, mon?"

"Huh?"

"You wearing a grin from ear to ear. Big as the moon."

I snap out of my daydream, spot Lewis behind the bar shining up the glasses in anticipation of the sunset rush. "Just thinking about my wife."

"You should have your wife here with you, mon. That what the islands are for. Romance. You leave your wife home alone you asking for trouble."

"Believe me, Lewis, I got plenty of trouble."

I look around, can't for a second remember how long I've been here on Devil's Cay. Three days? Four days? A month? Christ, seems like forever. Already there's been too much booze, too little sleep. Plus that fat broad over at the Devil's Cay Inn, casting spells and curses on me. I woke up last night sweating and panting like I'd just run a marathon. I had a headache so bad I couldn't get my eyes open. Felt better by morning, but when I told Lewis about it, he said, "Maybe it just something you ate, mon, but I bet you feeling the wrath of Mama Rolle."

Hell no, it's not the wrath of Mama Rolle, it's the wrath of God Almighty. The old boy's punishing me for my sins, for being such a despicable swine.

I finish my beer, then suddenly hear this high-pitched whine, like something between a chain saw and a dentist's drill. "What the hell is that, Lewis?"

Lewis, calm as some Buddhist monk, just keeps rubbing those glasses. "Sound like Milo to me."

"Milo? Who's Milo?"

"Roland Milo. He's a local pilot. Sound like his plane."

"Plane! Pilot! You never told me Devil's Cay had an airport." All this time I thought I was safe from attack by air. Another fricking thing to worry about.

"Oh no, mon, no airport. Milo land on the water. Got himself a seaplane. Very wild guy, Milo. Flies like every flight is a kamikaze mission. I wouldn't get in no plane with Milo, mon. Not if my life depended on it."

I grimace at the noise, then wonder who Milo might have aboard. I head across the bar, peer out the picture window. Sure enough, there's an old seaplane taxiing across the harbor. I squint, try to see if maybe Sarah's in the co-pilot's seat. Come, she has, to rescue me, carry me home, make love to me up in our bedroom with the windows wide open and the warm late summer breeze blowing across our faces.

"Be right back, Mr. Weston," says Lewis. "I got to go see if maybe Milo brought some folks in need of a room." Lewis goes out the front door.

The seaplane, its pontoons floating over the calm water, pulls up to the public wharf. Immediately, as if by magic, the entire population of Devil's Cay appears from the shadows, descends upon the plane. Exactly the same way they did when I arrived on Captain Ahab's stinking diesel mailboat.

The seaplane door swings open. Out flies an anchor attached to a long length of steel cable. The anchor bites. The plane stabilizes. Out climb the humans: three of them, two males and a female. The tall black one must be Milo. The other two: just a couple of whiteys with dark tropical tans. The woman looks nothing at all like my sweet. Shorter. Older. Bleached blond hair. Must be another honeymoon couple come to Devil's Cay for the sport of fornicating on some far-flung island paradise.

I slide back to the bar, wait for Lewis to return, draw me another brew. Wonder if maybe I should ask this Milo the Pilot fellow to haul me back to civilization. But what'll I do once I get there? Give myself up? Turn myself in? Throw myself at Iron Kate's feet and beg for mercy?

A few minutes later Lewis returns to the hotel with only Milo at his side. Milo is tall, easily six feet six, skinny as a beanpole. In his youth he starred on the Bahamian National Basketball Team. His greatest moment came when he slam-dunked up and over Kareem Abdul-Jabbar, the premier NBA center of his time. But Milo was too frail to play in the NBA so after a couple of years riding the bench, he came home to the Bahamas. He spent the money he'd made playing hoops on a pilot's license and an old Cessna. Used that Cessna to make his first of many cocaine runs from Exuma to rural Georgia and other out-of-the-way sites in the States.

Roland Milo slaps Lewis on the back as the two step into the bar. "Gimme the tallest glass you got, Lewey. Fill it halfway with light rum, halfway with dark rum, and maybe spit in it for a little local flavor."

Milo has a big, booming, happy voice. An accent that sounds half British and half American, barely Bahamian at all. And a huge smile filled with gleaming white teeth. Smooth, dark skin. Not that dark. Light chocolate. Somewhere along the way some horny white guy must've slipped it to one of Milo's black ancestors. Probably some stinking slave owner.

Sex and Money.

"Who's this cozied up to the bar?" Milo comes right up to me.

"Roland Milo," says Lewis as he uncorks a bottle of rum, "Eddie Weston. Eddie Weston, Roland Milo."

Milo extends his long, lanky arm. I give his hand a shake.

"Weston, huh? Any relation to the famous black and white photographer of the same name?"

I'm impressed the guy has heard of my photographic mentor. Decide to tell him a small lie. "Distant cousins."

Lewis sets the mixture of light and dark rum on the bar in front of Milo.

Milo does not waste time. He lifts the glass, takes a long pull. The glass stands half empty when he returns it to the bar. Smacks his big lips together and says, "I love that shit Weston did in the early forties. You know the photos I mean. Along the Pacific coast. Monterey. Point Lobos. Dreamy stuff. Almost surreal. No one had ever made photographs like that before. While all the other white motherfuckers in the world were out shooting each other dead, Weston was patiently shooting some of the finest pictures ever made. Unbelievable what that guy could do with a camera. I guess you'd have to call him a genius." Milo says all this in a loud, boisterous voice, and when he finishes, he picks up his glass, polishes off the rest of the rum. "Another one of those, Lewey. Exactly the same."

I know all about Weston and his Point Lobos work. Been studying his stuff for years. Was out this morning, just after dawn, stalking the beaches, searching for images of similar depth and visual power. "How do you know so much about Edward Weston?"

"Hell," answers Milo, "I studied the arts. Painting. Photography. Fell in love with Weston's stuff while stoned on mushrooms over in Mexico. There was this big exhibition in Cuernavaca. I bought some of his prints. Done by the man himself. Very expensive. One of them cost me twenty-five Gs. Had it hanging in the front foyer of my grand oceanfront hacienda up in Spanish Wells. That's when I had money. Big Money. Cocaine Money. Right, Lewey?"

Lewis set another glass of rum in front of Milo. "That's right, Roland."

"I used to wipe my nose with hundred dollar bills right here at this bar. I tell you true, Weston, I made more successful cocaine runs between the Bahamas and the States than any man in the islands."

"Yeah? So what happened?"

"What happened? Shit. I got busted, that's what happened. Damn DEA caught me. Threw me in jail for three and a half years. Took my house, my boats, my planes, my artwork, even took my woman. Well, they didn't actually take her, but she upped and split once the gravy train ran dry. But hey, fuck it, I'm having a good time. Right, Lewey?"

"Right, Roland."

"I got me that little puddle jumper now. Carry folks back and forth between the islands. Just brought a couple over from Nassau. Claim they want to do some fishing, bonefishing, but I got a feeling they're running from something." Milo drains another half a glass of rum. "What about you, Weston? You running from something? No other reason to land on this godforsaken cay."

I gear up for an answer. But too late. Milo's a talker, not a listener. Turns his attention to Lewis. "So what happened, Lewey? Couldn't get that couple to book a room here at Lewey's Swanky Seaside Hotel?"

Lewis shrugs. "They went to Mama Rolle's. I guess they called ahead. She's got that ad in the Vistors' Guide."

"Fuck 'em," says Milo. "A couple of clerks from Atlanta or some such place. I don't know what crime they committed, but it ain't no big deal. Probably extorted some dough from an ATM. Think they're fucking Bonnie and

Clyde now." Milo drains his second glass of rum. "Say, you boys hear about the hurricane?"

I barely hear the question. The word hurricane doesn't have much impact on me. Never been in one, never even seen one except on TV.

But Lewis, he knows about hurricanes. Ask him and he can recall David back in '79, Agnes back in '72, Flora back in '63, even Donna back in 1960. Knows enough about hurricanes to pay attention when someone utters the dreaded word. Especially in August and September: prime months for killer 'canes in the islands.

"I haven't heard a thing," he tells Milo.

"Then you better start listening to the radio, Lewey."

"Why? What's up?"

"The usual. Some crazy shit off West Africa. A tropical depression."

"They got a course yet?"

Milo shows off that big smile again. "Lewey," he says, "if it comes, it's coming your way!" Then he turns, heads for the door. "See you boys around. Got to get back to Nassau. Got some sweet young white thing waiting for me at the roulette table at Merv Griffin's Paradise Island Resort and Casino. If those two twits over at Mama Rolle's wonder where I went, tell 'em I'll be back when I got time. Ciao."

Lewis and I watch him go. We keep staring at the empty doorway long after he's gone. Milo's high impact.

Finally I say, "That guy just drank about sixteen ounces of straight rum. Now he's going to fly an airplane?"

The answer comes before Lewis can open his mouth: the sound of Milo's plane winding up for action. The low din quickly escalates into that chain saw–dentist's drill whine. I cup my hands over my ears, push away from the bar. "Hold any and all calls, Lewis. I'm going upstairs, see if I might lull myself to sleep."

❧

Soon after Sarah and I started making love, Maggie Jane came down from Boston for a visit. They hit it off right away.

"She's a real sweetheart," Maggie said to me that night. Then my little sister asked, "What does she see in you?"

I tried to look indignant before listing all my best qualities.

"And what do you see in her?"

I mentioned things like beauty, sincerity, a sense of humor.

"What about the money?"

"What about it?"

"How motivated are you by the money, Michael?"

We had spent the day up at TREETOPS.

"I'm not motivated by the money at all."

"No?"

"No."

"Maybe a little?"

"Forget the money, Maggie. I love this girl."

"Do you think you'd love her if she worked at the A&P, drove an old Chevy, and had a kid to support on two hundred dollars a week?"

"That's not really fair."

"Maybe not," said my little sister. "But I'm a lawyer, Michael. And you're my brother. You and I have always been honest with each other. I just think those are some questions you should ask yourself. I can see the attraction between you two. A blind person could see you guys are in love. I just hope you love her for the right reasons."

"I think I do."

"Then you're a lucky man. Especially if she loves you back the same way."

"I think she does."

"And don't forget."

"What?"

"She has a kid. He's part of the deal. Now and forever."

I didn't mind Maggie's interrogations. In fact, I expected her to work me over.

But she didn't have to worry about Tim. Tim and I got on great. He was a little jealous at first because I took up so much of his mother's time, but more and more we included him in our plans.

I remember Tim was there the day Sarah told me about her father. The three of us had ridden the horses down to the Black River for a picnic. Tim fell asleep on the blanket after we ate.

We watched him for a few minutes, then Sarah said, "This is so good for him."

"What?"

"Having you around."

"Graham told me he doesn't get to see his father much."

"Try never."

"Does Tim miss him?"

"I don't think so. Timothy was pretty little when his father left."

I sat close beside Sarah, my arm around her waist. A cool breeze blew across our picnic. We had on sweaters for the first time in months.

After a minute or so I asked, "What about you, Sarah? Do you miss your father?"

She glanced at me, then looked out at the river. "I do, yes. Every day."

She told me then about her father. Thomas Browne. Direct descendent of Peter Browne. Co-founder of Crawford & Browne. Husband of Katherine Browne. Father of Sarah Browne. Her best friend. The most important person in her life. He came from Money. And he made some Money of his own. Millions. Quite a guy. Smart. Funny. Adventurous. Loved to ski, ride horses, tame wild rivers.

I sat there quietly and listened. And I could tell by the intimacy in her voice that she trusted me and that I had found a very special place in her heart.

She told me how her father had died while running the white water up on the Allagash Waterway in northern Maine: capsized, swept downstream, split his head wide open on a rock, and drowned.

"His death," she added in a whisper, "broke my heart."

She went on to tell me that her father's death had led directly to her marriage to Ricky Carlson. "I guess I married him because I didn't know where else to turn, didn't know what else to do. Of course, we never should've married. I wasn't ready for marriage. Neither was Ricky. He had so much pent-up anxiety and anger. On the outside so confident and successful. A Princeton grad from a long line of Princeton grads. His family was prominent in both business and politics. But inside he was a mess, in desperate need of therapy. His father had been physically abusing his wife and children behind closed doors for years."

On and on Sarah spoke about spousal and child abuse. I only half listened. Not because I wasn't interested, but because it forced me to think about all the stuff Stanley had inflicted upon my mother and my sister and me. And I didn't want to think about that stuff. Not then. Not now. Not ever.

"Ricky," said Sarah, "made me feel safe. Secure. I needed that after my father died. But I wasn't safe or secure. Far from it. Without knowing it, I had married a madman. At first he just criticized. Called me useless and inept. Everything I did was wrong. I washed the dishes wrong, folded the laundry wrong, made love wrong. I tried to ignore him, but that only made it worse. He started screaming and swearing at me, calling me all kinds of ugly, filthy names. Then one night he slapped me. Hard. Across the face. A few days later he hit me again. I begged him to stop. And for a while he did. But he was sick, Michael. I didn't know what to do. I kept blaming myself. Thinking it must be my fault. And then he hit me with his fist, with his closed fist."

Hearing about this abuse from Cracker had been tough enough. But listening to Sarah tell it, her head resting against my shoulder, I felt a powerful urge to protect her, keep her safe. I leaned down and kissed her eyes, her nose, her mouth. "It's okay," I told her. "Nothing like that is ever going to happen again."

She sighed, no doubt uncertain. "Just promise me, Michael. Just promise me you will never hurt me."

"I promise," came my immediate response. And believe me, I meant it. "I'll never hurt you, Sarah. Not in a million years."

A couple years anyway. Well, a little less if you want to get picky about it.

The more Sarah told me about her life, the more I wanted to tell her about mine. For a long time I just listened, thought it over, waited for my chance. My chance came when suddenly I realized I could trust her. No small thing for this boy to trust anyone. Until I met Sarah I could count those I trusted on one hand: Jessie, Maggie Jane, and Graham.

Then one evening I just started telling Sarah about Jessie. I told her how much I'd loved her. How much I missed her. How horrible it had been when she died. That's when the tears arrived. Real tears.

I had never told anyone before. Not like that. Not with that much emotion. Not with that much honesty. It had always been a tough-guy thing. "Yeah, my mother died when I was a kid." Cool. Detached. But Sarah heard the real tale, the whole tale, nothing held back. Nothing manipulated to solicit a response. Just the emotional pain I had experienced.

She held me tight, cradled me in her arms, told me she loved me. Just the way Jessie would've done.

Then Sarah wanted to know more. She wanted to know about Stanley.

But I couldn't do it. I couldn't open up. Couldn't dig that deep. So what did I do? I switched gears, shifted into superficial mode, an old trick I had been performing for years. I told a dirty joke, made a funny face, then very nonchalantly I changed the subject.

"I went to see your uncle."

"You did?" Sarah quickly forgot all about Stan the Man. "When?"

"A week or so ago."

"Why didn't you tell me? How did it go?"

"Pretty well. He made me sell him a pencil."

"What?"

"He handed me a pencil, told me if I could sell it back to him he'd give me a job."

My need to play the tough-guy, cool-guy role was fast returning. "Within fifteen minutes I'd sold him not only that pencil but a whole gross of pencils. Special, stay-sharp pencils. Plus a dozen of the brand new super-powered Standish electric pencil sharpeners with the titanium never-go-dull blade."

Sarah found all this amusing. Then wanted to know, "So did you get the job?"

"After my super sales pitch and a few minor lies, sure, I got the job."

"Lies?" The word crossed her up, even caused a slight knit in her brow. "What kind of lies?"

"You know, the usual job app lies. I told him I had vast sales experience: J&J, AT&T, IBM."

"And he believed you?"

"I guess. He made me an offer."

Which was really all that mattered to my sweet. Sarah found a way to justify my lies because they were lies told in her behalf.

"So when do you start?"

"A few weeks. I told him I needed to clean up my affairs at J&J." Then, even though Sarah did not so much as bat an eye, I added, "I only told him that so I'd have more time to spend with you."

To this my lover could relate. She'd been taking a few personal days lately herself from her work with the Literacy Volunteers of America.

"I also told him I could only work four days a week because of graduate classes in business administration down at Rutgers."

Sarah seemed momentarily shaken by the complexity of my deception. But she quickly shook it off, as new lovers will do when information of an undesirable bent creeps into the conversation. "So what's the job," she wanted to know. "What will you be selling?"

"I don't know. Land, I think." Then I put my arms around her waist, gave her a squeeze. "But we've got three whole weeks before I have to report for duty."

Those three weeks passed in a flash. Early autumn. Warm days. Cool nights. I remember sunshine. Lots of sunshine. Day after day of a golden glow. Not so much as a cloud in the sky.

Sarah and I couldn't spend our nights together, owing to her domestic situation, but during our waking hours we became virtually inseparable. We became pals, friends, buddies. Like Cracker and me. Only with more intimacy.

We played tennis. Went biking. Horseback riding. Both of us very physical and athletic. Often we brought Tim along. A very entertaining kid. And a much better horseman than me. Although he always sat up on his pony with a perfectly straight back like some proper English gentleman. I used to kid him about it. Did my best to loosen him up, make him more like a Western cowpoke.

A couple times Sarah even took me out on the fox hunt. I didn't actually get to hunt though. Didn't have the skills yet to jump fences or stay up with the pack. So I had to hang back with the hilltoppers who go around the fences, take things a little easier. This foxhunting business, I quickly learned, was not for cowards or the faint of heart. Once the hounds scare up a fox, you better be prepared for a full-out gallop through the woods and thickets, over streams and fences. Hard to slow down your four-legged beast once he gets a whiff of the chase.

Never good at hanging back, I tried to convince Sarah to let me ride up with the main field. "No way," she told me. "You'll kill yourself. Hilltop this season, practice jumping all spring and summer, and next season you can ride with the hunt."

Next season? She uttered the words innocently enough, but we both sensed immediately their profound impact. Did we really think we would be together a year from now? Is that what we wanted? What we silently had been anticipating? At that time we were much too insecure to answer these questions. So we just paused, then let the moment slip away.

But the moments kept piling up. One on top of another. A big one came the day before my tenure with Crawford & Browne began. It took place up at TREETOPS, inside the Brownes' elaborate mansion. Sarah had invited me for lunch, told me we would have the house all to ourselves. For the very first time.

I knocked on the back door early in the afternoon. To my surprise, young Lucy answered my knock. On her way out. "Sarah's getting dressed," she told me. "She'll be down in a jiff. Make yourself at home. Sorry I have to run. I'm late for class."

I said so long, then crossed to the refrigerator and pulled the door open. It was stuffed with juice, milk, sparkling water, fruit, bread, cheese, yogurt, various kinds of meat. Last time I'd looked in my fridge there might've been a couple slices of old pizza and a six-pack of beer. I pulled out a gallon of fresh-squeezed orange juice and poured myself a tall, frothy glass. The well-chilled juice slid pleasantly down my throat.

Glass in hand I wandered through the downstairs. The family room. The dining room. The living room. Took a long slow look around. Now I am not easily impressed by the things Money can buy, worthless doodads more often than not, but ambling through that Tudor, anticipating the arrival of my lover, I saw firsthand the Power of Green: the vast rooms, the high ceilings, the tall windows overlooking rolling hills and fenced pastures, the long sofa with its billowing pillows stuffed with the finest goose down, built-in bookshelves lined with leather-bound books, thick Oriental carpets covering hardwood floors, lamps and vases and original paintings by famous artists hanging on the walls. I stood there staring, wondering how much cold hard cash it took to own such things.

Was that, I wonder now, the beginning of my desire for more than just the woman? Was that my economic awakening to all that this love affair might bring if I played my cards right?

I do not know. I cannot say for sure. I had rejected Maggie's assertion that I was at least partly enamored by the Money. But I knew about the Money. Hell, it was always there, right smack in my face. Very tough to ignore the Money.

And then she appeared, beautiful and bright. She seemed to float across the living room. Wore tight jeans, a loose cotton sweater. Blue. Nothing on her feet. Toenails painted pink.

"Hello, Michael." She said my name as though she loved me, as though she wanted nothing more than to have me hold her tightly in my arms, plant a passionate kiss upon her lips. But that's exactly what she wanted, so that's what I gave her. And in no time at all we found ourselves sprawled across that Oriental carpet.

"Maybe we should go upstairs," one of us said.

I had not yet been upstairs. I had been waiting impatiently for weeks to see her quarters, to bury my face in her pillows.

But we didn't go. Not right away. Into the kitchen first, poured another glass of orange juice. I held it to her lips. She to mine. We set it down and kissed again. I had her pressed up against the refrigerator, my mouth all over her face and neck.

"Maybe we should go upstairs," one of us said again.

But not quite yet. First we took a tour of the Tudor.

Arm-in-arm we swept through the rooms, our feet barely making contact with the plush carpets and exquisite rugs and polished parquet floors. Everywhere we went we found old things in exceptional repair. The house was a virtual museum of early American antiques.

"Mother's a collector," Sarah told me. "Although lots of this stuff has been in the family for generations."

"Like what?" I asked, my innocence still intact.

"Like this," she said, picking up a simple pewter candlestick from a table in the dining room. "This was made in Philadelphia in the late sixteen hundreds. The family has owned it since it was cast. There probably aren't a dozen like it left in the world."

Hands still clean, I idly asked, "It must be valuable?"

"It probably cost a dollar when it was made," she told me. And then, somewhat reluctantly, she added, "It's worth more than a thousand dollars now."

"A thousand bucks for a candlestick?" My thoughts swirled: enough to buy that fancy new Nikon I'd had my eye on.

Sarah, unaware of my deviant thought, nodded. And then into the living room, where my sweet put her hand on a massive cherry chest-on-chest. An enormous piece of work. An impressive mass of handcrafted lumber. Huge carved feet. Nine rows of drawers reaching to within inches of the ten-foot ceiling. Sparkling brass hardware.

"This," Sarah told me, "is my favorite piece in the house. My great-great-great-great-great-grandfather, Jason Browne, had this chest custom-built for his wife's fortieth birthday. Can you imagine getting this for a birthday present?"

I could only shake my head, whistle softly. "Incredible." And then, still not a teaspoon of corruption in my cup, I asked, "What's something like this worth?"

Sarah threw me a sideways glance. A glance that said we here in the Browne family don't really discuss such matters. Very poor taste. Utterly inappropriate to have even mumbled the value of that pewter candlestick. Then a little laugh fell from her mouth. "It's invaluable," she announced. "Irreplaceable at any price."

That's right, Mikey Boy, irreplaceable at any price.

Carefully I laid a hand on the lightly oiled wood. The grain of the cherry circled and swirled around my palm. I stared into that grain, followed its contour like a man studying a road map. A road map to where? To nowhere. To hell but not back. Kept wondering what it might be worth: ten grand? twenty grand? fifty grand?

Sarah kissed me on the neck. I let my hand fall away from the wood. My fingerprints left a mark on the oil, faint but visible. I wanted to rub them off, make them disappear, but she wanted the tour to continue toward the bedroom.

On our way upstairs we slowed in the front foyer. Stopped to have a look at an arsenal of family photographs resting in solid gold frames on a long wooden tavern table. Sarah pointed out portraits of her father, her brother, her sister, aunts and uncles, cousins, nephews, nieces.

"Quite a crew," I said, wondering if there might one day be room for me. Part of the family. God, I longed to be part of a family again. And this one, I thought, this one has room for me: Man Needed to Take Up Slack.

So why, you dirty stinking Polack, why did you blow it?

In the back row, I spotted a photo of Tim as a baby in the arms of his father, Ron Cramer, Graham's brother. I picked up the photograph. "Ron looks like a happy dad in this shot."

Sarah, I noticed, did not look at the picture. "A regular Father Knows Best."

"It's too bad he doesn't see his kid."

"He doesn't deserve to see his kid," Sarah announced. And then, "Basically, Ron Cramer is a selfish, worthless shit."

That simple out-of-the-blue utterance stopped me dead in my tracks. Sucked the breath right out of my lungs for several seconds. Understand: in the weeks we'd been together, I had not heard Sarah mutter a single mean-spirited phrase. Oh, maybe a cross word or two for Tim when the youngster fell out of line, but nothing more than that. A mildness of manner that every day reminded me of Jessie. So I stood there momentarily stunned, then finally I pulled myself together, set the photo back on the table, and tried this on for size, "Graham told me things went bad, but he never really told me what happened."

Sarah shrugged, then, after several seconds had passed, she sighed. "What can I say? I made a mistake. My second mistake in the marriage department. I married Ronny on the rebound. I was young and stupid and lonely. I wanted someone to take care of me. That whole safe and secure thing again. Instead I wound up with another lunatic. A sick, needy nut case."

Whoa! I kind of wished I'd left that photo alone. Gone upstairs without this last stop. "I never really knew Ron very well," I said, shifting my weight from one leg to the other. "I guess he seemed like a decent enough guy."

Nope. Not so, Standish. Sarah agreed with Cracker. Ron was not a decent guy at all. Mean and ornery. A drunk and a drug abuser. Seems his relationship with Big Walt had left him an emotional cripple. Scarred for life. Never really developed beyond early adolescence: totally self-absorbed, the center of the universe, very little ability to withstand controversy or confrontation. Flew the coop long before the fox ever even rooted out the nest.

Were we chatting about Ronny C. that day? Or Mikey S.?

"So why did you marry me?" I'd ask her now. "Why did you marry him?" I asked her then.

"Because," she answered, "he could be so funny and charming and entertaining. The life of the party."

Another portrait of your man on Devil's Cay. But then, thank God, Sarah finished up with a few character traits belonging solely to husband number two.

"Life of the party one second but cruel and abusive the next. He felt so lousy about himself, so inadequate, that he constantly needed to strike out at others. A day didn't go by that he didn't criticize me, find some ugly way to put me down, make me feel bad. I put up with it for a long time. Too long. We had a child. I thought that might make him better, give him reason to feel good about himself. But it made him worse, totally unbearable. He started competing against his own son. When I couldn't take it anymore, I told him I wanted a divorce."

I stood there, not real sure what to say or do. Finally I just squeezed her around the waist, drew her close.

She relaxed, for a moment, then continued. "He couldn't handle being rejected so he twisted everything around. He started telling people that I was a bad mother, that he was the one who wanted the divorce. But when push came to shove he couldn't bear the confrontation. So one day he just fled into the hills."

I decided we had said enough. So I kissed my sweet on the mouth and led her away from those photos. In the direction of that long, wide carpeted stairway. She took the hint, led the rest of the way. Up to the landing and down a long hallway lined with more photographs of the family Browne. Into a large sitting room containing a big-screen Sony TV, an expensive Bose stereo system, a Stairmaster, a rowing machine, a stationary bike. Then another hallway with Tim's bedroom on the left, Sarah's bedroom on the right. Deep shag carpet covered the floor of her room. A large room with a bay window overlooking the tennis court and the swimming pool and the pastures beyond. But I barely noticed the view that day. I had something else on my mind. I kicked off my shoes, headed straight for the bed.

Our lovemaking reached new heights that afternoon. Slow and sweet and soft and intimate as always, but this time, just as I prepared to explode, Sarah latched on to me with a firmness and a fury I had not seen in her before. Our muscles grew tense and rigid. Our skin warm and wet. We came together. At the very same moment.

We stayed in bed that afternoon a tad longer than intended. Met Mama Kate in the front foyer as we glided down the front stairs, a couple of pixies so light and airy on their feet. The mother gave the new boyfriend the most heinous of looks, as though I had surely just raped her eleven-year-old virgin child. Offered not a word to either of us. Just a scowl and then straight into her study. A door slam to let us know exactly how she felt about our lascivious behavior.

Sarah heard all about it later. In great detail. After I had fled the scene of the crime. Not about the Sex. Oh no. Mama Kate never could have broached that touchy subject. She attacked from a different direction.

"You've been ignoring Timothy, Sarah. You barely spend any time with him at all anymore."

"That's ridiculous, Mother. We do things together all the time."

"Never just the two of you."

"Oh, I get it. This isn't about Timothy. This is about Michael."

"I didn't say that."

"I know what you said, Mother. But what you refuse to see is that Timothy likes Michael. He'd rather do stuff with Michael than with me."

Right on target there. Tim liked having another guy around. Sick to the bone of all those women telling him what to do and how to act.

Kate gave her daughter a moment to settle down, then laid this on her: "You may be right, Sarah, but I'm just not sure your friend is absolutely trustworthy."

"What is that supposed to mean?"

"Just some things I've heard."

"Oh? And just what have you heard?"

Katherine, we found out later, had heard from Allie Cramer. My old chum. The two of them had been chattering up a storm. "Just that Standish is not your friend's real name."

Oh yeah, here we go. The old girl had been putting up with me: out in the hunt field, out on the tennis court, around her dinner table, but let's not for a second think she actually liked me. In her mind I was nothing but a Polack with a name change. A closet racist, the Pilgrim Browne definitely held my roots against me. Also figured I was probably a gold digger, only after the Money.

Money and Sex. Sex and Money.

"Michael legally changed his name to Standish a long time ago, Mother. Partly so bigots like you wouldn't pass judgments on him. And will you please stop referring to him as 'my friend.' His name is Michael."

"Fine. Michael. I still think you've abandoned your life to chase this man."

"What are you talking about?"

"Family, friends, responsibilities. Everyone and everything abandoned so you can pursue this . . . this . . ."

"This what, Mother?"

"This doomed relationship."

"I think," said my sweet, "this conversation is now over."

Not quite. "You're just momentarily blinded, Sarah Louise, by his charm and his good looks. But soon enough you will see that this can't work. There is too great a divide between the two of you. This is not easy for me to say, but my eyes see more clearly than yours on this matter. And I see—"

"I think it's time for both of us to be careful, Mother. I think we should watch what we say."

"I understand, dear. But it's a mother's duty. And I see a man with virtually nothing in hot pursuit of a woman with practically everything. I'm afraid I see an opportunist."

"You're blind, Mother. You see only what you want to see."

Don't we all?

Mother needed the last word. "I'm only trying to help, Sarah. Believe me, I'm only concerned with what is best for you."

*   *   *

Sarah gave me the lowdown on that conversation later. After the fact. After work the following evening. That's right: work. Early in the morning I followed Uncle Colin out Interstate 78 to the Delaware River. He in his big green Mercedes sedan. Me in my company-owned Ford Taurus. We pulled into a small asphalt parking lot on the edge of a vast field. A vinyl-clad trailer sat between the field and the parking lot. Big sign out front said it all: DELAWARE MOUNTAIN ESTATES. DISTINCTIVE, CUSTOM-BUILT HOMES BY CRAWFORD & BROWNE OF FAR HILLS, NEW JERSEY.

Okay, but I should tell you: not a distinctive, custom-built home in sight. Not a one. Not even so much as a foundation anywhere out there on the horizon. Just some curbstones and the muddy beginnings of a few new roads. Also some earth-moving equipment. Idle and unmanned.

I followed Uncle Colin into the trailer. Pretty fancy digs. Set up and ready for business. Well stocked with food and booze. A couple leather sofas. A long hardwood conference table. Colorful brochures depicting what DELAWARE MOUNTAIN ESTATES would one day look like: winding roads, mature shade trees, lovely homes with lush green lawns, children on swings, moms tending flower beds, dads charbroiling beef in the barbecue, everyone happy happy happy.

Colin poured himself a tumbler of Old Grand-Dad. Must've been about, oh, nine or nine-thirty. Didn't offer me one. Didn't want one. We stood side by side in front of the picture window that took up most of the back of the trailer. We looked out across that vast, muddy field. More or less flat, a slight dip here and there, for most of a mile, all the way out to the banks of the Delaware.

"Doesn't look like much now, kid," said the boss. "But there's a hundred million bucks sitting out there." Colin swirled the ice cubes around in his whiskey. "Maybe more if we can get these goddamn real estate prices to climb."

"How many acres are there?" I asked.

"Two thousand," came the answer. "Two thousand pristine acres. And let me tell you, buddy boy, I bought 'em for a song." A wide grin spread across Colin's face as he uttered these words. A happy man. "Two thousand acres. Five-acre zoning. That's four hundred new houses. Use your imagination, kid, and you can see them out there dotting the landscape: boys and girls riding their bikes, fathers mowing grass, mothers planting Johnny-jump-ups. Four hundred brand spanking new homes with an average selling price of three hundred and fifty to four hundred thousand dollars. How's your multiplication, Standish?"

I couldn't come up with a number right away, but I knew it was way up there in the millions. "So we're going to build houses here?"

Colin let loose with a rip-roaring laugh. "Hell no! Too much toil in that. We're going to find some fool who wants to spend ten years or more busting his ass building and selling. We'll be long gone by then. But you have to see it to sell it. That's the key to selling, my boy, a clear and concise picture of the whole project. Right down to the insertion of the last screw."

I thought about Colin's metaphor, then asked, "So if we're not going to build houses, what's the plan? What do you want me to do?"

Colin put his arm around my shoulder, led me over to one of the sofas. Sat me down. Refilled his glass with Grand-Dad. "A couple years ago," he began, "I got wind of this place. I belong to a fishing club across the river in Pennsy. You fish, kid?"

I hate to fish. Hate to see the poor slithery creature struggling on the end of a barbed hook. Pretty cruel if you ask me. "Sure," I lied. "When I can find the time."

"We'll make time. I'll take you over to the club one of these days."

Great. Wonderful. I couldn't wait.

"Anyway," Colin continued, "a friend of mine in the club knew the old farmer who owned this land. Poor bastard had some nasty kind of cancer, stomach, I think it was. In no time at all, before he could get his affairs in order, he kicked the bucket. His wife inherited everything. They didn't have any kids. Or they'd had a kid but he'd been shot and killed in Vietnam. I don't know all the particulars." Colin took another pull on the bourbon. "You follow me?"

I nodded. "I think so."

"Well, this old farmer's cancer treatment went on and on for months. It wound up taking all their money, every last nickel, a couple hundred grand. When he died the old girl had nothing left but the land. That's when I stepped into the picture." Colin gave me a smug look.

Oh yeah, I was beginning to see that picture pretty clearly now.

Colin pressed on. "And I didn't step out of the picture until I had that old dame's signature in all the right places."

So, came the sudden realization of this dirty lowlife Polack, old Uncle Colin's nothing by a shyster, another shark in the pool. I couldn't help but smile. Colin Crawford: a man who thought his wad was his greatest virtue. Shit.

"How much," I asked him, "did you get it for?" I could feel him just itching to give me the facts and figures on his latest financial coup.

"An even million, son. One million dollars. Cash. Enough for that old girl to live the rest of her life in the lap of luxury."

I did some quick math. One million divided by two thousand. "Five hundred an acre. Sounds like a steal."

Colin showed off his grin again. "Damn close, son. Damn close. Would've made me feel bad to get it any cheaper."

I'll bet. Absolutely rotten. "So what's it really worth?"

"Hell, who knows? Real estate's a fickle commodity. Whatever the market will bear. Maybe we'll take a loss." Another big smile from the boss. "But I doubt it. This part of Jersey's booming. Everyone trying to get as far away from New York City as possible. I suspect we'll entertain some pretty interesting numbers. Six million. Eight million. Maybe we can push it to ten million."

So, came my next realization, almost an epiphany, this is how the Crawfords and the Brownes got so stinking rich. By ripping off little old ladies. "Then the plan is to just resell the land as is?"

"Not quite," said Uncle Colin. "We are a land development company, after all. I have my lawyers taking care of the subdivision work with the municipality. And we plan to lay the sewers and build the roads. Of course, these improvements will drive up the cost."

"Of course," I said, getting into the swing of things. "Absolutely." Then, "So how do I fit into the picture? What's my job?"

My job was to sell DELAWARE MOUNTAIN ESTATES to all potential buyers. I spent most of my four-day workweek hanging around the trailer waiting for people to pop in and offer me eight or ten mil. Unless I had prearranged appointments, most days went by without me seeing a soul. I read the newspaper, the latest photography magazines. Took naps and talked on the telephone. Usually with Sarah. Sometimes with Maggie Jane at her law office up in Boston.

When the weather was good I'd venture outside, shoot some film. I got some great shots of the wildlife and the autumn colors down along the river: deer, squirrels, chipmunks, groundhogs, ringneck pheasant, wild turkeys, crows, vultures, hawks, even a belted kingfisher flying low over the Delaware in search of lunch.

Once a week or so, Sarah showed up at the trailer. And when she did we usually hung out the CLOSED sign and locked the door. One cool, damp afternoon, in the heat of passion, someone knocked on that locked door. Loudly.

Sarah just about leapt off the leather sofa. Any and all thoughts of continuing our lovemaking instantly dissipated. I calmed her down, whispered in her ear. "Don't move. I'll get rid of them and be right back."

Maybe not. Another knock on the door followed by a familiar voice. "Mike, you in there? Open up! We got business!" Yup, it was the boss, Uncle Colin.

All color drained from Sarah's face. Scrambled off the sofa, literally dove for her clothes. In a frenzy she searched for discarded socks, panties, jeans, shorts, shoes.

"Colin? Is that you?" I called out with all the cool I could collect.

"Damn right it's me. Open up!"

"Be right with you! Just cleaning up the kitchen!" Did a little scrambling myself then. Pulled my threads together.

And finally, after what seemed like hours, Sarah sat ladylike on the sofa while I pulled open the door. Colin had that big grin of his plastered across his face. Son of a bitch winked at me as he rolled into the trailer.

Sarah stood. "Hello, Uncle Colin." A slight quiver in her voice.

"Sarah!" Colin smiled at his niece. "I thought that looked like your car out there. How are you, dear? Stop by to help Mike tidy up the office?"

I thought a little chuckle might've been in order, but my sweet had guilt all over her lovely face. "No," she said. "I was just in the area. Stopped by to say hello."

Colin gave me another wink. "Right. A little hello. That's nice. I heard you two were . . . pals." He gave us a quick smirk, then moved on. Money on his mind even more than Sex. "I hate to interrupt, but we've got a hot one on his way out. Some big wheel from Long Island. I've been working him for months. He's ready to deal."

I nodded. "Right. Okay."

"Yes, well," announced Sarah, "I was just leaving."

Colin squeezed her shoulder as she headed for the door. "See you later, kid. Say hello to Mom for me."

A small dig. Sarah did her best to ignore it.

I walked her out to the Bimmer. Could see she was pretty upset. "Sorry about that."

"It's not your fault. I just wanted him to wipe that stupid grin off his face. He can be so obnoxious."

A rather complex family dynamic existed between the Browne clan and the Crawford clan. At the time I didn't know exactly how complex. It seems Kate and Colin, brother and sister, were as different as fire and water. Their relationship had simmered with bad blood for decades. Thomas Browne, husband and partner, had managed to hold the two siblings together. But his sudden death had caused their lifelong rift to widen. Especially after Kate inherited half of Crawford & Browne Investments, Inc. She remains to this day a hands-off partner, leaving virtually all business decisions to her brother, but nevertheless taking her share of the profits. For years Colin has been trying to buy her out. Without success.

I gave Sarah a hug and a kiss, said goodbye, then headed back inside. I found Colin hunched over the conference table studying a thick pile of blueprints. "So we've got a hot one, huh?"

"I think so. The guy's a major builder. He's done a couple developments out in Nassau County this size. He must know what he's doing."

I nodded. Didn't know if I should say something about Sarah or not.

The boss went back to his prints. A good five minutes passed. Then, suddenly without even looking at me, he said,

"Listen, Mike, sorry about crashing your party. I had no idea."

"I was out of line. It won't happen again."

Colin found that one pretty funny. "Oh, I think it'll definitely happen again."

"No, I mean . . . it's just that, well, sometimes it's tough for us to, you know, get any time alone. She has the kid, of course. And then there's her . . . her . . . her—"

Colin kept right on laughing. "Her old lady? My lovely sister? Iron Kate?"

"Iron Kate?"

"My nickname for her since we were kids. Stiffest bitch east of the Rockies."

Iron Kate. I liked it. Used it from that day on. "She's kind of protective."

"Kind of protective? Shit! Tight as a pig's ass. Sarah'd still be a virgin if Katie had her druthers."

I permitted myself a small indulgence. "She's a pretty serious gal."

"I used to ask Tom, her husband and my best buddy, God rest his soul, if she ever loosened up. In bed I mean. Now Tom usually kept his own counsel, especially on personal matters, but he said enough to let me know that sister Katie was pretty damn tight in the sack. But that little honey of yours, my lovely niece, she seems quite taken by the act."

I didn't catch his drift. "Huh?"

That's when the bastard slapped me on the back, let fly another laugh. "I maybe shouldn't tell you this, Mike, but I slipped around to the back of the trailer when I first got here. Just to have a look around. Make sure there wasn't any trash lying on the ground. And lo and behold, when I glanced in the picture window I spotted a couple of bodies over on that plush leather sofa. Sarah looked active, son, like she was definitely having a good time. In the saddle no less. And to think, all these years I figured she was a tight-cheeked prude like her mama."

I came damn close to defending my woman's honor by landing a right jab on Colin's jaw, but then this image of the greedy, lecherous uncle peering in the window flashed through my brain. Made me laugh. Right out loud. Right in his face. I wondered how long he'd stood out there watching me make love to his beautiful and sensuous niece. We'd been at it for quite some time when that knock finally hit the door. So I didn't hit him. Didn't do or say anything. Not a word. Just stuffed the insult away in my Crawford & Browne file. A file growing thicker with each passing day.

In early November, after the rains and the north winds had wiped all but the most stubborn leaves from the trees, I donned a tuxedo for just the third time in my life. The first time I acted as Cracker's best man. Second time I led my pretty sister down the matrimonial aisle. Both times I wore a rental.

For my third black tie appearance I wore a borrowed suit. Borrowed from the deceased father of my lover. Thomas Browne, a dandy in his day, had several tuxes in a variety of styles and colors. All stored up in the attic. One day his daughter found one that fit me perfectly. Like a glove. All we had to do was let out the length in the trousers an inch or so.

The affair was the annual Hunt Club Ball ushering in the official opening of the winter foxhunting season. Oh yeah, headed for the club, Sarah at my side, behind the wheel of the Brownes' 1932 Rolls-Royce Phantom. Only got to take the Rolls because Iron Kate was out of town. We made the most of it. Took a long, romantic cruise with a bottle of bubbly. Arrived at the club fashionably late. All the local gentry had turned out for the event. Even those who did not participate in the rather childish, to say nothing of barbaric, practice of riding horses through the woods in pursuit of small, bewildered foxes. It was, after all, the Sport of Kings. And oh how badly many of these affluent folks wanted and needed to think of themselves as American royalty.

I met them all that night. And since I had the great good fortune to meet them on the arm of Ms. Sarah Browne, I attained instant respectability. Tall and straight with a firm handshake and a solid Anglo name to lead my introduction—I had all the proper credentials. The ballroom, after all, was chock-full of Anglophiles. Although in recent years, much to the indignation of the Old Guard, especially certain racist mothers-in-law who will remain anonymous, the club had been infiltrated by various Italians, Greeks, Catholics, and Jews. And now a Polack had slipped through the front door. God, what next?

Three topics pretty much dominated conversation: Horses, Sex, and Money. All else need not apply. The Horse talk was mostly gibberish: feed and farriers, trailers and tack, vets and vaccinations. I soon lost interest. Not my subculture. And the Sex chatter: it proved only slightly more interesting. Mostly melodrama. Infidelity. I had already learned at the Brownes' summer barbecue that everyone in these parts was sleeping with someone other than their mate. Or at least thinking about it. So I only half listened. Had heard it all before anyway. Everywhere I'd ever lived the rumor mills spewed out stories of love, lust, and impropriety. It gave bored and boring people something to gossip about.

But when talk turned to Money, my ears perked up. Hard to pinpoint exactly when, but recently I had become preoccupied with the dark green stuff. Didn't have any myself, but plans, I must confess, had been hatching in my head to get some.

How, I wondered, as I swung my sweet around the dance floor, did these swells get their dough? The answer came not all at once but in dribs and drabs. Doctors, lawyers, and other professionals held their lower-echelon niche: respectable but only relatively rich. Next up came the Wall Streeters and the entrepreneurs: maybe not entirely respectable, but awash with cash. And riding the crest: the Old Money. The heirs and heiresses. Trust funders. They ran the show, dominated the action. Some of them worked. Most of them didn't bother. My love, of course, was an heiress. So too was Mother Kate. They'd done nothing at all for their fortunes other than pull a royal flush during that all-important first hand of draw poker. Thomas Browne made millions, but even had he never made a dime, his wife and kiddies would've eaten from the golden skillet.

Quite a group, those hunt clubbers. Putting on a quite a show.

The music stopped. Time for the orchestra to take a break. Sarah slipped off to the powder room. I sauntered over to the bar, ordered myself a Dewar's on the rocks. Took a look around the room. Everyone laughing, smiling, imbibing. A thousand ways to make Money, I thought. One way: just marry it.

A hand slapped me on the back. Turned and found Colin Crawford. Tall and handsome. Cut quite a figure in his black pants and scarlet jacket. Cut across party lines as well: both a successful businessman and an heir. No one in that room walked with more of a strut than Uncle Colin. "Having a good time, Mike?"

I nodded. "Free food. Free booze. Dancing to a live band."

Colin laughed, took a quick look around the ballroom. "They can be kind of a snooty group," he said, "till you pour enough alcohol into them."

I shrugged, decided not to vent any of my cynicism. "Everyone's been plenty nice to me."

He laughed again. "That's because they're like dogs, son, just sniffing you out, getting a good dose of your scent. But watch yourself. One wrong move and they'll go for the jugular."

"I'll be a good boy."

"Room's abuzz with talk of you and my niece."

"Is that right?"

"Hell yes. What did you think? A complete stranger could waltz in and sweep up one of our most eligible young beauties and no one would say a word?"

I hadn't really thought about it. Just falling in love. Going about my business.

Time for Colin to turn his attention to business as well. "That land deal looks good. All we need to do is get the lawyers together and sign the papers."

That was the best news I'd heard all day. I'd spent two solid weeks wooing that Long Island land developer. Endless walks over the two-thousand-acre mud field, long lunches with blueprints spread across the table, a million phone calls to get all his questions answered. I figured if he bought the land I might have a commission coming my way.

"That's excellent," I told the boss. "How much did we get?"

"Seven and a half million."

The number caused a sudden whistle to stop through my lips. Did some quick math: seven and a half million, less one million for the farmer's wife, another half a million for improvements, maybe half a million for property taxes and legal fees . . . that left Crawford & Browne Investments, Inc., with a tidy sum of five point million dollars. Not too shabby, especially considering that Colin had taken title on the land less than nine months earlier. No wonder he strutted around the hunt club like some prize peacock with his plumes on display.

"Hell," he grumbled, "I should've held out for eight."

Yeah, I felt like telling him, life's a real bitch.

The orchestra returned. Struck up the music. I found my sweet. Rescued her from some dull conversation about stud fees. Swept her out onto the dance floor. Our moves more and more sexual as the hours slipped away. Sarah telling me to behave even as she provoked me to kiss her mouth and rub myself against her sequined thigh. We danced until the orchestra quit. And all the while I kept wondering how much of that five point five mil might come my way. Even one half of one percent would be twenty-seven thousand five hundred smack-a-roos. Not a bad payday. As we left the ball, practically the last to leave, climbed into our Rolls, my mind swirled with ways to spend the Money: cameras, lenses, clothes, trips to Shangri-la. I might need more, I decided. Much more.

November came and mostly went. Cold, raw, and rainy. The deal went through with the developers from Long Island. We closed the trailer, had it towed away. I started reporting to the office in Far Hills to tie up any loose ends.

Wednesday, the day before Thanksgiving, I went upstairs to have a chat with the boss. Found him practicing his fly fishing casts. He told me he was off to Chile in a few days to catch the big rainbows. I thought he might invite me along, but nope, not part of the plan.

I hemmed and hawed for a while, made small talk. Finally he got sick of me hovering. "What's the deal, kid? What's on your mind?"

I decided to go straight at it. No use pulling any punches. Told him I thought a commission might be in line after the big land sale.

"Commission!" roared Colin Crawford. "You must be shitting me. Whoever said anything about a commission?"

I took a step or two back. "No one. But I just thought since I helped put the deal together that—"

"What the hell did you do? You didn't do shit. Hung around in that cozy goddamn trailer porking my niece. Commission! Fucking-A commission!" Then he crossed to his desk, pressed a button on his phone. "Anne!" he shouted. "Put me on the intercom. I got something to say."

An instant later, Uncle Colin's voice boomed throughout the offices of Crawford & Browne Investments, Inc. "Listen up, people: I got a joker in my office who thinks he should get a commission on a land deal we recently completed. Anybody else thinks this joker should get a cut, get up here now and tell the old man about it!"

No one came.

"You see, Standish," explained the boss, "we don't work on commission around here. Commission's a dirty word. We work on salary. Right now you earn a pretty shitty salary, but that's because you haven't been here very long and because you don't do much. Put in your time, earn your keep, and someday you might make a few bucks."

So what did I do? What did I say? I probably should have clocked the bastard for humiliating me like that in front of my co-workers. But I didn't. Nope, I didn't do a thing. Didn't say a word. Just made my retreat. Back to work. Back to my desk. I had a different plan brewing in my head, an entirely different scheme for getting my cut of the green.

On Thanksgiving I popped the question. That's right. After the turkey had been carved and consumed. After the mashed potatoes and gravy. After the cornbread and the bean casserole. After the cranberry sauce and salad. After the vanilla ice cream and the pumpkin pie. After the coffee and the fifty-year-old port. After the football games. After all the Crawfords and Brownes, aunts and uncles and cousins, nephews and nieces, had fled TREETOPS. Gone home. After Timothy, exhausted, had dragged himself up to bed. After Katherine, satisfied all had been amply fed and entertained, had retired to her room. After the house stood perfectly still, empty except for the two young lovers sitting quietly on the sofa in the living room. After all that, I popped the question.

I had never asked anyone to marry me before. A couple times I almost had, but always, at the last second, I'd come to my senses. Almost did on Thanksgiving as well. All day long, with the festivities circling around me, I'd been working the idea over in my head. And not just that day but for the past few weeks. Did I really want to get married? To Sarah? What if she rejected me? Laughed in my face? Hell, I decided, I didn't really care about that. Besides, I didn't think she would. I felt pretty confident she loved me. Of course, things other than love could stand in our way. Marrying me would send her mother into a rage, and Sarah hated upsetting her mother. But I didn't think that would stop her. In fact, Iron Kate had grown so ugly with her attacks on my character that I figured it might actually cause the daughter to say yes partly out of spite. Not that I wanted her to marry me out of spite. Oh, so many different scenarios. So many different subplots. Tough to keep them all straight. The Sex. The Family. The Money. Oh yeah, the Money. Kept asking myself over and over if I just wanted to marry Sarah for the Money. Or was it Love? True Love? Sure, we had a good time together. A great time. Lots of laughs. Lots of romance. Endless discussions about everything under the sun. Incredible Sex. The best sex of my life. But my God, the Money, all that fricking Money. I couldn't pretend that it didn't have some slight influence. I mean, Maggie Jane was right, had Sarah been just another girl in the long line of girls, without the Bimmer or the Tudor or the trust fund, would I have been contemplating the Big Question? I don't know. Didn't know then. Don't really know now. Just know I finally fetched up the courage and went ahead and did it.

We sat on the goose down sofa, my arm around her neck, her hand on my thigh, our bellies full of food, our hearts full of fondness. A minute passed. Two minutes. Ten minutes. Sarah yawned, swung her legs up onto the sofa, put her head in my lap.

"Tired?"

She nodded. "I wish we could just go upstairs and go to bed."

"Yeah," I said, "me too."

She closed her eyes, nestled up against me. I looked down at her and felt a surge of emotion unlike any I had ever felt before. And right then the words came tumbling out. "So, I've been thinking . . . wondering . . . wondering if maybe . . . you know, what you thought about, about us . . . about us maybe getting . . . you know—"

Her eyes came wide open. She stared right into mine. Waited for me to finish, but when I didn't, couldn't, she helped me out. "I don't know, Michael. What?"

I took a deep breath. "You know, I just thought that, well, that you might want to get married."

She smiled, even laughed just a little bit. "My God, Michael, the M word. Are you actually asking me to marry you?"

I held her gaze for as long as I could. Then I glanced away. Shrugged. Trying with all my might to find my cool, my nonchalance. "Well, yeah, I guess I am. I'm asking you to marry me."

There. I said it.

And what did Sarah say? She said, after a second or two, "Do you love me?"

I nodded. Didn't even have to think about it. "I do. Yes. Absolutely. I love you."

She thought about it some more. A couple minutes. She held my hand. And then, "Of course I want to marry you, Michael. But I can't say yes. Not yet, not right away."

Another deep breath. Followed by a sigh. Probably I looked a little hurt. Maybe slightly relieved as well. "Right, of course, I wouldn't want you to say yes, not right away. I mean, you should think about it. We've only been together, only really known each other, for a few months."

Yup, that's all it had been: a few short months. But God, we'd unleashed years of feelings and emotions in that brief spit of time.

Sarah thought about it for a week. We both thought about it for a week. Just about every waking second we thought about it. We didn't talk about it; just thought about it. Silently. Inside of our own heads.

Sarah thought about how great it could be, how wonderful, how passionate. But she also thought about the pain if it didn't work out, if she discovered somewhere down the road that I was psychopath number three. Or maybe just some conniving cad out to get her Money. My sweet was no dummy after all; she fully understood the powers of deception. But then she thought about sleeping next to my warm, hard body night after night. About making love. Making babies. Oh yeah, we'd talked about making babies. In those few short months we'd talked about everything. And finally, she had to think about her mother. She knew Kate would be angry. Upset. Furious. But still, she would have to make up her own mind. Nothing and no one would stand in her way if she decided to say yes.

For seven days Sarah thought about all these things. Around and around she spun. Weighing the pros and cons. Filling and emptying and filling our cup over and over. She told me about her ambivalence later, after the die had been cast.

And then one morning in the first week of December, with a bone-chilling rain pouring out of a low gray sky, Sarah arrived at the cottage. Unannounced. With her answer. She knocked and entered. She couldn't find me in the kitchen or the living room. Crossed to the bedroom door, the bedroom I used as a darkroom. By that time she knew not to enter a darkroom without knocking. "Michael, are you in there?"

"I am, but don't come in. I'm with another woman."

"You're what?"

"I'm with another woman. I'll be right out."

"You are not with another woman," she insisted. And then, "I've decided."

My thoughts preoccupied with the work at hand, it took me a couple seconds to respond. "You've decided what?"

"I have an answer for you."

"An answer to what?"

"To the question you asked me on Thanksgiving."

That brought me to attention. "Should I sit down?" I, as you can imagine, had been having some ambivalence of my own. I wanted her to say yes because I loved and adored her. But at the same time I was worried I might not be worthy of her love. I mean, what if I messed up? Made her life miserable like those scumbags Cramer and Carlson? Believe me, I was riddled with fear and foreboding.

"My answer, Michael, is yes."

I slapped myself on the side of the head. "Yes?"

"That's right, Michael. Yes!"

In an instant my ambivalence vanished. My future, happy and bright, flashed before my eyes. I threw open the darkroom door. I stood there before my sweet as naked as the day Jessie had pushed me into the world. Great big grin on my face. "I knew you'd say yes. I knew it."

Sarah stared at me, at my nakedness. Confused, she peered into the darkroom, I suppose in search of that woman I'd mentioned. "Why," she wanted to know, "are you naked?"

I threw my arms around her waist, lifted her easily off the ground, kissed her hard on the lips. "Because it's hot in there, baby. Because sometimes I work myself into a frenzy." Kissed her again. All over her pretty face. "Come on, I want to show you something." I carried her into the darkroom. Put her on her feet. Right in front of an 11 x 14 print fresh out of the bath. Still moist and glistening. A full-color print of Katherine Browne. Iron Kate. My soon-to-be Mama-in-Law. A full head shot, from the neck up. Life size. Flattering of the old girl it was not. I'd snapped it with the Iron One in full fury, her jaw set in steel, her eyes narrowed and glaring.

Sarah practically recoiled from the image. "God! When did you take that?"

"A couple weeks ago. One day when she was grumbling about something."

Sarah stepped up for a closer look. "I love my mother," she said. "Love her with all my heart. But Michael, shoot me if I ever scowl like that."

"You never will," I whispered in her ear, "because you'll never have to. I'm going to make you smile, Sarah. I'm going to make you smile all the time."

We announced our intentions a couple weeks later at the Brownes' annual Christmas party. Prior to the party we told no one. Not Mother Kate. Not Uncle Colin. Not Cracker. Not his lovely wife, Alison. Not a soul. Oh no, wait, that's not right, we did tell someone. Of course we told someone. That very afternoon, after Sarah said yes and I put some clothes on, we went and told Tim. Actually we didn't tell him; we sat down on the edge of his bed and asked him what he thought of the idea.

"Married!" he shouted, so loudly Sarah put her index finger over his lips so that his always lurking grandmother would not overhear. "I've been praying every night for weeks that you guys would get married."

Sarah gave her son a hug, felt a tear roll down her cheek. *My sweet now had the blessing she most wanted. Plus a vow from him not to utter a word of this to anyone.*

And so, with the Christmas lights in the windows, with the Christmas tree trimmed and topped with a silver angel, with mistletoe hanging in every doorway, with the big Tudor once again full of family and friends, Sarah and Tim and I made our announcement. Must've been a hundred people milling around the house. Drinking red and green Christmas punch. Munching on red and green Christmas cookies. Singing Christmas carols. All this when, from the top of the landing in the center hallway, beneath the huge crystal chandelier, those partygoers heard a familiar voice calling for their attention.

"Please!" shouted the beautiful Sarah Louise Browne in her melodious voice. "If I could just have your attention for a minute! My son has a very brief announcement to make."

The crowd slowly grew quiet. Attentive. Their eyes glanced up. Saw the three of us standing close together on the landing. Tim in the middle. I had the feeling we already looked like a family. And then, out of the corner of my eye, I spotted Iron Kate. She came out of the kitchen. In a big hurry. Looking anxious. Confused. Spotted us up there in no time. Made eye contact with me. For a split second. I promptly looked away.

"I just want to say," said young Tim, "that this is going to be the best Christmas ever. The best Christmas because my mom," and he took his mother's hand, "and our best pal Mike," and the kid took my hand, "are getting married!"

Tim raised our hands up over his head. The crowd, for just an instant, gasped, then recovered with a rousing cheer. Hoots, hollers, and whistles filled the house. Of course, not every last soul could be seen beaming with joy and good cheer. Cracker looked confused. Alison looked downright pissed off. And Mama Kate, well, she stood there in her red and green apron, a long cake-cutting knife in her right hand. Looked like she might enjoy plunging that knife into the abdomen of yours truly. I watched as friends and family arrived at her side, offering their warmest congratulations. Kate had little choice but to smile, thank them all very much.

Coward that I sometimes am, I slipped away that evening before my future mother-in-law could get her hands around my neck. Left all parental explanations up to my sweet. A harbinger, I would gather, of things to come.

Kate descended on Sarah's bedroom after all the guests had gone home. Her iron fist pounded on my lover's door. "Sarah, are you in there?"

This part of the wedding announcement Sarah easily could have avoided. "I guess."

"May I come in?" Kate entered, closed the door behind her. "You at least could have had the decency to tell me ahead of time."

Sarah nodded. "You're right, Mother. I apologize. I just didn't want to listen to you belittle Michael. Tell me that I was making a terrible mistake."

"But marriage, Sarah, my God! You've only known this man a few months."

"I know him as well as I've ever known anyone."

"That's impossible. You're being ridiculous. You've never even met his parents."

"I told you, Mother. His mother is dead. And he is estranged from his father."

Tough, Sarah later told me, to tell who was more exasperated. Mother or daughter.

A loud, windy sigh from the mother, followed by, "So this is something you fully intend to do?"

"Yes, Mother, it is. I plan to marry Michael."

Iron Kate ever so slightly winced at the sound of my name. "I see. And may I ask when?"

"We haven't decided exactly."

"Tomorrow? Next week? Next month? Next year?"

Sarah felt pretty small, like a little kid. Just the way mommy wanted her to feel. "I'm sure it won't be tomorrow or next week."

"So sometime next year?"

"I suppose. Yes."

This back and forth, this pushing and shoving, struggling for position, went on for quite a while. Most of the night by Sarah's account. One small step at a time, the mother broke down the daughter. Katherine used all her oldest and best strategies to gain an advantage: guilt, anger, manipulation. Sarah grew more and more helpless under the continuing barrage. By the time Kate finally retired to her bedroom, she had turned her daughter into a little girl again, say seven or eight years old. A girl willing to bend to her mother's will. Bend but not break. She was her mother's daughter, after all. She had a strong, stubborn streak of her own. And so, as they parted company, she still fully intended to marry the Polack.

But on two other very important points, she had bowed to her mother's wishes. The first, one could conclude, was not all that big a deal: there would be no wedding until spring. April or May at the earliest. But the second point, make no mistake, had trouble, Big Trouble, scrawled all over it: Sarah agreed that after the wedding, the three of us, she and I and young Tim, would reside right there at TREE-TOPS. That, of course, meant the mother, the daughter, and the brand-new son-in-law would all be cohabiting under the same roof. Mama's roof.

"Just temporarily," went the Iron One's argument. "Just until everyone has a chance to settle down. Get acquainted. Just until we're all sure this is going to work out. No one ever regretted an extra moment of caution."

Sarah, exhausted, browbeaten, dizzy with guilt, caved in. Nodded her pretty head up and down. Without further discussion, she consented to this demand.

The Iron Bitch, down but definitely not out, packed up her ugly little victory and steered herself off to bed.

Now, as you can easily imagine, the long-range consequences of this seemingly innocuous agreement would cause all kinds of problems. Like maybe somebody should have consulted me. Let me know the options. And I ain't talking wedding plans here, I'm talking bedroom plans. I'm talking the location of where this boy lays his head at night. But no, I was just the future groom from the wrong side of the tracks. The stupid Polack who would do what he was told. Keep his mouth shut and his tail wagging.

Fine. So now I'm down here on this stinking Devil's Cay. Lost and all alone. And maybe I wouldn't be if that Bitch had minded her own business. Stayed out of our lives. Maybe come over on Sunday afternoons for a pork roast dinner.

Sure thing, Mike. If only Kate had stayed clear everything would've been just peachy. You would've been a good boy, stuck next to your woman through thick and thin, through sickness and health, till death did make the two of you part.

Look at me: nothing but a shell of my former cocky confident self. Sitting on my bed here at Lewey's Hotel. Staring at an 8 x 10 of my lover lost. God, what a sight! Pitiful.

And what about last night? You know what I did last night? I slipped into Lewey's office after he'd gone to bed and put his phone against my ear. Told myself a couple days ago I wouldn't do that, couldn't do that, but then I went ahead and did it anyway. Even went so far as to contact the overseas operator. But when she asked for the number I wanted to call, I came to my senses: told her never mind, put that phone back in its cradle, crept back up here to my room, tail between my legs.

I didn't sleep much. Hardly a wink. Restless. Agitated. Sweaty from the intense heat and maybe a fever. Feeling mildly delusional. Took a swim just after dawn. To cool off, get a little exercise. Swam out to the reef, did some snorkeling with a mask I'd borrowed from Lewis, peered through the plastic at some small fluorescent fish with huge bugged-out eyes.

Middle of the afternoon now. Tried to shoot some portraits earlier, but ever since Mama Rolle put that curse on me, no one on this crappy little island will even talk to me, much less pose for a photograph. That's not entirely true. Lewis still talks to me. Though lately, I've noticed, he keeps it brief.

So I sit on my bed, hot and bothered, thinking about my woman: her smell, her smile, her laugh, her pout, the way she wraps the tea bag around the spoon to squeeze out the water, the way she looks at me when we kiss, the way she always calls my name just before she comes, the way she likes to fall asleep on her side with my chest pressed up against her back . . .

I got it bad today. Real bad. I need to get out of this room. Now.

I wipe the sweat off my face. Change my shirt. Head down to the bar. Take my usual stool. Home sweet home.

Lewis, as always, rubbing those glasses. Doesn't he get sick of that? "What'll it be, Mr. Weston?"

"Bahama Mama, Lewis. Don't be shy with the rum."

"No mon, never shy." He begins to mix up the lethal concoction. "So how you feeling this afternoon, Mr. Weston? Over the grippe you had earlier?"

"I feel lousy, Lewis. My whole body aches. Plus I got a fever."

"Probably all the heat and humidity, mon. Does that to folks who ain't used to it. Wipes 'em right out."

"Plus this damn thing with Mama Rolle."

"Oh yeah, mon, that too, that too. That give you the chills, mon. Hot and cold and hot again all in the same minute."

I let out a sigh. Suck down half my Mama the second Lewis puts it in front of me. As soon as I pull my lips away from the straw, I hear the sound of that whiny seaplane again, the one belonging to Roland Milo.

Lewis confirms. "Must be Milo back to pick up that couple."

"Already? They just got here yesterday."

"I heard they put a call into Nassau this morning. Asked him to come over and pick them up as soon as possible."

I take another pull on the straw. Enjoy the momentary relief the sweet, fruity rum brings to my physical and emotional well-being. "Why so soon? What's their big hurry?"

Lewis looks across the bar at me. "Gotta be the hurricane, mon. Nothing else drive them off that fast."

"Hurricane? What hurricane?"

"The one Milo told us about yesterday."

I sit up, quit my slouching. "You mean he was serious?"

"Absolutely, mon. This look like the real thing."

"Jesus. When it's supposed to hit? Hell, where's it supposed to hit?"

"Excellent questions, Mr. Weston. Not too many answers yet. It has a name though."

"A name?"

"This one's a lady. They call her Bertha."

"And where is this Bertha now?"

"Off in the Atlantic, mon. Be here in a couple days if it stays its course."

"Come on, Lewis. Right here? On Devil's Cay?"

"Could blow right through the lobby, mon."

"So what the hell do we do? You know, if it hits?"

"We go down in the basement of St. Andrew's Parish. The only basement on the island. Put our heads between our legs and pray to God to carry us through. Even those who don't believe, mon, trust me, in a hurricane, they pray."

I can feel the adrenaline pumping through my body. Or maybe it's just fear. All I know for sure is that I didn't count on being part of some hurricane. That never entered into my plans. Another sigh from deep down in my belly, then, "Maybe I ought to catch a ride out of here with Milo."

"Not this trip, mon."

"Why not?"

"That seaplane full, Mr. Weston. One of the Rolles about to have a baby. Milo taking her and her husband over to Nassau to the hospital."

"Jesus!" I try to collect myself, calm my thoughts. "So maybe I can get him to come back. Yeah, that's it. I'll go tell him to come back and get me."

Lewis shrugs, goes on rubbing. I head for the front door. But the second I reach the street, I hear the engine of that seaplane working itself into a frenzy. I stop. Stare down the hill at the harbor. The seaplane taxis. I wildly wave my arms. A moment of desperation. But for naught. Up, up, and away goes Milo.

Lewis stands at my side. "Not to worry, mon. Bertha probably change her mind. They usually do. And if not, you maybe get some fantastic pictures."

Pictures. Right. Pictures of this useless little speck of an island leveled by the winds and submerged beneath the raging sea. To hell with pictures.

What about Sarah? Where is she? Any chance she might get here before that damn Bertha broad slams into us?

There she is: still riding in the passenger seat of that Lincoln Town Car. The one Glenn Sheldon, P.I., rented

over in Fort Myers. Almost midnight. Upper end of the
Keys. Islamorada. U.S. 1 South. Heading for Key West. Looking for me.

Sheldon sits behind the wheel. He sneaks a peak at my
sweet. Sarah sound asleep. She's been asleep practically
since they left Grandma Becky's house on Sanibel. Fine
with Sheldon. Gives him a chance to drink and drive fast
without her bitching and moaning. Reaches into the back
for his bottle of brandy. Good brandy has long been
Glenn's cocktail of choice for extended motor trips. He sips
it, barely enough to wet his tongue, feels the heat rush
down his throat. Just a nip every ten miles or so and the P.I.
can drive for hours. Thinks about turning on the radio,
searching the dial for some big band tunes, maybe some
Tommy Dorsey or some Glenn Miller. Figures there has to
be a station down here playing that old jazzy stuff, what
with all these old farts and blue hairs creeping around the
Sunshine State. But he's afraid the music will wake up his
client. So in between sips, Sheldon takes long, leisurely
looks at the sleeping beauty at his side. Goddamn, he practically says right out loud, I sure would like to get inside this
one's pants. Probably a bitch though. But maybe not. You
never know. Impossible to tell until the real action starts.
Another sip. Another glance. She half sits, half lies across
the big leather seat. Leans against the door, head thrown
back, wedged between the window and the headrest.
Breathes evenly through her open mouth. Sheldon thinks
maybe, just maybe, if I turn the wheel sharply, not too
sharply, I might just be able to . . . yes, here we go . . . a little more . . . yes, here she comes . . . Sarah's weight shifts.
Her whole body sways. Sheldon catches her with his right
hand, gently lowers her body across the seat. He manages
to settle the side of her head right onto his lap, practically
right smack on top of his maleness, without interrupting her
slumber.

Son of a bitch. I'll kill him when they get here.

Wait, she's waking up. Her head flies off Sheldon's lap. Grabs her stomach. A sudden rush of nausea. Her chest heaves. Her mouth sputters. Between sputters she yells, "Stop the car! Pull over! Stop the car!"

Sheldon, confused but obedient, steers the big Lincoln onto the shoulder of the highway. As soon as the car stops, Sarah opens the door and spills herself out onto the loose gravel. Hot out there, even now in the middle of the night. Hot like fire. And humid. Wet. But Sarah has no time to contemplate the heat. No, she gathers herself and retches into the weeds. Not much, just a moist little pile.

Immediately she feels better. Climbs back into the Town Car.

Sheldon looks a little bewildered. "You okay?"

Sarah, as always, perfectly calm. "I'm fine. Where are we?"

"Just south of Long Key."

"How much farther to Key West?"

"Maybe an hour. Hour and a half."

Sarah glances at the digital clock on the dash: 12:34. "I think we should find a motel, get some sleep. We'll go on to Key West in the morning." My sweet, I see, is feeling cranky. Maybe even angry. Angry at me, of course. Angry at herself.

"Why don't we just push on tonight?"

And angry at Sheldon. She can smell the brandy wafting through the car. In no mood to argue. "Because I want to stop. As soon as possible."

Her tone does not leave room for discussion.

They keep driving. Sarah turns on the radio. The word hurricane echoes through the car as she scans through the stations. The word has no impact on the occupants whatsoever. Abruptly, she turns off the radio. Thinks about being sick to her stomach. "My God!"

"What is it?" asks Sheldon. "Are you going to barf again?"

Sarah, indignant, shakes her head. "No, I'm not going to barf again." But she knows now the reason for her nausea. At least she thinks she does. She does not feel sick. Only nauseous. The same way she felt with Timothy. She counts the days, does some calculations. Realizes she's overdue, way overdue. She should have gotten her period the same day I disappeared. Thinks about it some more, goes over her addition once again. The numbers add up.

Just stay calm, she tells herself, it might be a false alarm. And if it's not? So what? We wanted to have a baby. We talked about having a baby. Michael said he wanted to be a father. He'll make a great father. But where is he? What if I can't find him? What if I'm pregnant and I never see him again?

Nice work, Mike. First-class. You should be tarred, feathered, shot between the eyes.

"Dammit!" she announces, right out loud. "This is all so stupid, so idiotic!"

Sheldon, startled, jumps. Takes a quick look at his client, then shifts his eyes back to the straight white line separating the two lanes of U.S. 1.

They drive onto Marathon Key. Plenty of motels. One after another lining both sides of the highway. Decide to try the Bonefish Bay Motel. A cluster of low, one-story buildings set back from the road in a grove of royal palms. Quiet, dark, private. Too quiet, dark, and private if you ask me. Place looks deserted. The palms sway back and forth, propelled by a hot, wet breeze blowing out of the south. Sarah and Sheldon don't know it but hurricane season has arrived in the Florida Keys, and all that moist tropical air blowing out of the Caribbean is a pretty good sign that very low pressure could be on its way.

Sarah goes into the office. Has to wake up the owner-operator, a gruff-looking old dame wearing a Miami Dolphins tee shirt over her skinny and wrinkled body. Two rooms. Rooms 10 and 12. Out back. Just across the parking lot.

Sheldon carries my wife's bag from the Lincoln to room 10. Sweat pours off his brow by the time he reaches the door. "It's like a damn sauna bath out there."

Sarah grants him a curt nod, takes her bag, goes into the room, closes and locks the door. Good girl. The room is a small somber affair, barely enough space to pass between the bureau and the bed: a lumpy-looking mattress covered by a ratty turquoise spread.

She tries not to think about it. Tries not to think about anything. About how much she misses Timothy. Misses me. About how much she hates me for leading her on this wild goose chase. Puts down her bag. Crosses to the sink. Washes her hands and face. Looks at herself in the mirror. Sees me standing there. "You told me you would love me forever, Michael. Love me and take care of me and make me happy."

A knock on the door.

Startled, she takes a moment to answer. "Yes?"

"It's me, Sheldon."

"What do you want?"

"I found your purse in the car. Thought you might want it."

Sarah sighs, crosses to the door, swings it open.

Sheldon stands there looking big and ominous. The bottle of brandy has been sucked dry. This P.I., look at him, feeling no pain. "How you doing, kid? Everything okay?" Slurs his words.

Sarah reaches out for her pocketbook. "Everything's fine."

Sheldon pulls the pocketbook back, just out of reach. Smiles. "I thought you might like some company."

His breath slams into her face. It feels hot, smells like fire. "Excuse me?"

"You know," he says, very suave, "someone to help dispel the loneliness."

Sarah snaps. In no mood for this. Reaches out and grabs her pocketbook. Tries to pull it away. Sheldon hangs on.

"Let go, Mr. Sheldon! Let go and then go back to your room. You're drunk."

Sheldon laughs. Remembers how her head felt resting in his lap as they cruised along in the Lincoln. Decides it might be nice to get that feeling again. He pushes her backwards, into the room. Follows her in, shoves the door closed with his foot.

"I hope you know what you're doing, Mr. Sheldon."

Sheldon nods his head up and down. "Oh yeah, honey, I know exactly what I'm doing."

All that booze has bolstered his manly desires. Testosterone practically shoots out of his eyes. He gives her a shove, pushes her toward the bed.

Sarah thinks maybe she should scream. But will anyone hear? It might just make him violent. She feels both angry and afraid; not at all sure what to do. No way, she decides, am I going to let him get me onto the bed.

He gives her another shove. Lightly. Nothing too rough. Still wears that boozy smile on his face. Grabs her shoulders. Draws her close. Tries for another kiss.

Sarah turns her head. Sheldon finds her ear. He sticks his fat, swollen, brandy-stained tongue into it.

My sweet pulls back. "Get out, Sheldon! Get out of my room, now!"

Sheldon clutches at her, rubs his sweaty palm over her breast, makes another attempt to find her lips.

Jesus, this bastard's going to rape her. But not without a fight. My wife slips out of his grasp, heads for the back of the room. He pursues, but not with any great agility. Look at him: the jackass has dropped his drawers. And now he's trying to get his grimy white dress shirt up over his head without undoing the buttons. Has himself momentarily tied up.

Sarah Louise, a hell of a lot more spunk than you might think, does not waste a second. Springs into action. Goes for the heavy brass lamp on the bureau. Sweeps it up with both hands. Brings it crashing down on Sheldon's head before the P.I. can tear himself loose from his shirt. A mighty groan spills from his mouth. He teeters there for a few seconds. Then down he goes. Straight onto the floor.

Sarah stands over him, motionless, struggles to catch her breath. Then, not wasting a second, she grabs her bags and heads for the door. Outside: the warm, wet darkness. And the Lincoln: locked. The keys: back in the room. Probably in Sheldon's pocket. She turns, takes a few steps, puts her hand on the doorknob. No, wait! This is not some rank horror flick where the creature gets one last shot at the maiden. This is my wife we're talking about here. Sarah does the smart thing: she gets the hell away from there. Runs across the parking lot of the Bonefish Bay Motel. North along Route 1: for home. No, south: for Key West. She stops, turns in circles. Where should I go? What should I do? Damn you, Michael. Damn you!

She spots another motel. A Days Inn. Fearing Sheldon might be close on her heels, she heads for the light of the motel office. The clerk, drowsy at this early morning hour, dozes behind the front desk. Sarah wakes him, asks for a room.

The clerk, a scrawny kid with a raging case of acne, hands her a registration card. Sarah takes a look at the requested info. Immediately she begins to fabricate a new identity: name, address, telephone number. All phony. All fictitious.

"All right," says the clerk as he looks over the registration card, "and how will you be paying this evening . . . Mrs. Cramer?"

Mrs. Cramer! What's up with that?

"Cash," answers Sarah. She hands him the money.

He hands her a key. "The room," he tells her, "is out back. Second floor."

Sarah thanks him, slips out into the night. Takes a look around. No sign of Sheldon. Wait! Was that the Lincoln, cruising slowly down U.S. 1? She's not sure. But she's not going to wait around to find out.

Once safely in her room, the door locked and bolted, she has to stop, ask herself what should be done next. Should I call the police? What will I tell them? How will I explain? Who should I call? What should I do?

She sits on the edge of the bed. Weeping and shaking. Finally, she picks up the telephone. After a moment, she begins to dial.

I would like to report that the phone rang here at Lewey's Hotel. Rang and I picked it up and informed my bride that I would arrive at the Days Inn on Marathon Key posthaste. ASAP.

But no, the phone did not ring here at Lewey's Hotel. The phone rang about fifteen hundred miles north of here.

Eyes closed, fast asleep, she hears it ringing. Thinks it must be part of her dream. Finally, along about the tenth ring, she realizes it's not. Her hand pokes around in the darkness. It's out there somewhere, on the nightstand. Forces one eye open. Glances at the alarm clock: 2:26 A.M. For chrissakes, who could be calling at this hour?

"Yes? Hello?"

"Alison?"

"Yes?"

"It's Sarah."

"Sarah!"

The name brings Cracker wide awake.

"I know it's late, but, well, I had to call. I guess it's an emergency."

"An emergency?"

Cracker hears this and his ears and eyes open wide.

"Yes," Sarah says, "an emergency." She's doing her best to stay calm. "I was wondering, if he's up, if I could possibly talk to Graham."

Normally Alison would react with no small amount of hostility if another woman called her husband in the middle of the night, but tonight Allie holds her tongue. Not only is this woman her hubby's ex-sister-in-law, but some tasty tidbits concerning the disappearance of one Michael Joseph Standish Standowski might come spilling out of Sarah's mouth. "Hold on a second. Let me see if he's awake."

"I'm awake," he says softly.

"It's Sarah."

"I heard."

Alison hands him the receiver. "She says it's an emergency."

Cracker nods. "Hello?"

"Graham. I'm sorry to call at such an ungodly hour."

"Sarah, what's the matter? Is everything all right?"

Right away, long-distance, she starts to sob.

"Sarah, what is it? Tell me what's happened. Where are you?"

"Florida."

"Florida!"

Cracker and Alison make eye contact. Alison strains to hear. Cracker presses the receiver to his ear so Sarah's words cannot escape.

"Yes. Florida. Marathon Key."

Cracker can hear her sobbing, crying. Her voice breaking. "Are you okay?"

More sobs. "I guess . . . I don't know . . . He tried . . . He tried to rape me."

"What! Who tried to rape you? Mike?"

The R word causes Alison's ears to instantly triple in size. She tries to worm her way closer to the receiver but Cracker fends her off, even throws her an evil eye.

"No," sobs my sweet, "of course not Michael."

"Then who?"

"Sheldon."

"Sheldon?"

"The private eye."

"What private eye?"

Sarah lets loose with a full-fledged bath of tears. She'd held it together during the assault and the escape, but now, safe and secure, her old friend Graham on the line, she breaks down. "Michael . . . he . . . he," the words catch in her throat as she tries to control herself. "Like you said, he . . . he . . . he left . . . Disappeared . . . He did something terrible, Graham, and now he's . . . he's . . . he's—"

"Sarah, just slow down. Take it easy. Are you safe?"

Sarah nods. "Yes," she tells him. "I'm safe."

"Good. I don't want you to explain. Not now. I just want you to tell me exactly where you are. Tell me where you are and I'll be there as soon as I can."

Now it's Alison's turn to cast an evil eye. "You'll what?"

Cracker, my best buddy, ignores his wife. "Tell me where you are, Sarah."

Sarah struggles to catch her breath. "You'll come?"

"Yes."

"Now?"

"Yes."

"The Days . . . The Days Inn. Marathon Key. Room . . . room 215."

"I got it, Sarah. Now just stay put. Don't go out. Don't leave the room."

"Alison," Sarah tells him, "I'm registered as Alison . . . Alison Cramer."

Cracker does a double take upon receipt of this news, but tells her again he'll be there as soon as possible. They hang up.

No choice now but to meet his wife's eyes. "What was that all about?"

Cracker sighs. "I don't know. She's in some trouble."

"She was raped?"

Cracker climbs off the bed. "I don't know. I don't think so. I think she's just upset."

She follows him into the bathroom. He snaps on the light. It nearly blinds them. "So what are you doing?"

"I'm going to Florida."

"You're going to Florida?"

"Yes."

"Just like that. Little helpless Sarah snaps her finger and Graham the savior rushes off to Florida?"

Cracker doesn't want to think about his motivations. Or the consequences of his actions. "She needs help, Allie."

"So why does she call you?"

"We're family, Alison. Christ, we're practically brother and sister."

"Bullshit!"

She's right, he thinks, that is bullshit. I never wanted Sarah to be my sister. I wanted her to be my lover.

God Almighty, the wild webs we do weave.

Morning now. Cracker on the move. He catches the 6:55 flight out of Newark bound for Miami. Daydreams all the way south. About renting a convertible, cruising the Keys with the top down, the wind in his hair, Sarah at his side. Imagines the two of them searching for me in the watering holes of Key Largo and Key West. But the scoundrel always one step ahead, Sarah upset, crying on Cracker's shoulder, the two of them growing closer and closer, sharing a kiss and maybe even . . .

The plane hits the ground. A little after ten. Cracker, his small overnight bag slung over his shoulder, heads straight for the Avis rental car counter. But when he gets there he doesn't ask for a convertible. Too much guilt for that. Instead he takes a Chevy Corsica with free unlimited mileage. Maybe the same Chevy Corsica I rented just a few days back. Was that only a few days? Seems more like a few years.

Cracker heads south. Reaches Key Largo early in the afternoon. He hasn't been to the Keys since college. Since the time he and I went there on spring break. Oh yeah, Cracker remembers that trip. His travel mate had like fifty bucks to last him a dozen days. Cracker shakes his head thinking about how I practically robbed my way from Miami to Key West.

That may be a slight exaggeration. Okay, I stole some food, maybe a pair of shorts, a couple tee shirts, a fishing rod from that tackle shop on Big Pine Key. Not that much, just what I needed to get through another day. Cracker, nervous, afraid I'd get caught, he'd get implicated, kept offering to pay, but hell, I didn't want to impose on him. Although, as Cracker soon realized, that was only half the story. The other half had to do with the fact that I enjoyed the thrill of pulling those small jobs, making off with a box of donuts or a beer mug from Captain Tony's Key West Saloon.

Now, thinks Cracker, the guy is on the loose again, wandering around the Keys without a care in the world, probably humping a different woman every night. But this time he's not going to get away with it. I'm not going to let him. This time he's messing with Sarah. This time he's going to pay for his sins.

Cracker scowls, concentrates on the road ahead. He spots a sign: MARATHON 46 MILES. Steps hard on the accelerator. The Corsica shoots forward.

When I covered those same miles last week, I drove my Corsica much slower, stopping every few miles to take pictures, stare out at the endless vistas of calm blue water. I had nowhere to go, no destination in mind. I was not, however, just wandering around the Keys, humping a different woman every night. Far from it. I was then, as now, lonely and troubled, constantly looking over my shoulder, worried I'd never see Sarah again. I stopped every few miles because I had nothing else to do, no one to see, no one waiting for me at the end of the road.

But Cracker doesn't know any of this. He still thinks I'm the coolest, most laid-back guy on earth, never worried about a damn thing. Ask him and he'll tell you life's troubles just roll off Standish like water off a duck's back.

He conjures me up again with his imagination. Sees me cozied up to some bar, sucking on a brew, hitting on some suntanned babe, giving her a line. He can't wait to get his hands around my neck. Can't wait to squeeze.

He keeps on driving. Faster and faster. He turns on the radio. Right away he hears the word: hurricane. "It's coming," announces some newsman's voice, "it's on its way. South Florida, batten down your hatches!"

Cracker whistles softly. He's never been through a hurricane before. Thinks it sounds kind of cool, romantic. An adventure. Like Bogie and Bacall, he sees himself with Sarah holed up in some old hotel with a bunch of bad guys while the winds batter the shutters and the rains pound the roof.

He tries another station. And then another. And another. Hurricane talk up and down the dial.

"Hurricane Bertha," another voice tells him, "now lies some six hundred and fifty nautical miles southeast of Miami. The storm is picking up moisture and rapidly gaining strength. Traveling northwest, it is presently recording winds in excess of one hundred miles an hour. If it maintains its present course and speed, it should hit the eastern tip of Cuba and the southern end of the Bahamas sometime late tomorrow afternoon. From there it will sweep across the

Straits of Florida, making landfall somewhere between Miami and Marathon Key. Emergency conditions now exist from Key West all the way north to Daytona Beach."

Cracker cruises the dial. Bertha is the only order of business. A twinge of fear rockets down his spine. Also a rush of adrenaline. He cannot believe he might actually take part in a hurricane. Until today hurricanes have just been something on TV. All his life Cracker's been an observer, watching important events from a distance, never actually participating. Never in his life has he felt he's been in the right place at the right time. But this time, he tells himself, this time it's going to be different!

He drives that Corsica even faster, wanting more than ever to play the role of Sarah's savior. Plans on saving her from Sheldon, from Bertha, and, if necessary, from Mike. From me.

Just after two o'clock in the afternoon he reaches Marathon Key. And there's the Days Inn, just beyond the Bonefish Bay Motel. Cracker swings the Corsica into the parking lot. Decides to go straight up to her room. Parks in the lot, steps out of the air-conditioned car. The intense heat nearly knocks him down. Sweat forms instantly on his brow and under his arms. He has a hard time even taking a deep breath. The humidity is ferocious. He crosses the baked asphalt, climbs the concrete stairs to the second floor. His heart pounds with anticipation as he reads the numbers on the doors: 209, 211, 213, 215.

He mats his hair, wets his lips, knocks on the door. No answer. So he tries again. Still no answer. He begins to worry. What could have happened? Where could she be? Am I too late?

He decides to go down to the office, make sure he has the right room. Turns to go. Across the parking lot he sees the motel swimming pool. A woman sits at the edge of the pool, her back to him, her long, thin legs dangling in the crystal clear water.

Cracker smiles. He'd know those legs and that auburn hair anywhere. Quickly, ignoring the sweat soaking his clothes, he makes his way to poolside.

So we did it. We got hitched. To appease Mrs. Katherine Pilgrim Browne, Sarah and I waited all winter. We waited till spring. The very first day of spring, March 20, but spring nevertheless.

We exchanged vows at the Pottersville Presbyterian Church, the Reverend David Sayer presiding. Okay, I might've been a Catholic in a Protestant sanctuary, a wolf in sheep's clothing, but I was at best a nonpracticing Catholic with little or no faith in the Holy Gospels of Rome. Those Presbyterians with their low-key service worked just fine for me.

Stanley received an invitation, but the bastard didn't show.

Maggie showed with her husband, Tom. Of course Maggie showed. She was part of Sarah's bridal party.

Cracker showed. He stood up there with me. My best man. He wasn't entirely happy about the affair, but he did his duty.

Iron Kate showed. Pissed off and barely hiding it.

Alison showed. She actually snarled at me from her seat in the second pew.

Uncle Colin showed. He brought his niece down the aisle on his arm. Whispered this to her when they reached the altar, "Remember, kid, this is your third trip to the plate. Three strikes and you're out." But later, at the reception, he gave us a check for five grand.

I got pretty well soused at the reception. I don't remember many details. My good buddy Cracker roasted the bride and groom for a while, all in good fun, of course. I laughed and had another glass of champagne. Sarah and I took the first dance. Later I danced with Maggie. And much later, although my memory might be faulty on this point, I even took a turn around the dance floor with my brand-new mother-in-law. No doubt she tried to lead.

Right after the reception we left on our honeymoon. To Sanibel with Tim and a visit with Rebecca. The first time I met the old dame. She'd been unable to attend the wedding due to some minor surgery. So we had to pay her a mandatory visit. After a few days we left Tim with her and flew over to the Bahamas where we spent the next three days at the British Colonial Hotel in Nassau. I lost over four hundred dollars playing blackjack at one of the casinos on Paradise Island. But it didn't matter. Sarah had piles of cash. And plenty of credit cards to boot.

From Nassau by boat to Eleuthera. Five days at the exclusive Runaway Hill Club on Harbour Island. God, what a spot. Three hundred bills a day. Not including meals. I got my money's worth. Sarah's money's worth. Made love to her morning, noon, and night as those ocean breezes blew through our lavender-scented room.

Then by plane to George Town on Great Exuma for four days at the Hotel Peace and Plenty. We snorkeled, sailed, and made love on a vast stretch of deserted beach with no one else but the pipers and the gulls in attendance.

One night, after dinner, while sitting around the hotel bar, feeling pretty good, nice and relaxed, I got to talking to a local named Kyle Bowe. I kept telling Kyle how lucky he was to live in such a peaceful, quiet, tranquil place.

He listened for a while. Smiled, nodded, polished off his beer, and said, "You ain't been to de real Bahamas, mon, till you seen dis place called Devil's Cay. Dat de real Bahamas, mon, if you wantin' peace and quiet. George Town a boomin' metropolis compared to dis Devil's Cay."

I brought Kyle a fresh brew. "So where's this Devil's Cay?"

"South and east of here, mon. Off de tourist trail. Dey still practice de white magic in Devil's Cay. Obeah. Not like on Exuma, mon. Here it only for de tourists. On Devil's Cay it de real ding."

On and on Kyle Bowe babbled about this Devil's Cay. He kept insisting if I wanted to see the real Bahamas I had to go to Devil's Cay. And believe me, I wanted to go. Of course I did. Right up my alley. But I couldn't just go. Not anymore. I was married now. Had a wife. And a job. And a kid.

The wife, in fact, was off talking to the kid on the telephone. So I bought Kyle Bowe another beer and found out he owned a fishing boat. Then I found out if I wanted to go to Devil's Cay, lo and behold, he could take me. For a small fee: two hundred and fifty bucks. Round-trip.

Slippery dudes, these Bahamians. The truth is whatever comes out of their mouths. Kyle Bowe figured I probably had pockets lined with cash. And an insatiable desire for adventure. He figured right. The second Sarah got back to the bar I started hounding her about Devil's Cay. Told her ten or twelve times I wanted to go there. See it. Live it. Take some photographs of it. She listened patiently, both to me and to Bowe, but in the end she nipped my plan in the bud. Nipped it by reminding me that we had a flight back to the States the following afternoon.

"So what?" I asked. Such minor details had never before stopped me from doing exactly as I pleased.

"Timothy," she informed me, "needs to get back to school." And then she really took the wind out of my sails when she added, "And you have to go to work."

Jesus, she might as well have plunged a dagger into my heart. I turned to my good buddy Kyle Bowe and shrugged.

Kyle smiled, sucked down the rest of his beer. "No problem, mon," he said. "We all got de commitments. But, promise me, de next time you come to Exuma, we go to Devil's Cay. You and me, mon."

I assured him we would.

So the newlyweds returned to TREETOPS and settled into domestic bliss. With Kate, Tim, Dot, and young Lucy. Okay, bliss might be a tad strong. But we did settle in. Up in Sarah's suite. I brought my stuff over from the cottage. Not very much to bring. Mostly my clothes. My photography equipment. Sarah gave me a closet, a spare dresser. All I needed.

You might be wondering, however, how I reacted when Sarah first told me about the deal she'd struck with Iron Kate concerning our post-matrimonial living arrangements? And the truth, I must confess, is this: I hardly reacted at all. In fact, I had pretty much assumed we'd be living at TREE-TOPS. I mean, where else would we live? In the cottage on the Cramer Compound? Oh yeah, right. I could just see Sarah moving into that little dump.

I got a kick out of the way she told me though. Laid the news on me one very cold winter afternoon at the cottage after we'd made love. We lay nestled between the sheets, wrapped together, her tongue kind of licking my ear. "I guess," she whispered, free and easy, "after the wedding we'll live up at the house."

At that point she probably could've said we'd be living in an igloo up above the Arctic Circle and I wouldn't have offered much objection. She had me, I must admit, pretty well mesmerized.

But I did rouse myself long enough to ask, "Wait a second. You want me to move in with your mother?"

She had already prepared her defense. "Just until we find a place of our own."

I had visions of dining with Iron Kate. Of crossing paths in the bathroom. "But I can't live in your mother's house. She hates me."

"She does not."

"She does too."

"That's silly, Michael. She likes you just fine. And once she gets to know you better she'll love you. It'll work out. You'll see."

I shrugged, told her I'd think about it. Didn't want her to think she could just order me around. I had to maintain at least a semblance of control.

Oh yeah, I thought about it. But not very hard. The pros easily outweighed the cons. On the negative side loomed Life with Kate. But on the positive side I foresaw free room and board, a full-time built-in baby-sitter for the kid, and an excellent cook who also shopped and cleaned. Plus a first-class darkroom in the basement, a game room with Ping-Pong, pool table, and darts. And let's not forget the swimming pool and the tennis court and the horse stable. Very little end to the luxuries. Like staying free at a five-star resort.

Still, over the next few weeks, whenever Sarah brought it up, I did my best to sound dubious. I didn't want to seem too anxious. But finally, about a month before the wedding, I told her, "Okay, we'll do it, we'll move into TREETOPS. Give it a try. But let's not get too comfortable. Let's keep our options open."

It took me about an hour to make myself at home, make myself comfortable up at TREETOPS once we'd returned from our honeymoon. Katherine had made the transition especially easy for me by taking herself down to the sunny Caribbean for a three-week holiday.

But when she came back, brother, she came back with a vengeance. I swear to God: she started in on me almost immediately after walking through the front door. In fact, that very first night. At dinner she just had to tell us all about running into Mrs. Wilcox at some cocktail party on Barbados. This Mrs. Wilcox, I gathered, was an old friend of the family. Well, it seems her son, Donald, had just returned from London where he'd spent a couple years as an attaché with the State Department. "His mother," noted Katie, "insists he'll be an ambassador by the time he's forty."

I learned that Donald had been a prep school mate of Sarah's. Had gone on to do great and wonderful things. A master's in political theory from Princeton. A Ph.D. in diplomatic history from Harvard. A foreign affairs expert for one of those blue bloods with four names: George Herbert Walker Bush. And so on and so forth.

"Thirty-three and still single," Mama Kate made sure she told us, several times. "One of Washington's most eligible young bachelors."

This needling and not-so-subtle innuendo went on from there. Dinner with my mother-in-law inevitably contained some small morsel of information about one or another of the truly gallant and virtuous men Sarah had passed over in her decision to marry the likes of me. A truly ugly performance. Rude and boorish. One that really should've been booed and canceled, the lead actor driven from the stage. But the stage belonged to Iron Kate. The stage and all the props. No one else up there had the guts to shout her down, shove her into the orchestra pit.

Sarah even defended the Bitch when I complained up in the privacy of our bedroom. "She's just jealous that we're so happy," was my wife's explanation. Her advice to me, "Ignore her petty comments."

I did my best. But believe me, my best was nowhere near good enough. Kate was out to get me, drive me off that sacred hilltop. I remember this one Saturday morning, I didn't come down to breakfast until maybe ten o'clock.

Hey, I enjoy sleeping in, one of life's purest pleasures. By the time I reached the kitchen the family had dispersed. Sarah and Tim out for a horseback ride, Dorothy shopping, Lucy on an errand. But Kate, she was there. Pretending to pay some bills.

But in reality she was lying in wait for me. "Good afternoon, Michael."

I just smiled at her. She'd pulled this good afternoon stuff on me several times before. I poured myself a cup of coffee, warmed a croissant in the microwave, took a seat across from Kate, asked after my wife. I received an answer, sort of, nothing too specific. I tried to chat her up, worked my tail off to get her to smile. No luck. So I just sat there, sipped my joe, enjoyed the view through the open window.

A couple minutes went by. Five at the most. That's when the Iron One looked over her half glasses, gave me an evil stare, and asked, without the slightest twinge of irony, "So, Michael, tell me, how long do you plan to stay?"

I didn't catch on. Not right away. At first I thought she meant how long did I plan on staying at the breakfast table. Innocent me. Then I thought she wanted to know how long Sarah and I planned on staying at TREETOPS. So what did I do? I gave her an answer. "I guess till we find our own place. Or till you get sick of us. Whichever comes first."

She gave me a phony little laugh. "No, Michael, that's not what I mean. How long do *you* plan to stay?"

Oh, I caught her drift then. Tough to miss it. Like a right jab to the jaw. Made me dizzy. But only for a second. I don't get tagged without striking back. "God, Kate, I don't know." That was the first time I ever called her Kate to her face. "Maybe just long enough to see you sweat."

Well, that brief exchange was pretty much a declaration of war. After that, let me tell you, we battled almost daily. Sometimes I even enjoyed it. Especially if I got the old girl's goat, brought the blood rushing to her face. Victory, even a minor one, was sweet.

But inevitably it caused a strain between myself and Sarah. She could not stand to see the household in turmoil. And, of course, because she was her mother's daughter, living under her mother's roof, she usually cast the blame my way. "You provoke her, Michael. I'm beginning to think you do it on purpose."

Maybe I did. But the Iron Maiden needed a kick in the behind. Too many years getting her own way, having everyone kowtow to her whims and demands. Not me. I wasn't about to let her take random potshots at this boy, belittle me at every meal, cast aspersions on my motives. Hell no. She didn't own me.

Wait a second. Let's slow down here. I don't want to give the impression that the battle between Kate and me raged on night and day without pause. We had our moments of peace. Usually when Kate traveled. Which she did, thank you very much, quite frequently.

And when she left the nest, the rest of us did indeed experience the beautiful calm of domestic bliss. Sarah and Tim and I became a family. Tim and I did all kinds of stuff together. We went down to the beach to ride the waves. We went hiking up in the mountains. We went on adventures with Cracker and Molly and Tracy. I taught him how to dribble a basketball, throw a football, kick a soccer ball. I became more and more like the kid's father. I impressed myself with my patience and my ability to make him understand right from wrong. Maybe, I even started to think, Sarah was right, maybe I would make a good father. Maybe I didn't have to wind up the spit and image of my old man. We talked about having a kid of our own, talked about it all the time. We got more and more lax with birth control, just kind of letting nature take its course.

Yes, when Kate was away we did play. We gave dinner parties. Sarah's way of introducing me to her friends and acquaintances. Usually small, intimate parties with two or three other couples. Cracker and Alison came quite often, but Sarah's roots spread far and wide. I poured wine for all kinds of interesting folks. Folks who could converse on a wide variety of subjects: sex, poetry, politics, art. These folks took an interest in me, in what I had to say. They treated me like an artist, asked if they could see my photographs. I soon found my pictures, my precious black and whites, being bought and sold and hung in local galleries. And all because of Sarah, because of my sweet and generous Sarah Louise.

Oh yeah, life up at TREETOPS was good. Very fine. We had tennis parties and swimming pool parties and horseback riding parties. At night I used to dream of ways to remove Mama Kate permanently from the premises.

When she was around I kept my distance. After work I often played soccer or basketball. Several nights a week Sarah and Tim and I went out for dinner. I gave the old girl a wide berth.

I gave her brother a wide berth as well. Uncle Colin had me doing peon work for Crawford & Browne Investments, Inc. Had myself a small, cramped cubicle on the first floor. I didn't get to do much. I answered the phone. Ran errands. Drove around in my Taurus looking for large tracts of undeveloped land. Call me the low man on the totem pole. It might have been because I'd had the audacity to ask the boss for that commission. Or maybe he'd looked into my résumé. Found it bogus. I had no idea why I was on his shit list, and I didn't ask. Just stayed out of his way. Put in my time. Not too much time: four days a week, six hours a day. I only made above five hundred bucks a week, but that didn't bother me. I could've gotten by on half that. After all, my living expenses were virtually nil. I spent most of my salary on camera gear and taking Sarah out to dinner.

The real benefit of the job, besides the company car, was the company health plan. I put it into action the second my back went into spasm. Straight over to see a first-class orthopedic surgeon in Summit. He took X-rays, told me to bend at the knees, gave me a book of exercises that, if practiced religiously every day, would help eliminate the pain. The bill came to almost four hundred bucks. Insurance picked up the tab. Didn't cost me a nickel.

Then one morning, must've been around the middle of July, we turned another page. One hell of an important page. Plot details scribbled all over it.

Colin Crawford called me up to his office. He stood in the middle of the room practicing his putting stroke. "Mike," he said, without bothering to look up, "I have a little job for you."

What does he want me to do now, I wondered, be his caddy? Follow him around the links? Track down his errant shots? God, I was getting pretty sick of being his Boy Friday. "You're the boss."

"On the corner of my desk there's an envelope." Colin putted another ball. It missed the cup just to the right. "I want you to deliver it for me."

Oh yeah, that was me all right: Uncle Colin's delivery boy. "Where to?"

"Somerville."

"Bradbury & Owen?" Crawford & Browne's attorneys. I knew the way.

Colin laughed. "Not this time, kid. This one goes to Burger King."

"Burger King?"

"Right. The Burger King just off the Somerville Circle."

"And who do I—"

Colin cut me off. "Just drive into the parking lot. Park in the back. Shut off the engine and sit tight. Don't get out of the car."

A bit of intrigue. I crossed to the desk. Picked up the plain white envelope. The company letterhead was nowhere in sight. I could tell the envelope contained money, a pile of cold hard cash. Thought about asking a couple questions; decided against it.

Colin took another swing with the putter. The ball rattled into the cup. "So you got it?" he wanted to know.

"Sure," I told him, "I got it."

I drove south on Route 206 to Somerville. But I didn't go straight to Burger King. First I pulled off the road at a service station. The envelope sat squarely on the passenger seat of my Taurus. I looked at it, picked it up, felt its heft, wondered about the contents. Held the envelope up to the light, tried to see inside. Looked like hundred dollar bills in there, a thick stack. But how many? I tried to loosen the seal. Peel it back. But the envelope began to tear.

I tossed it back on the seat and drove to Burger King. As ordered, I parked in the back, shut down the engine, and waited. While I waited I leafed through my new photography magazine. Read an article about New Zealand, "The Islands Down Under." Beautiful color photographs of rolling surf and lush green hills filled the pages. I thought how easy it would be to take the envelope and make my way to the South Pacific. A change of clothes and my camera gear and I'd be all set. But then I remembered it wasn't so easy. Not anymore. All kinds of loose ends.

The passenger side door of my Taurus suddenly opened. Lost in thought, I jumped, tossed the magazine into the air.

A short, thin man wearing a crisp blue suit swept the envelope off the seat and stepped into the car. I saw he had a black, pencil-thin moustache. He slammed the door. "How ya doin', pal?" He had a tough-guy voice and black hair, slicked straight back. "This must be the goods?" He waved the envelope in the air.

I recovered, nodded. "I think so."

"The real name's a secret," the little man said, "but you can call me Vince."

Vince and I shook hands.

"I'm Mike."

"That yer real name?"

I quickly shook my head.

Vince laughed, pulled a penknife out of his jacket pocket. Unfolded the blade and used it to slice open the top of the envelope. Then, without bothering to extract the contents, he made a quick count of the cash.

I watched, tried to get a look inside. Definitely hundreds but difficult to tell how many. Fifty, at least. Five grand.

"Lookin' sweet," said Vince, as he folded the envelope and stuffed it into the inside breast pocket of his jacket. "Right on the nose."

I figured I should say something, so I said, "Good."

Vince gave me a look, then opened the door and stepped out. "Real nice doin' business with ya, kid."

That pissed me off. I was as old as him. Maybe older. "Right."

Vince started to close the door but stopped. Took out the envelope, extracted a single one hundred dollar bill, tossed it on the seat. "Here ya go, Mike. Have yerself a nice afternoon." Then he crossed the parking lot, stepped into a brand-new Lexus with gold trim and New York plates.

I just sat there and watched him drive away.

A couple weeks later I made another payoff. Same deal. Different locale. This time I rendezvoused with Vince at the

McDonald's over in Morristown. He slipped me another hundred dollar bill. I took it.

After the drop I drove over to the New Jersey chapter of the Literacy Volunteers of America. I used that hundred to take my wife out for a fancy lunch. I started to tell her about the Money, about the Payoffs, about Vince, but at the last second I changed my mind, moved the conversation in a different direction. No use stirring up the in-laws.

A couple weeks later: here we go again. Colin called me into his office, handed me another plain white envelope. "This one goes to the White Castle hamburger joint out on Route 22 in Green Brook."

I took the envelope. "Any chance you want to tell me what makes our friend so valuable?"

Colin had a good laugh over that one. After he'd settled down he put his arm around me, buddy style, walked me across the office. "Let's just say, partner, that this is part of the price of doing business in the Big Apple."

Partner. Right. Partners in crime.

But that was the deal. Crawford & Browne had a huge real estate project pending in Manhattan, something in the neighborhood of a hundred mil. I didn't know then, don't really know now, but definitely those payoffs were going to one city official or another. Or maybe to one of the powerful construction unions. Just another kind of investment capital.

Halfway to the White Castle, I had to know. So I pulled over, picked up the envelope. This time I didn't even hesitate. I carefully broke the seal, lifted out the cash. Found not fifty crisp new hundred dollar bills, but two hundred of them. Two hundred hundreds. Twenty grand. Damn near as much as I made in a whole year.

Half an hour later Vince climbed into the front seat of the Taurus. Right away he saw the envelope had been messed with. After he counted the money, made sure nothing had been pinched, he laughed. "So you finally got curious?"

I shrugged. "I guess."

"Just a delivery boy, huh?"

I felt like tweaking his moustache, telling him to fuck off, but before I could he handed me two of those crisp new hundred dollar bills. Then, before opening the door, he said, "Listen kid, we got a few more transactions before everyone'll be happy. But I want ya to know somethin'. I'll be around even after this is a done deal." And right then and there is when Vince pulled the infamous scrap of paper from his pocket. Not a business card. Just a scrap of paper. It passed from his hand to mine. Nothing on it but a large V and a telephone number.

I stared at it, hard, then heard him say, "Ya wanna make some money, ya got somethin' cookin', all ya gotta do is call Vince. When it comes to doin' business, kid, I'm yer best friend."

And with that, Vince disappeared back inside his Lexus. I sat there for a while thinking it over, staring at that scrap of paper and at the face of Benjamin Franklin adorning the front of those hundred dollar bills. I might've sat there all afternoon, save for the rancid odor of hamburger grease wafting through my open windows. I stuffed all that paper into my pocket and drove away.

So, thought I, over and over again, Uncle Colin Crawford is a dirty dog. Surprise, surprise. A man willing to do just about anything to further line his silk pockets with the Almighty Dollar. Even deal with a lowlife sleazeball like my pal Vince.

Was I really surprised? Hell no. The accumulation of vast sums of Money is, by design, a business for dirty dogs. A business wherein one daily sells his soul to the devil. Very tough to keep your hands clean.

The women managed to keep their hands clean. Iron Kate and Sweet Sarah and all the other Crawford & Browne gals. Turned a cold shoulder to any and all dirty dealings. Pretended as though those dealings simply did not exist. *Money from Heaven* the name of their favorite home movie. Just give them a fancy new car from time to time. A new horse. A new summer wardrobe. A first-class ticket to ride around the world.

Me, I just wanted someone to pay for my dental work. No problem. Sarah told me where to go. Assured me she would take care of the bill. In no time at all I'd run up a tab of almost twenty-eight hundred dollars. Hey, I hadn't been to a dentist for over ten years. Had my teeth cleaned and polished. A full set of X-rays. X-rays that uncovered an oral disaster area. I needed a root canal, two crowns, and half a dozen cavities drilled and filled. All that stuff cost Money. Big Money. But it didn't cost me a dime. Never even saw the bill. Straight to my lovely wife. She never mentioned it, except to ask if everything was working to my satisfaction.

I showed her my pearly whites, assured her everything was working just fine.

But Mama Kate, believe me, she mentioned it. During one of our late morning chats around the breakfast nook.

"So, Michael, what's your plan?" Katie always spewed a little venom when she pronounced my name. "Is your plan to get your teeth and your back and any other ailments taken care of and then slip away in the middle of the night?"

It had been maybe five months. That's all. Just five months under the same roof. But let me tell you: I was sick and tired of listening to her line of attack. So what did I do? I poured myself a glass of orange juice. Filled it right up to the brim. Carried it carefully over to the breakfast table where my mother-in-law sat leafing through her gardening and horsey magazines. I put the glass down just a couple feet from Katie's face. Then I leaned forward. Put my mouth around the rim and literally slurped the juice right out of the glass. Sucked it right down my throat as loudly as I could. Very poor manners. Totally gauche. But it got the Bitch's attention.

Oh yeah, I had my weapons full of ammo. Ready for a full-scale battle to the death. "Tell me, Kate, why don't I ever see you with a guy?"

She tried to ignore me, pretend as though I did not exist.

But no way was I about to back off. Not after her "slip away in the middle of the night" remark. "No, really," I asked, "how come? What's the story? You're a good-looking woman. Smart. Attractive. Rich as royalty. But I've been coming around here for a year or more now, and, correct me if I'm wrong, I don't think I've ever seen you go out on a date, you know, with a man."

"Men," she informed me, couldn't help herself, "are pigs. Swine."

I wiped her spittle out of my eye, then agreed with her. "Some men, yeah. But not all men."

"Most men."

"Gimme a break, Kate. That's just a massive generalization."

She put down her horsey magazine, prepared to duel. "Look at the statistics, Mr. Standish. Or whatever your name is. Men commit over ninety-two percent of all crimes. For every ten people in jail, nine of them are men. Men start wars and engage in fistfights in bars. Men rape, rob, and beat women. How many women do you think rape men? None, that's how many. Zero. Men are big, filthy, powerful animals. We should keep them locked out in the barn with the cows and chickens."

"And the horses," I added. "Let's not forget the horses."

She resisted my attempt at humor. Carried on her tirade. "I've seen what men have done to my daughter. And these were decent men. Brought up in proper families with all the advantages. And now you. You will be the worst of all. You'll hurt her worse than the others. You'll—"

That about did it for me. I'd heard all I needed to hear. "What kind of crap are you spreading now, Kate? Sitting there calling Ricky Carlson and Ron Cramer decent men. Christ, one of them beat her up, the other one treated her like trash. Decent men from proper families! You're nothing but a rich, racist snob. My mother, God rest her soul, had more class and more guts than you'll ever have. You want to gnaw away at Sarah's relationship with me, go ahead, do your damage. But I think you're just pissed off and unhappy because you're all alone. I think you want your daughter's relationships to fail so you can keep her trapped up here with you on this fancy hilltop estate forever. But I see the petty game you're playing, and I think it sucks. Keep it up, honey, and you'll lose her. Lose her entirely to me."

Want to know what Iron Kate did? Want to know what she said? She didn't get mad. Didn't get upset at my barrage of foul language. Nope, she just waited for me to finish, then she took a deep breath and calmly predicted the future. "No, Mr. Standowski, you're the one who will lose. You will self-destruct long before you have any chance of winning."

Then she got up and just as calmly walked away from the table. And oh, by the way, she pronounced Standowski perfectly. Right on the Money.

"She's driving me crazy," I told Cracker a couple days later.

"Who's driving you crazy?"

We sat at the bar at the Tewksbury Inn sipping cold ones, eating burgers.

"Iron Kate."

Cracker laughed. "Problems with the mother-in-law, hey, Standish?"

"She hates me. We fight all the time. I'm not used to this shit."

"She's a tough old girl, Mike. You should've seen it coming."

"I have to get out of there. No way I can go on living in that house."

"You think you're going to get Sarah to leave TREETOPS? I don't think so. She's as attached to the place as her mother."

"All the bitch does is belittle me. Every day she works on me. Pokes me in the eye. Asks me all the time how long I think it'll be before I leave. Accused me the other day of getting ready to slip out of the house in the middle of the night."

"I wonder about that myself sometimes."

"Screw you, Cracker. Why does everyone think that?"

"Yeah, I wonder why? Might have something to do with your track record."

"Look, pal, I'm not leaving Sarah. Not now or ever. We're great together. The question is, how am I going to get her out of that house? Away from her goddamn mother? I agreed to live there, but now I see what a lousy idea that was."

"So you'll have to find your own place. Why don't you buy a house?"

"Buy a house. Right. On my twenty-five grand a year."

"Twenty-five grand? Is that all Colin pays you?"

"That's it."

"Jesus. Slave labor."

"Tell me about it. Plus he makes me feel lucky to get that much. Treats me like a stinking stock boy."

"It's not that, Mike."

"Then what is it?"

"Colin figures you're a Browne now. And as a Browne you're living high off the hog on money he has to give Katherine since she still owns a hefty chunk of Crawford and

Browne. He's probably handing her over a million bucks a year, so he figures he can get by paying you next to nothing."

"You really think that's it?"

Cracker nodded, sipped his brew. "Damn likely."

"It's not like I'm seeing any of that cash."

"Maybe not, but you're living a pretty cozy life up there on the hill."

"Yeah, but I want to get Sarah off that damn hill."

"Sounds to me like you're in a bind, old buddy. Up the freaking mother-in-law creek with only twenty-five grand a year in your pocket."

Cracker thought this was plenty funny. Had himself a good, long laugh. But I didn't see the humor. I sat there at the bar frowning, scratching an irritation on the side of my face. Ordered myself another beer. Plus a shot of tequila. I suddenly felt a powerful desire to tie one on.

Then came the night just a few days before yet another Christmas. Would wind up being another page turner. A giant step down my road to Wrack and Ruin.

It started with a little white lie. Told not by me but by my sweet. The whole family getting ready to go to a Christmas party. Over at the Cramer Compound. But a few minutes before heading out the door, Sarah announced she didn't feel well. She had felt a cold coming on and suddenly it had arrived. Or so she said. She thought it would be wise to stay home, get some extra rest. Asked me if I'd stay with her. I told her of course I would.

But then, to my amazement, just seconds after the rest of the crew had piled into Kate's Range Rover, Sarah popped up off the couch and declared her sickness a hoax. "I'm not sick. I just thought we needed some time alone."

Indeed we did. We hadn't had any time alone, except in bed at night, for weeks. So much going on. So many things to do. We needed some private time.

Sarah made omelets. I opened a bottle of wine. We dined on the living room carpet in front of a roaring fire. Sipped the wine, enjoyed the silence. Neither of us mentioned Kate or my growing desire to abandon TREETOPS. We'd been talking that subject to death.

We finished our omelets. I moved over close to Sarah. "So, beautiful, what do you have in mind now?"

Sarah smiled at me in the firelight. "I want to get naked and chase each other around the house."

"Sounds kind of risqué."

She giggled. "But I don't want to just rip off our clothes."

"No?"

Sarah shook her pretty head. "I want to play strip poker."

"Strip poker. Haven't played that in a while."

"What do you mean, in a while? I've never played it."

"Well," I told her, "it's high time we changed that."

We stood up, set off to find a pack of playing cards. "I'll check the kitchen," said Sarah. "You try my mother's study. I think there might be some in her desk. At least that's where she used to keep them."

I went down the hall, into Iron Kate's personal domain. The one place in the house I rarely went. Flipped on a light. The room a mix of modern high-tech electronic components and eighteenth-century simplicity. A computer sat beside a two-hundred-year-old fountain pen. A fax machine and a copier occupied the same table as a pair of silver candlesticks made before the United States had a constitution. The telephone answering machine sat on a solid cherry stand that had been built before Thomas Jefferson was born.

But I was not there that evening to contemplate the dichotomy between past and present. No, I had Sarah's naked body on my mind.

I crossed the solid walnut kneehole desk. Pulled open the top left-hand drawer. Nothing but stamps and envelopes. Tried the middle drawer, pushed aside the pencils and paper clips. Didn't see any playing cards, but right then is when I noticed a manila envelope marked: Selective Insurance Company. Homeowners Policy. Just out of curiosity, I took a peek. Slipped the contents out of the envelope. The first two pages were a bunch of mumbo jumbo about costs and liabilities. I did note, however, that the premium cost $16,684 a year. A soft whistle spilled from my mouth. All the stuff I owned in the world wasn't worth close to sixteen grand.

A listing of contents began on page three. Item number one was a Goddard Townsend walnut highboy built in 1782 and valued at one hundred thirty-two thousand dollars. My eyes just about jumped out of my head. "A hundred and thirty-two grand for a dresser!" I figured the highboy had to be that fancy-looking piece up in Kate's bedroom.

Item number two on the list was a solid cherry chest-on-chest built in 1739 and valued at one hundred sixteen thousand dollars. It had to be the one in the living room. The one Sarah had told me was her favorite piece in the house. A hundred and sixteen grand!

"Michael! Come on. I found some cards in the kitchen."

I heard her coming down the hall. Quickly I stuffed those pages back into the manila envelope. Just as I closed the clasp, Sarah appeared in the doorway. I acted like I hadn't heard her call. "I can't find any cards."

She held up a deck. Totally unaware of my deception. "I found some."

I carefully replaced the envelope. Closed the drawer. Went out into the living room, stole a glance at that cherry chest-on-chest, then sat beside my wife in front of the fire.

We played five-card draw. I lost the first hand. Removed my shirt. Sarah lost the second hand. Removed one of her socks. She also lost the third, the fourth, and the fifth hand. Yup, old Mike was cheating, pulling cards off the bottom of the deck, hiding cards behind his back. I couldn't help it. Cheating at cards came naturally to me. And watching my love get naked, well, I just couldn't resist.

It didn't take long before Sarah sat there on the floor with nothing on but her panties. "I feel like a floozy."

I gave her a devilish grin.

"You dirty old man."

"Just one of the many reasons why you love me."

I dealt the cards. Time for me to disrobe. I lost the next several hands, lost until I didn't have on a stitch of clothing. Then I dealt one last hand: three jacks for myself, a pair of tens for the little lady. She stood up, pulled off her panties, and fled for her life. I gave her a head start, then set off in hot pursuit. Up the front stairs, along the hall, and down the back stairs she raced, screaming and giggling every step of the way. I followed, but she proved too quick for me. So I hid upstairs behind the guest room door, waited for her to make another pass. She came through a second time, much more cautiously this trip. Knew I lay in wait. Through the crack between the door and the jamb I could see her coming. She tiptoed along the darkened corridor. I waited for her to pass. And the moment she did, I sprang out with a mighty roar. She screamed. And fled. I chased her back into the living room. Where we made love, lustfully and athletically. Sarah started on top, but we rolled over and over, back and forth. Our thin, hard bodies enjoyed the struggle. My sweet came first that night. Long before me. After she came, I fell into a nice, slow, steady rhythm, one that gave us plenty of time to gaze into the fire and into each other's eyes. Finally I came. The wine had made us drowsy. Arm-in-arm, side by side, we drifted off to sleep.

Car doors slamming woke us up. Woke Sarah up anyway. She leapt to her feet, gave me a kick. "Michael! They're home."

I stirred. Thought about it. Didn't much care. I would've enjoyed watching the expression on Katie's face when she strolled into the living room, found us lying there in the buff. Too bad my love was not about to let such a thing happen. She shoved the fireplace screen in front of the fire, then scrambled around picking up our far-flung clothes. I yawned, slowly got to my feet. She grabbed my arm, steered me into the front foyer. Up the wide stairs we fled.

Iron Kate, probably smelling the sex and the sin, nipped at our heels. So close, in fact, that she came through the front door just as we reached the top step. Oh yeah, the old witch caught a glimpse of our bouncing white butts just as we hit the landing and slipped quickly into the upstairs hallway.

"Sarah!" Her tone sounded both outraged and horrified.

Sarah did not respond. No way. She kept moving, a naughty little girl on the run from her mommy.

I laughed and laughed. Devil that I am.

The Pilgrim Browne had the nerve to follow us upstairs, right to the threshold of our bedroom. But when she reached our closed door, she stopped. Maybe she came to her senses. Maybe she heard me laughing. For whatever reason, she knew not to take another step. Way beyond her bounds already. So fuming, spewing fire, Katie turned in retreat.

So now we come to a rather titillating little sideshow. One of those indelible twists in the plot that spins the action in an entirely different direction. Don't ask me to explain. Just something that happened. One of those small moments in life when the battle between Good and Evil rages within us.

It happened that very same night. Just a few hours after Kate's retreat, after everyone at TREETOPS had been fast asleep for quite some time. My bladder woke me up. Probably the wine. I pulled back the sheet, headed for the bathroom. And while I stood over the bowl, I had this powerful urge to once again see that manila envelope down in Iron Kate's desk.

So instead of slipping back into bed, I slipped on a pair of sweat pants, slipped out of our bedroom, slipped along the hall. The house did not make a sound. Everyone down and out for the night. Except Mike. He tiptoed down those carpeted stairs, into his mother-in-law's study. Not knowing exactly why, assuming nothing more than curiosity, he opened the middle drawer, drew out that manila envelope. For the next several minutes he studied the list of valuables: furniture, paintings, jewelry, gold, and silver. Total value: almost two and a half million dollars.

So okay, what did he do next with his curiosity?

I crossed the room, locked the door. Switched on the copier. The engine whirred, began to warm up. I wondered what I'd say if Mama Kate suddenly waltzed into the room. I didn't know. Didn't have a clue. I just stood there and methodically copied all sixteen pages of the insurance policy. One by one I slipped those crisp white sheets into the copier.

And when I was finished, I put everything back just the way I'd found it. Neat as a pin. Then silently out of the study and up the stairs. My own personal copy of Katherine Browne's homeowner's policy folded neatly in my right hand. I placed those pages in the bottom of the dresser drawer where I kept my sweaters, brand-new cashmeres and alpacas that Sarah had bought for me. Then I slipped between the flannel sheets and warmed myself on the still naked body of my beautiful wife.

That night occurred just eight months ago. Eight short months. Approximately two hundred and forty days. Two hundred and forty nights.

Now here I am, between the sheets again. In bed. But not our bed. No, Lewey's bed. At Lewey's Hotel. All alone. And all I can do in this bed is moan and groan. Sick as an old dog. Middle of the night here on Devil's Cay. At least I think it's the middle of the night. But since I barely have the strength to open my eyes, I can't be sure.

The first wave of nausea hit me not long after Roland Milo's seaplane rose into the sky and disappeared into a bank of low clouds. I made it back to the bar, ordered myself a beverage, then turned to Lewis and said, "I'm feeling a little queasy." And all at once I felt my strength fast slipping away.

Lewis looked concerned. "Maybe, Mr. Weston, you need to lie down. No color at all in your face."

"Yeah," I said, grabbing my stomach, "maybe I should." I stepped off the bar stool. Weak and wobbly. Wanted to lie down right there on the floor, spread myself out on those cool white tiles.

But just then the late afternoon crowd started to file into the bar. In no time at all a dozen or more black and very animated islanders surrounded me. Hurricane talk buzzing all around them.

"Be right back," I mumbled to Lewis. "I have to go upstairs for a minute."

"No problem, mon. You let me know if you be needing anything."

"Right." I mustered what little strength I had left to drag myself out of the bar, up the steps. Doubled over the whole way. Practically bent in two. When I reached the second-floor landing, I had no choice but to go down on all fours and crawl the rest of the way to my room. Collapsed on the small oval rug at the foot of the bed. Quite a lot of time passed. How much time, I don't know. I measured time by the waves of nausea sweeping over me. Every couple minutes. Every thirty seconds. Then every few seconds. Oh yeah, I knew I was going to puke. Just a matter of when.

I felt that intense trepidation one feels when one knows puking lies in the not too distant future. The trepidation that incorporates both the fear of puking and the promise of relief that puking will hopefully bring. So I curled up in the fetal position on that small oval rug and waited. And waited some more.

One second I would lie there drenched in my own sweat, my whole body wet and glistening. And then, without warning, the sweat would turn cold and I'd be overcome with chills and uncontrollable shivers. Sweating and freezing, freezing and sweating, hour after hour.

Little by little, an inch at a time, I crawled toward the bathroom, toward the white porcelain bowl I knew squatted at the end of the rainbow. By the time I reached the bowl the nausea no longer came in waves; with me now all the time, every second, my constant companion. And when finally the retching began, my arms hugging the bowl, my face practically right down in the puddle of water, I begged God to let me puke, to let the pain and misery pass. Let me puke or let me die!

Surely you know of what I speak. We've all been there. Our dignity squandered by a parasite in our belly.

And so, finally, I puked. And I felt better. And I thanked the Lord.

Now, all these hours later, I still lie here on the floor of my room. Three times so far I've gone through the trials and tribulations leading up to the oral release. Three times and counting. I'm so small and weak from the effort I can't even pull myself up onto the bed. The oval rug has become my cradle, the porcelain bowl my best friend. I think of little else.

Although I do manage to wonder from time to time exactly what demon has invaded my body. This is definitely more than just an overindulgence in rum. I got the devil in my gut. "Out, devil, out!"

It must be something I ate. Probably all that rubbery conch. Conch stew and conch soup. Conch burgers. Broiled conch. Cooked conch and raw conch. No wonder I feel like I'm going to die. But maybe it's not the conch at all, maybe it's some kind of bug, something in this foul water these people drink. The booze, the food, the water, the stress. Whatever it is, it's making me sick, making me want to flush my body down the toilet. Maybe it's fat Mama Rolle and her damn curses. Maybe the fat lady does have black powers. No way. I don't buy it. God's doing this to me, punishing me for the crap I've pulled, for the way I've treated my sweet sweet Sarah.

And with that thought rolling around my head, I crawl over to the bowl for another round. Nothing at all left in my stomach, so it's mostly just the dry heaves, but nevertheless my whole body convulses like a man in the midst of electric shock treatment. After a while my body relaxes. I crumple to the floor.

I rest for a few minutes, then crawl back out to the relative comfort of the oval rug. Something has changed. Before the room was perfectly still, not a breath of air or a wisp of wind. But now, suddenly, the thin white curtains blow about the room. The breeze floats in through the open windows. Not a nice breeze. Nothing pleasant or cool about it. Hot, in fact. Hot and damp. Stirs a pile of papers on the bureau. Ruffles the sheets on the bed. Even runs an invisible finger through my hair. A hot finger. Causes sweat to immediately form on my brow, run down my face. Never in my life have I felt such a breeze. Something terrible and surreal about it. Or maybe I'm just losing my marbles, hallucinating with fever and protracted guilt.

I slip into a restless slumber. Right away the nightmares begin. Nothing I can do to calm the storm, either in my head or lurking out on the stormy Atlantic.

My old pals Colin and Vince star in this nightmare. They sit in the front seat of Vince's gold-trimmed Lexus. I, the lowly delivery boy, sit in the back seat. Colin and Vince wear suits made of hundred dollar bills. Vince says, "The envelope, please." I hand Vince the white envelope. Vince pulls out not his little penknife but a long Bowie knife with a sparkling blade. Slices open the top of the envelope. Colin turns, winks at me. Vince pulls out the contents of the envelope. It's an arm! A man's arm. The whole damn arm from the fingertips right up to the shoulder. I scream at the sight of it. But Vince and Colin laugh and laugh. Then Colin hands Vince another envelope. Vince opens it with his Bowie knife. And sure enough, he pulls out another arm, still bloody and with the fingers still moving. This time I puke, all over the floor, all over the back seat of Vince's Lexus. "Oh gross!" shouts Colin. "That's really disgusting, Mike," says Vince. And with that, both men, clad in their hundred dollar suits, throw open their doors, evacuate the premises. They toss those arms into the back seat as they go. I scream as one arm lands on my lap. The fingers of the other arm brush against my face. I scream again, reach for the door handle. I need to escape. But I can't get the door open. You see, I have no fingers, no hands, no arms. How can I get the damn door open without any fingers or hands or arms? "Help!" I shout. "Help! Let me out! Let me out!" Colin and Vince stand outside laughing and pointing and making faces. I try like hell to reattach my arms, but no good, they've been severed. I throw my armless body around the cabin of the Lexus, trying in vain to break free.

"Please!" I plead. "Please help me! Somebody please help me. Sarah! Sarah!"

Lewis, not Sarah, rushes into my room. "What is it, Mr. Weston? What's the matter? You screaming so loud, mon, you wake up the whole island."

Slowly I come around, creep out of my nightmare.

Lewis crosses to the small oval rug. Kneels at my side. Puts a cool hand on my hot and sweaty face.

I reach for my arms. Find them and visibly relax. Then I look up at Lewis, directly into his eyes. "Where am I? What's going on?"

"You right here, Mr. Weston. Just a nightmare." Lewis sniffs the air. "And you been sick too, mon. Plenty sick. Smells like the death in here."

I let my head fall into his hand. "You're my best friend, Lewis. My only friend in the whole world."

Lewis smiles. One of God's chosen few. Helps me off the floor, into bed. "You got to get some sleep, mon. In a few hours you feel better."

I manage a nod. "I'd like to feel better, Lewis. Be wonderful to feel better."

"You need rest, Mr. Weston. Almost dawn now. By dusk our friend Bertha be paying us a visit. You got to gain some of your strength for that."

"Bertha? Who's Bertha? I need Sarah."

"Don't know about Sarah, mon. Bertha's a hurricane. And she be coming."

Hurricane. Right. I feel a river of fear ripple down my spine. "Are we going to die, Lewis? I don't want to die without Sarah."

"Oh no, mon, we not going to die. We going to hide. Down in the basement of the parish."

"That's good. Down in the basement. God will guard us there."

Lewis shows off his impressive set of white teeth. "That's right, mon. God will guard us there."

And with those words floating on top of that hot and suffocating breeze, Lewis backs out of the room. I want to ask him to stay, to maybe sit for a while at my side, but I don't. I tell myself to buck up. Act like a man.

I lie back. Close my eyes. Search for Sarah.

There she is: in the company of one Graham "Cracker" Cramer. My oldest and best buddy. A man I can fully trust to watch over my wife. Maybe even guide her to my side.

They've navigated Cracker's Chevy Corsica most of the way down U.S. 1 to Key West. They've crossed Seven Mile Bridge. Sped through Big Pine Key. Summerland Key. Sugarloaf Key. But along the way they've missed most of the sights. Haven't seen the soaring birds or the sailboats or the fishing boats. Have barely seen that endless horizon of blue-green sea. They've seen nothing but the road dead ahead, occasional glimpses of one another. Ever since Cracker tapped my sweet on the shoulder, back at the swimming pool of the Days Inn on Marathon, these two have been pretty well preoccupied.

Oh yeah, Cracker has heard an earful. All about my exploits. How I had more than likely been the one who burglarized TREETOPS back in March. How I had fled when evidence of my guilt began piling up at the back door. Cracker just listened, didn't say much, frequently shook his head, sighed his powerful WASPy sigh.

Now, as they cross the last bridge onto Key West, Cracker has heard the whole story. Knows exactly what his old crony Mike has done. He has heard and, alas, is not surprised. The story Sarah has told him over the last couple of hours is nothing less than what Master Cramer expected all along; really ever since I first told him I had the hots for that tall, thin, long-legged girl with the auburn hair.

A crook, he thinks, I allowed a stinking, petty, Polack crook to weasel his way into the family.

As they drive onto Key West, Sarah spots a sign for the airport. "I think we should go there first."

Cracker turns south on Roosevelt Boulevard. "We know he dropped his rental car at the airport, right?" All business. He wants now to find me. Wring my neck. Bring me to my knees. Maybe crack me right between the eyes.

Sarah nods. "Avis."

Key West International Airport occupies a pretty piece of real estate on the southeast side of the island. It has just one terminal: a long, narrow, bunker-like affair housing a bar, half a dozen rental car companies, and the handful of airlines that have found it profitable to fly in and out of the Keys.

Cracker parks the Corsica. Sarah immediately swings into action. The incident with Glenn Sheldon, P.I., has been erased from her mind. Much more important things to think about now. She gathers her pocketbook and her manila envelope filled with photographs of her husband, and climbs out of the air-conditioned car. More of that wet and oppressive heat surrounds her. She marches quickly across the hot asphalt for the airline terminal.

Cracker follows close behind.

They go straight to Avis. The young woman behind the counter has her face buried in some thick romance novel. She does not bother to look up until Sarah clears her throat. Sarah wants information. This girl has none to offer.

The duo from New Jersey spend the rest of the day at the airport interviewing practically every person who works there, even the guys up in the traffic control tower. Sarah will not be deterred. She's on a mission. She shows my photograph to everyone, even the baggage handlers sitting in the shade at the edge of the tarmac.

Several people recognize the guy in the photo, but no one can remember where he came from or where he went. He returned his rental car, but he left no forwarding address. Nor did he rent another car, at least not under his own name.

Cracker suggests they go into town, have a look around. "Maybe we'll stumble upon him just sitting in some bar." My old roomie still expects to find me making the moves on some bar bimbo. No idea that I only have eyes for my wife.

Fortunately, Sarah's not ready to give up, not quite yet. She visits each of the airline counters one more time. "I think he may have been traveling under the name Weston," she explains to the ticket agents. The poor woman looks desperate so they treat her kindly. Besides, there's little else for them to do. In fact, the whole airport has been buzzing for the last couple hours with talk of this tall, good-looking woman trying to find her runaway husband.

Finally, at American Eagle, a stroke of luck. A young man has just come on duty. Sarah shows him the photograph.

"Yes," he says, after a quick look, "I remember him. He seemed anxious, very nervous and impatient. He wanted to fly up to Miami right away."

"Miami?"

"Yes, he wanted a ticket on our first available flight."

"Can you tell me when that was?"

The young man thinks about it. "A few days ago, I believe. What's his name?"

"Standish," answers Sarah, "Michael Standish." But they already checked for anyone named Standish. "No, wait! Try Weston, Edward Weston."

The young man taps his computer keys. "Date?"

Sarah gives him the date the rental car was returned.

"Sorry, no one named Weston traveling to Miami on that day."

Sarah sighs. "Maybe the next day. Try the next day." She sounds very close to frantic. Most of the airline terminal is tuned in to her performance.

The young man does some more typing. "Yes," he says, "here's a Weston. But not Edward. This ticket was issued to a Cole Weston."

Sarah lets out a hoot. "That's him! Actually, it's his son. Edward's son. Also a photographer. Worked in color, mostly. But that's him, definitely. And you're sure he flew to Miami?"

The young man checks his computer screen. "Yes. He purchased a one-way ticket. Paid cash."

"Any connecting flight?"

The young man shakes his head. "No ma'am. Just one way to Miami."

Sarah thanks the ticket agent, then turns to Cracker. "We're going to Miami."

"Now?"

Sarah nods. "Right now. Just as soon as we can."

"But Miami's huge. We'll never find him in Miami."

Sarah remains calm, almost serene. "Don't worry. He'll leave us a trail."

Count on it.

After an uneventful flight from Key West, they walk into Miami International Airport through the American Eagle gate. "I don't know the long-range plan," says Cracker, "but the short-range plan is a beeline for the bathroom."

They make their way into the terminal. Cracker spots the restrooms.

"You go ahead," Sarah tells him. "I'll wait right here."

Cracker nods, heads for the men's room.

Sarah works her way out of the heavy stream of human traffic. Hordes of people come and go, arrive and depart. She doesn't know it but there's a hint of panic in the air.

Hurricane panic. People fleeing for the interior. My sweet finds safety with her back against a thick concrete pillar. She tries not to sigh, not to think about what will happen if she cannot find her man.

Her eyes wander vaguely around the terminal. Dead ahead she sees the ticket counters: Delta, United, American, Air Jamaica, BahamasAir. Something familiar about Bahamas-Air. Very familiar. But what? And then she remembers: yes, we flew BahamasAir on our honeymoon. The memory slaps her across the cheek.

She makes her way quickly to the BahamasAir counter. No passengers wait on line. Of course not. No one's flying to the Bahamas with Bertha pounding on the back door. There is no ticket agent behind the counter. Sarah does not hesitate; she climbs right over.

This kind of behavior is not taken lightly at airports. We have developed a keen sense of paranoia, a built-in fear that sees terrorists with bombs everywhere. Up and down the terminal ticket agents spot Sarah's antics. They press their emergency buttons underneath their countertops. In distant corners of the airport, security guards mobilize instantly.

Sarah, oblivious, pounds on the door that says: BAHAMASAIR PERSONNEL ONLY. It takes several seconds for the door to open. And when it does, Sarah finds herself face-to-face with a tall, snarling black man. "Who are you? What do you want?"

"I need to get out to the islands. Please! I have to. Now. This evening!"

"No more flights today," the tall black man tells her. "Our last flight is backing away from the gate at this very moment. Now if you will please return to the other side of the counter, I will see about getting you a ticket for tomorrow. But as I feel sure you know, a hurricane is supposed to hit the Bahamas tomorrow. Most people are departing the islands. Very few are arriving."

Several armed security guards descend on the BahamasAir ticket area. They surround Sarah, guns at the ready. Without uttering a word they frisk her, search her person and her bags. Hundreds look on, curious and hopeful that something exciting might go down.

Nothing does. This woman is harmless. Merely distraught. All she wants to do is find her husband. She explains the whole situation to the security guards and the ticket agent. And because she is beautiful and desperate, a woman in distress, they hang on her every word. Men will do anything for beautiful, desperate women. Even sell them tickets on airplanes that have already secured their doors and started to back away from the gate.

Once airborne, bound for Nassau, Sarah explains the situation to Cracker. "I know where he is," she tells him. "I'm sure of it."

"How can you be sure?"

"Because I can feel it. I can feel it in my bones. Call it a woman's intuition. Call it anything you want. But I know where he is. I can see him suffering."

"Okay. So where is he?"

"Some island called Devil's Cay."

Bingo.

"And where is this Devil's Cay?"

"I don't know exactly. Even the ticket agent wasn't sure. Somewhere south and east of Eleuthera. The airline doesn't fly there. As far as he knows, the island doesn't even have a runway. You have to go by boat."

"Great," mumbles Cracker. "Miami. Marathon. Key West. Nassau. And now someplace called Devil's Cay. Someplace you say Mike wanted to go while you two were down here on your honeymoon?"

Sarah, perfectly calm but trembling with excitement, nods her head. "Yes, he wanted in the worst way to get out to this Devil's Cay. I forget exactly, something to do with pirates or voodoo. He was all upset when I told him we didn't have time." She almost smiles at the memory. Can feel now I am no longer quite so far away. "In so many ways Michael is like a little boy, a bundle of energy and mischief. But he's out there. And he needs me. He's waiting for me."

That's right, Sarah Louise. Waiting and ready.

Cracker doesn't say a word. He has a raging headache. Too many beers and too much stress. Plus he misses his kids, maybe even a little bit his wife. He thinks he probably never should have come. Should have stayed at home where he belongs.

I should have stayed at home where I belonged as well. Unfortunately, life sometimes goes awry.

Kate saw Sarah and me bounding naked up the front stairs upon her return from the Cramers' Christmas party. And the following morning, as an added insult, she stumbled upon my discarded silk boxers while tidying up the living room. Found them draped across one of her precious lampshades. Where they must've landed during our strip-poker-off.

Kate, as you can imagine, did not enjoy thinking about her daughter fornicating on the living room furniture. Sarah Louise was not that kind of girl. So the Iron One had no choice but to conclude that it must be the evil influence of her husband, that dirty, stinking, no-good Polack. Only Polacks, Italians, and dogs, in Kate's worldview, fornicate on the living room furniture.

From that morning on our private war escalated beyond control. Kate never mentioned my boxers. She just returned them on a silver tray, left them right outside our bedroom door.

Christmas and New Year's came and went. I discussed with Sarah more than ever my desire to move away from TREETOPS. Almost every day I mentioned it in one breath or another. It became a bone of contention, a source of many an argument between myself and my sweet. She felt my desire unwarranted. I felt her attachment to the family homestead obsessive.

It quickly turned into My Winter of Discontent. Suddenly I found myself being swallowed up by Crawfords. I spent my days cooped up in the office with Uncle Colin, my nights cooped up at TREETOPS with Mama Kate.

Then Rebecca took ill down at Casa Rosa on Sanibel, and my wife flew down there to nurse the old girl back to health. Nothing very serious. Some strain of flu. But it kept Sarah away for almost two weeks at the end of January. One night during her absence it snowed. And it kept snowing. Over a foot. For two whole days I was snowbound with Pilgrim Browne. With the drifts piling up two and three and four feet high, no one could get up or down that long and winding drive. Finally one of the heavy plows owned by the town came in and dug us out. But not before Kate and I had very nearly torn each other's heads off both verbally and physically.

It got worse. Oh yeah, the truly low point came near the end of February when Sarah flew off to San Diego for a Literacy Volunteers of America conference. Another week gone. That mean another week across the dinner table from Iron Kate while she glared and snapped at me. And worst of all: the whole thing, at least in my mind, was a damn setup. Originally the plan had been for me to attend the conference with Sarah. A week of fun in the San Diego sun. But at the last minute good old Uncle Colin decided there was too much work for me to do around the office, so he nixed my vacation. I felt sure Sister Kate had something to do with his decision. But my bride called my notion "silly and ridiculous" and flew off first-class to the West Coast.

A couple days after her departure, I went into the bottom drawer of my dresser to fetch a sweater. And what do you think I stumbled upon while there? Ah yes, my very own copy of Iron Kate's homeowner's policy. I took it out. Had myself a look. A long and leisurely look. And right then and there, I tell you true, my imagination began to wander, began to dance to some very unconventional tunes.

And it kept wandering all that day, and all the next day, right up until the lunch hour of the day after that. That's when I dug that scrap of paper out of the back of my desk drawer, slipped away from the office, and went around the corner to the pay phone outside the Sports People ski shop. I stood there quite a while with the receiver in my hand and thought the best thing for me to do was just stymie my imagination, stop dancing to these unconventional tunes, turn my butt around lickety-split, and get back to the office.

In fact, for the next several weeks, as circumstances escalated out of control, I told myself daily to bring this insanity to a halt. Trouble is: I never listened. I've never been good at controlling my urges. So I just kept putting one felonious foot in front of another. Mike Standowski: stupid, self-destructive Polack to the bitter end.

But enough analysis. I did what I did. I went ahead. Took the number off that scrap of paper and dialed away. The phone rang five or six times before he picked up, plenty of time for me to hang up, walk away.

"Yeah?"

"Vince?"

He hesitated, suspicious. "Could be. Who wants to know?"

"Mike. From Crawford and Browne."

I could hear him relax. "Yeah, Mike. How are ya?"

"Pretty good."

Enough small talk. We got down to business. I spoke as softly as I could, my eye darting around for any would-be stool pigeons.

When I finished outlining my basic plan, Vince said, "I need to think about this, Mike. Check out my options. Call me in a couple days." Then he hung up. Didn't say goodbye. Just hung up. Hey, it was business. Sleazy business.

Two days later, just one day before Sarah returned from San Diego, I called Vince back. From a different pay phone. In a different town. Sneaky Mike.

Vince told me he liked the deal. "But I gotta tell ya, kid, till I see the goods, no firm compensation can be agreed upon."

"No problem."

"Just as long as we understand each other."

I assured him we did. We hung up. I found my hands trembling, my heart bouncing around inside my rib cage, rivers of sweat running off my forehead even though it hadn't been above freezing since Christmas.

Okay, I had my conduit. Now I needed a plan. It took me a couple weeks to put the whole package together. Things fell into place quite nicely. Almost as though the entire event had been preordained. A foregone conclusion. Nevertheless, I worked long and hard on the details of my plan. Left nothing to chance. I felt like a general plotting his strategic moves for an upcoming battle. I knew I'd need a dash of luck along the way, but I counted on precise execution to assure success.

On the ides of March I finalized the exact date for my attack: ten days later, on the twenty-fifth, just a few days after our one-year anniversary. One year of wedded bliss. I fully expected many more. Dozens more. Decades more. Already I had bought my wife an anniversary gift: a fine gold chain to drape around her lovely neck.

I picked this date for my attack for two reasons. First, because both Kate and Dorothy would be out of the house, out of the state. Kate down in the Old Dominion hunting foxes, and Dorothy off to Ohio or Iowa to visit her sister. And second, because old Uncle Colin had done me the great good favor of informing me that I also would be out of state. Up in Albany, New York, taking care of some business for Crawford & Browne Investments, Inc. Permit business. Yup, I would be out of town on that date, nowhere near TREE-TOPS. The perfect time to strike.

Two days before D-Day, nervous and jumpy with anticipation, I went over my checklist one last time. I'd only been going over it about twenty times a day for the past two weeks. Still, once more wouldn't hurt. Everything was in order: bags packed, hotel reservations squared away, space reserved under an assumed name up at the self-storage facility in Mahwah. I had my new duds. My maps. My list. Everything I needed. Everything but the truck. Had to call and reserve the truck. Had been holding off on the truck till the last minute. Just in case I decided to back out, get a grip on reality. But the last minute arrived and I had done neither. I knew the number by heart of the U-Haul dealer up in Suffern, New York. I slipped out of the office to the pay phone by the ski shop and dialed the number. I made that call.

A woman answered. "U-Haul of Suffern. May I help you?"

"Yes, I need a truck. Tomorrow."

"No problem, sir. What size truck would you prefer?"

I hadn't thought about size. Should've thought about size. "Oh," I said, trying hard to think on my feet, strike a chord of indifference, "I don't know, nothing too big. I just have a few things."

"Our smallest model holds approximately one roomful of furniture."

"Maybe something a little larger."

"All right, that would be our medium-size truck."

"Yes, medium-size. That would be fine." Believe me, I sounded like a criminal.

"And will this be one way or local?"

I knew the answer to that one. "Local," I answered. "I'd like to pick it up late tomorrow afternoon and return it the following day, probably around noon."

"That's fine, sir. And so that I can reserve this for you, would you give me your name, address, and a major credit card."

My heart skipped a beat. A couple beats. A major credit card! I almost hung up without saying another word. But then I made a few quick calculations. "I'd like to pay cash for this, if possible."

"Yes, of course," said the U-Haul agent. "But I'll still need a major credit card to guarantee the reservation."

I stood there: sweating, fidgeting. Knew I stood at a crossroads, a place where I could easily foul this whole business up. I took a deep breath, plowed ahead. Reserved that truck with my Crawford & Browne American Express card.

Then back to the office where I pretended to be just another honest, hardworking white boy.

Early the next morning I kissed my beautiful wife and her handsome young son goodbye. Told them I would see them in a day or two, just as soon as I finished my business up in Albany. Sarah gave me a squeeze, told me she loved me, asked me to please call later so we could say good night. I assured her I would.

And this, I think, is interesting, and maybe a little bit sick: I turned my back on them and went out through the front door without the slightest twinge of doubt or guilt. I felt confident the job would go off without a hitch. I felt absolutely certain I would soon return to the bosom of my loving family. I definitely did not feel as though I was embarking on a criminal mission. After all, I had myself fully convinced that this crime was being perpetrated as much for them, for Sarah and Tim, as for me. I believed that. I really did.

Do I still believe it? I don't know. I'd have to say less and less, what with the way things have turned out.

I drove up the Garden State Parkway and the New York State Thruway to Albany. Swept past the Poughkeepsie exit without a glance. The trip took about five hours. Arrived around noon. Checked into the Albany Hilton on State Street. Made a point of striking up a conversation with the young fellow at the front desk. I told him a lewd joke about the Pope and the President. Disgusting stuff. Not even close to funny, but I felt sure he'd remember me. Putting in place my alibi. Just in case. Then up to my room. Hung my clothes in the closet, left a razor, some deodorant, a toothbrush, and a tube of toothpaste in the bathroom. Pulled back the blankets and the sheets, fluffed up the pillows. Then I locked up and left.

I walked across Empire State Plaza, passed the Capitol. The Permit Bureau was on Hamilton Street. I found it without difficulty. Went in and asked for Florence, a woman I'd been dealing with on the phone for the past several weeks. It all had to do with Crawford & Browne's big real estate deal down in Manhattan. The one involving the payoffs to Vince. But we weren't paying off Florence, at least not as far as I knew. She was simply our government liaison, someone to help unravel the miles and miles of red tape. I spent an hour or so with Florence, a perky middle-age divorcee with blond hair and dark roots who had found harmony and bliss working in the state bureaucracy. I left her office with a thick mass of papers, assuring her I would be back tomorrow, "sometime in the middle of the afternoon."

God willing.

Florence gave me a smile, happy she'd been of help, but sad I wore a gold band on my finger. Her days pursuing married men were long gone. My days of pursuit were gone as well. I had my one true love waiting for me at home. Only half a day away and already I missed her smile and her squeezes.

Still, I had a plan. I had to stick to the plan. I walked back to the hotel. Climbed into my Taurus and drove as fast as I dared back down the Thruway. Kept reminding myself I did not need a speeding ticket. Drove straight to the U-Haul dealer on Route 17 in Suffern. I went inside wearing dark glasses and a baseball cap. Gave the man behind the counter my name. My truck, he said, awaited. I told him I also needed a dolly, a hand truck, and two dozen furniture pads. The man, polite and efficient, placed the requested equipment in the back of the truck. Then he had me sign all the proper papers. When I finished he took an imprint of my American Express card. My heart came to a dead stop as the piece of plastic passed through the machine.

My hand visibly shaking, I took back the credit card. Mumbled, "I'll pay cash when I return the truck tomorrow."

The U-Haul man thought this sounded perfectly reasonable. "No problem," he assured me. "Pay cash and we'll just throw away all this credit card business."

Yes, an excellent idea. A paper trail was not something I wanted to leave behind. I walked out through the glass door feeling somewhat relieved. Crossed to the Taurus. Grabbed my gear, including all the papers Florence had given me. Then I locked up, climbed into the U-Haul, and drove south on 17. Over the border and back into New Jersey, the Garden State.

I drove directly to the self-storage facility in Mahwah. You know about these places. Nothing but row after row of one-story cinder block buildings divided up into bunkers: fifteen-by-fifteen-by-ten-foot cells where humans with too many possessions can store the ones they don't want or need. I checked in with the security guard up front, got my key, then drove out back, and, after a few wrong turns, I found my bunker. Used my key to unlock the tall garage door. Raised the door and found a cool, empty space; my very own storage space paid for in advance for the next thirty days.

Satisfied, I locked the door and drove the U-Haul back across the border to New York, the Empire State. Checked into the Big Apple Rest Motel just off Route 17. Registered as Richard Jones. A nice, benign name. Paid cash for the room. An old, kind of crummy motel, exactly what the doctor ordered.

For the next couple of hours I did my best to concentrate on those permit applications. I knew it was vitally important that I complete the permit work. It was the key to my cover, my alibi. Those applications had to be back in Florence's office no later than tomorrow afternoon.

Around eight o'clock I needed a break. Drove north along Route 17 until I found a tavern where I could get a burger and a couple beers. Sat in a booth near the back, kept my banter with the waitress to a minimum. I didn't need her remembering my mug. The tavern had a pool table, one of my favorite diversions, but I wisely decided to put off any desire for instant gratification. Two beers and a burger and I was out of there. On my way.

Back in my room at the Big Apple Rest Motel by nine o'clock. Worked on the applications for another hour and a half. My eyes grew heavy. I put my head down on the desk, just to catch a few winks, just for a few minutes. But then, suddenly, I snapped to attention. Remembered I had to call Sarah.

She picked up on the first ring. "Hello?"

"Hi, it's me."

"Michael! I knew it would be you."

"I was just getting ready for bed. I wanted to say good night."

"I'm so glad you called. I've been waiting all day." She sounded so sweet, so kind and loving. I wanted to reach through the phone line and give her a hug.

"I miss you," I told her. And meant it.

"I like to hear that. I miss you too. When do you think you'll be back?"

"Hopefully tomorrow night. The day after at the latest."

"I hope it's tomorrow. Where are you anyway? You didn't tell me where you were staying."

That gave me a moment's pause. "The Albany Hilton," I told her. "Room 316."

"Do you know the phone number?" she asked. "In case there's an emergency."

I hesitated, but not for long. "It's not written here on the phone, but if you need to call I'm sure you can get the number from information."

"Okay. I just wondered. I'm sure everything will be fine. The house is so quiet with you and Mother and Dorothy all gone. I like it better when you're here."

"I like it better when I'm there too."

We rattled on like this for a good twenty minutes, lovers longing to hold one another close, lost and lonely after just a few brief hours apart.

We finally hung up after whispering, "I love you," about fifty times.

I wanted to go straight to bed after that, knew I had a long day ahead of me, but I also knew I had to get those damn applications completed. I'd be in deep trouble if I didn't. In the end I didn't turn out the light until almost two o'clock.

In some ways I might've been lucky. By the time my head hit the pillow I was so tired I didn't have the energy to think about what I planned to do come dawn. Fell asleep in an instant. Didn't wake up or move a muscle until my small travel alarm clock brought me wide awake at 5:55 A.M.

I took a cold shower. Pulled on brand-new clothes no one had ever seen me wear before. Fancy, upscale duds. Ralph Lauren stuff mostly: light blue chinos, a cotton flannel shirt, black baseball cap, leather boots, leather jacket, Ray-Ban sunglasses, a pair of black leather Coach driving gloves. Gloves intended to keep my fingerprints off of everything for the remainder of the day.

I took a look at myself in the mirror. Looking good. A real dude.

Gathered my belongings. Took one last look around. I did not want to leave a trace of myself behind at the Big Apple Rest Motel.

By 6:30 I was back in Jersey, driving south on Route 17. By 7:00 I'd hit Interstate 80. Heading west. Careful not to exceed the speed limit by even one mile per hour. Plenty of time, I kept reminding myself. All the time in the world. Patience and a sense of inner calm would see me through the day.

Just after 7:30 I reached the exit for Route 206. Swung that U-Haul through the exit ramp. Headed south. Still had plenty of time. Right on schedule. Enough time even to maybe stop and get a cup of coffee and a donut.

"No! You stupid moron!" I shouted right out loud as I glared at myself in the mirror. "No stops! Someone might recognize you."

But already I felt the pangs of hunger. A portent of bad things to come.

I kept moving south. Nice and steady.

A couple minutes before eight o'clock I reached the intersection of Route 206 and Pottersville Road. Twelve minutes ahead of schedule. Not bad. "But now what do I do?" I told myself to stay cool. Better early than late.

I drove south for a few more miles. Down to Bedminster. Then I turned around at the Texaco station and headed north. I had this bad feeling that my U-Haul stuck out like a great big giant dump truck loaded to the top with dead and rotting bodies. I felt certain every passing motorist knew exactly what I had in mind. But I was just paranoid. No one noticed my crummy little truck. Everybody was too busy trying to fight their way to work, earn their piece of the American pie.

At ten minutes after eight I returned to the intersection of 206 and Pottersville Road. Pulled over safely onto the shoulder. Unfolded my map. Pretended to study the highways and byways of the Garden State. But I had zero interest in those zigs and zags. I peered over the top of the map at the line of traffic along Pottersville Road, idling, waiting for the light to turn green. And at 8:14, one full minute ahead of schedule, I spotted Lucy in her paradise green VW Cabriolet. And sitting right beside her: young Tim, looking spiffy with his hair slicked back. Both of them on their way to school. Lucy swung the Cabriolet out onto 206 South. I watched them glide by. Their eyes didn't even glance my way. I watched them until they disappeared over the first rise.

Two down, thought I, one to go.

My sweet, as usual, was running a little late. I should've spotted her Bimmer by 8:15, 8:20 at the latest.

8:25 and still she had not appeared. I started to sweat. I could feel the nervous energy soaking through my cotton flannel. A part of the plan beyond my control. I knew Sarah was supposed to be over at the Literacy Volunteers in Morristown by quarter of nine. Usually the drive took her about thirty-five minutes. So where, I kept asking myself, is she? Maybe she's sick, maybe she's not going in today. 8:26, 8:27. I'd been sitting there almost twenty minutes. Pretty soon a cop would stop, ask me if I needed help. That would be it. The jig would be up. 8:28. 8:29. Wait! What's that? A green BMW? Sarah's Bimmer? Yes! There! Fourth in line at the traffic light. I could see her sitting behind the wheel waiting for the light to turn green. Looking oh so sweet and beautiful. I kept my face hidden behind the map. The light turned. The Bimmer rolled forward. Right past my perch. Sarah didn't even cast me a momentary glance. She accelerated. And in just a few seconds, out of sight.

I immediately put the U-Haul into motion. I drove over Pottersville Road and down into the small town. Went right by the church where we had one year earlier tied the marital knot. Right by the bank where we kept our Money (okay, mostly Sarah's Money). Right by the post office where we got our mail. Right by the little general store where we bought our milk and bread and beer. Believe me, I slouched low in the seat, my hat pulled down over my brow, my head pushed down into my shoulders. No one, so far as I could tell, noticed me or even gave my truck a second glance.

I drove up Fairmount, turned left on Hollow Brook Road. All the way up Hollow Brook I didn't pass a single car. And then I turned, yes, I did, turned up the Brownes' long and winding drive. Up and up I climbed, as I so long ago described, up through the woods, still brown and bare from the long winter. Into the clearing. Dirt and gravel turned to smooth macadam. I shoved that U-Haul into low and pushed on toward the big Tudor.

So now what, I ask, might I add to what I've already told you about the events that transpired up at TREETOPS on that chilly March morning? I've told you I was up to no good. You know that now. And you know the reasons why. I've told you I had pillaging and plundering on my mind. Told you sweat poured off my brow even though I had the windows wide open and the air conditioner on high. Told you my nerves were all a-jitter. That I had second, third, and fourth thoughts about calling the whole damn thing off. But that I eventually settled down, went about my business. That I slipped into the big Tudor, pulled out all the most valuable goodies, wrapped them carefully in swaddling cloth and packed them securely in my U-Haul. I've told you all this, and so I see no good reason to rehash the whole operation again. A felon, or so I've heard, may enjoy re-creating his crime, telling his sordid tale, but more than once I fear might be overkill. As well as bad luck.

So let me just reiterate: I cleaned out the house. Packed up my truck. Took a last look around. And drove away. Down that long and winding drive. No one saw me come. No one saw me go. A job well done. Free and clear.

I drove back down Hollow Brook Road. Back through town. Back to 206 and started north. Nice and easy. A little behind schedule but still okay. I remember it started to rain. Just a few drops at first, but then harder and faster. No choice but to slow my speed: thirty-five, even thirty miles an hour. Falling further behind schedule every second. The sweat, let me tell you, the sweat really began to flow.

Just over an hour later, I made my big mistake. My colossal error. And like many of the mistakes and errors we make in life, I didn't even realize I'd made one. I screwed up royally, then went merrily about my business.

About ten miles from the self-storage facility in Mahwah, my belly whining and rumbling, I decided I had to have something to eat. No way around it. I knew it was getting late, but a body needs fuel, and mine was screaming on empty.

So what did I do? I pulled the U-Haul into a diner along Route 17. Must've been about 11:30. I sat in a booth near the back, hid my face behind the large plastic menu. Ordered a turkey club, french fries, a root beer. While I waited for my chow I watched the door. No familiar faces came in or went out.

The waitress set the food on the table, asked me if I needed anything else. I told her no thank you, didn't meet her eyes. She left the check, went away. And what did I do next? I pulled off my black lightweight leather Coach gloves so I could dine like a gentleman on my turkey club and fries.

A gentleman. Right.

Hungry, half starved, and in a very big hurry, I wolfed down my food. I barely tasted it. Only half chewed it. Kept checking my watch: 11:31. Dammit! Took another bite. 11:33. Jesus! Should've been halfway to Albany by that time.

Stuffed those greasy fries into my mouth, gulped down the root beer. Salt and fat and sugar. I glanced at the bill: $7.32. Pulled my wallet out of my pocket. Found a ten. Left it on the table and blew out of that diner as fast as I could. Blew out of there, friends and neighbors, without looking back.

Too bad. Oh yeah, too bad. Had I taken a little extra time, looked around to see what personal items I might be leaving behind, maybe, just maybe, I would've seen those black lightweight leather Coach gloves lying there next to my empty plate.

Refueled, I drove straight to the self-storage facility. Backed the U-Haul up to my cinder block bunker. Time to go to work. No time to think. Full speed ahead. Threw open the door of the U-Haul and began immediately to unload the booty. My hands all over everything. My black lightweight leather Coach gloves all but forgotten. In much too big a hurry to notice the missing mitts. Getting that furniture stored away and making haste for Albany occupied every nook and cranny of my little brain. Leaving fingerprints behind was the last thing on my mind. I pushed and shoved the stuff out of the truck, into the bunker. Hands and fingertips right out in the open. For all the world to see. Oh yeah, no doubt about it, I left great big giant prints all over that old, oil-soaked wood.

It didn't take long. Twenty, maybe twenty-five minutes. I stepped back, took a look. The few things I'd pilfered filled only a corner of that cinder block bunker. But so what? Those ten or twelve pieces of antique furniture were worth somewhere in the neighborhood of half a million bucks.

Or so this moron thought.

I locked the door. Hit the road. Back across the New Jersey–New York border. Back to the U-Haul place in Suffern. Paid for the truck. I watched as the man behind the counter, a different man from the day before, tore up and discarded the credit card slip. I gave off a little smile, maybe more of a smirk, took my receipt, and skedaddled.

Back in my Taurus and on the Thruway by 1:15. I took the time to pull over and call Florence. Told her the permit applications were taking longer than expected, but I hoped to be at her office by three o'clock, three-thirty at the latest. She assured me she'd be there until five. I hung up. Back in the car. Pedal to the metal all the way to Albany.

A little after three I reached my room at the Hilton. The maid had come in, made the bed, tidied up the bathroom. I washed up, changed clothes. Figured someone would be getting home about now, probably Lucy and Tim. They'd discover the front door hanging wide open. The mess in all the rooms. They'd call the cops, call the cavalry, call Iron Kate down in Virginia. But no time for me to think about that now. I was safely away in Albany, my alibi quite nicely tucked away.

I stuffed my burglary duds (boots, chinos, flannel shirt, sunglasses, baseball cap) into a brown paper bag. Then I grabbed the bag and the permit applications and made my way quickly across the plaza. Just before entering Florence's office, I threw the paper bag into a large trash can. Several hundred bucks' worth of clothes, but I felt better getting rid of the evidence.

Now you might think I would've missed the missing gloves at that point, but nope, didn't give the damn things a thought. Too busy being a cool customer, a felon on a roll.

Florence spent almost an hour checking over my work. "Everything looks excellent," she kept telling me. "You're very meticulous."

I smiled. Thanked her. Sat back and caught my breath.

By five o'clock I was back at the hotel. Went to the front desk. "Any messages for Standish?"

No messages. Surprised Sarah had not yet called, I went up to my room and called Colin at the office.

"You still up in Albany?" Colin, the tyrant, wanted to know. "I thought you'd be back by this time. Sounds like you're milking me."

"I've been busting my butt," I assured him. "Didn't think I'd ever get all those forms filled out."

"But you've got it licked?"

"Pretty sure."

"So when are you coming home?"

"I'm at the hotel now. I'm pretty beat. Thought I'd come down in the morning."

Uncle Colin laughed. "You find some loose lips up there, kid? And my poor niece down here all alone pining for you."

"Nothing like that, boss."

Colin laughed again, then he hung up without bothering to say goodbye.

I set the receiver back on its base. Almost immediately it rang. I let it ring a couple more times, then I took a deep breath, pulled myself together. Picked up the receiver. "Hello?"

"Michael! Thank God you're there." She sounded frantic.

"Sarah! What is it? What's the matter?"

"Someone broke into the house! We've been robbed!"

I drove home right away. It was close to midnight by the time I arrived. The cops had already come and gone. Sarah told me they'd taken some pictures, dusted for prints, walked through the house a couple dozen times.

"Who would do this?" my lovely innocent wanted to know. "Over thirty years we've lived here. Never has anything like this happened before."

I shook my guilty head, held her close to my chest. "I'm just glad no one was home when it happened. Someone might've gotten hurt."

We locked the house up tight and went upstairs to bed. Tim slept in with us that night. Sarah feared the culprits might come back.

The cops returned in the morning to take statements. While I was making mine, telling the detective that I'd been up in Albany for a couple days, the matron of the household arrived bleary-eyed after an overnight haul from Virginia. One look at Kate and I knew she knew I'd done it. No doubt in her mind. But also no proof. Not a spot. I had my alibi all sewed up. She had to stand there and listen to me tell that detective how Sarah had called me with the news at my hotel room at the Albany Hilton. Nothing she could do. Not a damn thing.

Later we sat around the kitchen table with Police Chief John Rawlings. "It looks to me like a pretty clean job," he told us. "Very professional They probably staked the place out. Watched you coming and going for a few weeks. Then, when the time was right, they moved in."

"So," I asked, "you figure it was more than one person?"

Iron Kate scowled at me.

"I'd say definitely," answered Chief Rawlings. "Some pretty heavy pieces were moved. I'd say two people minimum. Maybe more."

I nodded.

He continued, "As I'm sure you know, this kind of thing happens around here from time to time. Usually in these big, isolated houses. Very tough to prevent. And even tougher to track down the perpetrators." He checked his notes. "I see you have a burglar alarm. Do you know if it was turned on?"

Kate did not hesitate. Her eyes fell immediately upon her daughter. I felt the oxygen catch in my lungs.

My sweet sighed, shrugged. "I could've sworn I turned it on yesterday morning before I left. Really. I thought I did." We could all see she was upset. Blaming herself for the burglary, for the whole mess. "But when I got home last evening and saw the door broken open, I checked the alarm. And no," she dropped her eyes, wouldn't look at her mother, "it wasn't on. I must've forgotten."

A shudder of relief swept through me as my wife made her confession, all but absolving me of any connection to the crime. But within just a few microseconds that feeling of relief dissipated. I glanced at my sweet, saw her pretty face all knotted up with pain and guilt. Right then and there I wanted to confess. I wanted to. I really did. But I didn't. Nope, good old Mike suddenly turned into a mute. Didn't utter a sound. Deaf and dumb from that moment on.

A couple weeks came and went. Life up at TREETOPS got back to normal fairly quickly. After all, a few pieces of furniture had been stolen, valuable antique furniture, sure, but just furniture nevertheless. It wasn't like someone in the family had been raped or murdered in their sleep.

I had a couple run-ins with Kate wherein she more or less accused me of either pulling the job myself or hiring someone else to do it for me. I just laughed at her, told her I refused to even acknowledge the insult.

Then, one warm and sunny spring morning in the middle of April, I met my business associate, Vince, up at the self-storage facility in Mahwah. He pulled up in his gold-trimmed Lexus. He had an old guy with him. Gray and bent with super-thick eyeglasses. Looked to be about eighty. Introductions were not made.

I opened the door to the cinder block bunker. Exposed the booty to the light of day for the first time in over three weeks. The stuff was still there, undisturbed, just the way I'd left it. The old boy went in without being asked, started giving the goods the once-over.

Vince and I waited outside.

"He's my expert," Vince told me, as if I didn't know.

The expert stayed in there about forty minutes. When he came out he walked right by me, didn't say a word, didn't even glance my way. Went straight to the Lexus and climbed inside. Vince joined him.

I paced around the parking lot: nervous, pissed, paranoid.

They sat in the Lexus ten, maybe fifteen minutes. Then Vince got out. The old guy stayed in. Vince crossed to me. Got right in my face. Didn't mince words. Straight to the heart of the matter. "The stuff's worth seventy-five grand."

For a second I didn't think I heard him right. Kind of shook my head as if to clear my ears. "Say what?"

"The shit's worth seventy-five grand to me. Not a penny more."

Oh yeah, that's when I lost my cool. "Seventy-five grand! Christ! That damn cherry chest alone is worth a hundred and a quarter!"

"Maybe so," said Vince. "On some piece of paper. But I ain't a piece of paper. I gotta get ridda this shit, friend. And that ain't gonna be easy. Now I don't wanna know, but I figure we got stolen merchandise here. I figure this shit's hot. That means risk. And it's me gotta take that risk. I hand over the dough to you and you're free and clear. All of a sudden you don't know from nuthin'."

I paced around in a circle. No, I marched around in a circle. "Seventy-five grand! Seventy-five fucking grand. I did this for seventy-five grand? This stuff's worth close to half a million bucks, pal. I was looking for a cool quarter mil."

"Yer dreamin', kid. Outta yer mind. Seventy-five grand: that's my one and only offer. You don't like it, go somewheres else."

I paced around some more. Jittery. Uptight. Rubbed my face and my neck and my arms. "Fuck," I kept saying, "fuck, fuck."

"Let's go, friend. Make a decision. I got work to do."

"A hundred. Gimme a hundred."

"Screw you," announced Vince. "Seventy-five. Take it or leave it."

He knew I'd take it. The son of a bitch knew I had to take it. What else could I do? What choice did I have? Vince was no dope. He knew when he had a chump by the scruff of his neck, a chump way in over his head.

Okay, you know it and I know it: I took the seventy-five grand. Vince had the cash, right in a briefcase in the trunk of his Lexus. Seven hundred and fifty hundred dollar bills. We sat in the back seat and counted them. He threw in the briefcase so I'd have some way to carry all that dough.

"Now gimme the key to the garage door," ordered Vince. "I'll be back in a day or two to haul this shit away.

Don't come up here and fuck wit it, 'cause if you do, I'll be forced to come around and fuck wit you."

I found the courage to snarl at him. Then I climbed into my Taurus and drove away. My tail, I can assure you, tucked tightly between my legs.

So what, you might be wondering, did I do with the Money? I didn't run off with it, I can tell you that. Didn't want to run off with it. I wanted only to stay with my woman and her little boy. Our little boy. I just wanted to use the Money to buy our way out of TREETOPS, liberate ourselves from Iron Kate. So I put the Money in the bank. Several banks actually. More than a dozen. I needed a small notebook to keep track. I opened checking accounts and savings accounts all over central Jersey. Kept these accounts tidy and unobtrusive, never more than three or four grand in any one vault. Plus ten grand cash locked in my safe in the darkroom. For emergencies.

Emergencies, right.

Oh yeah, I had nothing but the highest motives. The finest intentions. Going to buy my sweet a house, emancipate her from under the heel of Iron Kate. I had one small problem, however: how to explain this sudden influx of cash? Oh look, boys and girls, I just won the lottery. The Lotto Jackpot. Seventy-five thousand. Aren't I lucky? Oh no, that's just a coincidence that I possess the winning number a mere one month after the big Tudor fell prey to burglars. Pure coincidence, I assure you.

The thing is: I must've foreseen this problem long before I pulled up to the front door in that U-Haul. And if I did foresee it, if I knew it would be extremely troublesome putting the cash into circulation, then were my intentions truly the purest in the land? Or did I all along have something besides selfless love up my sleeve?

It began to seem more and more likely to me, especially as I lay wide awake in bed in the middle of the night, night after night, right beside my beautiful bride, that perhaps I had pulled the Job not for Love but for the Money; as well as for the simple pleasure of ripping off my bitchy mother-in-law. By ripping her off I was avenging the Standowskis for all the Fascists and Bigots who had controlled and shackled us over the eons.

So which was it? Love or Money? Who was I? Some noble, modern-day Robin Hood? Or just another petty thief looking to make a quick score? My answer changed every couple minutes around the clock.

If I was a crook, I reminded myself in way of justification, then I was by no means the only one. Oh no, those affluent rolling hills were crawling with crooks of the white-collar variety. My sweet had told me so herself, pointed out the swindlers and the shysters at parties and at black tie benefits on more than one occasion: lawyers, businessmen, investment bankers. They all bent and twisted the rules to their own financial wills. And what about the Crawfords and the Brownes? Nothing, really, but a bunch of high-class thieves. Oh sure, they hid behind their Ivy League educations and their WASPy heritages and their dandy manners and their hilltop estates, but behind all the bullshit: crooked scumbags. Old Uncle Colin might not've pulled a U-Haul up to his sister's front door, but the guy had no qualms about ripping off little old ladies and making payoffs to sleazeballs like Vince. "All part of doing business, Mike," he used to tell me. "Just another day in the office here in America where money is the only true measure of a man's worth."

I guess I could babble on from now till Doomsday, but it ain't going to change the facts: I burglarized my mother-in-law's house. Stole all her best stuff.

Okay, so I lost plenty of sleep at night lying awake worrying about my motives, finding ways to justify my actions, but during the day life rolled along in a fine and pleasant manner. I went to work. Went horseback riding with Sarah. Went bicycle riding with Tim. Played softball on Sundays with Cracker and a bunch of other guys. I took photographs. Worked in my darkroom. Made love to my beautiful wife, told her I wanted us to have a baby. A whole slew of babies. I even coached Tim's Little League team, a gesture that believe it or not brought praise and smiles from the youngster's grandmother.

"You see," Sarah told me, "time takes care of everything. She was just a little skeptical in the beginning. Now that she sees you're honest and committed, she'll love you like her own son."

I sighed and nodded and wished I'd never stolen the old girl's fancy antiques. But I had stolen them. Stolen them and sold them to a fence for a pittance. Couldn't deny it. The Money, the evidence, lay scattered in banks all over the state.

I slipped a little of that Money into circulation. Spent it on clothes, restaurants, camera gear. Didn't spend much. Afraid to touch it. Afraid if I touched it, it might jump up and bite my head off.

Spring came and went. Summer arrived. Hey, I'm talking just a couple months ago now. Eight weeks. Just over fifty days. Hot and dry. We played tennis, swam in the pool. Looked around for a horse I could ride this year in the hunt. Found one too. A gentle, Dutch warmblood. Named him Thunder. Easy to ride. Perfect manners. Took the fences with little or no fuss.

All through June and July Sarah and I worked harder than ever to make a baby. Day and night. We began to wonder if something might be wrong. We even went to the doctor to find out.

"Nothing that a little persistence won't take care of," she assured us.

At the end of July we went on vacation. Sarah and Tim and Mike. Drove up to Maine, stayed in a cabin on Kezar Lake. Swam and fished and water-skied. At night we cooked fresh trout over an open fire. Then we headed over to the coast where we camped in Acadia National Park. I paid most of the bills. With some of the cash I had stashed away in my safe down in the basement. I enjoyed paying the bills, pulling out my wallet. Sick and tired of Sarah paying all the time. I also enjoyed being a family man. It made me feel calm and necessary. Gave me a purpose. Someone to think about other than just myself. Of course, it helped that I loved my wife. Loved her more than anything or anyone in the world. I'd give up everything to have her here with me now.

Every night of that vacation we worked on making babies. In the cabin. In the tent. Under the stars. On the beach. Worked our fingers to the bone.

So you see, it would be perfectly logical to assume, if Sarah really is pregnant, that she became so during our trip to Vacationland. Hell, it makes sense. The timing is right. That trip, after all, took place only a few weeks ago.

Just a few short weeks. Hard to believe. So much has happened in such a short span of time. Oh yeah, let me tell you, events spiraled out of control rather rapidly after we returned home from our summer holiday. We had not even unloaded the car when Mama Kate came dashing, yes dashing, through the front door, greeted us with the wonderful news.

After hugs and kisses, even a quickie for me, she said, "You won't believe what happened!"

We waited.

"They found our chest."

"What?" This came from Sarah's mouth, but it just as easily could have come from mine. I stood there in the driveway, a large suitcase dangling off the end of each hand.

"Our cherry chest-on-chest. They found it!" Kate was all worked up, intoxicated with happiness. She practically did a little jig there on the macadam.

"They found our chest?" Sarah again, but it could have been me.

"Yes! Actually it was Mary Cramer who found it."

"Mary Cramer? When? Where?"

"In Manhattan," came the answer. "Just a few days ago."

"You're kidding?"

Kate, her smile a mile wide, shook her head. "I absolutely am not. The whole thing happened quite by accident. Pure luck really."

Sarah put on a nice big smile as well. "God, Mother, that's fantastic. Tell us what happened."

Yes, Mother-in-Law, tell us. Please.

"Well, you know how Mary loves antiques . . ."

No, as a matter of fact, I didn't

"She has several shops in the city she frequents. Very exclusive ones along Fifth Avenue. Open by appointment only . . ."

Of course.

"She was in Conner and Blair, on the corner of Fifth and Sixtieth Street, just browsing, when she saw this exquisite chest. Just the most extraordinary piece. And it looked so familiar. She knew, of course, that ours had been stolen. It didn't take her long to put two and two together . . ."

No, I suppose it didn't.

"She called me right from the shop."

"This is unbelievable, Mother. Isn't this unbelievable, Michael?"

My fingers had started to cramp from the weight of those two suitcases. I set them down on the driveway, managed a little nod. "Yes," I answered, almost in a state of shock, "unbelievable."

"Well," continued Kate, "to make a long story short: I drove into the city the second Mary and I got off the phone. I knew it was our chest the moment I laid eyes on it. Then, right in front of Mary and the shop owner, I pulled out the secret drawer and produced the tattered bill of sale dated 1735. It was signed by both the man who had built the piece and by our ancestor, Mr. Jason Browne."

I had to keep from swallowing my tongue. "Secret drawer?"

Oh yeah, I heard all about that secret drawer. Tucked away behind one of the three drawers at the top of the chest. Just a small, narrow drawer. But large enough to hold that bill of sale. Proof positive the piece belonged to Katherine Pilgrim Browne.

"So," Sarah wanted to know, "are we going to get it back?"

"Eventually," answered her mother. "At the moment it's in police custody being held as evidence."

I had a pretty good sweat going by this time. Hot out there on the driveway, sure, but this was a nervous sweat. A guilty sweat. A fear-of-being-caught-red-handed sweat. "Evidence?" I asked.

"Yes," answered my mother-in-law, who really was beginning to accept me into the family. "It seems the chest is covered with fingerprints. And not just on the brass handles and the drawers, but all over the sides and back as well. The police think the fingerprints might belong to the thieves who removed it from the house."

I felt something heave up out of my stomach. Thought I might have to leave it right there on the driveway. But then I remembered the good news: I had gloves on during the heist. Black lightweight leather Coach gloves. The best Money can buy. I couldn't possibly have left any fingerprints. No way. An audible sigh spilled out of my mouth. Figured those prints must belong to Vince's henchmen. The cops would never be able to connect those lowlife skunks to me.

"So," I heard my sweet ask, "we might actually find the creeps who stole our furniture?"

Mama Kate nodded. And, without irony, she answered, "We'll keep our fingers crossed."

As you might easily imagine, I didn't sleep very well that night. Didn't sleep a wink. I couldn't even keep my eyes closed. Jumpy. Nervous. On edge. I got up. Went downstairs. Paced around the living room. The dining room. The kitchen. Replayed the entire day of the crime over and over in my head. Looking for any cracks. Any little seam I might've left open. Any puddle of oil where I might've slipped, left some clue connecting the crime to me. Damn near dawn by the time I started to reconstruct the scene up at the self-storage facility in Mahwah. I could see myself perfectly: running around, half in a panic, trying to off-load the goods, get them out of the truck, into my cinder block bunker. Oh yeah, moving like a machine. Pushing and pulling those big heavy pieces. Then, just as the first light of a new day filtered through the kitchen windows, reality hit me. Punched me right between the eyes: the Gloves! The black lightweight leather Coach gloves! I didn't have them on! Why the hell not? Where the hell were they? I could see my hands. The flesh: bare, uncovered. My fingers: all over that antique furniture. My prints: prominently on display.

After that it didn't take me long to search through my memory banks and find those black lightweight leather Coach gloves resting on the table in the diner where I had devoured that turkey club. No, not long at all. Just a minute or two. And a few seconds after that, I had my first of many armless nightmares. In that initial horror, I found myself running down the Brownes' long and winding driveway, both my arms severed at the shoulder. Kind of strange, running without arms, rather awkward, but I kept running anyway. Had to. Iron Kate, wielding a cleaver, was in hot pursuit.

Alas, I settled down. Got a grip. I still had hope. I was not a convicted felon. My fingerprints had never been documented. Not even during my juvenile delinquency. If my fingerprints were not on record, I rejoiced, then no one would ever know the prints on that cherry chest belonged to me.

My last best hope did not last long.

A week slowly slipped by. Every day an agonizing mental ordeal. Into August now. Just a couple weeks ago. Dog days. Sleepless nights. Nothing but nightmares if and when I drifted off for a few brief seconds. Nightmares and heavy sweats. I did not, do not, make a good criminal. Jessie endowed me with too massive a conscience. I was so stifled with fear and guilt that I couldn't even get an erection. Suddenly and utterly impotent. Every night Sarah wanted to make love, but Mikey Boy couldn't help her out. Couldn't perform. Started, for the first time in my life, making excuses, searching for reasons to avoid intimacy.

"I'm so tired tonight, sweetheart."

"I have the worst headache."

"My stomach has felt queasy all day. Is there any Pepto-Bismol?"

Sarah, patient and caring, never pushed, never raised a ruckus. Just kissed my forehead, rubbed my shoulders, told me she loved me.

Then one morning, let me see, it must've been ten or twelve days ago, Mama Kate made her terrifying announcement. It happened at breakfast. We all sat around the kitchen table: Kate, Sarah, Tim, Mike, Lucy, Dorothy.

"I spoke to Police Chief Rawlings this morning," Katie told us. "He would like us all to come down to the station."

I just about choked on my whole wheat toast.

"For what?" Sarah, thank you dear, wanted to know.

"To be fingerprinted," came the immediate response.

That's when I did choke. Coughed and sputtered. Needed Tim to pound on my back. A long pull of orange juice to wash down the crumbs.

"Are you all right?" my lovely wife wanted to know.

I assured her I was just fine.

She gave me the sweetest smile, then turned to her mother. "Why do we have to be fingerprinted?"

Yeah, I wanted to know, why? But I knew why. Knew damn well why.

"For the police investigation," answered Kate. "The police detectives in New York would like copies of our fingerprints so they can tell them apart from the prints possibly belonging to the thieves. All of us, at one time or another, have touched that chest. But according to Chief Rawlings, it is extremely unlikely that our prints would be all over the sides and back."

Sarah nodded. "Yes, I see. That makes sense."

The others thought so too. I did as well. Although I doubt any of them had the urge to get up from the table and run for their lives.

"I'm going to the station this morning," Kate informed us. "Dorothy is coming with me. I would appreciate it if the rest of you would go as soon as possible. The sooner we can get this done, the sooner we can get our chest back."

Iron Kate glanced at Sarah and Lucy, then she fixed her eyes on me. At least I thought she did. Maybe it was just my imagination.

Sarah asked me after breakfast if I wanted to go to the police station later that afternoon. I told her I had things to do at work but that I would try to get home early. This sounded perfectly reasonable to my bride.

Off I went. Drove around most of the morning in my Taurus. Wondering what I should do, where I should go. I found myself stopping at several of my banks. Making small cash withdrawals. A thousand here, a thousand there. Just as a precaution, I told myself, just in case things turn ugly.

Hell, I knew the fingerprints all over that cherry chest-on-chest belonged to me. And everyone else would know it too the second I walked into the police station and stuck my fingers on that ink pad. So I drove around for a couple more hours, visited a few more banks, repeated over and over to all those who could hear, "I refuse to be fingerprinted on the grounds that it will definitely incriminate me."

I didn't get back to TREETOPS until almost seven o'clock. Apologized to Sarah, told her something had come up at the office. She didn't seem to mind. Didn't even mention the fingerprint gig.

That night, around midnight, a nearly full moon blazing outside our bedroom window, I finally fell asleep. From sheer exhaustion. But the nightmares began almost immediately. Vivid and horrifying. In the first one Iron Kate hacked off my arms with a dull axe.

The story went something like this: we all drove down to the police station in Kate's Money Green Range Rover, the entire Family Browne. Singing songs along the way: "Row, Row, Row Your Boat," "She'll Be Coming 'Round the Mountain When She Comes," "I'm a Yankee Doodle Dandy," swell old tunes like that.

Then, just before Kate pulled the Rover into the station, I mumbled, "I can't have my fingerprints taken."

"Why not?" they all wanted to know.

"On the grounds that it might incriminate me."

"What is that supposed to mean?" Iron Kate demanded.

Right then and there, her eyes burning into my soul, I broke down, made a full confession. "I did it," I said. "I pulled the job. I stole the furniture."

A collective gasp. And then the Iron One calmly asked, "Do you have any last requests before I pass sentence?"

"Only," I begged, "that you show mercy. I love the one with the auburn hair. I do love her. I love her more than life itself."

Iron Kate scowled at me. She didn't buy a word of it. Showed her contempt for my being by pulling out that dull axe. "Time, Standowski, to rest your arms across the dashboard."

I did as ordered. And without further adieu, Katie began to chop. First the left and then the right. Severed them both clean just above the biceps.

I could feel the pain, even in my sleep. Woke up with a start, sweating and breathing heavily; my arms, however, still intact.

At breakfast Kate asked us if we'd been to the police station yet. Lucy and Tim had. Tim said it had been great fun. The policeman had shown him his gun, his badge, and his handcuffs.

Sarah and I admitted that we had not yet made the trip, but that we fully intended to go that day or the next.

Sarah was the reason we did not go that day. She had errands to run, other more important things to do.

So for a little while longer I was off the hook. I made a few more bank stops. I began to amass a large collection of greenbacks. Had close to thirty grand by the time I got back to TREETOPS that evening. Then I paid a visit to my safe down in the basement. Found another seven grand. A nice little stash. I hadn't yet firmly committed to blowing town, making a run for it, but if and when I did make that decision, I wanted to have my finances secured. And let's face it: it ain't like I had a whole lot of options. Confess or run. That's about it.

All that night, between my armless nightmares, I lay awake and tried to find some other way out. Thought about altering my prints, maybe burning my fingertips with one of my darkroom chemicals. Thought about turning my bizarre nightmares into some grotesque reality. I'd chop off my arms so I couldn't possibly even have any fingerprints. That would solve everything; though it did seem a tad desperate. Still, I needed something. Some miracle. Or at least an explanation for why my prints were all over my mother-in-law's cherry chest-on-chest. And I needed that explanation pronto. ASAP.

I caught a break in the morning. Kate and Sarah had gone off with their horses before dawn. And the next morning, when Kate asked me if I'd done my duty yet, I replied, the lie like silk upon my lips, "I stopped by the station yesterday after work, but there was no one around to take my prints."

She accepted this explanation. Asked me only if I intended to try again today. I assured her I would. But I could see her mind working, going over all the details. Oh yeah, her suspicions were back in full swing. I could see it in her eyes: she knew damn well I was guilty. And I knew at that moment if she got the goods on me, she would prosecute me to the fullest extent of the law. I wondered then, as I continue to wonder now, if Sarah will be able to protect me from the wrath of Iron Kate.

Later that same day, riddled with guilt and trepidation, I went up to the spare bedroom. Called Continental Airlines. Booked a one-way reservation for the following evening for Edward Weston to Fort Myers, Florida. Tossed the scrap of paper with the flight info into the trash can. I even left one of Weston's photography books next to the telephone. All the clues my sweet would need to track me down.

And that night, unable once again to maintain an erection, I cried in my lover's arms. Spilled tears all over her breasts. She asked me a thousand times what was wrong. "Nothing," I kept telling her. "I just love you so much."

I could have told her. Should have told her. Should have confessed my sins. But I am nothing but a no-good dirty Polack. The Scum of the Earth. Everything Cracker and Iron Kate said I was and more. A scoundrel. A cad. A lecher. I am, let's be honest here, the Son of Stanley. Always have been. Always will be.

I proved all this the next day, when, instead of going to the police station, instead of acting like a man, instead of going home to my wife and telling her what I had done, I drove to Newark Airport, abandoned my Taurus in short-term parking, and boarded a southbound flight under an assumed name.

I rest my case.

Late morning here on Devil's Cay. Maybe early afternoon. I lie in bed in more or less the same position Lewis left me several hours ago. I continue to drift in and out of a feverish slumber. My muscles ache. My stomach growls and rumbles. My breath smells like vomit.

A serious wind whips through my room. If I could stand, take a look out the window, I feel sure I would see white-caps on the harbor, palm trees bent almost parallel to the ground. Even from here I can see the sky. Nothing but a swirl of high and scattered clouds. But I'll bet these innocent-looking puffs are forward scouts for Bertha. Wasn't that her name? The one coming to do its damage? The boys at the National Weather Center should've named this one Kate. Hurricane Katie Browne.

Maybe, if I'm lucky, Bertha's winds will pick me up, toss my miserable body out into the Atlantic a thousand miles or more from any landfall. That way I can just drown, become food for the fishes.

Oh yeah, I flew to Florida. Up there in my posh, first-class accommodations, I had a few drinks. Let the alcohol carry me up, up, and away. Wondered what I would do once that big jet touched down. Where would I go? How would I get there? Pretty much went on autopilot once I got inside the terminal. Once I reached the Sunshine State. Only semiconscious. Rolling along in a lost and lonely funk. Knew that another page had been turned. I rented a car. A white Chevy Corsica. From Avis. Left the airport. Found an interstate. Headed south. Dark outside. Close to midnight. Drove all night. Miami. Key Largo. Key West. Checked into the Southernmost Motel on Duval Street. Slept most of the day. Then walked into Old Key West where I got falling-down stupid drunk at Captain Tony's Saloon. Bought everyone drinks with the Money I'd more or less stolen from Kate. Made myself some new friends.

Then what? Only a few days ago but already getting tough to remember. At some point I know I realized that Sarah would need to find me, that I definitely did not have the guts to go back and fess up to my crime. I needed her to come and rescue me, bring me back into the fold. That's when I convinced myself that she would be able to find me here on Devil's Cay. You know, because of the clues I'd left behind: the scrap of paper in the trash and the book of Weston's photographs. And also because of what had happened on our honeymoon at the Hotel Peace and Plenty: my meeting with Kyle Bowe followed by a strong desire to visit this out-of-the-way cay. My sweet, I deduced, would easily fit together the pieces of the puzzle.

So I returned the Chevy to the Key West Airport. Flew up to Miami. Then over to Nassau. A mailboat out to Eleuthera. And finally, aboard Captain Ahab's stinking diesel tub, the final leg here to Devil's Cay and Lewey's Lovely Harborside Hotel.

Oh yeah, here I be. Now what? I answer by forcing myself to climb off the bed, the sheets wet with my sweat, and stand on my own two feet. This takes no small amount of effort, but eventually I get the job done. I head straight for the door, inch my way along the hallway, slowly steer myself down the wooden stairs, my arms wrapped firmly around the banister for support.

"Lewis!" I try to yell but my voice is pretty well shot from all the retching and puking. "Lewis!"

Lewis does not answer. Lewis is nowhere in sight. Not in his office. Not in the bar shining glasses. Not out on the front porch jawboning with one of his pals.

I make my way to the kitchen. Need some water. Maybe something to eat. Not much. Just a piece of bread. My stomach empty. Hollow. My head hollow. My heart hollow. Hollow and cold.

I take my bread and water, go out to the bar. Take a seat in front of the picture window. Sip and chew slowly. Very slowly. Stare through the glass. The wind blowing wild now. Blowing waves up over the bulkhead of the town wharf. The sky a funny color. Black and gray and furious. Threatening. No real rain yet. Just a few big drops splattering against the window. And out there along the cobblestone street: a steady stream of islanders making their way to St. Andrew's Parish. All of them laden with provisions. Lady Bertha must surely be on her way.

The bread and water hit my stomach. Right away I feel nauseous again. I lie on the floor. Curl up into a little ball. Search for Jessie's womb. For Sarah's breast. Find nothing. No, wait, there: sitting on the edge of her bed at the British Colonial Hotel in downtown Nassau. The same bed in the same room where we made love during our honeymoon. My sweet can be such a romantic. Don't worry, Sarah, I'm only a stone's throw away now. Closer all the time. Every second.

She and Cracker checked into the British Colonial late last night after arriving from Miami. She slept for a while but woke up early and has been on the phone for the past hour looking for a way out to Devil's Cay. She just confirmed that the island has no airport.

Cracker, my old buddy, knocks on my wife's door, enters. Poor bastard. Look at him: exhausted. Worn to a frazzle. Worried sick. Bags under his eyes. Didn't sleep a wink last night in that too warm room down the hall. All alone. The wind rattling the glass. Called home early this morning. No one answered. He figures Alison, angry that he flew off to Florida to save Sarah, probably packed up the kids and headed for Vermont to commiserate with her mommy.

Sarah looks at him. "Any luck finding a boat?"

He sighs, shrugs. "We can try a place not too far from here called Potter's Boat Launch. We might be able to catch a mailboat out to Devil's Cay. But it could take two or three days. And with this hurricane about to—"

"We don't have two or three days."

Half an hour later they leave the hotel, climb into a taxi. The taxi hurtles down Bay Street at breakneck speed. Cracker and Sarah sit in the back, hang on tight to the overhead straps. They fly by the straw markets, the fashionable boutiques, the government buildings all dressed up in pink and white.

"Bertha be comin'," says the driver.

Cracker and Sarah know all about Bertha. Sarah's already sick and tired of Bertha. Nothing but some other woman trying to keep her from her guy.

The taxi stops just before the bridge over to Paradise Island. The driver points to the long wharf stretching out below the bridge. "Dat Potter's Boat Launch," he tells them. "Where de mailboats leave for de Out Islands."

Sarah pays the man. She and Cracker step out. A hot wind blows out of the southeast. Here in Nassau the 'cane is still a long way off. But it's coming. Everyone keeps telling them it's coming.

Bags in hand, they cross onto Potter's Boat Launch. A dozen or more old and battered short-haul freighters line the concrete wharf. Men and machines load mail and various materials into the freighters. Virtually all the men are black. This causes Cracker some mild apprehension, but Sarah barely seems to notice. My sweet is on a mission. She will go anywhere, do anything, ask anyone anything to find her man. Cracker follows at her heels; he had no idea this mild-mannered young lady could be so assertive. She wants to know which boat goes to Devil's Cay. Takes a good half an hour to get a straight answer. Those black boys just ogle and whistle, offer her a free ride anywhere she wants to go. She ignores them. And finally, get this, she stands face-to-face with old Captain Ahab, you remember, the red-eyed, bad-tempered, rum-sucking skipper who landed me here on the shores of Devil's Cay not so many days ago.

"Does this boat go to Devil's Cay?" Sarah asks.

"Maybe. Why? You wanna go there?"

"It depends. How soon can you get us there?"

Ahab scowls. He's hungover, feeling plenty nasty. "If Bertha don't scuttle us, we'll set out for Eleuthera in a day or two. Then, if I feel like it, I might slip over to Devil's Cay. But it's a stinking, godforsaken place. Crawling with black magic."

"How soon before you actually arrive there?"

Ahab spits some slime out of his mouth onto the gang-plank. "Be four, five days, at least."

"Four or five days! I can't wait that long."

"Well you ain't gettin' there any sooner on this tub, sister."

Sarah takes my photograph out of her overnight bag. The one she took of me a couple months ago sitting out by the pool. "Do you recognize this man?"

Ahab takes a look at the photo. Spits again. "Maybe."

"Did you take him to Devil's Cay? Sometime in the last several days?"

"Maybe I did. Maybe I didn't. Who wants to know?"

"I'm his wife. I'm looking for him."

"Yeah? Well maybe he don't wanna be found."

"So you did take him."

"I didn't say that."

Cracker, nervous over this business of being out on this wharf among all these black dudes, reaches into his back pocket. Pulls out his wallet, extracts a crisp new one hundred dollar bill. Waves it at Ahab. "This might help jog your memory?"

Ahab looks at it. "Might."

Cracker hands over the greenback. "Well?"

"Yeah," growls Ahab, "I hauled him. Last trip out. A real landlubber. Puked all over my deck."

Sarah turns to Cracker. For the first time since my disappearance she wears a genuine smile on her pretty face. God, what a face! "I told you, Graham," she says. "I knew he was out there."

Cracker is impressed with her detective work, her intuition. Nevertheless, he remains our eternal skeptic. "But how are we going to get to this Devil's Cay?"

Sarah sighs, takes some time to think about it.

"Ain't no one gettin' out there," growls Ahab. "Not with this blow about to blast through the Bahamas. But after it passes you can always fly."

"Fly?" asks Sarah. "I didn't think the island had an airport?"

"No airport, sister. But you can take a seaplane. Seaplane take you anywhere in the islands you want to go."

Oh yeah, anywhere at all.

"But where," Sarah demands, "do you hire one of these seaplanes? Do you know anybody who has one?"

It takes another hundred bucks, but Ahab, sixty-three years in the islands, knows all.

They find Roland Milo's seaplane before they find Roland Milo. It bobs on its pontoons on the choppy water, tied up to a private dock over on Paradise Island. The man himself proves somewhat more difficult to locate. But finally, after hundreds of questions and a couple of straight answers, they find him cozied up to a baccarat table at Merv Griffin's Hotel and Casino.

Sarah taps him on the shoulder. The six-foot-seven-inch black man slowly turns around. "Excuse me, sir. Are you Roland Milo, the pilot?"

Roland takes a long look at Sarah. Enjoys what he sees. Still, he's learned to watch his back. Cops and narcs everywhere. "I could be. Who wants to know?"

"I'm Sarah Browne Standish. This is Graham Cramer."

Milo takes a quick look at Cracker. "Yeah? So?"

"We'd like to charter your plane."

"You would, huh? Where do you want to go?"

"Devil's Cay."

"An excellent destination. One of the great spots left in the Bahamas. When do you want to go there?"

"Today," says Sarah. "Right now."

Roland Milo lets fly his big booming laugh. Then he turns around, back to the baccarat table. "Sorry, missy, no trips to Devil's Cay today. I maybe take you over to the mainland, say someplace safe for me and my plane. But Devil's Cay, that'll be a disaster area by this time tomorrow. Haven't you heard? There's a hurricane coming to pay a call on the Bahamas. Weathermen got it blowing right smack through the middle of where you want to go."

"I'll pay you a thousand dollars cash to fly us there."

"Not a chance."

"Two thousand."

"Nope."

"Three thousand. They tell me it's only a thirty-minute flight."

Milo sneaks a peek at his measly little stack of chips. Decides it's time to turn around again, have another look at this white woman. "Forty-five be more like it."

"So an hour-and-a-half round trip," says Sarah. "Three thousand dollars for an hour and a half of your time." My sweet pauses, but only for a moment. She studied psychology up there at Vassar; knows what strings to pull. "What's the matter, Mr. Milo? Afraid of a little wind and rain? We heard you had more guts than any pilot in the islands."

Oh yeah, now Milo's ego has been brought into play. And a mighty large ego it surely is. He struggles to control it. Takes a look around. Sees that all betting has pretty much come to a halt. All gamblers waiting to see what Milo's going to do. A few diehards even make a quick wager.

But Milo is no one's fool. This old drug runner knows how to exercise control, how to haggle over price. "Four thousand," he announces. "Four thousand cash, up front, and we fly."

Sarah, my sweet, does not hesitate. She's no one's fool either. "Two thousand now. Two thousand upon arrival on Devil's Cay."

Milo agrees. Cashes in his chips.

Half an hour later, the winds howling, the sky growing ominous, Cracker and Sarah stand on the dock as Milo fuels up his seaplane, goes through a list of safety checks, prepares to take off. Cracker has more or less managed to keep his mouth shut since he arrived at the Days Inn on Marathon, but now my old buddy can barely contain his fear and foreboding. He visibly trembles. Still, he does not want to sound like a coward in front of the one true love of his life. But at the same time he cannot believe they're about to fly, willingly, into the heart of a hurricane.

Sarah, always in tune with those around her, feels his fear. "This is something I have to do, Graham. I simply have to. But you don't. There's no reason for you to get on that airplane."

Cracker sighs. "We could wait until the hurricane passes."

"No, Graham. The hurricane is exactly why I have to get out there now. Before it hits."

Cracker nods. He gets it. He understands.

"Let's go!" shouts Milo. "Come aboard!"

Sarah turns to her old friend and ex-brother-in-law. "Really, Graham, you don't have to do this. Think about Alison and the girls."

Cracker sighs, hesitates, rubs his eyes. All knotted up inside. Swallows hard and says, "I'm going, Sarah. I can't let you do this alone. He's your husband, but he's also my best friend."

You got that right, old pal. Best buddies till death do us part.

They cross the dock, duck their heads, climb through the narrow hatch. Sarah sits in the co-pilot seat, Cracker directly behind. Milo climbs aboard, settles in behind the controls, fires up the engine. "So why do you crazy people want to go out to Devil's Cay anyway? Not much of an island. Be even less after this blow."

Sarah shows him my picture. "Hey," he says, "I know that guy. Had a drink with him at Lewey's Hotel just a couple days ago. Said his name was Weston, Edward Weston. Like the photographer."

Sarah smiles, nods. "Do you think he's still there?"

"Damn likely. Not many ways off that rock. What did he do anyway?"

"He didn't do anything. He's my husband."

Milo accepts this bit of information without another word. Pushes the throttle forward increasing the rpms.

From the back, Cracker wants to know, "How long till we get there?"

"Shouldn't take more than thirty, forty minutes. But strap yourselves in. With these winds picking up it'll be plenty bumpy."

An hour later and still flying. Cracker makes a continuous search of the world beyond the scratched plastic windows. The poor, air-sick bastard has not laid eyes on land since they left Paradise Island. "How much farther?" He has to shout over the roar of that chain saw engine.

"Won't be long now!" reassures Milo in his booming voice. "We'd be there if not for this damn head wind. Bertha must be closing in faster than those weathermen predicted."

The small, light seaplane bounces up and down like a Yo-Yo in that jet black sky. Cracker's stomach leaps back and forth between his throat and his ankles. He clutches a barf bag with both hands. Waits to puke, and then to die.

Sarah stares straight ahead. She hasn't mumbled a word since takeoff. The bouncing doesn't seem to bother her at all. Barely aware of it, barely aware of even being aloft. Her thoughts float back and forth between Tim and me and our unborn baby. A girl; Sarah feels sure it'll be a girl. Going to name her Jessie. Jessie Katherine Standish. Hang on, my sweet. What about Jessie Margaret Standish? That has a real nice ring to it.

The invisible wind grabs the plane, shakes it unmercifully. Milo clutches the control stick with his right hand, the throttle with his left. A dozen years of flying and never has he encountered winds or turbulence like this before. He manipulates the rudder pedals and the trim levers in an effort to keep the plane flying level.

Almost two hours now and still flying. Wind and rain batter the seaplane. Milo flies low, just a couple hundred feet above the water. Nothing below but ocean, wild and passionate. Milo wonders how he's ever going to land the plane in this mess, but he pushes the thought aside. First he has to reach the island. Find the damn coral rock in the middle of nowhere. He can't help wondering if it's worth dying for four measly grand.

I know how he feels. And I know how my good buddy Cracker feels too.

Oh yeah, the sweet, pungent smell of vomit wafts through the cabin. Cracker sits back there filling one barf bag after another. He feels horribly weak, and pretty sure he'll soon be dead. Fears he will never see his wife or his two little sweethearts again. His head hangs between his legs, down around his ankles. He no longer has the strength or the desire to look out the windows.

But Sarah continues to look. She stares dead ahead. Has no thoughts of death; she knows with absolute certainty they will survive the flight.

My God! They have to survive the—

Wait! I think my sweet sees something. She peers through those rain-streaked windows, lets out a holler: "There! Look! Straight ahead!"

"Yes!" shouts Milo. "I see it."

Cracker, resurrected, manages to lift his head. He spots what they spot: terra firma. The hint of a smile breaks across his tortured face.

I tell you this: no wandering band of humans since Columbus and his seafarers has been so happy to feast their eyes on these sand and coral islands.

Milo flies directly over the harbor. Circles the island. Circles it again. Circles it a third time. Around and around, battling the winds.

Suddenly I hear the distinctive whine of that seaplane's engine. Slowly I lift my head off the barroom floor. Pull myself up onto my knees, peer out the window, now dripping with rain. I search the heavens. Visibility practically nil. I can barely see down the hill to the harbor.

"What's the problem?" Cracker wants to know.

"I'm afraid," answers Milo, "if I put her down that the sea will grab us and break us into a million pieces. In fact, I'm sure of it. Look at that chop."

Cracker barfs again. "I don't care about the chop! Land the damn plane! Being up here is worse than death."

Milo takes a quick look at the fuel gauge: fast slipping into the red zone.

But then, from the heavens, a miracle descends upon that seaplane. Call it a gift from God. Call it the calm before the storm, a brief respite before Bertha's full fury strikes its powerful blow upon this Devil's Cay. Where only moments ago sixty- and seventy- and even eighty-mile-per-hour winds raced across the sky, suddenly they diminish to nothing more than a stiff breeze.

Milo knows he has to make his move. "Hang on, people!" He circles the island once more, then begins a hasty and daring west-to-east landing. Still up in the clouds but rushing downward now, heading for the harbor.

Oh yeah, I can hear them coming! I stare into that black sky. Impatiently wait for that seaplane to appear. Deliver my woman into my arms! I wait and wait. And wait some more. Where are they? Where the hell are they?

"Mr. Weston!"

I turn around. Find Lewis, soaking wet, standing in the doorway of the bar.

"They're coming, Lewis. Did you hear the plane? They're coming!"

He looks confused. "Plane, Mr. Weston? What plane? Who be fool enough to fly in this terrible mess?"

I feel dizzy, weak. Grab the windowsill. Slide myself onto the floor. "Sarah and Cracker and Milo," I tell him. "They're coming. I heard them. Didn't you hear Milo's seaplane circling overhead?"

Lewis crosses the bar, kneels at my side. "Not even Roland Milo crazy enough to fly in this wildness, Mr. Weston. That little plane of his be ripped to pieces in this wind."

I look up at him, search his black face, the milky white of his eyes, wish he'd at least call me by my right name. "But . . . but . . . but . . ."

"Maybe Milo come and get you after the storm, Mr. Weston. But right now we got to take refuge in the parish. I almost forgot you, mon, so busy was I carrying food and water to the basement."

"No, Lewis," I insist, one more time, "I heard it. I heard that plane. Sarah's on board that plane. Don't you see?"

Lewis doesn't see. He gives me a blank stare. Probably figures he has a lunatic on his hands. Along with a hurricane at his doorstep.

Hope fast slipping away, I turn my head, stare through the wet glass. My last hurrah. Too bad there's nothing for me to see. Nothing but my absurd fantasy. A fantasy I've been promoting now for days, ever since I set foot here on Devil's Cay, really ever since I fled TREETOPS.

Call it: The Fantasy of the Phantom Clues.

Just take a peek out the window. You will immediately see the utter folly of my fantasy. There's no seaplane out there. No transport of any kind about to deliver my sweet Sarah Louise into my arms. Nothing out there but rain. Rain and wind. Wind I can't even see. Except that it has driven the mighty Atlantic into a rage, ripped the beautiful bougainvillea from the earth, bent the royal palms over until their fronds touch the ground, sent humans in a panic scurrying for safety.

No, Sarah's not circling, like some angel, overhead. Nor is my old pal, Cracker, my savior so many times in the past.

My God: the intricate fantasies we do concoct to deceive the demons within our fragile psyches.

Lewis grabs me under the arms, pulls me to my feet. I do not struggle. No more struggle left in this body. I put my arm around his waist. We cross the bar, go out into the lobby. "It going to be okay, mon," Lewis assures me. "By the time Bertha hit this place with all her power, we be safely in the parish basement. We weather the storm no problem."

Weak and resigned, I nod. Right at this second I don't really give a damn if we weather the storm or not.

We head for the front door. Walk right by the small office.

I suddenly have an inspiration. A deep desire. I stop. "There's something I need to do, Lewis."

"Now, mon? Not much time."

"I have to make a call."

"A telephone call?"

I nod. Pull away from Lewis under my own power. Head for the office. "Have to do it, Lewis. No way around it."

"I doubt the phone be working."

"Don't you worry, Lewis. It'll work just fine."

"I don't know, mon. Already this blow be knocking down poles and trees."

I ignore his pessimism, go into the tiny office, not much larger than a jail cell, slide into the wooden chair behind the desk. Pick up the receiver. Hear it right away: a dial tone! In no time at all I get an operator. She puts me on hold. A couple minutes pass. Lewis grows impatient. He wants to reach the basement before Bertha slams into us. I tell him to relax, hang on to his hat. Finally, an overseas operator comes on line. Her voice garbled with static. But I manage to pass along the number I want to call. She tells me to be patient, that it may take a few minutes. I assure her I'll stay on the line no matter how long it takes. Three minutes. Five minutes. Eight minutes. Ten minutes. A couple times I think the line has gone dead. The winds outside have grown ferocious. They pound the hotel, rattle the doors and windows. Somewhere upstairs we hear glass shatter. Lewis frets, begins to beg. I ask him for a little more time. Just another minute or two. He groans, paces, peers out the window, mumbles, "Soon it all be gone. Everything. My hotel. The island. Everything."

"Hello!" I keep shouting into the telephone. "Hello! Hello!"

And then, yes! I hear a voice. Distant. And very faint. "Hello? Hello!" Almost inaudible. Not much more than a whisper. But still a voice! A familiar voice!

"Tim!" I shout as loud as I can. "Is that you, Tim!"

"Mike?"

"Yeah, Tim, it's me, Mike!"

We both shout. Our long-distance, overseas voices snarled and overlapping.

I cannot believe it has taken me so long to make this call.

"Hey, Mike!" shouts Tim.

"Hey, Tim!" shouts Mike.

We both sound pretty excited to hear the other guy's voice.

And then Tim, cutting right to the quick, a child's innocence so perfectly lucid and complete, "Hey, Mike, you remember that big rat we saw running around down at the stable?"

No attitudes. No accusations.

"Sure," I shout, "I remember!"

"Yesterday Lucy and I caught him in a trap. One of those steel have-a-heart traps. He's still in there. I don't know yet what we're going to do with him."

I'm the one who was supposed to help him catch that damn rat. Not Lucy. Me. Just last week, just before I ran for my miserable life, I told the kid I'd help him catch that stinking rat.

"You'll think of something!" I tell him.

"Lucy and Gramma and Dorothy want to kill him, but Mom and I want to take him somewhere and let him go. I don't think he deserves to die some horrible death just because he's a rat. Do you, Mike?"

Oh yeah, I get the irony, every drip of it. "That's a tough call, kid! I guess I'd give him a break, let him go!" Damn right I would.

The phone line cracks and hisses. For a second I think it's gone dead. Don't hear a sound. But then I hear Tim's voice again. "So where are you anyway, Mike? Mom keeps telling me you'll be home any day now."

"She does?"

"Yeah. So why don't you hurry up! I miss you! And I know Mom does too!"

All choked up, I ask, "Listen, Tim, is Mom there? I need to talk to her!"

Again the line cracks, fades, reconnects. ". . . not home," I hear Tim say. "She's over at that place where she teaches people to read!"

"Mom's at work?"

"Yeah!" shouts Tim. "At work!"

Of course she's at work. Going about her business. Fulfilling her responsibilities and obligations. No running off half-cocked because of some ridiculous clue found, or perhaps not even found, in a trash basket. Not her style to go off half-cocked. Sarah Louise: calm, steady, strong. Patient and resilient. Like Jessie. God rest her soul. Of course Sarah's at work. Waiting. Hoping. Knowing all along her man needs to work things out. Make the next move. No way she can make it for him. Not after what he's done.

"Do you want to speak to Gramma, Mike? Mom's not here but Gramma is!"

I hem and haw over that one. Think at first: no way, not a chance. Then: what the hell? maybe I should. But in the end I don't have to answer, don't have to make up my mind. Nature takes care of it for me. Her wind severs the audio link connecting me to TREETOPS. The line goes dead. Tim's voice grows silent.

No choice now but to follow Lewis. Still, I feel better, stronger, knowing Sarah Louise is safe and secure at home. Not off performing in my fantasy. Not off on some wild goose chase with my old buddy Cracker. No, this is my struggle. It has been my struggle, my own private hell, all along. Mine and mine alone.

We go through the door, into the street. The Wind! My God! Blowing now a full-force gale. Lewis and I bend our bodies almost in half and plow straight into it. Slow going. Right smack in our faces. The sky close and black. Right on top of us. The rain spitting, slashing, coming down almost horizontally.

Lewis, caught up in his own hell, stops, turns around. So do I. We peer back at the hotel. His hotel. A hotel under siege. The shutters have all been ripped off the windows. The roof shingles have started to peel away. The porch leans and sways. It can't last much longer. We don't say it, but we both know it: slowly but surely Lewey's Hotel is being torn asunder.

Lewis just shakes his head. Not a word falls from his mouth. We turn, push on into the wind. Vast amounts of debris fly around the island: bicycles, brooms, lawn chairs, baby strollers, garbage cans, tiny specks of sand. I cover my head and my eyes, struggle forward.

Only a hundred yards from the hotel to the church, but it takes us the better part of five minutes. I half expect the wind to just pick me up and throw me into the sea. Another piece of debris. But finally we reach the front doors of the parish. We pull them open, rush inside, draw them closed. Calmer in here, out of the wind and the rain. But still incredibly noisy. Like being locked inside a kettle drum.

We make our way down the center aisle, between the pews. All the seats empty now. All the Bibles and hymn books removed from the pockets on the back of the pews. I follow Lewis past the altar, into an alcove at the back of the church. He lifts a wooden hatch in the floor. We go through the hatch onto a landing. Lewis closes and secures the latch, then starts down a narrow spiral stairway. I follow. The wooden steps creak, the iron banister bends against my weight.

And then, halfway down the stairs, in the dim light, I see them: the islanders, the residents of Devil's Cay. Every last one of them. Men, women, and children. A hundred or so black faces. The whites of their eyes staring straight at me. I stop in my tracks. Feel a powerful desire to retreat, even if it means going back into the teeth of that storm.

"Come, Mr. Weston," says Lewis, still the innkeeper, "we find a place for you to rest yourself."

But I don't move. Not right away. Sense hostility. Smell it in the air. "I don't know, Lewis," I whisper as softly as I can. "Maybe this isn't such a safe place for me, what with Mama Rolle's curse and all."

"This the only safe place for you, mon," Lewis tell me. "Besides, no more time for curses. This a very bad time. We all in this together."

I nod, unconvinced, take a deep breath, keep moving. See now these islanders have brought not only themselves but their friends as well: dogs, cats, chickens, even a few goats tethered in the corner. I look around. See cardboard boxes everywhere containing pots and pans, plates and glasses, all kinds of food and drink.

I reach the bottom of the stairway. Find the floor is nothing but dirt. The ceiling low. Barely enough room for me to stand up straight. Nothing but a couple of bare, low-wattage bulbs illuminating the space. Bulbs that crack and flicker. Preparing, I feel sure, to quit entirely at any moment.

I follow Lewis through the maze of humans, beasts, and belongings. He has carved out a little space for himself back by the goats. Just enough room for the two of us to squat on a couple of crates containing various canned fruits and vegetables, our sustenance, he tells me, for the long hours ahead.

I settle down quickly, do my best to make myself invisible. Those white eyes eventually stop staring. Voices start up again: low and grave. A whole roomful of folks dealing with their own personal hells.

I just don't want to die here, alone, without Sarah.

Several minutes pass. The tone of the voices around me changes. Sounds all of a sudden like some kind of weird chanting. Figure it must be black magic. Or white magic. Maybe Obeah. Or Voodoo. Probably trying to ward off the evil spirits. Drive this bitch Bertha away from Devil's Cay. But then I get paranoid, decide the whole bunch of them has got it in for me. I figure they figure this hurricane business is my fault; it's my arrival precipitated the entire mess. If they just sacrifice me to their rain gods and their wind gods, their island will be spared. Oh yeah, I'm feeling pretty wacked out, pretty certain I don't have a friend left in the world. Sure would be nice to see old Cracker slip down that spiral stairway.

But nope, not this time. He's back up at the Compound listening to his bitchy wife tell him, "I told you so."

Finally, my nerves right on edge with all this chanting, I turn to Lewis and ask, "Say, Lewis, what's all this hokum I'm hearing? Can't make out the words but it sure sounds like spells and curses to me."

Lewis laughs. So close I can smell his breath. Just finished a large can of fruit in heavy syrup. His breath sweet and peachy. "Oh no, mon," he tells me. "You got to listen more closely. No spells and curses down here. Like I tell you before, those for good times. These bad times, Mr. Weston. Very bad. Tough on everyone. You hearing the word of Jesus. You hearing the sound of people praying. Times likes this when we call out to Jesus for help and guidance."

That's what Jessie used to tell me. When things got rough, she'd say, "Reach out, Michael. Reach out for Jesus." I never did much reaching out. I guess I had a bad attitude about the whole religion business. Maybe because we'd come home from Mass, after praying up a storm, Mama and Maggie and me, and right away Stanley, pissed off and hungover, would haul off and slap Mama across the face or knock me down or give Maggie a tongue-lashing for leaving one of her toys on the floor. I figured this guy Jesus had to be a fake. Letting a prick like Stanley Standowski strike a woman like Jessie Buell. A fake and maybe even a sadist. But Mama told me it all had to do with faith, with believing, always, that things can get better, that people can be helped and saved and made to see the error of their ways.

So what the hell? I give it a try. Say a little prayer. Silently. For Jessie. Then one for Maggie Jane and her husband. Then another one, right out loud, for Sarah and Tim and our unborn child. God, I hope that child is not just another of my far-flung fantasies.

Then I really go wild. I say a prayer for Stanley and Iron Kate. Why not? Stan the Man could use all the prayers he can get. And then I have this rather bizarre thought, probably sacrilegious: maybe we could get old Stanley cleaned up, give him a haircut and a shave, take him down to TREE-TOPS, introduce him to Katherine Pilgrim Browne. You never know. Could be a match made in heaven.

I close that cynical thought out, go on with my prayers. Go through everyone I know a second time. And a third. I have to admit: the prayers somehow make me feel better. Like I might be doing a good deed. Something positive. I even send one out for myself. Ask God to let me live. Give me another chance. One more opportunity and all that jazz.

An hour passes. Two hours. Three hours. The lights go off and come on and go off again. Off now for quite a while. I doubt they'll be coming back on. Nothing now but darkness. The only light when someone strikes a match to fire up a cigarette.

And outside, upstairs, well, I can only tell you that it sounds like the world must surely be coming to an end. Try to remember the wildest wind you've ever heard howl, and now imagine a wind ten times wilder, ten times more powerful. That might give you an idea. At one point, a few minutes ago, I swear to God, I heard the wind pulling the nails right out of the beams holding this old church together.

The rain has found its way into the basement, but so far we remain reasonably dry. In only a few isolated spots has the dirt floor turned to mud. So far there have been just a couple mild cases of panic among the troops. But I wonder how much longer we can hold out. How much longer we can listen to that wind before we all go stark raving mad.

"Hey, Lewis," I whisper in the darkness, "how long for one of these hurricanes to blow through?"

He puts his hand on my knee, squeezes softly. "Until all the anger be gone, mon. Until it takes everything it want to take."

I guess that pretty much says it all. I lean back and listen to the wind some more. But then, suddenly, I spring to my feet. "Christ! Lewis!"

"Easy, mon. What's the problem?"

"My gear!"

"What about it?"

"I left all my gear up in my room!" Sure as hell did! My clothes, my cameras, my portrait of Sarah. The Money. The damn Money! "I have to go back, Lewis. I have to go back and get my stuff!"

"You go out there now, mon," says Lewis, calmly, "you die. You not come back here. And besides, you find nothing anyway."

But I don't listen. I head across the dirt floor, stumbling over bodies and boxes in the darkness. Angry words from those around me. It takes me a while but I finally find the spiral stairway. Slowly I ascend. Reach the rickety landing. Search around with my hand for the hatch. Find it and push. I need to get my shoulder behind it. Manage, after a struggle, to get it open. A few inches. The wind swirls right in, slams into my face. So does the rain. No, not rain. A literal cascade of water.

Below me a bevy of voices demand I close the hatch. I do as ordered. But not before I see what can only be a hallucination, a figment of my imagination: there is no church! No steeple anyway. No roof. Nothing but walls flailing in the breeze.

All night long Bertha pounds the island. More and more water finds its way into our underground cave. Dirt turns to mud. Thick and slippery. I cannot say I actually sleep, but off and on I doze. Wait for death.

But death does not come. What comes instead is silence. All at once, utterly and completely, it descends upon us. Pure silence. At first it sounds almost eerie. No one trusts it. After twelve hours or more of that constant bombardment, this sound somehow does not ring true. We listen to it practically without breathing for five long minutes. Then ten minutes. Fifteen minutes. Almost half an hour. We listen and wait for the horror to begin anew.

Finally, a few whispers. Wonder aloud if it might really be over. A few people stand. More time passes. More people stand. I stand. Lewis stands. We start to mill around. Stretch our stiff limbs. Someone starts up the spiral stairway. We wait to see what will happen.

The hatch is thrown open. Early morning light filters into our cave. A collective sigh spreads through the wet basement. And a long chorus, in which I, Michael Josep Standowski, actually take part, "Hallelujah! Thank the Lord! Hallelujah!"

Another door is thrown open, a cellar door leading directly outside. We begin to stream out, calmly and orderly, single file. No one pushes or shoves. The humans, the dogs, the cats, the goats and chickens. All seeking the light of a new day.

I follow fat Mama Rolle out into the wide-open spaces. And let me tell you what I see: complete devastation. I mean nothing less. Dim, early morning light. Not quite dawn. But enough light to paint a picture of perfect annihilation. Wrack and Ruin. I mean to say a major bombing operation by the United States Air Force could not have inflicted more damage.

The islanders stand silently and stare in awe at their ruined world. No one says a word. Not even the children. Innocence shattered.

Then I feel Mama Rolle's big meaty hand on my shoulder. I fear she might crush me. But no, her voice echoes loud and clear across the island. "Dis nuthing," she tells us. "I want you all to hear me now. Dis nuthing but broken-down piles of stone and wood and brick." And with a slow wave of her chubby hand, she sweeps away the destruction. "We live. All of us. Dat everything."

Then Mama Rolle turns her back on the wasted town. She starts into the dunes, ruined and ravaged by the winds. Others follow. Before long everyone is on the move.

Including me.

We make our way slowly over the dunes to East Beach. Or at least what is left of it. We reach the beach, spread ourselves out in a long, thin line. Bertha has left her mark: ripped the sand to shreds, littered the beach with debris and driftwood. But these islanders do not bother to notice. They look beyond the beach, beyond the surf still in turmoil, before the Atlantic rippling and heaving with whitecaps.

They, we, look out beyond the ocean, all the way out to the distant horizon. We cast our gaze out into the hazy gloom and we wait. It takes several minutes, but so what? We've been waiting for hours, all night long. We can wait a little while longer.

It will need to rise above those clouds. But it will. And it does. We see its potent glow shining through the mist. And the thing itself: Huge. Massive. Ominous. Blood red but full of light and life.

Another round of "Hallelujah!"s up and down the beach.

I feel myself smile. Know now she has saved my life. Twice. The first time up at TREETOPS. And, now, again. Here. On this lonely beach. Saved me both times with the simple uncompromising purity of her love.

I'm still here, thinking about my sweet Sarah Louise, and watching that sun rise into a brightening sky, when suddenly I realize I stand on this beach all alone. I look over my shoulder. See only the backs of the islanders as they slowly disappear into the dunes.

I begin to follow, but then change my mind. Turn around for another look. I see the sun spin from red to orange to yellow. It spreads its glow out across the surface of the sea. Oh yeah, it must be the same sun we all see every day.

Satisfied, I slip away, back into the dunes. And when I reach the edge of town, I am both amazed and mesmerized by what I find: a hundred pairs of hands already at work. Already busy shifting through the rubble. Sorting out their lives.

So very little left. Bertha did not move on until she had pretty much punished everyone, stolen everything. The town has been razed, leveled, demolished. Nothing left but chaos. Lewey's Hotel: flattened. Mama Rolle's Devil's Cay Inn: destroyed. St. Andrew's Parish: obliterated. I tell you, not a pew or a stained-glass window in sight. It saved our lives but lost its own. Along with everything else on this tiny island not protected by that hole in the earth.

The evidence of disaster floats on the harbor: blankets without beds, curtains without windows, bits and pieces of homes and boats. I see a doll floating facedown in the blue-green ripples. Everything looks ghostly, surreal, immaterial.

But the islanders keep moving, keep working. Mama Rolle starts humming in a deep, brassy voice. After a few moments, she begins to sing. Soon they're all belting out the words. Slowly. Emotionally. Listen:

"Amazing Grace! (how sweet the sound)
That sav'd a wretch like me!
I once was lost, but now am found
Was blind, but now I see.

" 'Twas grace that taught my heart to fear,
And grace my fears reliev'd;
How precious did that grace appear
The hour I first believ'd!"

Not knowing the words, I can only watch. And listen. My mouth wide open. It's true: we've been spared. Who knows why?

I go along the cobblestone street to where Lewey's Hotel used to stand. I find Lewis singing the next verse softly while he digs through the rubble that used to be his home and his livelihood.

> *"Through many dangers, toils, and snares,*
> *I have already come;*
> *'Tis grace that brought me safe thus far,*
> *And grace will lead me home."*

Lewis looks up. Meets my eyes. Manages a smile.
I smile back.
"Sorry, Mr. Weston," he says. "No sign of your gear."
I shrug. "It doesn't matter, Lewis. I'm better off without it."
His turn to shrug. A man with a few other things on his mind.
"And listen, Lewis," I tell him, "let's forget this Mr. Weston stuff. The real name is Standowski. Michael Josep Standowski. You can call me Mike."
Lewis takes some time to think over this name business. "Okay, mon," he says, finally. "From now on I call you Mike."
"Thanks, Lewis," I tell him. Then, "And thanks for pulling me through that storm."
Lewis shows me his wonderful set of teeth. "No problem, Mike."
Time now to go to work. We sift through the debris, looking for anything that might be of use once life gets back to normal.
I cut the tip of my finger on a piece of broken glass. Just a tiny cut. But enough to make me bleed. Enough to assure me this is not more of my fantasy. I squeeze the cut, watch

the blood run down my finger, into the tiny swirls that make my print unique in all the world.

Maybe, just maybe, the nightmares are over.

I feel pretty good. As good as I've felt in days. Weeks. Months. Maybe since last March. Since I pulled the job. More trouble than it's worth trying to get something for nothing.